ZACHAEL T.J. PRESGROVE

The Poem of Thearu, Line 1: World of Mirage

Contents

Dedication

For the ones who have lost it all, but continue to press on, I dedicate this story to you. May you move to a life of joy despite a history of sorrow...

To Papa Ted; this story is only possible because of you.

To my son; when your trials come, may your perseverance guide you like a star in the night.

Foreword

I would like to acknowledge that not everyone shares my beliefs. Not everyone sees things how I do. This is, most assuredly, okay. I don't expect the world to conform to my views or revere the same god(s) I do, and etcetera. What I do expect is that whoever picks up this book knows what they are getting themselves into, and that they respect what it features. Please understand, as I do, that there are religious undertones in my work, but there are also social views and personal beliefs that have just as much importance in shaping and inspiring this work of fiction as the religious undertones. I am a follower of Yeshua, but I am also a believer in science. I am aware that I don't have all the answers, and I will not pretend like my work is an answer book to important life questions: it's literally a fantasy novel.

However, readers should be aware that there are characters of diverse ethnical backgrounds represented, and there are characters of many sexual orientations represented - in heroic and villainous presentations. If this offends you in any way, please - put the book down and don't read it. You'll keep yourself from wasting my time or your time. Neither this book, nor future works, were meant for you, and that's okay. Leave it for the ones whom it was meant for.

As for those that do read it and aren't offended by content like what's above, I hope you're inspired, driven, and provoked by the tale this book tells. I hope you walk away with something to relate to, something to make you think, and something that speaks to the deepest core of your being. Life doesn't always go as we plan, and while we may have good intentions or a desire to restore our honor from the ways we've lost it, we don't always succeed.

And that's okay.

Readers, may I present for your literary enjoyment, The first line of the Poem of Thaerv and the tale it tells;

World of Mirage

Acknowledgement

There are many friends and family that helped get me to this point - too many to name in this section - but namely, I want all those who helped to inspire and shape this world of mine that know that this is the product of the love and labor they poured into me. Be as proud of it as I am.

To my Papa Ted, this is it. This is the story inspired from our long, deep conversations when I was young. The pages of this book and the ones that follow are telling the story you ignited in me, and I hope it brings you as much joy to read as it gave me to write. Thank you.

Thank you to my God, my friends, and my family that all supported me through every step of the way to getting to this point. I wouldn't have gotten here without you.

Literary by Zachael T.J. Presgrove

The Salom'Sileyu Trilogy
The Kult of Salom'Sileyu
The Tribes of Enthedrill
The Ascent of Majjai

The Poem of Thaerv Series
World of Mirage

I

The Vial

Memories, like dreams, unfold space and time, and transcend the laws of reality.

London, England

April 18, 2024

12:00AM

She gawked.

Unsure of what to make of it, she gawked at the glowing vial with a puzzled look. There she sat, frozen, at a desk in the far upper room of a massive mansion in London. The room was dim, its beige walls and oaken floors illuminated by an old lamp, painting the serene image of an old, wealthy Victorian home. The glowing, cyan-hued liquid encapsulated the center of her focus. She did the research, but nothing she found helped her understand what she looked at…

Or the feeling she had in her heart...

...A feeling that she was the one who was supposed to drink it.

Her research led her to tragedy. Around this time, on this day, trauma happened to an entire city in 1906. America's western coast-line experienced a catastrophe like no other. Beside her, the laptop was lit up on the desk with pages opened, struggling to give her some sort of clue that she wasn't able to find. Nothing helped. No amount of research gave her the answers she sought. Nothing that explained a luminescent drink of that haunting color, or people with powers that bent reality in the way that *he* did...

Rather, from all the clues she uncovered, it only brought her to documents and records of the great earthquake. There were countless missing, countless more dead. Just fourteen years before the prohibition, at the dawn of the heroin epidemic, she pondered the supernatural. It was a perfectly natural disaster, but something kept tugging at the strings of her heart, as though it wasn't what it seemed to be. There wasn't anything that stood out to her, so why was she entranced by that event?

In her hand was something alien, foreign;

4

something her research couldn't explain. She didn't understand why the liquid was glowing, and she didn't understand why the glass felt cool in her hand. Her hearing was so sharp from the adrenaline pumping through her veins, she could hear her own heart beating.

She was alone for another couple of hours, from what she knew. *He* wasn't going to return for a little while, not with guild matters to attend to. His mansion was big enough that if she felt like she needed to, she could hide away in an obscure room before drinking it, but she knew that she *had* to drink it.

She took a deep breath, and then roiled all her tension and nervous emotion with a long and dramatic exhale. All her senses were heightened with anticipation, and she knew she couldn't put it off any longer. She looked at the label one more time and read its gripping message, written in the finest penmanship; *The right one will drink it at the right time.*

Without delay, she popped the cork and flinched - the sound echoed louder than she desired. Then, she heard a door slam from down the stairs in the most hurried fashion, followed by a clambering of footsteps. She couldn't hesitate; he was home earlier than expected. He must have found out her intentions somehow. Perhaps it was the gods, or perhaps it was his cunning intuition. Regardless, she needed to be quick.

Things seemed to move in slow motion as the moment drew near. Her hands were unsteady, quaking with fear as the door slammed open. She knocked back the bottle with her shaking hand and chugged the sweet, cool drink until it was all gone. The effects were immediate; her veins began to glow through her skin, and it felt as though her nerves were set on fire. Her muscles tensed, and pressure accumulated in her head. Her heart pounded in her chest so hard, it could rival a blacksmith.

She stumbled out of the chair and onto the floor, and suddenly, she heard frantic whispers and voices everywhere. Her chocolate-colored locks draped past her face as she tried to crawl forward. Her eyesight was blurry, and her mind seemed to escape reality as visions exploded forth of a time and world she had never seen before. She couldn't see it, but she could feel the tears start to pour out from her eyes. She felt like her heart should have burst.

"What have you done?!" He yelled, though she could barely hear him. All she could see and hear now was a world with fantastic beings and a forgotten magic. It was as if the memories were her own in that strange mirage that scrawled before her like a film. Amidst her terrorized state, and as she faded from conscious thought and into the visions, she heard one soft and gentle voice that comforted her in her journey, gently repeating a single phrase:

Everything is going to be alright...

II

The Tragedy

...Nothing is as it seems...

Fateful, Tragic Day

"Jack, no!"

His brother's voice shouted in sheer panic, desperately trying to stay his hand. There Jack was, fighting once more, fighting those that represented everything he hated in society. He was angry, always angry. Every insult about his Jewish mother, every name thrown at his Irish father, all of the tense emotion unleashed with every furious punch on the rich man's face.

A rich man that looked down on him for the last time.

He refused to take it anymore. He was fifteen, barely into his prime, and he was already suffering the weight of English judgments on American soil, where his father fought so hard to make a life in. He was tired of having to smile and take it, and if it took him pounding on this snobby Englishman to inspire others to stand up against such wretched judgments, he would play the role of the martyr.

Only, this was not the time he'd hoped it would be. This wasn't the glorious revolution he fantasized about starting, nor would it be a moment of love and adoration from his dear family. Instead, it would be a moment marked by pain, hatred, and a twisted fate that would shape his future in ways he could never predict.

His mother was a beautiful young Jewish woman, barely into her mid-thirties. She was eighteen when she had his eldest brother, twenty when she had Jack, and twenty five when she had their youngest. Their father loved her like they'd never seen a man love a woman before, and it was an inspiration to the three of them.

But this day would mark a tragedy for their family as their mother tried to chastise him. "Jack Owens, get off of that man right this instance!" She hollered. Adrian, his eldest brother, tried to hold her back, but she was quick to slip out of his embrace. She ran into the street, but didn't notice as the lawmen rode up on their horses.

Everything happened so suddenly.

Jack turned and watched in horror as the startled horse reared onto his hind legs, kicking his mother's jaw and knocking her to the ground. Everything seemed to move in slow motion. Adrian tried to rush to their mother with an outstretched hand, and Jack stood to his feet as he let go of the beaten rich man. The horse, unaware of what horrible act it was about to commit, followed gravity's pull and readied its hooves to land on the road beneath.

The crunch of their mother's sternum pierced their ears louder than any sound. Jack watched through misty, shocked eyes as she reached out to him with nothing but love and sorrow in her gaze. It only lasted for a few brief moments, and then her spirit lifted from her body with invisible grace, leaving her lifeless.

Was it raining? He hadn't noticed. The storm rumbled above, but all he could see and hear was his mother's corpse, lifting with the panicked horses' foot as it tried to get away. The lawman quickly leapt off the horse and rushed to their mother, while Adrian rushed to Jack. There was a moment of silence, then his cries filled the streets with their mournful, pitiful howls. Adrian tried to help him up, but he was quick to break free

13

and stumble to his mother.

"Stay back, son-"

"MOTHER!!!" Jack cried, falling to his knees and holding her close to his chest as he wept. The rains that were supposed to sting as they fell on his face were weightless. The storm, though it raged, was nothing more than a background. No, the only things he could feel in that moment was the pain of her death, and shame of his violent outburst that caused it.

Yes, shame. That was what he felt. Shame, sorrow, and guilt. It was his fault. She lay dead in his arms with a gaping hole in her chest because of his anger. He wanted to blame the Englishman. He wanted to blame the lawman and his horse. He wanted to blame so many other things, but it didn't negate the fact that she rushed into the streets because he was beating someone so badly, she felt like she needed to stop him.

As more lawmen put their hands on his shoulders and Adrian's shoulders, they sobbed over her corpse. He wondered what twisted fate saw this as an appropriate action to take in his life and her life. As the thought of God entered his mind, he immediately rejected it with burning anger. There was nothing that he knew of that could soothe the shame and guilt he now faced.

So, as the tears fell, he resolved in that moment

to live his life standing up for what was right. He would fight for those who couldn't, get himself in trouble for those who didn't deserve it, and do everything in his power to spare those from experiencing the pain he now felt. He no longer cared what happened to himself, as long as no one else went through what he was going through in that very moment.

"I'm so sorry, mother," he whispered, stealing himself back to reality.

…I'm so sorry…

10 Years Go By

Smoke hazily drifted throughout the diner. Jack leaned back in his seat, full and satisfied with his breakfast, and sipped on his steaming mug full of coffee. It wasn't often he got to sit in for a meal at the diner. Too often, he was busy working at the factory, or he couldn't afford to go out. Conditions were rough, but he made it by without getting himself into too much trouble.

There were always fight to have. Whether he had to fight against his older brother after being accused of being the one responsible for their father and youngest brother returning to Ireland, or to defend a poor sod being abused at the hands of their society's aristocracy. San Francisco was no stranger to the troubles and toils of their society's divisions, but in that city, things were different. People cared about each other a bit more, and the police cared more about the cities they patrolled than most. He recounted the officers and lawmen that helped him and his brother when their mother died, and when they should have been arrested and locked away, they were granted amnesty.

He breathed in deep the smell of burning tobacco and hot food being shuffled about, and slowly gazed at the crowds that accompanied him in the humble eatery. After a few moments, his eyes rested on a particularly beautiful sight; a woman only a few years younger than him, dark hair flowing in bouncing curls over her shoulders as her crystal-blue eyes longingly stared out the window into the busy streets. He knew that look all too well.

Despite her tasteful attire, she was a factory worker like him. He recognized that aimless stare, a longing in the pupils of a woman's eyes that preached to her desire to break free of the harsh conditions of working a hard factory. She kept herself well fed, and put herself together. Too often, men, women, and children were left malnutritioned, more slender than a skeleton. She wasn't, though. She was just right, an alluring figure and a pretty face full of makeup he wouldn't expect a woman working the factories to own-

He blinked in surprise, realizing only then that he knew who she was; Elizabeth McOwens. He called her Liz, and worked beside her at the very same job in a clothing factory. It made sense, of course, that he didn't know who she was initially; she was almost always covered in dirt and grime, wearing a humble apron over an old, ratty dress she didn't care about. His face flustered, and he quickly looked away before she had a chance to catch him staring.

Emotions stirred in his heart. Emotions he hadn't really felt before. He'd had crushes before, but never felt motivated or worthy enough to pursue those relationships in any fashion. Something in his heart stirred like he'd never felt before, though. But how would it work? In his time, families still arranged marriages. His family was all but demolished... Ever since his mother... Ever since he caused her death...

Was her family still around? Would they ever approve of a man like himself? He wanted to go over to her, indulge in the fantasy of them making something work, but he hesitated. His heart burned with shame, a shame he carried with him for so long. How could she ever want to be with someone like him? He needed to spare her from experiencing that burden.

Then, something else stirred in his heart.

There was a shift in the air around the diner, something that just felt wrong deep inside him. His eyes quickly scanned the room, analyzing each guest, until they rested on a couple back in the corner at a booth all by their lonesome. He recognized their deeds; a young couple that, like himself and Elizabeth, worked a pauper life at a factory. Their poverty led them to meeting each other, and their love bounced between them like electricity.

It was beautiful to watch, and for a moment, he found himself smiling, unaware that Liz had seen him and followed his gaze to the budding couple. That wasn't the feeling in his gut, though. No, something was about to happen that generated an unspoken panic in their eyes as they searched around the room.

Then, the unthinkable happened; officers casually entered the diner with their glares fixated on the woman. They pulled out their batons and calmly made their way to the couple, their intent on aggressive arrest. There was a look of terror in her eyes, and he finally knew what was happening; she was being considered a prostitute. It wasn't uncommon anymore; his generation was tired of the standard of arranged marriages. They wanted love to flourish naturally, but the aristocrats and wealthiest of their society didn't like it.

So there they were, with the police having the excuse of accusing her of offering sexual services for goods in return - at least, according to a rather ambiguous statute, they used that excuse. She was now caught, and would be taken to jail for the crime of love. A fire burned in his heart. A fire that quickly grew into a raging inferno. He couldn't stand to see it happen, and he hated how those with influence and riches used their status to walk all over those like him.

He calmly stood to his feet and kept his steps hushed, ignoring the confused looks from those all around. For a brief moment, he looked over at Elizabeth for one last mental picture, and caught her looking back up at him. They locked eyes, and it seemed like she knew what he was about to do. Worry filled her irises, but he gave a reassured, cocky half-smile with a wink, and turned his attention to the officer whose shoulder he tapped.

Confused, the lawman turned, and without warning, Jack threw a tightly clenched fist into his jaw, knocking him over. "I'm willing to gamble you officers aren't quick enough to catch me, dogs," he spat.

He wasted no time. Adrenaline pumped into his veins, and he watched as all the police in that diner, including some who were disguised as patrons, turned to face him with a violent spark in their pupils. He snickered and quickly dashed out of the diner, throwing chairs to block their path.

He broke into a mad dash down the street, but for the briefest moment, he turned and assured himself that every one of them gave him chase. The couple was safe, and that was all that mattered. He could hear his heart beating in his ears, he could feel the cool spring breeze that whisked across his face. The hard path beneath his feet were hard against his soleless boots, but he didn't care. For once, he felt he did something right. For once, he felt like he stood up for someone who needed it.

The couple could embrace love, and his life found meaning again. He found a fight that didn't end with death and pain, but in justice for a young woman and a young man born into a poverty they didn't choose. He helped protect their desire to choose who they would love, and in his core, he believed that was a righteous fight to take up.

He imagined, as his heart beat louder and louder, and as the wind rushed past his face with supernatural agility, that his mother smiled upon him from her rest in paradise...

…Perhaps, for once, he could find a little grace for himself as well.

12:00PM

Five years had passed since Jack found a greater cause in his fighting. Five years, within which the unexpected happened... Love had found him.

Love...

And tragedy.

Everything began at noon, when he took a leisurely break from the noise and oily scents of the toxic factory he and his coworkers begrudgingly subjected themselves to. "I'm going to eat lunch, Liz," He said. He grabbed his brown coat and slung it over his shoulder, and then grabbed his flask and lazily started to stumble over to the pile of palettes over by the front door. There she was, the girl from the diner that one fateful day. The girl that captured his undivided attention for the briefest of euphoric moments. She rolled her hazel-blue eyes at him as she flipped some of her dark-brown hair over her shoulder. They had known each other for years, and had grown to be more than the best of friends.

Neither of them could afford to marry, though, so they kept their romantic relationship a closely guarded secret and resolved to strictly be called 'friends.' Just like the couple he helped protect at the very same diner. He didn't want to attract the attention of law enforcement, who made a persistent habit of jailing women who were taken out to eat with a man they weren't married to.

"You and your damned drink," she scolded as she wiped her dirty hands on her equally dirty white apron, which she wore over a modest blue dress that matched her eye color. "Your brother tells you too often about such vile poisons and their hazards. If our boss hears of you leaving the job, he's going to send you off," she added with a tone of voice that made his brothers' rebukes pale in comparison. He could barely hear her youthful vocals over the machinery around them, though.

"I'm just sitting down! I'm not leaving the job, Elizabeth. I would simply like to have a few moments off my feet," Jack refuted as he passed her by. Many of the other machines shut down as others took a moment to get their lunches as well. They, however, didn't find a seat to sit at; they just ate where they were. It wasn't uncommon. In fact, Jacks' behavior was the more uncommon, and many of his coworkers knew why – he wanted to drink somewhere away from those he worked beside each day. They never told his boss... unless the pompous foreman asked, of course.

His cosmic destiny began, though, as his boss unexpectedly made his way down to their floor, puffing away on a white cigarette. "Where's that cur, Jack?!" He barked at Liz as he stomped his way over to her. She ducked her head and shied away from him as he tightened his chest and shoulder muscles. Jack heard him even over the loud machines, and could smell his musky tobacco scent, even as far away from him as he was. He knew there was trouble.

"I'm over here, boss!" he called as he rushed to her and wedged himself between them. The boss was a cruel man, and he wasn't going to let him degrade or hurt Liz.

The man eyed him up, scrutinizing and judging his nappy blonde hair that was tied into a bun behind his head. Loose strands soaked with sweat dangled over his face. His white button-down shirt was dirty, and his suspenders held up his black pants snugly. Jack couldn't help it. He could barely afford a place to live with the rent split between himself and his older brother,

Adrian.

They stuck together through thick and thin. His brother had common sense and a sensitivity to spiritual things, and he was ridiculously smart. Jack was smarter, but couldn't truly grasp his brother's religion and spirituality. It became worse with the death of their mother, and led to his drinking, his fighting, and his inability to avoid troubling situations.

"Are you occupied, Jack? I'd speak with you privately... unless, of course, you would rather if I enact the wage penalties on your *lovely* young friend here-"

"I'm going to interrupt your rather childish demands there and assert my defense against you for our sake: you'll not lay a finger on her or her blasted wages, swine. Your threats don't frighten me; they amuse me as a fighting Irishman. Quite the contrary, I'll ensure our safety and your absolute humiliation in front of all these fine men and women here that you weigh on undue oppression," Jack threatened. Everyone around them turned their machines off as the tension began to rise, watching as the silence between Jack and the predatory man grew louder. He was surprised the lawmen weren't around. He couldn't stand for it any longer, though. Too long had he and Liz been bullied by him. Too long.

This was the last string to be plucked. Rage began to burn in his chest, and his vision tinted with a slight red.

"My apologies. I forgot that we here are graced by the presence of a drunken Celt." He spat after he looked around to see all who were watching. It was clear he had made a scene, and he needed to correct the issue. Jack's brow furrowed at his disrespect, and his fists clenched tighter.

"Jack…" Liz cooed. She gently placed a hand on his. "It's alright. He's a blasted cur, and everyone in this city knows his reputation," Liz spat. Everyone around them gasped as their eyes bounced between him, Jack, and Liz.

"You'll learn to keep a civil tongue in that mouth of yours, you wasteful wanton whore!" He barked. Something clicked in his head, and he couldn't hold back anymore.

"You shut your fucking mouth!" Jack barked. "You talk to us all like we're your property! I won't have this blasted *fucking* treatment any longer!"

"Child, you'll not survive long enough on the streets, what with the wolves of the downtown alleys! If you leave, you had better crawl back into the dead womb of that Jewish whore-"

He didn't let him finish - he struck him with such fierce strength, the foreman fell backwards

27

and clenched his jaw as he groaned in pain. Angered, Jack's fists were clenched and raised, poised for a grueling fight where he'd make his boss eat every word he ever vomited. There were gasps and whispers. Everyone in the factory gathered to watch. Some of the girls quickly ushered Liz away from the ring they formed, and the tension was so thick in the air, people struggled to breath.

"Get up! I'll see to it that your bloody neck is wrung like a filthy washcloth! I'll make sure you're never a foreman over a campus again when I report to the courts the abuse you heap on us!"

You'll never get to, Jack.

Before he had a chance to look around to see who whispered that into his ear, his boss's meaty hands grabbed Jack's shoulders and threw him back onto the floor. Every strike, every movement, every wretched breath his foreman took registered to him on an emotional level. There wasn't a thing the pompous bastard did that didn't enrage Jack.

Everything moved slowly, and Jack's mind began to think faster. He got to his feet and dodged the rampaging behemoth, shoving him as he passed by. Jack raised his hands as his boss threw a wild punch, and he brushed it aside with an immediate retaliation. He threw his hand forth with a jab to his boss's chin, which wasn't expected. His boss stumbled backwards and collected himself, then charged again at Jack.

Once he was close, he picked Jack up and slammed him on the ground. The boss tried to pin him down, but Jack was too quick. He moved his head out of the way of the foreman's punch, grimacing when he heard it land on solid concrete. His boss screamed and grabbed his hand in pain, and then got off Jack.

Then, the young factory worker took the advantage; he tackled the foreman to the ground, nearly knocking over one of his coworkers in the process and pinned him with his knees on his hands. Rage took over at that point, and Jack started to beat on his face until it was bloody.

Then, suddenly, he was pulled off the boss by a desperate Liz.

"Jack!!!" She screamed as she stood in front of him and held his arms at his side. Jack, breathing heavy, began to collect himself. "This is not who you are!" She cried, tears starting to stream down her cheeks. "Let him threaten us! Fate will repay him accordingly! Don't let the wickedness of such a brutish brood make a murderer out of you!"

Jack was silent as he looked up at his boss, and suddenly, any emotion he'd felt washed away. His boss held his face, crying from the pain. Jack was sure that it hurt; he hit him hard. But in his introspection, he realized how little he cared that he inflicted so much pain. Jack was a bitter man, and while he had the capacity for goodness and love, the life he'd lived *made* him the way he was. While he instinctively disagreed with her, he knew she could see things about him that he himself couldn't.

"You're right…" Jack said as he turned around and walked away. Not knowing what else to do, Liz followed him, and they left the building together. The factory workers tended to the foreman, but not because they cared. No, they shared Jack's feelings, and didn't want him to suffer for something that they considered to be an appropriate emotional response to an overlord so vile…

…If only they knew how little it mattered.

3:00PM

Two hours pass them by. No law enforcement arrived on his doorstep, no detectives, no investigators. They were there in an uneasy peace as they waited for Adrian to come home. His stomach churned with impatient anxiety as he anticipated the worst outcome, so he instinctively paced around the living room before collapsing onto his chair. The apartment was small and cozy; a two-bedroom on one floor. The living room had birch planks on the floors, with a soft rug in the center. There were two armchairs on either side of a coffee table with stacks of books around.

On the far side of the room was a bookshelf with books stacked in every space on and in front of it. The walls behind were a deep maroon color, and broke on the opposing wall to make room for a fireplace. An open doorway led into a kitchen area with a small table, and beyond that was a hall that led to the bedrooms. The entire apartment was a mess, yet it showcased their wild intelligence and cunning intuition. They experimented with the wild subjects they read about through various broke-man's inventions, with elements left bare on their table, and pages of notes and scribblings strewn over every surface that wasn't needed to cook or eat.

"When was it your intention to repair this crazed mess of a home?" Liz finally asked after sitting, walking around, and looking for things to do while Jack replayed the fight over and over in his mind. Her voice, gentle even in her insults, broke his review of the day's events.

"Everything is exactly where we remember it," Jack said plainly as he looked up at her. His voice was smooth and slick, like anyone who was refined in their speech. This, of course, was also because Jack had sobered up. His intelligence glistened like finely polished china and was represented in his eloquent mannerisms - when he wasn't under any kind of influence of alcohol or narcotic.

"Why is it like this? What are you searching so hard for in these books and these... things in this apartment?" Liz asked as she walked over to the kitchen table once more. Jack reached over for his flask and went to take a sip from it, only to find that it was empty. He swore as he set it back down.

"What are we looking for?" Jack asked, turning his attention back to her. He stood up and walked over to the window.

"No, what are *you* looking for? There's clearly a deeper meaning to all of this," She pointed out. Jack felt he could appreciate how her mind worked. No one else cared about how other people thought quite as she did.

"...I suppose I just want to know how everything works," he finally answered after he pondered his response.

"How everything works? Jack, your texts study advanced mathematics and science. You've volumes on chemistry and physics, and your experiments grossly elaborate the intense research you've clearly done into the bodies of animals. How could you possibly still not understand how everything works? Your rent aside, I can see where your excess in pay goes when it's not pouring out strong drink," She pointed out with an exasperated smile. "You should be working towards a doctorate at a university and going on to discover whatever is next to discover. Something that will propel our society by hundreds of years."

"Your exasperation is complimentary," he responded politely, "Yet you mistake my meaning. If someone thinks they know all things and they are not God, they are a fool to the world and to themselves. As much as I could study, and as much as my brother and I can research in all sciences, mathematics, philosophies, and even religions, we would still know nothing about the universe. As much as I've seen, as much as was taken from me, I come to this realization; I understand nothing. Pain blurs my vision and compromises my emotion. When that is unreliable, I must turn to intellect for answers. Thus, it is my endless quest to know how everything works... I've lost too much to give up on this pursuit."

"You're a mad, paradoxical fool Jack... But your devotion to such pursuit is inspiring as it is ambitious," Liz complimented, and then she sighed. "When do you think the lawman will come knocking on your door?"

"Certainly not any time soon," Jack answered calmly.

"While I wish you wouldn't have ended our work there with such violence... I am grateful for how you stood up for me," she revealed. His ears perked at her comment.

"I'd have done it all over again if I had to."

"But why does it have to be through violent efforts? Could we not have ignored his insult and simply left?"

He was taken aback. "And let the man insult my dearest friend, as well as disrespect my deceased mother and my proud heritage? Absolutely not! He sought an emotional response, so I answered his request with an appropriate solution."

"I'm sorry… It's just that he's merely one man. Your mother… she wouldn't want that from you. I don't want that from you. He controls you through your untamed emotions, Jack…" She cooed.

He was silent as he pondered the weakest argument he could muster in the face of truth. "You would not understand it." The words burned like a viper's venom as they left his lips.

"If you offered me an opportunity to understand, you might be surprised…" Liz said as she walked over to his side. "Again… I'm grateful for you defending me."

Jack didn't say anything; he simply embraced her. They stood there, looking out the window as horse-drawn carriages passed by with creaking wheels and clacking hooves. Some people passed by on the sidewalks; women with elaborate and colorful dresses, while men wore tailored suits.

Of course, pauper citizens such as themselves were dressed as one would expect; dirty clothes stained and worn. Many men and women were covered in dirt and grime from the machinery.

His heart burned unpleasantly when he watched the aristocrats of society flinch as poorer workers of all skin colors passed them by, but even more so when they reacted more dramatically to the colored men and women. He shook his head, disgusted with society. His mother was treated harshly for her middle-eastern heritage as well, and his father fought as viciously for her as Jack did against the foreman. His heart sank, though, when he remembered once more how miserably he missed his mother.

"Let's go to the bakery; we're low on bread, and we could use a savory treat," Jack offered, pulling his mind from the maelstrom of depression that hid just beneath his psyche. "Besides, a little fresh air might calm our nerves"

"We cannot simply leave without seeing if the lawmen come for us, Jack-"

"Trust me," He interrupted, his expression calm.

"I hope we aren't going to find your delivery man," Liz said, shaking her head light-heartedly as she turned to walk out the door with him.

"He might be a stop on the way," He joked.

5:16PM

They both emerged from the bakery laughing,
Jack having finished a simple joke his brother
used to tell him when he was little. He carried
a large, brown paper bag filled with loaves of
freshly baked bread, which also hid a bottle of
whiskey that the shopkeeper sneaked in. He was
good friends with Jack and helped him out when
he was able to. Most people were charged a hefty
price, but Jack received a special discount.

The sun was setting, and there was less activity
on the roads as they made their way back towards
his apartment. Their spirits were lifted, and
they still managed to avoid trouble. Jack was
beginning to believe they were simply going to let
the whole event slide, and he was okay with that.
His worry, though, was over his public displays
with Liz. He had to be careful with how he

treated her in front of strangers. He didn't want anyone assuming something incorrect without there being wedding bands on their fingers, despite the growing trend of casual courtship when a couple was romantically interested.

"That was stupid," Liz chuckled, catching her breath.

"Stupid, but you must acknowledge that it made you laugh," Jack said with a snicker. "My brother used to repeat that to me when my mother was sick, and I was in distress. It made me laugh every time," He added. His heart burned a little with pained emotion as his thoughts drifted to happy memories of her.

"That's very sweet… Perhaps it's not so simple and stupid after all," Liz added with a soft smile. Then, she looked up at him and said, "You're a good man, Jack. You've stolen this pauper woman's heart."

"A heart I'm honored to cherish," he added in a hushed tone. She looked down with a smile as they walked.

"Do you think they'll still be after us?" Liz asked as she looked up at him. She held her other arm and caressed herself nervously. A carriage passed by, with its driver holding his nose in the air as if he were too great to be bothered by the gazes of passerby's. The clacking of the horse's hooves was just enough to fill the awkward silence as Jack thought of an appropriate response.

When it passed completely, though, he froze; across the street stood a creature – humanoid in appearance – with dark, coal-colored skin. It was taller than any human, with unnaturally long limbs and ghastly appendages on its hands that resembled the fingers of a sort of skeletal specter. Men feared demons, but this creature looked as though it was something worse. A stale scent in the air filled his nose, and fear paralyzed his body.

On its head, which sat on a long and thin neck, were two horns curved to almost make a perfect circle, covered in red eyes that focused directly on Jack. Its gaping maw twisted into an angry snarl, lined with and unnatural amount of needle-like teeth.

For a moment, he felt Liz tugging his sleeve, but he could barely hear her calling his name. It was all a vain effort; he ignored anything else or feel anything else as the thing pointed a long, bony finger at him. Then, as if he were suddenly experiencing a nightmare, its jaw opened beyond what any normal creature was capable, and let out a blood-curdling shriek that sounded like the pained screams of all an infant, a child, a young man, a young woman, and an old man and old woman at once. As it wailed at him, a black smog began to flow from its feet and spread. Jack was frozen with fear, unable to pay attention to anything else around him. He screamed in terror, but he couldn't hear his own voice.

Then, as another carriage passed, it was gone. In front of him stood a startled and concerned Liz. Jack gasped, realizing that he wasn't breathing after his utter shriek, and then leaned on his knees as he caught his breath, having dropped the bag of bread. He could hear everything again, from the sounds of people walking by to Liz gently asking Jack "Are you okay? What happened?"

"I don't know," Jack said with a shaky voice as he stood upright. "Honestly, I don't know... I just had the strangest hallucination."

"Are these frequent?" Liz asked as she gently placed her hands on his cheeks and looked into his eyes.

"Not typically..." Jack said as he looked back over her shoulder. Her eyes followed his, examining the area for what he might have seen.

"What did you see?" She finally asked.

"I cannot explain it... I just... I cannot," Jack said. She looked down at the bag of bread that hid the whiskey, and then back up at him with a look of sarcastic disbelief on her face.

"Perhaps it was the drinks? Or maybe the lack-there-of?" Liz pointed out in a hushed tone. Many people who were barely in range of his loud cry finally passed them by, straying as far from them as possible as they gave concerned, fearful looks.

"I haven't had anything like that ever happen to me when I've had to go without drinking," Jack defended. Liz paused for a moment and looked back over to where he was staring, and then she started to walk down the sidewalk again.

"Alright; let's get back home before law enforcement decides to investigate those frightened cries," she said with a nervous tone in her voice. He picked up the bag and followed closely behind her. Occasionally, though, he turned to look back where the creature was. In the empty space where it stood, his scarred mind continued to envision what he saw, wondering what was going on in his head.

8:23PM

Laughter erupted at the dinner table, cleared of its mess by Jack and Adrian, as the eldest brother shared a story from their childhood. Liz and Jack drank most of the whiskey, while his chestnut-haired brother only had a few glasses. "Truly I declare, Jack was a trouble-maker his whole life," Adrian added, his voice deeper than Jack's.

"I knew he was, but not to such an extent," Liz commented as she took another sip of whiskey, with a sheepish grin spread across her flustered face. Jack snickered and poured another glass.

"What more could I say," Jack added; "I never knew how to do good things, so I just did what I wanted, and sometimes I misbehaved along the way. Our youngest brother was quite upset with how his coat was torn. If he were here and not in Ireland, he'd still be trying to make Adrian get him a new one, despite my hand in damaging it!"

His brother chuckled and took another sip of his drink as his crystal-blue eyes drifted into memories of their times together. He was a broad-shouldered, tall man with a fine physique. He kept himself as healthy as he was able to, but he could only do so much working at a factory.

"But you ruined the guy's suit by throwing a broken pen on him!" Liz pointed out with a chuckle.

"Correct, but I stand beside myself; he deserved it."

"As much as you deserved every beating mother gave you," Adrian added. "Anyways, I'm going to retire. I've had enough drink, and I don't need a pounding forehead in the morning when I have to go to the factory. You two enjoy the rest of your night," Adrian said as he stood up from the table and walked back towards his bedroom.

"I'll see you in the morning!" Jack called out. Adrian smirked and shut his bedroom door behind him.

"I'm surprised no lawmen ever came to our doorstep after that incident today..." Liz commented as she leaned forward on the table.

"It's as I predicted; that swine wouldn't have the courage to attempt to bring such judgment down on us."

"I guess we should be grateful he didn't try to come here himself, then," Liz added.

Jack erupted in laughter. "I'd greet him at the door," Jack spat. "I wouldn't let him come near us, Liz."

She grabbed his hand and started to gently caress it. "I know you wouldn't, Jack… You know, I've never had a man so instinctively interested in my well-being before you," she admitted.

Jack's eyebrows furrowed. "What do you mean?" He asked calmly.

"I mean, no one has ever really been so nice to me. My parents raised me well enough, but I've always been a shy and quiet girl. Always quiet… Always listening to the rules and learning to mind my manners and pay attention to my own matters rather than involve myself in the business of others. Many people in my life took advantage of that. Remember how cold and frigid I was when we first met?"

"Quite," Jack confirmed as he listened intently to her.

"I wasn't ready to open up to you. I thought you'd be just like everyone else. But you… you were different. You didn't treat me like I was a tool to use."

"…I'm sorry other people couldn't have been

so kind to you…"

She didn't say anything. Instead, she stood to her feet and calmly made her way over to him, and then started to rub his back. "So, when I choose to give you myself… It's because you didn't try to force yourself upon me or use me like everyone else did," she said. His heart leapt into his throat.

"You know I wouldn't do that to you," Jack cooed. He stood to his feet and wrapped his arm around her, placing his hand on the small of her back. His mind buzzed and his heart burned in his chest with passion. Suddenly, he forgot about the strange creature he hallucinated. "…I love you… So very deeply…"

It was just Elizabeth and him.

"Are you sure you want to have me like this, Jack? You don't want to let the alcohol fade first?" Liz asked softly.

Longing filled his eyes when he looked at her. He admired her soft lips, her smooth skin, and the curves of her figure. She was an elegant artwork to him, something the divine hid in the mire of the pauper and the poor. His heart throbbed as he entertained his passionate fantasy with her. Was this his reality? Was he truly this fortunate, to have been blessed with such a powerfully elegant and beautiful creation in his life? He decided not to question it.

"I don't need alcohol to know how I feel about you, Elizabeth," Jack whispered back with a sly half-smile. Liz looked down as she broke away and turned around as she held her arm nervously.

"Why now, though?" She asked, keeping her back facing him. "Why confess these strong emotions to me now? Why, when there's such strong drink in your stomach? Why not when we first laid down with each other?"

"I don't have an answer for you... I suppose in some ways, I thought I was obvious. In others, I wasn't sure what your reaction would be..." Jack admitted as he approached her and started to gently caress her arms. She took a deep breath, turned to face him, and then pressed her lips to his.

"Wasn't I obvious enough, Jack?" She asked as she kissed him again.

Jack didn't answer, instead he placed his one hand behind her head and the other behind her back, pulling her closer.

"I think we like the guessing game a bit too much," Jack said with a smirk. He took her hand and led her back to his room. The door closed behind them, and they led each other into the night, drinking deep of the euphoria of each other's intimacy. Jack had no regrets.

…They were in this life together.

April 18, 1906 - 5:06AM

Jack!

The voice woke him out of a dead sleep. He looked over at Liz who slept peacefully beside him, the sheets covering her modestly. He didn't know why, but an unsettled feeling came over him. He quietly put on his pants and shirt, then walked out of the bedroom. He gingerly made his way through the kitchen, the only sounds breaking the silence coming from the soft padding of his bare feet against the hardwood floor. The dark was eerie to navigate, imposing an element to the air of some impending doom.

The kitchen was empty, as well as the living room. Jack's heart began to pound faster as he walked over to the window and moved the curtain aside. Then he froze, fear gripping him once more. Across the street, standing ominously on the sidewalk, was the creature from before, staring directly up at him.

"Jack?" Liz asked from behind, jolting him as though she had spoken with a voice of thunder. She had tied the sheets around herself, and delicately played with her fingers. He could tell she was probing for answers to the feeling she caged in her chest. A feeling just like his. Jack exhaled. His nerves began to calm after seeing her face. Then, to his dismay, he could hear her breathing increase before erupting into an ear-piercing scream.

He turned around to see the monster floating just outside the window, glaring angrily with all its eyes focused directly on him. He backed away slowly as the creature began to phase through the window and wall. It hovered into the apartment, and a faint glow splashed the darkened walls with a hint of crimson red.

He didn't hesitate; he ran to Liz and tried to rush her to safety, but just as quickly, he dropped to the ground and the world around him started to shake violently.

"BETRAYER!!!", the monster screamed in its multi-toned voice. The crimson light glowed brighter, and cast its evil hue onto the walls around them. Liz shrieked in terror, and the apartment shook with violence and force. Jack looked up, and suddenly, the monster had red light glowing through cracks all over its body.

With a loud boom, the creature shrieked in bitter rage, and it burst into nothingness. The light, however, remained. Jack glanced at it once more, but instead of the beast, a fearful symbol took its place; an inverted cross, with a bleached core, and glowing with a tone as red as the blood pumping through his veins.

Horror.

Horror gripped their hearts, and the world around them shook and crumbled with a force they'd never heard of before in their entire lives.

Horror, and the wafting air of death's decrepit approach.

...Nothing is as it seems...

5:12AM – The San Francisco Earthquake of 1906

Jack was desperate, Liz was terrified, and Adrian woke without any idea of what was going on. They were together in the kitchen during the final moments, all witnessing the bright, inverted cross glowing in their living room. Jack held Liz close, covering her from anything that might fall overhead. Adrian joined him.

The only thing they could hear was the sound of the earth shaking. Jack could barely hear Liz's terrified screams as he tried to keep her safe. They didn't know what was going to happen, but they knew it couldn't be good.

Everything's going to be okay, a quieted voice said in his mind. It was quieter than all of the chaos around them, and yet it was louder than everything.

Then the roof began to collapse around them.

Tell them to close their eyes.

"CLOSE YOUR EYES!!!" Jack yelled obediently.

Now you close your eyes. Jack obeyed, hoping they did as well. He heard everything collapsing around him, and then he heard the screams of the people outside.

And then... He heard nothing at all...

All faded into darkness, and he wondered...

Did I just die?...

No, Jack. Your tale has just begun...

III

A Cosmic Fantasy

Here be no logic humans can recognize.
No laws we know. Magic exists where our
imagination can't explain.

Awaken

A cool breeze gently caressed Jack's face while the sounds of strange animals could be heard from afar. There were the smells of pine and forest, and thick grass served as a polite bedding under him as he started to come around, which created a humble barrier between him and the rough ground. He was content to ignore it and treat everything like a bad nightmare, but the strange and fantastic noises of the world around him filled him with worry and fear. Did all of that really happen? Did the entire world crumble around them? Did they just lose *everything*?

His eyes shot open, but quickly reduced to a squint in the brilliance of the bright sun. Blue skies unanimously coated the background like a canvas, with puffy white clouds that slowly passed by overhead. The colors were crisp, and the glare from the sun created an image that would permanently etch in his mind until the day he died.

He sat up and looked around. There were stone bricks too large for one person to carry, scattered all around in the ruins of an ancient temple. Nature reclaimed it with winding vines and green leaves, leaving the temple bare and exposed to the clearing it sat in. A forest was beyond it, but what his eyes were drawn to was a tree taller than the tallest building he'd ever seen. Red leaves rustled in the winds above, leaves that he predicted were larger than any on earth.

He couldn't help but to notice the steady increase in his heart rate, or the burning in his chest as panic settled in. The sensation of tiny needles pricking his skin stole his consciousness from his gawking, and his arms and legs started to feel heavy. Why did this happen to him? Why was he the one that creature shook the earth over? All he'd ever done was try to survive and stay hidden. He wasn't a hero, wasn't a man of noble character. No, in fact, he was a mixture of two things his American society hated; Irish and Jewish. He was an outcast, tossed aside, forgotten.

He inhaled sharply when his lungs started to throb with the pain of starvation, reminding him to breath. "Liz," Jack said with a raspy voice as he crawled over to her unconscious form, still covered by the torn sheet she had turned into a gown. His clothes were stained and dirty, and his suspenders dangled off to his sides. Dirt and grime stained her pale skin, but it couldn't mar her beauty even then. His heart throbbed with both pleasure and pain, aching with hope that she was still alive.

He gently shook her shoulder, trying to wake her. After a few moments, her eyes squinted a little, and he sighed in relief. She started to cough as she sat up, Then Adrian followed suit. They all stood to their feet, startled by the strange, foreign environment they now found themselves in.

"What is this?" Adrian asked in rhetoric. The two stared in disbelief at the massive tree behind them. Liz reached out for Jack's hand and gripped it tightly.

"I have no idea, Adrian," Jack said quietly. They were lost. Their home was destroyed. He had no idea what happened, how they were there, where they even were or what he was going to do to get them home. His heart sank in his chest with dread.

He was lost.

He'd lost.

Everything was lost.

"We need to find someone, Jack," Liz said with

a sharp inhale and an unsteady voice. "What was that thing? And what did it do to our home?" She continued. Jack was silent. Tears began to well under her eyes. "What happened to all those people? Or our friends? Our home?" She cried.

"What was that light?" Adrian asked. A fiery rage burned in his eyes, and elevated the tone in his voice. "Why did everything shake like that?"

"Why was that creature snarling at you?" Liz pressed.

"What aren't you telling us? Did you start a fight again?! This is the same reason why mother died!"

"Why did it call you a betrayer?"

"What-"

"I DON'T KNOW WHAT HAPPENED!!!" Jack screamed with clenched fists. This time he couldn't stop it; the tears flowed freely from his eyes. He did everything he could to maintain his composure. "I don't know what that thing was, and I don't know why everything started to shake! I don't know!" Jack stammered. Panic set in. "I know that everyone is gone, and I know our home was destroyed, but I don't know any more than either of you!"

They paused, then Liz calmly rested a hand on his shoulder. She released her roiled tension in an exasperated sigh, and then looked up at

Adrian.

"Whatever that thing was, obviously it was after Jack and the two of us. I think we should just start looking for clues. Perhaps something around here will have an answer?" Liz suggested.

Adrian laughed. "We wake up in some new place without any idea of how we got here, and we think we're just going to find clues to what happened? Look around, Elizabeth! The way I see it is *we're dead!* This is the afterlife!" Adrian barked as he turned and kicked one of the massive stones that belonged to the ruins.

Jack stood and took in a deep breath, calming his nerves.

"Being emotionally distraught will serve us no good. I don't know anything about where we are, but before everything fell silent, I *did* hear a voice telling me that we weren't dead... So, wherever this is, maybe we're still very much alive," Jack revealed.

Adrian approached him and grabbed his collars, picking him up off the ground. "Everyone is dead, Jack! Dead! Whatever that thing was, it's your-"

"STOP!!!" Liz shouted, interrupting him.

Jack quickly wormed his arms under Adrian's and shoved him away. "I agree! Fighting each other is the worst mistake we could make right

59

now!" Jack barked.

"Then what do you propose, *oh wise and omnipotent one?!*" Adrian spat as he brushed off his stained shirt. "What *possible* solution could you offer that will keep me from *beating you into the ground* like the god-forsaken weasel you are?!"

Jack turned away, unable to look his brother in the eyes. His words stung, and invoked a bitter rage he could barely contain. It wasn't what they needed right now. Fighting *would* make things worse. Emotions were the highest they'd ever been, and he had to remind himself that Adrian didn't mean the things he said. He *needed* to remind himself of that. If he didn't, they would fall apart, and they would never make it to *any* home.

"Both of you: stop it! This solves nothing! We need each other! We can't lose each other in our anger!" Liz shouted.

They were silent. Adrian folded his arms and faced away from his brother.

"Look; Jack didn't cause an earthquake, Adrian. That's not possible. Whatever that *thing* was – that's what did it. So, if you're going to blame anything, blame that creature! Jack, you shoving your brother and trying to fight with him does nothing but get him more angry! We need each other in this situation! It's not your fault those people are dead, so stop blaming yourself! We're here, and we're alive now," Liz shouted.

Jack and Adrian exhaled their tension and rage, but when he saw the slip of white in Jack's pocket, his temper flared up again. He snatched a letter with Jack's name on the front, written in the finest penmanship.

"What's this?" Adrian barked as Jack backed away, bearing a frustrated and surprised expression on his face.

"How should I know?" Jack snapped back. He quickly snatched it back and opened it.

Jack,

Please understand, the terrors you and those with you witnessed needed to happen. I know you're confused, and I know you don't know where you are, but just trust in me. Everything will be okay. Don't be afraid. Look for a short, crimson-maned elvish woman named Ayela. She will tell you everything.

Sincerely,
Ruat.

Post-Script; Nothing is as it seems.

Jack's brow furrowed. So many questions swirled in his mind. Who was Ruat? Who was

Ayela? Elvish? Were they in a land ruled by elves of ancient myths and legends? He didn't have an answer, nor was he able to come up with one. All he knew was that he held a clue in his hands...

A clue that had given them no direction save for one...

"...I don't think we're on earth anymore," Jack finally said. His gaze fell on the letter and lingered there. A lingering line from the note burned like the glaring sun as a mental image in his mind...

...Nothing is as it seems.

The World of Thaeru

They spent hours navigating the woods. Their feet hurt from walking, and their bodies hadn't recovered from the trauma of their home collapsing around them, but they carried an alertness that kept them from stopping to rest. The creatures echoing through the woods left them alone, and despite the darkness in the distance, the sun above kept the forest floor well-lit. Their path, though it winded like a serpent, remained relatively level. Smells of pine and other scents Jack couldn't recognize filled his nose, fueling his anxious state of mind.

With a sharp stone in hand, he felt a little more at ease knowing he could defend himself and the others if needed. That feeling, though, only went so far. His heart beat rapidly in his chest, pumping his brain full of adrenaline. Anxiety was his dominant emotion, and he whipped his head back and forth at even the slightest sound. If a twig snapped underfoot, or a branch was snapped from a tree in the distance, he noticed with paranoia.

To his relief, however, the trees broke. They reached the end of the wood, and were faced with a clearing full of golden grass as far as the eye could see. Wherever they were, the cool breeze grazing across their skin and the deathly scenery before them implied an autumn season. Jack took a deep breath, and could feel the cool air rushing down his throat and into his lungs.

Just beyond the endless field, past their apparent horizon, were silhouettes of mountain ranges that rose above the landscape like teeth. Only a single opening laid before them, a break in the mountains that forced them to take that direction. The only problem was that a dark storm loomed over it, unmoving yet constantly shifting. He hadn't noticed when the sky shifted from clear to cloudy, but in that moment, it didn't seem to matter. They were forced by the world around them to waltz into a storm that instilled a sense of dread in their hearts.

"How welcoming…" Liz finally said, breaking the silence.

"It seems we either go back or we go towards

it," Adrian noted.

Grand. Everything was grand. The grass seemed taller than it would normally have been on earth. The mountains in the distance seemed so far away, yet so much larger. Who knew whether the creatures that ruled this land were greater than earth's humble predators as well. Thunder rumbled in the distance, echoing in the massive, stationary storm that lingered ahead. There was an ominous veil that slowly draped over the three, creating an uneasy awareness in their hearts. The hairs stood on the backs of their necks.

"What is this place?" Jack asked rhetorically as he took his arm off Liz and stepped forward, as if that would help him get a closer look. The breeze started to blow harder and roar a little louder in their ears.

"Whatever it is, I think we all know we're supposed to go there…"

"Yeah…" Jack said as he started to rub his pounding head. He wasn't sure what was causing it: perhaps it was the chaotic orchestra of events that happened the previous night, or perhaps it was the world they suddenly found themselves on.

"What, now you're going to tell me that you need a drink?" Adrian barked. "Your drinking gets you in so much trouble- Why do I even bother? You never listened to me before."

Adrian's comment took him by surprise. "What?" He stammered, confused.

"Your head's pounding, which usually happens when drunks go without their alcohol for any period of time-

"Adrian; that's not how the signs of a drunk going without a drink works! You think a small headache is what I'd be going through if I were addicted? I wouldn't have even left the ruins we woke up in!"

"I don't need lectures from a hypocrite, Jack!"

"You drank with us last night!" Jack defended. He couldn't believe what he was hearing. Of all the things to attack him for, he was astonished that Adrian would pick alcohol.

"But that's the thing, Jack; I don't drink every day! I show restraint!"

"BOTH OF YOU, STOP SHOUTING AT EACH OTHER!!!" Liz screamed with her fists clenched. Her voice echoed off unseen walls, reverberating in their heads as the silent shock and tension settled in their minds. Jack was unsure how to respond. "Here we are in the middle of a world we don't know, with a storm we don't recognize over the horizon, and maybe even with wild and violent animals that we've never seen – and you two want to pick each other apart like vultures?! SHUT YOUR FUCKING MOUTHS, YOU IDIOTS!!!"

Her indignant expression pierced through the hair that the strong and sudden breeze pulled across her face. She was justified, and entirely correct; the two of them were acting like children. After a few moments, the chill of the hastened wind danced across her exposed arms and shoulders, and she shivered as she held herself. He looked down, and the guilt of not having something to keep her warm overcame him. Like the storm ahead, his emotions swirled in his chest with an uneasy burning, making him feel as though he needed to be guilt over something.

Then, in a spiral, his thoughts swam through memories of his mother and the hardships of their lives. The guilt of all the things he hadn't been able to do for himself, his brothers, his father, and for Liz raged in his heart, and threatened to send him over the edge of insanity. They were like a roller coaster of ups and downs, unregulated emotions in their most extreme forms. He didn't have the knowledge or strength to know how to control them, despite how hard he tried. And though the sensations of pleasure the whiskey wrought were enough to help him sleep and carry on with their lives, it made his emotions and feelings that much harder to control.

"I… I'm sorry… I know I've gotten worse lately, but you don't understand the weight… It's too much to bear. I try to stop drinking, because I don't want to become addicted, but the weight of the emotion just feels so heavy, and it's so hard to care anymore… It was always hard, and my emotions were always heavy, but once our mother died… And once our brother moved away… It just got worse. I have guilt that I cling to, and I know what these feelings are, I just don't know what to do with them, and it manifests itself in erratic, obnoxious behavior… And now this? This world? That terrible earthquake? The amount of pressure this induces just makes it worse. I'm trying to retain myself, I just don't know how," Jack admitted. Their silence implied their sympathy and understanding.

"I'm sorry, brother…" Adrian consoled. He put a hand on his shoulder and looked upon him with care and concern, then pulled him in for an embrace. "We're just lost, confused, and suffering from what we just went through," he added. Liz gently grabbed his hand.

"Let's go find this Ayela… Let's find a way to get home," She said with a gentle voice. Jack took a deep breath and looked back towards the storm clouds in the distance. The howling wind was steadily getting louder as they stood there.

"What fairs this weather? Why is the sky the way it is?" Jack pointed out as he looked around.

"I don't know. Perhaps we'll find out the further we walk," Liz suggested. Jack nodded, and they continued to press forward...

A Storm Unmoving

Time was irrelevant. Whether they emerged from the magical wood in the morning or not didn't seem to matter; they'd spent what-felt-like the entire day walking through the golden sea of autumn grass.

They were far away from the forest – to the point where it was barely visible behind them. All they could see in their surroundings was the circle of mountain ranges, and the hastening of the dark storm ahead. They were passing through the opening of the mountains, and Jack's heart seemed to beat a little faster when he saw the darkened silhouette of rooftops peering over they furthest hill.

That hope was quickly dashed, though.

It only took seconds for him to realize the only reason he could see the silhouettes was because of the orange glow of flickering flames beyond. Whatever town they managed to stumble upon, it was wrought with destruction. Liz clasped her hands over her mouth, and Adrian's fists tightened with anxiety. Jack, however, picked up his pace and broke out into a race to the top of the hill.

Before he could make it to the top, though, a clap of thunder burst with such force, the three of them were knocked onto their backs. Then, in an instant, the skies were cleared and the breeze had stopped. Everything was so sudden. Everything was eerily silent, save for the crackling of flames lapping up the last bit of life from the wooden homes they smoldered.

"What the hell," Jack growled. As soon as he was on his feet, he was racing down to the town. All it took to stop him, though, was a quick glance at the pillars of smoke above. Hovering over the charred remains was a symbol much like the one that destroyed his home, emulating a blue hue from its white cores. It wasn't the same upside-down cross he saw, but it didn't matter. Whatever shook the earth clearly came from this world.

His heart pounded in his chest, threatening to break out of his rib cage as he struggled to catch his breath. The others came up behind him, gawking at the same symbol that had stolen his undivided attention. They were all at a loss for words. They were all frozen in fear and awe.

Just as quickly, though, he was brought back to the land of the living when he heard the distant screams of a child. There wasn't an ounce of hesitation. He leapt over the charred, crumbled gate with Liz and Adrian close behind, frantically searching for anywhere a child might be hiding. Her screams grew louder and louder, and his movements sharpened with adrenaline and urgency.

They leapt over a pile of charred wood and onto a road, and just when he thought they were too late, he heard a loud "HELP!" From one of the homes still in flames. Jack burst through the door, and the three of them rushed around the house searching everywhere a child might hide.

If it wasn't for what happened next, her life might have burnt up in the fires of destruction. Jack tripped over a piece of wood laying in the middle of the floor, and crashed onto his chest. He groaned, but before he was able to get up, he saw a young bundle of child wrapping her arms around her stained legs, as though she were waiting for the inevitable. His heart leapt in his throat.

"Found her! Get out of here!" Jack yelled. Adrian and Liz obeyed.

He crawled over to her and held out his hand, but was met with an ear-piercing shriek, followed with an image of her backing farther away. Then he noticed it; pointed ears poking through curtains of nearly-black hair, and frightened violet eyes.

"Take my hand, child!" He called out.

"Uh-uh!" The girl cried as she cowered further away from him.

"This place is going to collapse! Let's go!" He shouted. Time began to slow down, and as she held herself tighter, he could feel a shift in the air.

A dangerous shift.

He scrambled onto his feet and ran to her, swooping her out of the closet as he turned and dashed like his life depended on it. He leapt over the growing flames, and stumbled as he slipped on the soot-covered ground outside. She rolled a couple feet ahead, but he didn't give them a a single moment to catch their breath. The wood creaked, and the roar of the flames grew louder. Their time was even shorter than he'd anticipated.

"Go! Go!" He yelled to the others as he lifted the girl into his arms once more. She buried her face into his chest and clung tightly to him. They ran with every ounce of strength left in their legs, boosted by a rush of oxygen from the charred air.

They ran, and the fires around them crept out of the homes they consumed, lapping up the remaining flesh from the blackened bones that once were people. The fires set their sights on them, giving them chase with a voracious appetite. The gate they came through was there in sight, though, struggling to stay open long enough for them to make their escape. With a final push of strength and energy, they jumped through the opening, and rushed towards the top of the hill they descended down.

Once they were at the top, the town behind them exploded with a violent blast. The force of the sudden burst threw them all forward and sent them rolling down a shaken hill, safely away from any flames that threw themselves at the group. The girl cried from her pain, covered in scratches and cuts, while the three of them groaned and slowly pushed themselves off the ground. He hadn't realized how sore he was until he felt his limbs shake with weakness.

They rose to their feet, though, and with pained movement, they climbed back to the top of the hill. Jack held out his hand to the little girl, and with as warm of a smile as he could muster, he pulled her into a reassured embrace while she wept into his shirt.

"Jack…" Liz called with a shaking voice. His ears perked, and he could hear an strange, super-natural hum from somewhere above. He turned to gaze at a cross like the one in their apartment. Even its hue was the same crimson color.

"What… *is* this?" Jack asked as he stood to his feet, exasperated. "What's going on? Why are all these symbols popping up?"

"Um, excuse me…" The little girl interrupted with a timid, quaky voice.

"Wait- how do you know to speak English?" Adrian asked abruptly. The girl flinched, and Jack held out a hand to his brother as if to stop him from asking anymore questions.

"…I guess…" She answered shyly. "You don't look like normal people. Are you gods?" She continued, rubbing her pointed ears.

"We're humans," Liz responded. "What are you?"

"I'm… I'm a elvish girl… *Humans?*"

"Correct," Jack answered. "That's our species… Our race. *Elf* is your species?"

"I guess…" she said. Tears began to well in her eyes, and shortly after, she burst into pained sobbing.

Jack's eyes drifted towards the symbol that hovered over the ruined town. He dropped to his knees and pulled her into a hug while she wept on his shoulder.

"Momma and papa... They're all dead," she cried as she gripped handfuls of his shirt.

"I know, little one," Jack whispered soothingly. "What happened?"

"My town was... It was judged," She revealed. The air seemed to thicken from the tension. They didn't know what it meant for a town to be judged, but as he looked back at the charred remains of the town where flames once engulfed, he couldn't imagine what caused such destruction. What kind of being would inflict such destruction upon such a people? Stranger still, how did this girl *survive*?

"Judged?" He finally asked.

"Uh-huh... They come in the storms that don't float away, and they pick if the people they float over are worth passing by... No one has ever been worth it... When it came, papa hid me in the closet and said I'd be safe. Everyone screamed so long..." she answered.

"What is it?" Liz asked. She walked over to the girl and dropped down to her knees.

"...Papa said no one knows... But we call them aethrils," she said. There was mystery and an eldritch horror that surrounded the name. Jack's skin crawled as he imagined what the creature must have looked like. Fearing the worst, he shook his head and cleared his mind.

"What's your name, little one?" Jack asked.

"I'm Zesha. My momma's name was Sesha, and my papa's name was Vröm," Zesha answered. "Who are you?" Jack and the others exchanged glances.

"We're... San Franciscans. I'm Jack, the girl beside you is Liz, and the guy behind me is Adrian," Jack answered. But before Zesha could respond, a grumbling noise in the distance caught their attention. They turned around and noticed a strange object flying towards them.

"Run!" Jack yelled as he scooped up Zesha once more, and the three of them quickly dashed towards the burnt ruins of the town. With the flames gone, they were able to find a place to hide with relative ease. The heat lingered, but it wasn't unbearable. For the time being, they would need to put up with it.

They hid in the first empty building they could find, with Jack keeping watch. It felt like mere minutes before the sounds of spewing fires louder than anything they'd ever heard blended with alien noises from a technology none of them understood. Jack kept himself as hidden as he could, and peaked up at a boat hovering in the air. It was built with metal, and massive engines protruded from the rear that spewed out cyan.

His heart was in his throat, and terror gripped him to his core. They all covered their ears, all but himself. He shouted for them all to go hide, but he couldn't even hear himself think. Instead, he took Zesha and hid in a corner while the others found their own places to hide, and hid her away from any strange creature that might drop out of the airship. When he looked upon her face, though, he saw a hopeful smile. He'd hoped that meant they were going to pass them by.

To his dismay, though, it meant quite the opposite.

Lights flashed, and figures dressed head-to-toe in metal armor burst into the building they were hiding in. Each of them moved quickly and violently, and trained strange rifles on Jack and Zesha. Others went throughout the building and found Liz and Adrian, and dragged them into the soot-covered living room.

"Wait! Wait!" Jack pleaded, placing himself between them and Zesha, but it was to no avail. With on swift motion, the figure took the butt of his rifle and smacked Jack on his forehead. The force of the impact was powerful, and he quickly felt hid consciousness flee to the recesses of his mind. Once more, his reality faded to black, and he was left to swim in the black seas of unconscious dreams...

IV

A Deathly Empire

When evil tips the balance, wicked men
will always wield undue power.

The Imperial Interrogator

Gasp!

His eyes shot open once again to suddenly shrink to a squint. Once more he was in a strange environment. Once more his head pounded, his body felt weak, and confusion gripped his unstable mind. There were no creatures surrounding them, though. Not this time. He didn't find a bedding of soft grass, but rather, the shrill cool and discomfort of a metal table. He tried to move his arms, but his wrists and ankles were bound.

He looked around, trying to get a sense of his surroundings, but only found strange walls with a slick, glossy coating, and fantastic machinery. Everything was clean, glistening, and reflected the brilliant light that shined onto his face. His heart sank when he saw Liz and Adrian, still unconscious, bound just like he was. Zesha, however, was nowhere to be found.

"What the hell," he stammered. He tried to sit up, but couldn't.

"I wouldn't do that if I were you," said a deep, powerful voice from the far side of the dimmed room.

"Where am I?" Jack asked with a raspy voice.

"You're somewhere secret until I get answers."

Footsteps filled Jack's ears as a darkened figure slowly approached. The pain from getting hit by the rifle throbbed against his skull, but nothing compared to the panic that throbbed in his heart. Fear and anxiety were his emotions. He worried for their safety. He worried for Zesha. He did what he could to keep himself from imagining what their captors might have done to her. In the midst of the chaos, his heart added a third emotion; anger.

"First… What are you?" the figure started.

Frustrated. He felt frustrated. Were there no humans at all on this world?

"I'm a human. How do you people – you know what; never mind. Who are you?"

There was a deep laugh, and then his captor spoke. "First, you'll answer my questions. What were you doing at the wreckage of that town?"

"That's a good question. I'll get back to you on

that when I figure out what world I've stumbled into."

"No, you don't get to speak in disrespectful tones here. What were you doing at the wreckage of that town?"

Jack took a deep breath and mulled over how he was going to answer him. Who was this man? Where was he? Were they safe? He certainly didn't feel like it. He was confused and afraid, but he needed to maintain his composure. Their lives were at stake.

"Where am-"

"NO! ANSWER MY QUESTION! WHAT WERE YOU DOING AT THE WRECKAGE OF THAT TOWN?!" He barked with ferocious rage, slamming his fists onto the table loud enough to wake a mountain. Clearly Jack was in no position to start a fight.

"I don't know… We just woke up here yesterday and were looking for help. We saw the smoke rising from that town after these strange clouds vanished from over it, and then we rushed over to help. That's when we met that little girl… Where is she?"

"She's fine. She's being cared for. We're beginning the process of zoning her now. She'll be placed in a loving home. As for you, *human*, you're here with us until my superiors decide that you're no longer worth sparing."

"Look, whatever you're planning on doing with us, it's not worth it-"

"You will not speak unless spoken to, understood?" He interrupted. Jack was silent.

"UNDERSTOOD?!"

"Yes," he stuttered compulsively, shaken by the thunderous volume of his interrogator's voice.

"Good. Your cooperation is in your best interest, I assure you. If not, we will resort to our next procedure rather quickly. I won't lie to you; it will be painful. Answer my questions truthfully – I'll know if you were lying – and we may spare you any pain. Don't, and you'll all be tortured until either dead, or you give us what we want. Understood?"

"Yes."

"Good. Now, what nation are you from?"

"The United States of America," Jack answered truthfully. The interrogator paused.

"Not good enough," he retorted. "We'll try again. What nation are you from?"

"I assure you, I speak the truth," he insisted.

"Perhaps... Your accent resembles a native from Durinveii, however, and your tattered appearances from when we came across you could have been a ruse. See, we ran blood tests on you three. You're carbon-based lifeforms, like us, and your blood contains similar iron levels. We both bleed red. I don't buy into this 'human' ruse. It sounds like an unoriginal attempt at disguising covert operations to infiltrate Enthedrillan society. Only a few times in the past have other nations tried to send in teenagers with modified ears and augmentations to retain their youthful appearances. Only, we learned from the past. It won't work again this time," the man explained.

"What? You seriously don't believe me?"

"We're at war. Why would I trust anything you say? We're being invaded by two nations, assaulted by a rebellion, having secrets exposed by a hidden society in our own borders, and some alien race decimating our towns quicker than we can rebuild them, and then we find you three there at the wreckage with a survivor – a child that could have easily made up her story so that she would have survived an attack by you... And if you are humans, as you say, which seem to be alien to Thaerv, then it would seem the likeliest of cases that you are indeed responsible for the alien attacks on our towns... Are you understanding me now? You can stop this ruse. You're not fooling anyone. Either confess your nation or tell us why you're invading if you're truly alien. We ensured that you can't escape."

"Clearly... Don't you think that, if we were

aliens like the ones you think we are, we would have escaped these cuffs by now?"

"Put away the attitude. It serves you no bene-ficial purpose. I've considered it, but when we were able to knock you three out and take blood tests, we were confident our tech can indeed retain you," the figure growled as he walked back over to the door and pressed a button on the wall. In an instant, the bright lights shut off and the normal lights for the room cut on. Jack squinted once more, and took in the glossy walls and floors, bleach-white and contrasting black panels with red and blue lights glowing through them. There were no windows, and the room was small. There was a counter with cabinets over them, and a strange sink and faucet.

The shadowed figure, once illuminated, looked like the fiercest warrior Jack had ever seen. His black hair was short and combed neatly back, and it glistened in the light. His skin was tanned and rugged, and he had crimson eyes and ears longer and more pointed than Zesha's. He was tall, nearly seven-and-a-half feet, and was built like a Spartan. He wore a tightly fitted, long-sleeved black shirt with black pants and matching boots. On his neck, and what seemed to stretch all over his torso, were black lines precisely etched into his flesh.

"Soon, we'll find out how you're able to project such vivid holograms and manage to lay waste to our people like you do. We'll figure out what technology you're using, and when we're done analyzing your DNA, we'll have a better understanding-"

"*Holograms?* Aside from the particular detail that I don't even know what that is, how would we possibly be able to articulate them if we're similar in biochemical makeup, and you're not able to reproduce them? Of course, I assume you can't reproduce them."

"You assume correctly," the man said as he looked down. "It was obvious, however, that there are differences between us. Once we have examined your DNA, we'll have greater insight. As for right now... I've had enough of this ruse you continue to play. I demand straight forward answers, or I'll resort to crueler methods."

"Are you daft?! How have I not been obviously honest with you?! How do we even look like anything other than what we are?! Look at our attires!" Jack pointed out as he dropped his head back. His head started to pound even worse, then his mouth started to feel dry. His stomach growled from an intense hunger, and the stress of their situation stung his nerve endings like pin needles under his skin.

"I can see that. Quite frankly, I don't care. Disguises are an often thought of tactic when infiltrating a country or planet," He said as he pushed himself off the wall and started to walk back over to Jack, his arms folded across his chest. "As far as I'm concerned, you're a threat to our nation and world. For the good of the Reman race, I would very much like to kill you."

"Here we are, having a normal conversation, and you want to just kill us? After showing that we're intelligent lifeforms, too? A different race than your own?"

"With the situation I find our nations and world in, I have no reason to trust anything you say. Anything. The most beneficial thing you could offer us, if you are indeed aliens, is silence."

Jack looked over at Liz, wondering how she wasn't awake yet. Adrian was more excusable – he could sleep through a tornado. "Not only are you wrong, but even after you kill us, it won't stop the towns from being destroyed... And you'll have made yourselves no better than the ones responsible for killing them."

At that, the man paused. "Everyone has guilt in their hearts. We both kill. This is war. All that matters is who you kill for."

"You're a legitimate psychopath."

"We'll do much worse to you and your friends

if you don't give me what I want," he growled, getting close to Jack's face. Then, he backed away and looked over at Liz with a twisted smile. "Maybe I'll start with her."

"You keep your *fucking* hands off her!" Jack barked. He tried with all his might to yank his hands from the cuffs. The man smiled and walked over to her unconscious form. He slowly traced a finger over her exposed jawline. She groaned a little before turning her head over.

"Shh… You'll wake her up," he taunted.

"I'll cut a smile in your face from ear to fucking ear if you do anything to her, cur!"

"Then give me what I want, and I won't have to do anything to her," he demanded.

"I already did! What more would you want? My name? JACK!!! There! Satisfied?!"

"It's a pleasure. I'm Kozek. Now tell me what I want to know," he ordered once more as his fingers delicately brushed over her skin until they rested over the knot that kept her sheet-gown snugly over her body. Jack felt his chest burn, and he clenched his fists as he struggled even harder to break free from the cuffs.

"Isn't she like a child to you, bastard?! You'd do that to a child?!" He spat. Jack's heart pounded wildly in his chest. There was nothing right about this situation. Nothing. They were helpless, subject to the whims of a brute that unfairly saw them as a threat. He prayed in his thoughts, angrily, savagely, that something would happen that would pull him from his wicked actions. He struggled and struggled, wishing and hoping that the amount of noise and clamor her made would wake them up.

"If your tales are true, she's very much an adult. Inasmuch, no teenage girl is as-"

He was interrupted as a device rumbled violently in his pocket. He held it to his ear. "Speak," he ordered. For a few moments, Jack thought he could hear voices coming from it. "I'll be returning shortly... Don't move," Kozek ordered sarcastically. Then, as suddenly as he tried to undress Liz, he rushed out of the room.

Things couldn't have been more wrong than they were now. Perhaps they were dead. Perhaps the world fell apart and it did kill them, and he was just dreaming everything in the last second of his life... But that didn't equate for the creature he saw in his apartment before it happened – nor the word it screamed at him. What had he done? Why was it so angry with him? Why were they here to begin with, on this strange world with no sense of direction, seeking some person named Ayela under the orders of another person named Ruat?

Gasp! Liz woke with a startlingly sudden inhale, followed by Adrian just seconds after. Panic immediately set in as they tried to shake free from their bonds.

"Jack? Are you there??" Liz panicked as she began to rattle her cuffs harder. "Jack-"

"I'm here, Liz... I'm here," Jack said as he looked down at his own cuffs.

"What is all of this?" Adrian asked, startled. "Why are we bound? Did we find their police?"

Jack sighed nervously. "No – worse still. Wherever we are, we're in an empire," he revealed. "And they're no friends of ours."

Breathing heavy, Liz asked, "What do we do?"

Let me help.

In the blink of an eye, the cuffs clicked and fell off them all. "What was that?" Adrian asked as he sat up. Jack didn't answer. Rather, he quickly climbed off the table and snuck over to the door, peering through the skinny window into a well-lit, white-walled hall.

He looked back over at Liz and Adrian, who were quietly getting off their tables. "I don't know where we are, but whoever just released those cuffs will probably lead us out of here," Jack whispered as he peered through the window again.

"Jack, Liz; take these," Adrian softly ordered as he handed long-bladed scalpels to them. Liz took hers with shaking hands.

"A surgery room?" She asked rhetorically. "Or a torture chamber?"

"Perhaps both…" Adrian answered in a haunting tone.

"Are we ready?" Jack asked as he held his hand over the panel the interrogator pressed to open the door. Liz and Adrian nodded and gripped their tools with white knuckles. They were determined, focused, and prepared for anything. He took a deep breath and pressed his hand against it, and the door hissed and slid up with blinding speed.

Cautiously, he peaked his head through the doorway and looked both ways. Both directions seemed endless and threatened to be nothing more than a steel maze of advanced architecture.

Liz peered through with him. "Which way?"

Left.

"There's that voice again," Jack whispered to himself.

"I heard it too," Adrian stated. "And I'm willing to bet that Liz did as well. Perhaps we should trust it."

"Whoever they are, they're on our side," Liz added. Jack nodded and started to run. The others followed.

There's a hall on the right. Take it, or you'll be discovered.

On cue, Jack noticed the passage branched off. Following the guidance of the voice, they ran to the right.

Now run faster. The exit is at the end of this winding hallway, and the interrogator has noticed your absence.

Obediently, he broke out into a mad dash, leading them through its long twists and winding paths. Chaos erupted with an eerie alarm. A mechanical voice spewed words they could barely understand. Their skin crawled and their faces felt numb with fear.

His heart was pounding in his ears almost as loud as the alarm, and his breathing was heavy as he pushed himself to run harder and faster. Behind him, he could hear the armored footsteps of soldiers gaining ground on them, and them barking orders at each other as they approached.

"They're gaining on us!" Liz yelled as they tried to keep up, but the exit was in sight. He couldn't stop, so he ran faster in hopes that it would push them to keep up his pace.

The soldiers caught sight of them. "They found us, Jack!" Adrian yelled as Jack pushed harder. Liz was as fast as he was, but Adrian was falling behind.

He's not going to escape with you.

They were approaching the door quickly and it opened once they were close enough. Jack didn't have time to react. He and Liz jumped as the voice spoke, and they escaped.

But not Adrian.

"Adrian!!!" Jack yelled. Desperately, he tried to get to his brother, but he was too late. The soldiers dogpiled on top of Adrian, though, and Jack's face was covered with despair. All the pain he felt at his mother's death rushed onto him like a wave, crashing down onto his heart and piercing the scar that never truly healed.

"RUN!!!" Adrian screamed. The door shut before Jack could make it. He slammed his fists over and over, pounding to the rhythm of every pained heartbeat he felt pounding in his chest. He was too late. Once again, he was too late. Everything was his fault. His mother's death, his father and youngest brother leaving, and now his eldest brother's capture. He needed to fix it. He needed to fix it all. How could things have gone so wrong?

He hadn't noticed when Liz stood up. He barely felt her hand on his shoulder, or the light tugging on his shirt. He almost didn't hear her sniffling, or the light sobbing as she tried to pull him from his pain. "...Jack..." She whispered. He didn't answer. "Jack, we need to leave... They won't stop with just him... I know it hurts." They'd lost so much already. He couldn't lose his brother too. He *couldn't*. He had to get him back. He'd failed so many already.

Though he wanted to find a way back in, he didn't deny her logic. There would be time to mourn later. There would be time to plan. Right now, they needed to run as fast and as hard as he possibly could. They needed to survive, or all hope truly would be lost. He struggled to fight through his panic, his mental maelstrom. He fought hard against the swirling emotions and the racing thoughts. When they turned to find their avenue of escape, they were stricken by the alien beauty of the city around. Ivory towers reached for the heavens with their golden trimmings. Elegant, elvish in every sense of the word.

There were machines and vehicles of similar color palettes soaring through the air, with loud engines pounding a strange tune in their ears as they passed overhead. They could hear the voices of crowds of people passing by far in the distance on the other side of the wall. When it seemed they'd stumbled into a trap of a small garden on their side, they noticed a ladder built into the wall that climbed to the top, at least twelve feet above them.

Liz looked Jack in the eyes with the same dumbfounded expression, and then looked back out at the city. He wanted to move, but an ominous feeling swirled in his gut, churning and twisting with every dark force the universe wrought. He instinctively turned to the tower once more, and when his eyes scaled to the top - taller than every other building in sight, his entire body went numb.

Atop the tower, glowing with a hue of blood, was an inverted cross like the one in their apartment.

"What does this mean?" Liz asked with a shuddered voice.

Jack reached over and took her hand.

"I don't know, Liz…"

Go find Ayela.

The command was clear, and it was their only direction. They couldn't try to rescue Adrian, not as they were, and it didn't matter who Ayela was. That was their only lead, and possibly their only way home.

"Ayela, then?" Liz asked as they turned to face the wall with the ladder.

"Ayela…" He responded with a determined expression. He stepped forward, trusting that whoever was guiding them was a friend, and not a foe…

V

Destiny's Prime Directive

When something is meant to be, no law of nature can stop its coming.

Ayela, The Destined Meeting

A barrier of trees surrounded the tower, offering them a reprieve of cover while they made their escape. There was no doubt in their minds that whatever police this empire contracted would be searching for them with every effort they could muster. They kept the noise they made to a minimum, and wandered through the bushy woods as quietly as they could. To their advantage, crowds along the sidewalks were thick and noisy, and none seemed to care about two humans escaping arrest.

Elves of all shapes, sizes, skin tones, and hair colors moved to and from, busily making their way to whatever duties this society laid upon them. If they dared to venture out of their cover, they would stick out like a sore thumb. He wasn't sure how they were going to make it, and their anxiety nearly struck them in a panic attack. Was this the end? Was he going to face retribution for his mistakes? Was she going to have to suffer for his failures? He silently prayed that wouldn't be their reality. He hoped that wouldn't be their fate.

Many of the elves dressed in the most revealing clothes he'd ever seen. Women wore pants so tight, they were practically a second layer of skin. Some wore hoodies, some wore shirts without sleeves and deep necks that revealed more of their skin than any woman back home would ever dream of showing. Some even wore shirts that covered the upper half of their torso, but were accompanied by a strange fashion of belts and straps arranged in crossing patterns across their exposed stomachs, reaching down to a wide belt at their hips.

The males wore outfits that matched the women for the most part. Pants were baggier, but didn't contrast with the women's choice. Some wore hoodies, some wore shirts with strange patterns across the chests, and others wore plain sleeveless tops like some of the women wore. Some of them carried pistols at their hips. Others had packs strapped onto their backs. Jack questioned if they were ever going to find a moment of safety or peace for themselves with so many elves bigger than them, and so many that were armed.

Time was irrelevant as they wandered. No, instead, only their fears were what mattered. Their fears, which amplified when they saw the end of the woody park ahead. Roads extended beyond it to the beginning of the trees on the other side, leading to a massive, heavily guarded gate that led into the tower's fortifications.

"We're trapped, and it's only a matter of time before those people catch us and drag us back to their facility," Liz panicked. Jack inhaled deeply and frantically searched for a solution.

"We don't even know where we're headed, Jack."

"I'm aware. Perhaps that voice will give us some direction…"

"Maybe we're supposed to blend in with the crowd," Liz suggested. Jack blinked and gave her a stupefied look.

"Blend in? How exactly are we going to do that?"

"Maybe we knock out a man and a woman, and then take their clothes?" Liz suggested. Jack looked out at the crowd and shook his head.

"There's way too many people here. The moment we step out in the open, they're going to-"

"Jack! Over there!" Liz exclaimed with a hushed tone as she patted his shoulder. He followed where she was pointing. A young couple, budding in their passionate love embraced and eased their sexual tension. They kissed, and the girl started taking his shirt off. Jack looked back at Liz and then back at them.

"It's too convenient," he commented. He cautiously sneaked over, carefully hiding behind the trees and in the tall bushes that surrounded the couple.

It was one of the more difficult tasks Jack had to accomplish, but to his fortune, the couple was so engrossed in passion that Jack was able to carefully snatch their clothing so carelessly tossed to the bushed. Theirs was a vision of pleasure free and fulfilling, unshackled by the chains of society. It was a pleasure he longed to have publicly with Liz so desperately, for the briefest moment his worries faded under the hope of that kind of freedom for themselves.

As quickly as he sneaked over to them, he made his way back to his humble lover. "Are you sure this will work?" She asked as she picked out the girl's clothing.

"We don't have a choice. They're going to be the runaways our captors are searching for," Jack said as he quickly undressed. Careful to make sure their privacy wasn't compromised, he threw on the clothing quickly, surprised at how comfortable they were. The white hoodie he wore was snug on him, but long enough that it dropped down to his legs. He adorned the black harem pants, and slipped on the shoes that felt strange compared to his boots.

Liz's outfit was a bit more feminine but matched his. She also wore a hoodie, which fit her well and accented her figure. Her pants were tight, but the hoodie was long enough that she didn't feel exposed. The final part of her attire were shoes that matched Jack's. Finally, they clipped the belts around their waists, and carefully fit the holstered pistols to their hips. It seemed foolish to leave themselves without any sort of protection against whatever might be hunting them.

They calmly and discretely emerged from the small woods and vanished into the crowd, holding hands so that they didn't lose each other. Jack was immediately overwhelmed with the noise, the amount of people so close to him, the strange smells and looks. He gripped Liz's hand ever tighter, unsure of where they were going, except that they needed to get away from the park as quickly as possible.

Deep in thought, Jack wasn't paying attention to where he was walking until *SMACK!* He walked right into a red-haired girl so hard, he not only knocked her down, but himself and Liz as well. His hood fell off too, and everyone around them noticed.

Jack panicked and briefly looked at the girl, who wore a mixed expression of confusion and frustration on her face. Liz stood to her feet and helped Jack up as he pulled his hood back over his head. They didn't speak – they simply tried to maneuver their way around the girl and walk past.

"Hey, aren't you going to say anything? No 'I'm sorry,' or 'excuse me'?" The girl asked. She spoke with a slight accent that was something akin to French. Their attempts to move around was hindered, though, when she side-stepped in front of him and blocked his path. She was pretty, and appeared to be about his age. Her crimson hair was tied into braided ponytails behind her head, and had straight bangs that parted in the middle, showing a freckled, pale forehead. Her face was soft, easy to look, and her eyes were a beautiful violet. She was shorter than most of the elvish women, reaching only a few inches taller than Liz, and she looked like she was a healthy athlete. She was dressed in an almost exact outfit to what Liz was wearing.

"I'm sorry, but we're really in a hurry," Jack said. He tried to force his way past once more. The girl stubbornly stepped in his path, and stared into his eyes as if she were trying to read his thoughts.

Her brow furrowed, and she asked, "What *are* you?"

He wasn't given a chance to answer. At the part of the forest they emerged from nearly twenty minutes prior, a considerable distance away, hovercraft descended with orange lights flashing. More of the soldiers he'd seen earlier emerged from hovercraft with high-powered rifles trained at the young couple emerging from the forest. Both Liz and Jack panicked as they tried once more to force their way past the girl.

"Listen, we're not trying to harm you," Jack said. The girl ignored the commotion and kept staring at Jack.

"I know you..." She said as she tucked her hair behind her pointed ear. She continued her furrowed glare into his eyes. "We've met before, somewhere..." He barely noticed her eyes widen with revelation.

"That's impossible- Listen, we need to go! We can't be here! I need to find a way-"

"To get your brother," she said interrupting him. Jack was dumbfounded. Who was she? He couldn't stop to think about it... Unless...

...Unless this was the one they were supposed to be searching for.

"How could you possibly know that?" Jack exhaled.

"Come with me," the girl ordered. Jack and Liz followed without questioning it; they came to accept strange things happening to them at this point.

Things became increasingly difficult, however, when some in the crowds began to shout and point in their direction. "Don't look at them!" The girl barked, stopping them from turning around. "Follow my movements."

She turned the corner into an alley between two shops and broke into a mad dash. Neither Jack nor Liz put any second thought into it; they ran as fast as they could to keep up with her—and her speed was nearly inhuman. They kept up, nonetheless, dipping around each turn and corner to stick to the alleys. They didn't stop to see if anyone followed or even listen for footsteps. They just maintained their speed.

Without warning, the girl stopped in front of a doorway on the side of a smaller, more run-down building compared to the rest. It was old-looking, with black bricks assembling the walls that broke only for windows with bars in front of the glass panes. The door reminded them of home: a black metal doorway with a knob that twisted to open it. She fumbled around in her pockets until she found the key, twisted it, and rushed them inside. She calmly closed the door behind them and kept watch as a few clueless policemen in armored uniforms dashed by.

"Come," she ordered, making her way towards the stairs. Obediently, they followed, and for the first time in however many days it had been, they felt a moment of relief...

To Hide In The Sun

Hers was a cozy apartment with the bed and kitchen all in one room, and a small restroom closed off through a separate door. It was a slight mess, but they understood that she did what she had to do. Two windows overlooked as much of the city as it could, garnering a view of sidewalk vendors and streets bustling with life. Her bed was snugly placed on the opposite wall of the windows.

The kitchen, which was the first thing they walked into when they entered the apartment, was cute and cozy. There was a small refrigerator, what appeared to be an oven with electric power, and cabinets likely filled with all sorts of foods they wouldn't recognize. There was a sink and a faucet, as well as a metal rack with dishes standing in it, and a washing rag beside it.

Outside the kitchen, there was a small dresser, a bookshelf, and a strange rectangular object with a glass pane across the front of it.

The girl emerged from the restroom, tossing her hoodie onto her bed and then adjusting her black sleeveless shirt. She sighed as she folded her arms across her chest and analyzed them with a deep, penetrating gaze.

"How do-"

"No, I'll be asking the questions first," she interrupted as she placed her hands on her hips. Her expressionless demeanor made her difficult for Jack to read. She carried herself like a woman that had spent the last few years in Hell, but had come out stronger for it.

"Alright," Jack conceded with a furrowed brow. "Ask away."

"First, a statement: I know your identities. You're Jack, a person from some land called 'San Francisco.' And you're Elizabeth from the same land. That's all I know, but that's because I've had strange dreams many years ago about the same moment when I ran into you two... My name is Ayela, if that helps to ring any bells."

Ayela! Jack thought to himself. *I guess Ruat is behind some of this.*

"Next, I received a particular message on my phone from that someone telling me that I'll be

113

going to the store one day, and I'll run into you. Literally all it said. I just didn't think they were being *that* literal when they mentioned it. Then, I have another dream where you're begging me to help you find your brother, and I agree, for gods-know whatever reason. And now we're here. My first question - What are you, Jack from San Francisco?"

"We're humans. We're almost anatomically identical to you elves. I suppose the main difference that I know of for now is that our ears look different, and you have different hair and eye colors than us, mostly," Jack answered.

"Fascinating. So, you're an alien?"

Jack didn't stop to think for a moment that he might have been the alien on their world. He'd been so caught up in trying to find a way home for the three of them, he didn't think for a second that he would be treated exactly how he would expect to treat a strange creature showing up unannounced to his home.

"Correct," Jack answered curtly. "We're alien. We're from a planet called earth, where San Francisco... thrives..."

"Earth... Such a strange name... Well, you're on Thaerv now, and you'll find I'm one of the more compassionate of my species, near-remans."

"I'm Jack Owens," he responded, introduc-

114

ing themselves properly, "And this is Elizabeth McOwens."

"Owens and McOwens? Are you two related?"

"Not really. The relation is very far up our ancestry line. The son bearing the name Owens was an adopted son, while McOwens was a royal heir," Liz explained. "Even though they were in the same family, they weren't related by blood. It's how we became friends, by joking about our names."

"So, then you two are lovers?" Ayela asked as she crossed her arms.

"Yes," Jack answered. Liz blushed at his quick response and smiled as she looked over at him. "That was a pretty good guess."

"Life for remans is a cruel one; we're here, then we die. Life is relatively short for us on a cosmic scale, so for friends to be close like you are, it's assumed you're lovers." The elvish girl paused and furrowed her brow. "To the subject of importance: Where is your brother, currently?"

"In that tower with the inverted cross hovering over it."

"By 'inverted cross,' I assume you mean the Gramatoginon. And if that's the case, it's going to be nearly impossible to get him out by ourselves..."

Liz folded her arms across her chest and furrowed her brow. "Why?"

"Because that's the Emperor's tower. Are you aware of anything going on in this world?"

"Not exactly…" Jack started. "I mean, we were told about some wars going on… Really, we just showed up."

Ayela sighed as she looked out the window. "Allow me to educate you; the land you're currently in is the nation of Enthedrill; a great empire whose borders carve out the western half of the continent of Enthedrill. The border extends all the way to the huge desert of Rök that covers most of the eastern half of the continent. North of the desert is the kingdom of Korok, the oldest civilization on Thearv. It borders the desert, while the rest is bordered by the sea. To the south is the Republic of Dominov, also bordered by the desert and the rest by the oceans. Dominov and Enthedrill have established a strong trade relationship because their seaports are so close. Korok is very self-sufficient, but occasionally trades with the other countries – because they know how to play nice.

"There are two smaller continents west of Enthedrill, one to the north called the Sovereignty of Songriveii and one to the south called the City-States of Durinveii. Songriveii is a wasteland continent with a massive, old, sacred forest in the center – which is also where the Sovereign's city-fortress hides, and Durinveii is a technological wonderland with beautiful cityscapes like the world has never seen. There's also the Latvian Islands between Durinveii and Songriveii, full of sea-faring folk… This world is ravaged by war against most nations. Enthedrill wages war against Durinveii and Songriveii, and there's a rebellion living somewhere in the desert. There's also a loosely organized band of vigilante's hacking our government servers, exposing politicians and military generals, and organizing internal militias that resist the empire, all from within its own borders. It's a mess.

"Now, here are we – the elvish race, or remans, by our scientific title. We're like you humans… I mean, from what it looks like, we're pretty much the same as you humans. I'm obviously a girl, and our men look like you, Jack," she finished explaining.

"I gathered as much," he commented.

Ayela continued, "we have many races in our species too; light skinned, dark skinned, and those in the middle. The light skinned races are called ivory elves, darker skinned races are ebony elves- or dark elves, and those in the middle are either mixed, or they're called Dwarves."

"So, you're an *ivory elf?*" Liz asked, raising an

eyebrow.

"Yes. Specifically, I'm a sangran elf, which are natives to Songriveii, our homeland. Sometimes, though, we get called 'blood elves' as an insult," Ayela added. "Enough of the history lesson, though. The reason you can't get your brother back is because of the Emperor's tower, and with the wars and rebellions, it's the most guarded place in the world... And on top of that, strange happenings have occurred around the country and in this city."

"Elaborate."

"Towns burnt to a crisp with Gramatoginon left hovering over them, just like the one over the tower. People are quick to blame the Emperor, and they have good reason to," Ayela explained as she picked up a wand from a table beside her bed. There were several buttons on it, but she pressed the large green one. Suddenly, a screen on the rectangle flickered to life, showing a man seated at a desk with all sorts of images floating around and behind him.

"The Emperor, in his latest today, has issued a decree that the people of Enthedrill can no longer legally hold protest, peaceful or not, and began ordering the arrest and possible execution of anyone who gathers in rallies against his campaigns with banners

and loud chanting. His comments were particularly pointed at groups of ebony elves and dwarves that regularly spoke out against his ivory-supremacy laws and amendments. In addition, the Emperor has imposed additional taxes on citizens who were previously detained or charged for any minor criminal offense, and has boosted law enforcement with further equipment upgrades, ensuring definite militarization, and has granted immunity so that they may open fire on citizens they deem-"

She just as quickly turned the screen off. As the newscaster spoke, though, an image of a man appeared on the screen with short, black hair and a dark mustache, and with eyes as red as blood.

"That was the Emperor – the picture on the screen," Ayela pointed out. "His name is Gorvon Komin. He's a tyrant that, especially in recent years, has been removing liberties from the people, silencing or executing those that would speak out against him, and invading other countries…" Ayela sat down on her bed and leaned her elbows on her knees as she looked out the window. Jack and Liz casually made their way to either side of her and sat down beside her. "It's no wonder the people think he's been burning towns throughout Enthedrill. A man like him – immature, self-centered, filled with vanity – he's so unpredictable that it's easy to believe he'd start attacking his own people… He lets crime run rampant in some of the major cities, and doesn't do anything to help struggling families in the country… He's so unlike his father, Emperor Sephen Komin."

"…Is there anything we can do?" Liz asked. Jack looked over at her. *Was she really thinking of getting involved in their world?* He thought to himself. Ayela had a shocked expression, and narrowed her eyes.

"What do you mean?" She asked suspiciously.

"I mean exactly what I said," Liz responded, her tone firm and determined. "We want to go to our world pretty badly… But if going home means we help you out first – especially if one of our own is captured by the Empire – then we'll do it… And besides, I can't abide wicked men… I can't simply walk away while one ravages an entire nation of innocent people all for an unspoken ambition."

"Why would you want to help us?" Ayela pointed out.

"I just explained-"

"But you literally have nothing to do with this… None of these events are your responsibility…" She pointed out, looking into Liz's eyes. "Why fight a fight you didn't start?" The words echoed in Jack's heart. He felt an urge he had begun to think he wasn't worthy of, one that he promised his mother he'd take up.

"Why walk away from someone hurting when there's something you can do about it?" Liz retorted gently. "We don't really have anything else to lose... We've lost everything already, it seems."

"What could you possibly do about our situation?" Ayela asked with a smile of disbelief on her face, as if she couldn't believe what she was hearing.

Liz paused. She was right, and Jack knew it. Still, Jack felt his lover's fiery heart. "They have my brother... It doesn't matter what we could possibly do; everything that we could do is now a possibility." He answered. Ayela was silent as she contemplated his words.

"We need to find a way to infiltrate the tower... But we can't do that here. Not today... I'm going to ask a friend to come to the city. Once she arrives, we'll try to figure something out," she said. "We can't move forward without a plan... You're sure about this?"

"What have we got to lose?" Liz pointed out.

"...More than what you already have..." Ayela answered woefully. "You're trying to go home? You might not make it... You're in love with each other? Thaerv is a cruel world..."

"So is earth… And I see things set in motion beyond these wars… Beyond these alien attacks. Our arrival here can't have been an accident – we were brought here for a reason," Jack said, feeling the energy from his motivated emotions. "We'll find out along the way."

"I hope you know what you're asking, humans… Still, I can respect you. You both have good hearts. Anyway, you'll be needing somewhere to stay, and since it's apparent we were meant to find each other, I suppose my place will have to do. You two can have the bed, just please- no sex, alright? I imagine it's pretty standard between humans and elves, and I don't need the specifics," Ayela begged. They both blushed, and Liz put her hand behind her head.

"It's the same way you-"

"I don't need to know! I don't need to know! Gods!" She interrupted as she walked past them. Before she made it too far, though, both Jack's and Liz's stomachs grumbled violently. She paused and looked at them with an over-the-top concerned expression. "When was the last time you two ate?!" She exclaimed.

"Well… Not since we've arrived here, I suppose," Liz admitted. They both smiled awkwardly.

"What do you two eat on earth? Meats? Vegetables? Fruits?"

"Well, all of those, really. But are they the same here?"

"Okay... We're going to take a culinary risk," Ayela offered. Jack shrugged and Liz gulped.

"What do we have to lose?" He dismissed.

She stood at the stove with a skillet over top of it, stirring away at a savory smelling mixture of blue and green vegetables with a bright white meat. Occasionally, she would add spices of a variety of different flavors, but the smells and the sizzling popping sounds of the boiling grease caressed their senses of smell and hearing with pleasure. Their stomachs made their wait that much longer. Ayela knew it too, trying to cook as fast as she could.

"You could watch some television, or read something if you'd like," she offered from the kitchen when she noticed them sitting there, staring longingly at her skillet.

Jack looked over at the books while Liz picked up the wand. He casually walked over, but when he picked up one of the books and opened it, he realized he couldn't read any of the characters on the pages. Liz also had a hard time figuring out the wand to the device Ayela had turned on earlier. He smiled sympathetically and sat down, and gently rested his hand on hers. She looked up at him apologetically.

"I think we'd do best just waiting…" He declared.

"Suit yourselves," Ayela shrugged.

Ayela walked over after she'd finished cooking with food that resembled the steak cutlets and sautéed vegetables of a fajita mixture, and even handed them green tortillas. She handed them three-pronged forks before heading back to the skillet and making her own plate.

Jack and Liz didn't wait- no, they couldn't wait. They quickly forked the mixture into the tortillas and rolled them up. They were nearly half-way finished consuming them before they realized the taste: savory, zesty, and spicy. Jack had a friend from the Middle East, and the food reminded him very much of Mediterranean delicacies. There were just the right number of flavors mixed together, and it filled Jack's stomach just enough. It was probably the most delicious food they had ever eaten, especially with them being as hungry as they were.

"What is this?!" Jack exclaimed. "It's so good!"

Ayela blushed and smiled as she sat down beside them. "Thanks," she said as she took a bite. She looked out the window as the sun gave its last dim lights to the twilight hours.

"You both must be exhausted," the elvish girl pointed out. They didn't realize it until she said it, but they were. So much had happened to them, and with their chance to finally get some rest, he realized just how exhausted he truly was. His emotions were spent, and he just wanted to get the day over with.

"You're right," Jack admitted.

"I wouldn't blame you. You've had a long day. Would you mind helping me clean the dishes? After that, we'll get some sleep. Tomorrow, I'll pick up some things for us and we can talk about what we need to do to start getting your brother back… Sound good?" Ayela asked as she stood to her feet. They both nodded and followed her to the kitchen. Cleaning only took minutes, and before they knew it, they were climbing into the comfortable bed Ayela offered them, while she took a couple sheets from her bathroom closet and set herself up on the floor.

Jack lay there in the dark, his arm around Liz as their heads rested on the pillow. She fell asleep quickly, holding his hand over her heart. He, on the other hand, kept his eyes open for a little while longer, praying and hoping his brother was safe. As his world began to grow dark, sleep creeping over his mental horizon, he heard a distant voice calling out to him.

Jack...

Don't be afraid, Jack...

Trust in my voice...

Nothing is as it seems...

VI

Confusion In Clarity

Answers do not make a clear sight ahead,
only resolving confusion will accomplish
this.

Who Understands?

Rough days passed them by. They weren't really able to leave Ayela's apartment, and their activities were limited to resting, trying to read, or figuring out how to work the television. There was no shortage of panic and outburst from Jack, worrying over what their waiting was going to solve. He had no time to wait. He had no time to sit and think. His brother was at the mercy of the empire, and he needed to fix it. He needed to fix it all.

The morning of the fifth day started slowly for them. He was eager to stay in bed, while she had already gotten dressed with one of Ayela's more unique attires; a blue, cropped tank top fashioned with straps around her exposed torso, and a long, orange skirt with a slit that exposed her leggings underneath. Ayela offered they wear matching attires that day, and while the color schemes were different, they could pass as sisters.

"Jack," Liz demanded, her eyes glued to the television. Ayela was out that day, picking up more clothes for them. "Look at this."

Jack looked up at the screen and watched as a map of the massive country flashed across the screen. A woman stood in front pointing at various towns dotted across the landscape.

"Tragedy struck six days ago, when an unassuming town was hit by another Aethril attack, making five total this year. Nassah, home of the spice cake, was enjoying a casual Jieridas when a frightening anomaly loomed overhead, seemingly out of nowhere, as described by a young girl who was the town's sole survivor. Zasha Morae was safely relocated to Ih'Dejj, with plans to see her inserted to a willing family who will look after her. She said the terrifying being was indescribable, unlike anything she'd ever seen. She said she thought she saw a giant in the storm that – and I quote – was "made of really dark clouds." She said it "was also surrounded by storm clouds that whirled and turned, but hovered in place, and it had a glowing halo and a gramatoginon floating over its head." Officials have yet to release a public-"

"That's... disturbing. How is that even possible?"

Jack commented. Liz shuddered, and they tried to envision what it must have looked like.

"I mean, we've seen boats that fly and hover above the ground, horseless carriages with six wheels and big enough to carry a dozen men in the back alone, men that are at least six-and-a-half or seven feet tall at their shortest, and women that are only a few inches shorter than you. We have seen little slab-tablets, like what Ayela- an elvish woman- has, that show all these pictures on the one side of it, and can take pictures out of some small lens on both sides, and can be controlled by touching the screen on whatever little picture you want- all of this is out of a fantasy, Jack. None of this should be possible... We're literally seeing the impossible all around us," Liz pointed out.

Jack paused as he considered everything she said. "You're right. How do we blend in with people like this?"

"We can't. The most we can do is find a way to get through it all. Once we get Adrian, we can try to find a way to get home. Maybe we should go back to the forest we arrived at. That giant tree seemed important."

"Perhaps. At the very least, we can breathe the air here, drink the water, and eat the food. It could have been much worse."

131

"I don't want to think about that," Liz interrupted. Before he could respond, Ayela opened the door and entered with a few bags full of goods.

"Glad to see you're both awake," she said as she closed the door behind her and locked it. She quickly set the bags on the counter and made her way over to the bed, letting out a long sigh of relief once she collapsed on it.

"Much to procure?" Liz asked.

"Yes. I quit my job and went out to get a couple things we would need," she admitted. "They didn't seem to care all that much, which surprised me. You'd think losing a web developer would be a big deal."

Jack and Liz looked at each other with confusion. "web?" Liz asked.

"Yeah. You know, comp- you know what, never mind. From what you've told me, your planet doesn't even have computers."

"Not at all."

"Figures. Anyway, I have some new clothes for you to try on. Jack... The style of pants you're wearing is probably the only thing you'll be able to wear without sticking out. Liz, you have more freedom. I picked up some new pants and a skirt for you to try..."

"What's the purpose?" Jack asked. "We so

132

obviously do not belong."

"That's not entirely true. You look like budding young adults here. With the exception of Liz's proportions, most girls in their early twenties are about her size. She was lucky to be the same size bras as me. And most boys that are the same age are about your size," Ayela explained. "As long as you don't show your ears without these clasps I got, you both pass for growing young ivory-"

"Proportions?" Liz asked as she crossed her arms consciously, her face turning red.

"Yes, proportions," Ayela said with a flustered smirk. "I wouldn't be ashamed of it. Just means that the other girls wish they had your body."

"Oh?" Liz retorted.

"Yes... I filled out the same way when I was fourteen," Ayela admitted with a flustered expression. "I was looked at pretty differently growing up. I guess I just learned how to ignore the lingering gazes and the judgmental rumors."

"You grew up beautifully, though. Truly. You're so gorgeous. How old are you now?" Liz complimented.

"Twenty-eight years. And thanks," Ayela said with a blush.

"I can imagine how the other girls might have been intimidated by you."

"Thanks. I-"

133

"Did we forget I'm in the room?" Jack stammered. Both the girls giggled.

"Having an issue?" Ayela teased.

"Not at all," he responded curtly as he stood up and walked over to the window. He needed a moment to collect himself. "I appreciate you taking care of us, but I'm not so sure it's safe for us to go out there." He finally said.

"Things have calmed down a little," Ayela said. "It's fine if you go out. And don't worry about people seeing your faces. I've already thought through everything. Trust me; you both can blend in easily."

"Unless someone speaks to us."

"Your manner of speech is nothing to worry about. My accent is the one that sticks out, honestly. Besides, you both seem to have adjusted to me just fine," Ayela pointed out. "Don't worry so much. I bought these clasps that will make your ears look like ours."

"Clasps?" Jack asked with a raised eyebrow. She smirked as she leapt up and quickly walked over to the bags and fished through them. She pulled out two small, black boxes. Jack and Liz opened them, and were stunned by the intense, intrinsic detail etched into the silvery metal. They were ornaments that would cover the top half of their ears and give them a much-needed extension to make them appear like remans, cleverly disguising them as natives to Thaerv.

"It's a popular fashion trend here in the capital," she commented.

"Impressive," Liz said as she looked at herself in Ayela's small make-up mirror.

"Now you two don't need to be so cooped up inside my tiny apartment... And we don't need to sneak around when we go to Kamille's. Now, let's try on your clothes."

Liz was first, trying on the skirt Ayela picked out as well as a white blouse with a low-cut collar. Jack blushed. She was beautiful. The skirt was short, though. Women on earth wouldn't have dared to show nearly the amount of their legs that she was showing. It cut off almost half-way up her thighs. The blouse was pretty; white with gold-trimming. It was tight, hugging the curvature of her figure. He could tell how uncomfortable she felt, and she put no effort in hiding it as she raced back to the bathroom and changed back into her other clothes.

"It's fascinating how similar our races are," Ayela commented, "and also how different we are. Humans grow hair on their legs?"

"You don't?" Jack asked, raising an eyebrow.

"Not at all. We have head hair, men have facial

135

hair, but body hair? How are we going to cover this?" Ayela panicked. "The top is fine, but you need to wear those pants for now."

Liz sighed in relief. "Thank God."

"Truly, though, you look so pretty," Ayela complimented. "I don't know why you're so scared of showing off a little."

"Didn't you say that I'd get made fun of?"

"Wear it as a badge of honor," Ayela urged.

"I suppose…" Liz said half-heartedly, nervously tucking her hair behind her ear.

"So, where exactly are we going today?" Jack asked as he emerged from the bathroom, dressed in the same style of pants that he wore before, but with a short-sleeved shirt over his black tank top. He kept the hoodie he wore handy in case it got cold. Ayela blushed as she examined him, and then cleared her throat.

"We're going to explore the city a bit, and maybe get some shaving blades so that you can get rid of the hair on your legs. With a new attire, you should blend in a little better. Liz, I'm going to tie up your hair into a bun so that you don't look so recognizable. Jack… You're fine as you are," she said. Occasionally, he caught her quickly glancing over at him.

"Good," Jack said as he pulled his hoodie over his head. "Let's scope out the tower."

"What?!"

"Jack, we will be spotted if we go near there. Just because we can go out now doesn't mean we-"

"I know that, Ayela. I'm merely saying we spend some time near the tower so I can get a full, calculated, studied view from around it. I'm not interested in wasting time exploring while my brother is suffering God-knows-what at the hands of a larger, stronger species..." Jack said in a cold, mono-toned voice. Ayela sighed. She stood up and looked into his eyes.

"We're in enough danger as it is... We – I – can't be seen near the tower. There are things set in motion you know nothing about," she explained. Jack sighed in frustration as he turned and looked out the window. "We can't stay cooped up in here until we find some way to break in. We'd literally be here for years. You need to take your mind off things, and then tomorrow, we'll meet up with Kamille and we'll start to figure out our plan."

"What if we sneaked in by one of their vehicles?" Jack suggested, ignoring her comments entirely.

Ayela rubbed her temples. "No, people tried that already."

"Climbing the least-watched side of the towers and breaking in through one of their windows or vents?" He continued.

"The windows are reinforced to withstand gunfire, too high, and the vents are too small even for children," she retorted.

"Impersonating guards."

"Retina scans, hand print readers, voice detection, and x-ray scans. I doubt humans look exactly the same as elves on the inside."

His brow furrowed. "Prisoner impersonation."

"You'd be exposed immediately."

"Assassinate the front-"

"No, no, and no! Don't you get it?! That tower is impenetrable! If it were so easy to get in, the rebels waging war with the Empire would have broken in and killed the Emperor by this point! There's technology in that tower that the public couldn't even dream of seeing be a reality! We have no way of getting him out by ourselves!"

"THERE HAS TO BE A WAY!!!" Jack raged, his fists shaking, clenched so tightly.

Liz stood to her feet and walked over to him and placed a hand on his shoulder. "Jack... Adrian is as extraordinarily intelligent as you. He'll figure out a way to stay alive... He'll make it out of there."

"You should listen to her," Ayela suggested. She put her hands on her hips and shifted her weight.

He was silent as he kept thinking of a way to

get in. "You don't understand," he said, finally breaking the silence. "It's my responsibility… It's… It's all my fault…"

"Actually, I understand better than anyone else," Ayela retorted as she stepped forward. "You have nothing else… You were ripped from your home to a land you know nothing about – a place you don't belong– with nothing to your name except a voice in your head telling you which way you should go… I guess the difference between us is that you had a sibling who came with you… You even have a lover's comfort to cushion your downfalls. I had no one for most of my life. The things I've been through… I'm the one who brought it on myself, for the most part. Just by being who I am."

Jack looked over his shoulder at her, suddenly sensing an air of familiarity. She was right. "And I'm sure Liz understands just as well… You both have each other," she added as she folded her arms across her chest. He looked around the apartment she lived in, finally seeing it; a small place she couldn't call home, a lonely life with no one to be there for her, and a drive to fix the injustice of her world. She had a pure heart that no one wanted anything to do with, yet she wanted everything to do with everyone around her, because she still loved a people not her own.

And no one shaped her view. No man or woman affected how she viewed things. She shaped herself, and didn't really have anyone to share these self-discoveries with...

What a painful life to live.

"Then let's go," Jack said as he set his emotion aside. Their arrival threw him into such a state of chaos, and his emotions were so uncontrollable, but now that they were here. He needed to control himself once more. He sighed as he turned to face them. "Let's get our minds off of our current predicament."

"You won't be disappointed," Ayela said with a smirk as she turned and led them out the door.

Ayela, The Dancer of Songriveii

He wasn't sure what day it was, but the crowds seemed less busy than when they escaped the tower. Ayela casually led them into the market district, where they gawked and stared in awe at the shops and towering citadels. Everything was grand, elegant, full of art and grace. People seemed to give their full attention to their devices or their friends and partners. Cars passed by on the roads while hovercraft of all sizes and shapes soared quietly overhead. He was surprised by how calm the city was, despite how busy it seemed to be on other days.

The sky obtained a familiar red-orange hue as the sunset began to overtake the hours of the day, signifying the transition from day to evening. Liz and Ayela maintained casual small talk, sharing details of their worlds while Jack followed along silently, observing everything around him. The scenery mirrored the artistry of the sky, golden trims on most of them to complement their polished white surfaces, and a gray road with white sidewalks. Trees were planted strategically along the wide walking paths, and the doors to all the vendors and restaurants lined the side opposite of the road in parallel.

How could such a corrupt government maintain such a beautiful city? How were its citizens oppressed when they wandered about with as much freedom as they did? There seemed to be so much time for them to go about their long days without having to work their jobs. There was freedom for them to love whomever they wanted, without the worry of if they were going to be arrested for false crimes. He struggled to see the oppression at play, but perhaps his view was only limited to what he saw around them. After all, the news painted a much grimmer picture.

He thought about the other ways she explained, how many elves her age couldn't afford to live by themselves. She was fortunate for reasons she wouldn't share, but many weren't. Many who lived in the socially-split cities like Ih'Dejj or Ebonveii struggled to find a place to live, or a way to feed their children. Law enforcement was murderous in too many regions across the country, and those in power held ties to much darker forces than what was seen by the public, as she explained.

The emperor, too, led the people with mixed interests, and offered more confusion than clear leadership. People that looked like him lived relatively easy lives. They were left alone, didn't have to worry about where they might have to work, or whether the police would brutally attack them. Many of them believed the emperor and the businesses that fueled his power had their best interests at heart, and some were so devoted to him, they believed he was a sort of Messiah.

Messiah, Jack thought to himself. It was a deeply Jewish concept, and one he embraced with all his being- as his mother so passionately instilled in his heart when he was young. On the same hand, though, many tirelessly tried to eradicate his people on behalf of who they believed his Messiah was. It sickened his heart, and while he waited like any other good Jew, he was simultaneously repulsed by it. He didn't want to wait. He didn't want to care. So much death was brought on behalf of the one that Liz's religion proclaimed. So much pain, so much violence. If it was the one Liz believed in, he had questions for him. Pained, scarred questions.

This emperor, though... How could he know

who was telling the truth about him? Was Ayela, who knew more about her own world, right? Was he the tyrant the news portrayed him to be? Was he someone that needed to be righteously fought? Was he a man in power that shouldn't have been? Despite the questioning, his own experiences and intuition taught him *yes.* Absolutely. This man brought into official position those who would treat outsiders like they were animals. War or not, how could that be justified? How could it be considered military standard for anyone performing interrogations to attempt to violate a woman's body the way Kozek tried to do to Liz? His heart began to burn with anger-

"Jack!" Ayela shouted, grabbing him by the shoulders. He snapped out of his thoughts and realized that he had almost ran into her again.

"Sorry," he said with an embarrassed chuckle.

"You went somewhere pretty far there, didn't you?" Liz commented. "Want to go in this store with us?"

He looked up at a small shop she was pointing to; a vendor that sold confections and sweets of all sorts, with bottles of expensive wine in the back of its strangely Victorian-themed interior.

"I'm good," Jack declined with a smile. "I would like to remain outside for a time. You two go have fun."

144

"You sure?" Ayela urged. "You look like you could use a distraction from your… distractions."

"I'll be quite alright. Pick me out something, please?" He asked. Liz nodded with an excited smile as they went into the store arm-in-arm. He smiled, and then casually leaned against the window, watching the people pass them by. The air was cool, and felt good gently caressing his skin. He hadn't really taken the time like he did now to appreciate the beauty of their alien world. And he could appreciate it, and it felt as though he was close to earth.

"Hey, kid!" A man yelled from across the sidewalk near the road. Jack raised an eyebrow, but paid him no serious mind. "Don't ignore an adult when they're talkin' to you! Where's your parents?"

"Not here, obviously. What do you want with me?" Jack retorted coldly. The man marched over his way, trying to appear intimidating.

"You better learn some manners, kid! You know where you are?"

"I merely wanted to know why you're talking to me in the first place. Did I threaten you somehow?" Jack spat.

"Jack!" Liz called from the door to the candy shop. He looked over to see her and Ayela standing just outside the door.

"He with you, blood elf?" The man spat. Ayela's brow furrowed and lips flattened. Clearly, he chose the wrong words to say.

"Watch it, *ivory*. What did he do to you that got you so pissy?" She spat as she rolled up the sleeves of her shirt.

"I watched him scratch at me!" The man revealed. There were a few gasps from the citizens that happened to pass by. Jack raised an eyebrow in confusion, while Ayela slapped her forehead with her palm in embarrassment.

"Oh no…" She murmured. "Jack… Did you scratch behind your right ear with your index and middle fingers?"

He shrugged, truly not knowing, or caring, if he did or didn't. He sighed with frustration. "Look, I had an itch. I-"

"You looked back at me and then scratched, kid! You clearly don't know how to pick your fights!" The guy interrupted. Jack could feel his head pound with the irritation.

"My sincerest apologies?"

"No, Jack, that won't fix this," Ayela began to explain as the man stomped closer to him with his fists clenched. Liz gasped and covered her eyes when he threw a wild punch at Jack's face. He was slow, though. Too slow. Jack ducked out of the way and side-stepped. "That's the worst kind of insult in this country."

"Gee, you'd think something a little more obvious like holding up a middle finger would have done the trick!" Jack shouted as he dodged another hit.

"Now you're gonna have to fight this one out," Ayela stated as-a-matter-of-factly with a nervous shrug and smile. "Don't worry, though; you're moving pretty quickly."

"Hey, girl! Shut up or you're next!" The man shouted as he tried to hit Jack one more time. This time, though, he landed a hit in his chest and sent him flying backwards. People began pulling out their devices and recording the fight.

"Hell," Jack swore as he got back up on his feet and held up his fists. He took a deep breath, and then let it out slowly. As he did, time began to slow, and his mind kicked into overdrive.

He visualized it clearly. First, he would let his opponent throw another wild punch. Jack would dodge and brush the attack towards his left side – his dominant side. Once the boisterous elf was in position, he would weave his foot around while simultaneously placing his left palm on his chest, knocking him over onto his back. Once there, he would pin him at his wrists and land several jabs into his face. Once successful, he would assess the situation and offer the chance for his foe to yield to the fight, and then continue his stroll with his current company. Mischief will have ended.

Unfortunately, Jack didn't make it past throwing the man to the ground; he was just too strong. The hulking, seven-foot elf threw him off and got back to his feet as quickly as possible while Jack stammered. It was going to be difficult, but he saw that he was not strong enough to make brute force calculations against this opponent.

Jack's routine of visualizing his opponent's moves continued, and almost the entirety of their fight, he was correct in his predicting. He would often dodge punches, retaliate with a quick jab somewhere on the elf's body, searching for a weak point. Each time was unsuccessful until he tossed a strong kick into the man's rib. His opponent grunted and doubled over, and Jack grinned, his point of focus acquired.

But in the steady stream he'd begun to anticipate, yet another unpredictable factor was added into the fight when Ayela leapt in front of him and spread her arms wide, attempting to halt the elf from hitting Jack any further.

"Out of the way, runt!" He barked in a condescending tone.

"No, you back off!" Jack barked, trying to shove his way past Ayela, who suppressed him with surprising strength.

"Don't do it, Jack. He's not worth it."

"You think I won't hit a woman?!"

"No, guy, I don't! Because-"

Ayela was cut off as the back of the man's hand struck her across the face. She whimpered and stumbled out of the way.

This must not be allowed to go unpunished. Jack thought to himself.

It was like a switch in his head was flipped. His emotion was suspended, and he felt nothing. For that brief moment he calculated his next move. As predicted, the ivory elf went in for another punch, but Jack dodged once more, acknowledging that he simply didn't have the strength to block it effectively. Then Jack moved in to land the hardest hit his body could muster, shoving his closed fist into the his rib with all his strength. The guy gasped from the pain and stumbled backwards, grunting as he held his side. Jack assumed that there was a fracture before, but after Jack's punch, it either worsened or broke.

The guy was resilient, though, and straightened up to rush at Jack in a full-on charge. He readied himself all in vain, however, as Ayela dashed in between them and started to move as if she were reciting a dance rehearsal, and then she landed her open palm onto the ground. Once it hit, an near-invisible wave of energy emerged in a sphere around her with its highest concentration towards their opponent, throwing him back nearly as it bent the light that passed through it like a heatwave. The rest of them barely felt a slight gust blow back their hair.

She didn't wait, though; she continued her routine, spinning three times and then throwing her hands into the air as she stomped her feet down shoulder-width. The reman was thrown into the air a few feet, but slammed back onto the ground with brute force as Ayela threw her hands down. There were surprised gasps all around from their growing crowd of onlookers. Their attacker quickly rose to his feet, fear gripping his expression as he looked on at the redhead. Ayela wore a fierceness in her expression as she clapped her hands twice, slowly spun her arms in opposing circular motions, threw them forward with a step out, and then dramatically pulled her closed fists back in. The ground between herself and him – and only that ground – shifted towards her with the him still on it, as if it were some sort of rolling track built into the ground. It took only a second, and then the man who was ten feet away flung to her open hand, defying the laws of nature and reality. Her hand closed around his throat and tightened, and the ground shifted back to its

150

original state, leaving him at her mercy.

"Leave… Now…" She ordered in a firm voice. He whimpered when she let him go, and then took off in a mad dash, disappearing into the frightened and astonished crowd. Jack and Liz stood there, gawking at her. "We need to leave, too," she suggested. They began with a hastened walk, then they broke out into a run, trying to get away from the public eye as soon as they were able.

Time.

That was what they all needed at that moment. After Ayela's brilliant display, they took a long detour back to her apartment, and made it home at a very late hour. Police prowled the streets for them, searching long and hard anywhere they could, but they remained safe at the moment.

"We need to try and sleep," Ayela urged as she left the blinds slightly open. The lights were off, leaving the apartment barely illuminated by the light pouring in from the street lamps. Liz and Jack curled up together on her bed while she covered herself with blankets on the floor. The sounds of intimidating, unnatural sirens filled their ears.

"I'm so scared," Liz admitted. Jack didn't speak;

151

instead, he held her tightly and tried to comfort her.

"Tomorrow we'll meet Kamille," Ayela reminded them. "Once we meet her, we'll get out of town... I promise you both, this world isn't as bad as it seems." Jack could hear the pain in her voice, as if she had to try and convince herself that it was true. He didn't blame her, though.

As his eyes grew heavy, his thoughts drifted to Adrian, and then to his late mother, his father, and younger brother... He missed them so much... In his heart, though, he knew things wouldn't be the same. Maybe it was the voice that told him nothing was as it seemed. Maybe it was because they didn't even know how they had gotten there... All he knew was that his life was changed forever.

One thought continued to race through Jack's mind, though, carrying him into the seas of the unconscious...

...Just who was this Ayela, really?

VII

A Friend of Trustworthiness

To earn the trust of a friend is a desirable goal, but to earn the trust of a friend's friend blesses the soul.

A History Unknown

Sunlight peered through the blinders on the windows, pouring rays that lit the apartment with a warm amber glow. Though he longed for more sleep, the rising of the dawn stole it from him. Liz and Ayela had silently gotten up already, quietly packing everything they thought they would need for their trip. It was clear the apartment was meant to be abandoned.

With a deep yawn, he wiped his face and sat up. The grogginess of deep sleep hadn't fully faded from his demeanor, and it became increasingly obvious they hadn't had a truly good night's sleep for the entirety they'd been there. Even watching them scurry about exhausted him, but he knew he needed to get up and join them.

"Good morning, sleepyhead," Liz greeted with a smile. He returned it as he stood to his feet.

"Good morning. I see where getting ready to leave rather early," he noticed.

"We are indeed. Kamille should be in town, and we need to get out of this city block as soon as we're able to. Mind helping me pack?" Ayela asked.

"Sure."

"So, what's the date today?" Liz asked, clearly eager to spark up conversation after having to be so quiet for so long.

"Today is Jieridas, the third day out of the week. And today specifically is the twenty-fifth day of Serudmer, the fourteenth month of the year three-thousand, four hundred and eighty-three," Ayela answered.

"Fascinating," Jack commented as he tried to understand how time functioned on Thaerv. "Why three-thousand and four hundred years? What happened that many years ago?"

Ayela looked over at him. "The last Aethyrian. He was a hero of the people, and many who believe in Korism regard him as the "Hero-Prophet of Rök" that delivered the world from the oppression of the daethrils."

"Daethrils? What are they, a usurping and wicked variant of aethrils?" Jack snickered.

"You laugh, but most religions here talk about them. In most religions, they simply existed since the beginning of the universe. In Korism, they were once aethrils that turned evil and rebelled against Rök... As the legend goes, three heroes rose to the challenge: Shan'Hadai, the Aethyrian; Lukrinael, the Seyafin, and the last was Mikalael, the Ar'Kai. They defeated the daethrils in their first reign and freed the world from their grip."

"What does the rest of the world believe?"

"Shan'Hadai was a wise man and a fierce warrior who fought off an invasion of beings from another world, much like what we're fighting now."

"Allow me to present a new inquiry," Jack began.

"Go ahead."

"What's an aethril, and who's Rök?" He asked. His question was enough to stop her dead in her tracks, forcing Jack and Liz to pause as well. She turned to face him with a grave look on her face, as though she'd personally experienced something that shaped the faith she now had.

"What do you think they are?" She asked, looking into his eyes with a piercing glare.

"That they were the second phenomenon we encountered on this world-"

"Describe it," Ayela demanded. Jack closed his eyes and sighed.

"A swirling storm that hovers in one place, that

which leaves a town engulfed in flames when it vanishes. It leaves behind a cross made of a glowing red light hovering upside-down over the town after it's destroyed. We didn't really see any physical body; it disappeared too fast. But we've seen that light which they leave before."

She paused, as though she were reliving memories. He could see it in her eyes, the trauma she'd experienced. His mind buzzed with curiosity, yearning to know more about what happened to this girl that shook her to her core. What sort of horrors had she experienced, that his description would force her to relive something so dark?

"And Rök?" She continued.

"A god of some sort?" Liz probed.

"Not just any god... They're the creator-god. The chief of them all, king in the Blind Eternities. He's the one Korists claim to worship," Ayela explained.

"...We have a god like that... There's a few groups that worship him, but two of them have used that worship as a means of violence and dominion... My people have suffered at their hands for thousands of years," Jack explained. Ayela's gaze drifted to the brightening sky outside.

"...Ours was not the first to worship him. Korism descends from an elder religion based on a dead language called Khebreh. I've... I've

158

seen the horrors you describe- the aethrils. I've lost people to them... And if I hadn't met Rök, I wouldn't have kept my faith in him.

"So you're a Korist?"

"Not legally speaking... I'm not religious. The empire outlawed the religion, along with most others."

"That's horrible..." Jack said. Suddenly, he felt a deep kinship with her. "I'm sorry you went through that."

She analyzed him at his response, as though she were seeing someone she knew long before they met. Then, with a quick shake of her head, she continued to pack. "It's alright, Jack. That's in the past now. I'm doing what everyone of our faith does; survive. We keep our beliefs private, and we keep our heads down. No one bats an eye or suspects anything. It's how we've been forced to live. As long as the Gramatoginon hovers over the tower, our faith and culture is a dead one in Enthedrill..."

"That symbol... So, I understand what your religions and people say about these aethrils, but what *are* they?" Jack asked, circling back.

"Honestly; no one knows what they are. They call them aethrils because we don't understand them. No one sees anything except something surrounded by clouds, and there's almost never a survivor. We can't talk to them – no one understands what they say or even the voice they speak with save for a few. We can't touch them, so we can't hurt them, and we can't run from them. There seems to only be one motive they have in mind - destroying our kind through what some call 'judgment.'"

Jack's brow furrowed. He could hear it in her voice; that wasn't entirely true. She'd seen things, survived attacks, or seen them herself. Perhaps it was because they didn't know each other well enough yet that she kept those details hidden, but he didn't want to prod.

"We need to get going in a moment," Ayela urged. She pressed her ear against the door to her apartment. Once she was sure the coast was clear, she tossed them each a wrapped bar of some sort of sweet food to eat. She made sure that no one was eavesdropping into their conversation. "Also... I think they're beings from another world, existing in some higher dimension or something."

"You mean to say extraterrestrials?"

"Are you so surprised? I'm sure, to you, I'm technically an alien," she pointed out. Jack hesitated to respond, almost forgetting that she was indeed an alien to him, despite all her human-like qualities. Without waiting for a response, she turned and walked out of the doorway with them following close behind.

Their journey truly had just begun...

A Meeting of Bound Souls

The city was a steel forest, and the further they wandered from the emperor's tower, the harder it became to find it behind all the other buildings and complexes, reaching for the impossible in the sky. Their world was such a marvel of technology and fantasy, he never dreamed he would see anything like it. For a moment, he forgot his troubles and the overwhelming pain he carried with him, and saw the beauty of the world they drifted into. He could get lost and never have to worry about his demons ever again.

Alas, he knew he wasn't able to stay lost in the fantastic escapade for long. Soon, his feelings overwhelmed him again, and he began to notice the red streaks in the sky as the sun climbed higher and transformed the morning into a full day.

Red.

Like the color of the blood in his veins.

Red.

Finally, they arrived at a small collection of residential complexes deep in the outer rings of the city. It felt like they'd been walking for hours. With heavy feet, they walked up a stairway leading to one of the duplex buildings, and Ayela casually pressed a button on a panel beside the door, reminiscent of their home once again. The building was a smooth, polished, glistening black-brick structure with plenty of windows, keeping in similar theme with the rest of the city while giving a slight contrast. There were people walking around, but not nearly as many as the main streets. Jack assumed this was a residential district.

"These people are so advanced," Liz stated, awestruck in the expression on her face. "Humans could learn so much from them."

"We barely discovered electricity a little over twenty years ago, and here these people are with flying and hovering carriages, thin rectangles that manipulate light, long-distance communication without cables or anything, and even advanced weapons. I can't imagine what they're-"

"Don't, Jack," Liz interrupted. "Don't try to

think of what's happening to Adrian right now."

"She's right. You can't do that to yourself. Fight to get him back until you know for sure he's not there, but don't try to predict the future. It's impossible," Ayela encouraged. "I-"

"Ayela!!!" Shrieked an ebony-toned, leggy and muscular elvish woman. Her shriek startled all of them, and she had the thickest of cockney accents. She was about the same height as Ayela, but only a little taller. She was pretty, strong, and had an air of structure and regiment about her.

"Hello, Kamille!" Ayela said with an embrace. When they pulled apart, Kamille's attention was directed towards Jack and Liz.

"Who are they?" She asked, raising an eyebrow.

"I'll explain everything inside. For now, let's get out of the public eye," Ayela answered in a rushed tone. Kamille didn't say anything as she motioned for them to follow and disappeared back into the apartment-home. Jack and Liz followed in cautiously.

"So... You two aren't elves... And your brother is captured by the Empire?" Kamille investigated after listening to Ayela tell her everything she knew.

"Yes... We aren't entirely sure how we arrived here. We awoke in some ruins in the woods, and then we were captured by the Empire after an aethril destroyed a town full of people, and then after all of that, we ran into her. Certainly, this situation might be bigger than us-"

"You got that much right – this is much bigger than you or us. I'm not surprised Ayela didn't explain anything to you, though," Kamille interrupted as she folded her arms across her chest.

"Are you sure about this? Asher isn't here to help us-"

"Shh! I haven't said anything yet! Don't just assume things, love. I don't know what to think of this yet…" She interrupted with a hushed tone.

"What do you mean? My brother is trapped in that tower, and it's clear we're no friend of this Empire! Can you express a little trust?" Jack asked in an aggravated tone. It was apparent how exhausted he was with everything. "We've been in an apartment for the past couple of weeks, and we've had no progress until now… Give us something to hold on to!"

Kamille blinked her eyes in surprise at his tone of voice. She quietly stood up and walked up to him, getting in his face. "We run this operation, *human.* You're an outsider to this world. Neither of us know each other, and I've been fighting for a long time. I have no clue what you were on your world or what you've been through, but here, we're the queens, and you're the reinforcements. I call the shots. So put that tone somewhere other than your voice, understand?"

Jack kept his expression emotionless as he straightened himself. "I'm not scared of you," he declared blatantly. He could see it in her face; he was getting under her skin.

"Jack, enemies are not the greatest of things to make in our current circumstance," Liz advised.

"Wise girl. Should listen to her." Kamille spat.

"Listen carefully; I didn't arrive in some obscure part of the universe and have my life threatened by an alien race, and have my brother captured – maybe even killed – just to get into a competition with someone who spits on me before she gets to know me," Jack growled, snarling a little.

"Both of you– stop! This is stupid! You've only just met, and you're ready to tear each other down?!" Ayela barked. Kamille looked over at her with a slightly nervous expression, and then back at Jack with a glare. Without saying a word, she went back to her sofa, as Ayela took a seat beside her. Jack folded his arms across his chest, keeping an expressionless gaze at the two of them.

"What secret are you both fighting hard to keep?" He finally asked, announcing his suspicion. "Why are you talking with such hushed tones?"

"It's... complicated. I promise I'll tell you when I'm ready to. Right now, with so much going on, we need to make sure we can trust you first," Ayela explained.

"There's a number of things you don't understand about our world, especially the wars going on. For all I know, we shouldn't even really care what happens to you. You're just an inconvenience. You'd almost be better off with Captain Lunar, but you're here with us. Our little red-haired girly here insisted you were too much of an opportunity to pass up, so I left my cozy little home over in Lythia to see what the fuss was about," Kamille retorted curtly, her expression cold.

Liz scratched her head, and in an exasperated tone, asked, "Captain Lunar?"

"He's the leader of a massive fleet of airships and soldiers that are also trying to overthrow this government, officially dubbed the Majjai. It's the rebellion I mentioned in the desert," Ayela explained. Jack placed his hands on his hips as he walked over to the window. His gaze drifted down to the people scurrying about their busy lives.

"So what does this have to do with us?" He asked.

167

"It doesn't, and yet it does. You're here, and we were led to each other by someone who has a powerful mantle of divine logic," Ayela said.

"There's so much going on," Jack complained as he rubbed his head. "Divine logic?"

"Yes. It's what I used in that fight last night."

"What, are you telling me elves have supernatural prowess now?" Jack asked with a frustrated tone.

"No, it's not entirely supernatural. Throughout history some people have this energy about them that grants them a sort of control over some parts of reality. Some theorize it's because of the gamma radiation of our sun, others believe that religion is the reason – especially Korists, since theirs is one of the only current religion to produce those gifted in it. Others still think it's all just myth since there are so few of us who use it," Ayela explained as Kamille pulled out her tablet and began to swipe her thumb on it.

"That doesn't make sense; if it's radiation, then wouldn't it affect your entire race, and not just a few?" Jack asked.

"Unless it's a genetic mutation that responds to the radiation in such a way. After all, everything always boils down to genetics and quantum mechanics," Ayela responded.

"But to have a mutation that shifts your body's

168

matter into another form of matter seems entirely fictitious," he retorted.

"And yet, here you both are. Are you sure that your people aren't advanced? You're talking about atoms and particles like you're a studied academic."

Liz snickered. "Jack has volumes on the subject. He reads quite a bit. Only recently have great men been publishing thesis statements about major scientific findings with atoms and waves – as he's constantly informing me."

"We-"

"Oh, my gods," Kamille interrupted, lifting her eyes from the screen the screen of her device. Without saying anything, she grabbed a remote and pointed it at the wall, and then pressed a large red button on it. The wall slid down, revealing a screen hidden behind it that flickered to life and revealed the newscaster they watched several times before, but this time with a blurred image of the three of them from the previous night.

"Late last night, two dangerous criminals were spotted running with a female songrivan woman as authorities attempted to arrive and arrest them after a fantastic and violent fight outside the Wü'Shæ Sweet Shop. The Emperor has decreed a substantial reward for turning in the criminals to the Capital Tower as

soon as possible, as he believes they are suspected spies from enemy nation Songriveii. Any leads may be reported to local authorities and will also be rewarded. It is advised not to speak to the criminals, who are accused of sabotage, murder, and are considered a threat to Imperial security. Thank you for your ongoing-"

"We have no time to think… We need to leave the city," Ayela suggested. Kamille blinked in surprise, and Liz looked around anxiously.

"What about my brother?" Jack worried.

"I assure you; he's going to be alright. We will do everything we can to get him out. There is nothing we can do now, though. We need to regroup. We need to find Asher, and then start searching for the one who started it all… Ruat," Ayela suggested. He had enough. He barely heard what she said, and though he knew she was right, he couldn't settle in his heart to leave Adrian trapped by an alien race. It consumed his thoughts so much that he didn't even notice the name she had mentioned.

"This can't be our plan," Jack protested.

"Jack-"

"THAT'S NOT GOOD ENOUGH!!!" He barked with clenched fists. Calmly, Kamille stood to her feet and approached Jack, and then gently placed a hand on his shoulder.

"Look, I know you're in pain and you're worried. I know you want to get him out now, but there's nothing we can do. You'll get all three of you killed. We've all lost people to the Emperor and the chaos his reign has brought. We all have. My family was killed... My boyfriend's entire family murdered by the police. Ayela here lost a boyfriend *and* a girlfriend within three years of each other, while the military simply overlooked their towns and deemed them non-essential," she said softly. Jack's rapid breathing slowed to a normal pace, and he watched Ayela's expression fall downcast. He saw her pain. Liz walked over and took his hand, drawing his attention to her.

"We're going to get through this, Jack. We're going to get him back. Let's just... Listen to these two. Ayela has done nothing except look after us since we ran into her, whether someone told her to or not doesn't matter. We don't really have any other choice. If we were in their position, would we have been so gracious? Would we have gotten so involved with their troubles on top of our own?" She challenged gently.

Jack sighed and then nodded. "You're right," he admitted. The words were bittersweet. "Who are we going to find, again? Asher was his name?"

"Yes, and then we need to find Ruat," Ayela

added. Jack's eyes narrowed and his brow furrowed. This time, he heard what she said.

"Ruat?" He asked inquisitively. "How do you know that name?"

"How do *you* know that name?" Kamille asked with a raised eyebrow.

"I... It doesn't matter. Let's focus on our first step; finding Asher," Liz interjected.

"It's not that simple," Kamille answered. "What Ayela isn't telling you is that the city is barred and guarded. There are walls taller than most buildings around here, and there are no gates – not that there should be. The city sits on top of a mesa, with the walls towering on top of the cliffs. Only airships and warbirds enter and leave. And there are creatures that live in the wilds that have grown more feral in recent years and are crueler than anything we'd find in this city - aside from the possibility of an aethril's Judgment. There's only one way out, and it's almost as dangerous as the wilds themselves..."

"What's that?"

"The sewers. Beasts live in the wilds, but in the sewers... We need to be fast, or we won't make it," Kamille warned.

Jack sighed. "My intuition whispered to me that this wouldn't be an easy journey..." He said. His gaze turned to the window. He wondered what kind of things lived on this world that made their lives so hazardous. Or was it not always that way?

"Asher is in D'Vnora, one of the major cities to the east. But before we go there, we should stop at Shamol, a town at the base of the cliff. They're sympathetic to... us. My boyfriend is there- he'll help us get on our feet," Kamille suggested. "We should get moving. Ayela... Are you ready to leave this city behind?"

"...No... But I know the dreams I had... I know that these two are worth it," Ayela confirmed.

Kamille took a deep breath. "I hope you're right," she said as she packed her things. Jack looked out at the city once more, gleaning a long, dreamy vision of a city he would never truly understand. Perhaps this world was how he made it right by his mother. Perhaps their journey wouldn't take them back to their wrecked apartment...

...Perhaps they were meant to be there until the end.

Under The Surface Of A Mountaintop

Nightfall had come much slower than Jack anticipated, but it offered them cover for the long hours they sneaked around. He was following the three ladies leading the way to a secluded street that they could drop down into the sewers. The four of them had their hoods up, and they traveled far enough apart from each other that they didn't look like a suspicious group of hoodlums.

The evening cityscape was as majestic as it was in the daylight - polished and reflective of the lamps that illuminated the streets and the stars that dotted the black night sky. Not many people roamed in the nocturnal as they did in the day, but the ones that did paid them no mind.

He kept replaying scene after scene of everything that had happened to them, trying to make sense and analyze it all. As he silently shifted through the darkness, he couldn't help but notice the several armored soldiers roaming casually through the streets.

He had a feeling the heightened security was because of himself and Liz, considering how adamant the government was with trying to retrieve them. He hadn't stopped to think about the public disturbance it would cause them if they simply announced that *more* aliens existed, or that they were trying to kill them. From what he gathered, there was already so much unrest in their country, so many outcries, so many protests and rallies that anything could almost cause another full-scale rebellion among the people.

The Emperor seemed to only care about wealth, power, and a reputation as a powerful leader. He seemed to act so much on imposing a powerful regime, even at the cost of his own citizens, that it seemed he was oblivious to his obvious inability to responsibly hold a leadership position. It was clear this leader sought to keep everyone who opposed him either dead, or under a supremely oppressive thumb.

But Jack could see behind the scenes. The Emperor wanted to increase the divide of the rich and the poor for a specific reason. Citizens were overworked, and likely taxed out of what they earned. Status was a luxury, and no matter how hard they strived, it would always be just out of reach of the ones who lived to achieve it. It was all intentional. Someone needed the attention off of the government and focused on other issues among the population. There was a game being played, and it went deeper than war, politics, and citizen unrest.

"Jack," Ayela whispered as they turned the corner, pulling him from his thoughts back to reality.

"Ayela," he whispered back sarcastically.

She rolled her eyes. "We're here."

Indeed, they were. He quickly followed Kamille to the sewer entrance – a subtle maintenance hatch on the ground between the backsides of two community buildings. He hadn't noticed the massive wall that loomed over the horizon behind a maze of other buildings. He began to understand what they were saying about it. He knew they were close, though.

Before they could get it open, they all heard rough and grunted voices started to grow louder as they drew closer. They immediately assumed they were authorities.

"Trouble," Ayela said as she turned and looked

into the dark of the alley, searching for anything to hide behind. "There!" She whispered urgently.

They plopped themselves onto the ground behind a large orange dumpster and stayed still while their scarlet-haired friend peered around the corner. She ducked back behind, however, as they flashed beams of light down the alley, whispering among themselves that they thought they heard something. Both Ayela and Kamille covered their mouths and noses with their hands and motioned for Jack and Liz to do the same. They obeyed silently.

"Nothing. I'm telling you, these visor sensors are malfunctioning," One of them said as they put their flashlights away and continued on. Jack peaked over the top silently and carefully to get a view, watching the hulking and intimidating suits continue on their way, holding rifles in a resting position across their chests.

"What law enforcement dresses like that when patrolling the city?" Liz commented.

"Ever since the Emperor has entered this role, he's had any sort of armed force – law enforcement *and* military – fully armored and fully armed. Under severe penalty, no one can speak against the Emperor any longer; no one can pursue careers outside of family trades; no one can choose certain religious beliefs. Anyone suspected of committing crimes of even the slightest degree are imprisoned without the possibility of release until time is served, and anything remotely severe means certain death. The happy ones you see… They're the successful ones who stayed within the confines of the laws the Emperor set in place. The further away from the tower – the center of the city – the worse things look…" Kamille explained, confirming what Ayela had said before.

"He sounds like he's intoxicated with power and coin," Jack commented.

"It's no coincidence that the 'judgments' on smaller towns and villages started to occur as the Emperor rose to power. Once he started to outlaw Korism, that's when we knew things were going to get worse. And his ambition is to take over all the known lands – hence these wars he engaged in. He wants total control of all resources, all cultures, all properties… He wants the world."

"It's clear why the Majjai have sprung into action," Jack said in admiration.

"While I'd love to discuss political issues with you, we need to move. Let's open this hatch and get out of Bavylune," she ordered curtly.

"Let's all be very cautious; there are… *creatures* down there. They're creepy – no, they're daethric-looking. They're fast, strong, carnal, and very – very – hungry. Keep up with us and follow our lead and we'll live. Linger behind, they'll rip you apart." Ayela explained in a rushed tone.

He nodded and obeyed Kamille. They twisted the metal wheel that controlled the locking mechanism, and then pulled up on the thick metal plate and revealed a long well that led to the deep tunnels of the sewers. Jack's heart pounded into his throat as he wondered what sort of creatures awaited them, but he knew they had no other choice.

"Get in," Kamille ordered. One-by-one, they disappeared down the ladder. She waited until last, and once they were all in, she followed suit, closing the cap above them while trying to keep the metallic thud as silent as possible.

The street laid bare and wet as rain started to fall. There was no sign that it was going to rain; no warning. Yet, it came none-the-less. They weren't aware of the storm they set in motion, nor what it meant for the world they were on, but he couldn't shake the feeling that whatever was going on, he was there for a reason...

But for what reason, he didn't know.

VIII

Insurgency In Inquisition

Dreaded are they, those whom the Emperor trusts, though they plot behind his knowing.

Banil, The Ghost Of The Empire

His presence demanded the respect of the officers, soldiers, guards, and scientists that he passed, though they knew absolutely nothing of who or what he was. Professionally, he made his way through the bland, greyscale hallways, lined on both sides with doors that led to the many interrogation chambers of the Tower. No one dared to stop him or question him. They saw he wore an Imperial uniform, but they didn't recognize the order it was from. He kept a strong composure, however, as he heard the screams from men and women who were accused of rebellion: screams that caused his heart to sink. He didn't want this. He didn't want to hear elves in such pain, but such was the price of war. He understood that, though he didn't understand his Emperor.

His Emperor was a powerful man, talented in the ways of undeserved divine logic. Many thought the Uri'Kai returned when the Emperor took the throne, but when he revealed he was not of the legendary bloodline, the nation quieted with unnerving tension. The Emperor was a powerful practitioner of a strange magic that only a sacred order of adepts once wielded, or so they thought. Once the Emperor started to establish a tyrannical reign, he knew he needed to figure out a way to stop him.

But his place was not to rise up in opposition just yet. No, he was to serve obediently, acquiring as much information and as many allies as he could before it was too late, then he would assume his destiny from within. He believed it to be so. He was a believer of Rök, a Korist. He followed the precepts of the ancient texts and let the Creator shape his life's purpose.

He observed the signs of the times, acknowledging the wrath of Rök falling on the nation because of their hardened hearts and the rebellion of its leader. The aethrils were carrying out his judgment, just as the text prophesied. But the appearance of these new beings - beings who appeared to be like elves - this he did not fully understand. He knew what was written:

The hero of Rök's Memoriums – that is, those who

follow the ways of Rök – will rise, and no one will know from where the hero went. But that reman will preserve Rök's followers, while those who did serve the fallen one will return to their maker and redeem their names. Those who followed Lukrïnæl will eternally be his slaves, even in the end of all things. Let the name of Rök be praised, he who has no beginning, and will have no end.

He knew that either he – Banïl, The Emperor's Advisor – or Captain Lunar were destined to be that hero. But he didn't know where it was written that these two near-remans would take place. There was nothing more written in the book of Endwær that described them or their very strange arrival... Nothing except one fleeting passage that mentioned nothing more than someone called 'Rök's witness,' who would record what they saw for the future generations yet made.

He stopped in front of the thick, slate-colored door outlined with orange-and-blue stripes and sighed. He slicked back his jet-black locks and rubbed his pale-skinned forehead as his orange-colored eyes examined the blue computer screen on the door. It displayed the famous face the interrogator everyone talked so much about; the one who let them escape. Banïl wasn't so careless, though. He was an inquisitor. His duty went beyond standard military protocol. Nothing he did was recorded. He had no public identity. He was second only to the Emperor, and though only government authority appeared in enforcement systems, there was no name or rank or title. He didn't exist.

But as for this human, as they called him - there was more to this being's story. Banïl was certain of it. He straightened his slick, velvet black coat that draped down to his feet, buttoned from his right shoulder down to his right hip. Scarlet outlined the edges of the long sleeves with Victorian-styled embroidery. His boots glistened in the white light with a polished shine. At his hip was a ceremonial, katana-like sword with a black hilt complete with a crimson handguard, sheathed in a black scabbard. He was certain of his intimidating appearance, and it was appropriately placed; he was one of the most dangerous men in the Empire.

He took in a deep breath once more, breathing the stale air of a section of the Emperor's tower that barely had interaction with the world above them, and tensed as his heightened hearing picked up even the smallest sound of the other reman guards around them whispering rumors about Banïl and what he was. He smirked.

Then, he waved his hand over the screen, and

once it opened, calmly placed them behind his back as he stepped into the simple room. His gaze was met with a glare from the human as the door shut behind him, enclosing them in utter silence save for the rustling of the being's clothes as he shifted around in his chair. His hands were cuffed to the table.

"You stated your name is Adrian Owens," Banïl began with a calm tone of voice; a voice that sounded like a shrewd assassin. "And you claim you're something called a human."

"Correct," Adrian responded curtly. His black, curly hair fell over his eyes as he looked down at the table. The light glistened off his greasy hair. He hadn't been given a bath for the many long days he'd been held captive. His eyes were blue colored, and his skin was only a little darker than Banïl's. Scabs from cuts lined his arms, and his clothes were torn at the sleeves and all over his torso. The interrogators were cruel to him as they tortured him, and his exhaustion was apparent. They gave him the minimum that he needed to survive; water, meat, and bread. He knew the first few days of his capture were filled with intense questioning, but when he didn't give an answer they liked, they resorted to pain.

"There were two others, and somehow, they escaped," Banïl said calmly as he sat down across from him and crossed his legs. "You say you don't know how."

Adrian didn't answer; he merely lifted his hands palms up as high as they could go before the cuffs restricted his movements. "Can't say that I do, specter," he spat. "Your guess is as good as mine."

"The interrogators tell me you told them that the cuffs simply turned off, and a mysterious voice guided the path to escape – at least, for the other two. But you were not able to. I find this curious."

He looked up at the inquisitor, squinting at him, as if trying to read his mind. "What are you getting at?"

"Oh, nothing you need to concern yourself with. I must apologize for the treatment of the interrogators. They claimed you were a spy from one of the nations we're at war with and treated you as such. I was called in after they filed their reports - after they mistreated you," Banïl explained. "But I have no interest in such harsh methods when it comes to your case. Rather, I find it absurd they didn't bring your files to a higher authority the moment they brought you in."

"Is this supposed to woo me? Are you using honey-comb words to goad me into telling you something I haven't told anyone else?" Adrian spat.

"Not at all. But your presence has higher implications," Banïl responded, un-phased by Adrian's smart attitude. He stood up from the chair and fixed his coat. "I merely wish to know you better, to see if you can be trusted."

"And pray tell how you intend to do that?"

"I'm an inquisitor, my friend. Drawing out the truth and covering up secrets is what I do," Banïl answered with a smile. He liked the human. "So, who were the two that escaped?" he asked, as he turned his back to Adrian.

"Can I opt to not tell you?" Adrian growled.

"Then I will opt to use unnecessary methods to draw out the truth," the inquisitor answered bluntly.

"I suppose you'll just have to get to work, then. Or you could just ask the interrogators. I was entirely honest with them."

Banïl's brow furrowed at his response. He was quick as a whip, stubborn, and hardened by the pain he'd endured. He pondered the details the Interrogator's report gave: a brother, and the brother's... Wife? Lover? Partner? Those details were important, but regardless, he needed to hear it from his own lips.

"No... Clearly those methods didn't work before, and I prefer to take more civilized actions," Banïl insisted. "I understand that you may have been honest with the Interrogators, but I would like to hear this tale from you."

"Why?"

"Because the Interrogators are fools. It is common practice for them to employ harsh tactics on anyone they suspect of being rebels. And their reports do not give me all the details I need. As I'm sure you've heard, we're at war on four fronts, plus an invasion of higher life-forms. You are a second life-form to appear, and are one who can communicate and reason with us – even understanding our culture since your own is so similar – and may even be able to give us something we need in our current endeavors; an advantage," Banïl elaborated.

"Alright, for the seventh time, I am Adrian Owens from a city called San Francisco. I arrived here in a ruins in the middle of a forest, and somewhere off in the distance stood a giant tree with red leaves that reached taller and was wider than any building I've ever seen. I also came here with my brother, Jack Owens, and his friend – or lover, I should say – Elizabeth McOwens. They're courting right now, which is unique for them, because both our parents and hers aren't really in our lives-"

"Let me interrupt you there; you said a tree with red leaves?" Banïl asked.

"Yes. I didn't stutter."

"You have no idea of the implications of this. Did you turn around to see if the tree was still there when you three left the forest?"

"Honestly, we were all bickering at each other and not really concerned with where we came from," Adrian admitted.

"It's apparent your presence here means more than previously assumed," he said, turning to face him. He calmly approached the table and leaned his hands down on it, looking directly into the human's eyes. "I would like to see to it that your stay here is more than adequate – much better than how we treat true criminals. But in order to do that, I need your cooperation."

Adrian's eyes narrowed. "What's your thinking?"

Banïl blinked in surprise, having rarely encountered such deducing prowess. But it all could be a ruse. "Elaborate your question."

"You come into this room, employing these tactics of mystery and allure, attempting to extract information from me as if there were more to extract, when your interrogators beat me even after giving them the truth. Once I told you all I told them, you tempt kindness towards me, and allude that there's a place of better care for me, should I comply with you. I would expect your motives are different than that of the interrogators. If you're anything of a high government position, you would have used much harder, much more painful methods to acquire the 'truth.' I can tell by looking at you and listening to you; you're brilliant. A genius. But you're also a believer of whatever it is you believe. I've met people like you. I've met believers, and I don't mean religious fanatics – I mean people who believe in what they're doing. And I can tell based off our conversation it's not the Emperor you believe in, so what's your plotting for?"

Banïl didn't know how to respond. The human was entirely accurate in his deduction, and sniffed out hidden motives within. He straightened himself and turned away, hiding his smile.

Rök was smiling on him this day, he was certain of it. Everything he'd studied in the texts, in the Alldweii; the ways his maker spoke to him… His patience was rewarded with a being that was clearly more intelligent than most of what he could find on Thaerv, and he was certain this human could help him initiate his plans to bring down the Emperor and end his tyranny over the people he loved.

"Your ability to sniff out the truth in others

will serve you well, Adrian," he complimented. "I would like to make you an offer…"

Adrian looked up at him as he turned around. "Listen, if it'll help me find my brother and his maiden, and if it'll help fix this situation we're in, then I'm willing to listen."

"Good. We will need to get you out of here safely without raising suspicion. I need you to act as though I'm taking you to be tortured further," Banïl ordered as he took the cuffs and clapped them together, releasing Adrian's attachment to the table.

"You still have failed to tell me what your endgame is," Adrian commented.

"It's simple, really… I intend to free my people from *his* rule. As for you, I read the reports: you're not as strong as a reman. You will need to train. We need to present you to the Emperor as one who is not only useful to him, but trust-worthy as well. If we work together, we will see to your safety and your freedom will become a reality. You must become an inquisitor," Banïl revealed. "Once you are one of us, no one will question your presence with us."

The inquisitor opened the door and offered for Adrian to take the lead, watching as he walked out somberly with his shoulders hunched over and his face downcast. Banïl kept his strictly emotionless expression as he followed, his hands held behind his back and his posture tall and proud. The guards suspected nothing as they walked by. There were no questions, no looks, no suspicions. They knew nothing more than a high government official had come to take a prisoner to what they assumed was certain death.

But Banïl had other designs in mind. His designs, if constructed correctly, would build a new life for his people. Certainly, some had to die for this to happen, but once he removed the Emperor from the throne, it would be worth it. In the end, it would all be worth it. As the doors opened to the elevator, he reminded himself that his purpose was determined by Rök, the One who created all...

Even if his fool of an Emperor banned their belief in him.

Kozek, Dog Of Failure

Kozek splashed his face with water, washing off the dirt. He was the interrogator who questioned the humans; the interrogator that let them escape; the interrogator that failed his Emperor and his country. But that didn't matter; he was going to get them back. It was a primary objective now, and one he intended to fulfill to the best of his reman ability.

He slicked back his hair and walked over to his bed. His room was simple, accommodating for anything he'd need; a bed with a sheet, blanket, and pillow, and a bookshelf filled with books about physical science, mathematics, probability, the history of Enthedrill, and even a holy book from one of the few state-sanctioned religions left. There was also a closet with all his clothes, which were standard uniform attire and casual pants with white shirts. There was a sink there as well with a mirror, and bright white lights on the ceiling that illuminated the gray walls and floor.

He was a simple man with a simple desire. He only wished to apply his knowledge and skills to the nation he grew up in. He knew that the Emperor made difficult choices, but those choices were necessary for the common folk. The Emperor did more for the people than they realize. He sifted those who were leeching off the government, wasting precious tax-payer's sigil when they needed to be out working like the rest of society. Those who did work, who did pay their taxes, who were law-abiding – they were the ones who needed the government's support.

Sure, some places spiked in crime, and even D'Vnora had grown worse in its rates within the last few years, but he knew his Emperor was going to deal with it appropriately once the four wars they were fighting were at an end. Those murderers, gangs, thieves, mafiosos, and thugs would get what was coming to them. Kozek knew what he'd do if he ever saw any in the streets; he'd cut them to pieces for the world to see. There would be bloodshed. He cared about reman life, but not so much that he was willing to spare those who preyed off the innocent.

His political opinions were irrelevant for the things he needed to accomplish. First, he needed to correct his failure. He needed to apply his intellect to gathering resources and sweeping the rest of the city for those humans. His Emperor demanded it through the many warrants he put out. Perhaps this would also allow him to root out and find those rebels who had been causing as much trouble as they'd been – the Darklings. He could snag two bags in one swipe.

As he sat on his bed and contemplated his next course of action, a knock on his door stole him from his thoughts. Without hesitation, he walked over and opened it to find a young woman, fully dressed in her gray uniform, holding an envelope in her hands.

"Interrogator Kozek; the Emperor has important information for you," she stated plainly. He admired her beauty as he took the papers from her, examining her curly, golden locks and her smooth, pale skin. Her eyes were like the deepest of sapphire crystals. She had an attractive figure that men would swoon after. But to him, she was one of his closest childhood friends… Before they moved up as far as they did in their positions.

"Ynsigna Lorrin," Kozek responded as he looked through the files she handed him, professionally stating her rank and name, "please come in. There are matters we can discuss."

"I can't stay long, Kozek. We're analyzing data from every recording device in the city connected to Enthedrill's network and searching for the escaped humans and that blood elf," she said gently as she followed him into his quarters. The door slid shut behind her.

"That's why I'm asking you to come in, Lorrin. I know you're a busy woman, and I won't take much of your time. But I want as much of the data as you can collect brought to me," he said as he set the files down on the book shelf. "We're going to hunt for this *blood elf* first, since the humans are with her. We'll turn the tides of these wars once and for all. Once we have the humans back, we can put an end to them. Who knows what they can do?"

"Kozek..." Lorrin said softly as she walked over and sat down beside him on his bed. "You're so worried about duty. Don't lose yourself in your mission. Don't go so far that you can't come back after. We've been close for so long; I don't want to see my oldest friend disappear within the machine of this operation. You were never meant to lose yourself to this."

"I know, Lorrin... But I must correct this failure. An official arrived to take the human today, and I couldn't help but think that if we had done our job... If I hadn't..."

"You have a heart that craves justice," she complimented. Kozek was never good at taking compliments.

Changing the subject, he asked, "How's your boyfriend?"

"Don't deflect the conversation, Kozek. He's good, though. We're celebrating our two-year anniversary this week."

"Good. I hope things work out even better, Lorrin." Kozek said, unable to hide that his thoughts were still on the humans. Lorrin could tell.

"Don't beat yourself up over that, Kozek. You still kept one of the humans, and at least you enforced appropriate discipline for their attempts to escape on him."

"I'll spook them a little next time and make them think we're going to feed them to something," Kozek said with a childish snicker. Lorrin sighed and shook her head as she chuckled.

"All this happened for a reason. Don't forget that."

"Thanks, Lorrin. You've always been a good friend."

"And I always will," she reassured as she stood up and straightened her skirt. "I need to head back, now," she declared as she made her way to the door. Kozek nodded at her as she left.

His spirits were lifted now, and he opened the envelope with the documents he'd received from the Emperor. There was direction, and with that direction, an assurance of success that he was eager to obtain. They would not escape him this time.

He shuffled through the documents until he came across a letter signed by the Emperor's hand. He took a deep breath in relief as he carefully examined its words.

Kozek Naxios, Interrogator,

I give you full access to resources and databanks to fully acquit your new role as Inquisitor. Congratulations on this promotion. When you've finished with this letter, burn it. You will no longer exist in any recognizable capacity outside of the Inquisitor's Council and myself. I know there was failure when the humans escaped, but I am confident in your ability iven your exemplary military service. You have shown the same determination as the Council; Banïl, Semus, Körok, and Jürdæ. They have been notified of your new rank and arrival into your position. Your pay has been modified as well to adequately satisfy this position.

Know that there is not a higher position in our government except for Emperor that you have received. Your fellow Interrogators are now subject to your command when you are present with them, and they are not to know what office you now hold. You may use any means required to extract information, perform dark operations, access top secret protocols, and express judgment on my behalf – even crimes committed by you will be overlooked. I assign you this role for one reason; you are the one who captured the humans, and you are the one who must bring them back in.

News and media outlets will comply with your command, and the public will not know you exist. Even your new uniform will be an enigma to them. Embrace this role and understand that if another Interrogator had seen and done the same as you, they would not receive this special circumstance. I recognize your skill and intellect and seek to reward it. Bring the humans in, Kozek. Bring them in.

See Outfitter Kaimee for your new uniform, and see Ygmorath Kirmoan for the mandatory combat, reflexive, and mental training required for your new post. Due to previous military, special forces, and interrogation training, your Inquisitor training will last for the duration of one week. You're as a ghost in this. Good luck, and don't trust the Council.

Emperor Gorvon Komin.

Kozek grinned as he read the letter. He set the papers down and went over to his closet. He quickly threw on a white shirt over his black tank-top and rushed out his door. He made his way down the hall of the barracks, rushing to make his way to the dressing room.

He would not fail his Emperor again.

IX

A City In The Clouds

*A dreamy bride is she, the jewel of
Enthedrill, atop her lonesome mesa.*

The Sewers Of Bavylune

The pop and crackling of the blue flare echoed in the deep sewer tunnels, and sparks illuminated the darkness around them. Jack, Liz, Ayela, and Kamille had been traveling for hours, it seemed. The waters of the sewer, which Kamille used to lead them through the dark maze, formed a slowly moving river of contamination that traveled to various destinations, some of which were outside the city.

They disposed of their phones when they first entered the sewers, stomping on them and shattering them to pieces before kicking them into the filth-filled rivers. There was no way to track them that Jack and Liz were aware of.

"What were those things? We see them a lot, but I don't think you ever explained what they were," Liz asked finally, referring to the devices.

She rubbed her arms from the cold and looked down both directions of the wide and tall sewers cautiously, staying close to Ayela. Dripping could be heard all around close to them and far away, and there was even the sound of rushing waters far off in the distance. She whipped her head around to the path to their left as they crossed an intersection, convinced she heard padded footsteps rushing wildly in the dark.

"Those are called cellphones," Ayela whispered, her gaze fixed in the same direction as Liz's. It seemed Liz wasn't the only one hearing things. Jack simply gave the girls confused looks.

"You could call them cellphones. If you ask me, though, they're too much of a distraction," Kamille answered as she started walking in the opposite direction of the sounds. The others quickly followed.

"Cellphones... Alright, explain," Jack demanded.

"They're wireless communication devices. They utilize satellites, radio waves, even electric signaling. They're pretty advanced. Tech like this hasn't been around for long, either. We've been using them for the last five hundred or so years."

"Fascinating... The ability to communicate without a wire... That's incredible. We only just invented devices that could transfer replicas of our voices across distances through a connected wire. This fellow from Scotland, Alexander Bell, received a patent for it maybe ten years before I was born on earth," Jack elaborated.

"Your people are just discovering these things..." Ayela commented. "How did you get here?"

"Trust me; we're as confused as you are," Liz answered. "We were just factory workers... I can't exactly find a reason that dictates us being here."

"Neither of us can..." Jack added.

"...What do your people know of the atom?" Kamille asked without looking back.

"Other than it's what makes everything up? There are very well researched scholars that are making significant progress on the subject, but I could tell you that we understand so little about these things in the grand scheme of the universe," He answered. "As much as I study, apply mathematics, and research, I'm not the one to ask about it. I'm no practiced physicist. We're just common folk."

"Some of the greatest discoveries were made by the most humble of our people. I imagine it's the same for you," Ayela commented.

"You could say that," Liz agreed. Jack felt eager

to change the subject.

"So where exactly is this Asher?" Jack asked, walking up beside Kamille. Ayela and Liz continued to entertain each other with small talk, getting to know each other even more and distracting themselves from the creeping dread of whatever resided in the dark with them.

"I told you; D'Vnora. Once we leave this city, we have a long journey to reach an outpost where we have friends. Once we've stocked ourselves with supplies for the journey, we leave for D'Vnora. Once there, we'll regroup and figure out a plan. Asher's our guy, for sure."

"He'll know where to find Ruat?" Jack brought up. Kamille hesitated to speak for a moment.

She bore a puzzled expression, as if she couldn't find the right words to speak. "Ruat is something of a mystery, Jack. The person has never shown their face publicly. Ruat has always been there, and is the reason my associates and I are together... but... they're an enigma..."

"So, we're hunting for a specter."

"That's a polite way of putting it, yeah," Kamille chuckled. "But if anyone knows how to find them or where to look, it'd be Asher..."

Jack silently pondered what she said as they progressed through the sewers. The sounds of the rushing waters grew louder and louder as they moved forward, ensuring they were headed the right way – or, at least the way that Kamille was confidently leading them.

Then, breaking the silence that ensued save for Ayela's and Liz's whispering and light-hearted conversing, a low and ominous grumbling disrupted their thinking and talking. They each slowly turned, and with heart-pounding horror they gawked at a monstrosity, hauntingly glowering over them by a few feet.

There, peering through the darkness, was a figure cloaked by shadow save for its three glowing yellow eyes. It stood several feet taller than them, with abnormally long and slender limbs, and a thin torso. It growled as it stepped into the light of the flare, revealing charcoal skin and a face that had no mouth. Its hands were outfitted with sharp talons that made the blood drain from Jack's face.

"We need to run! NOW!" Ayela shrieked in a panicked voice. No one second-guessed her. They all ran as fast as they could, doing their best to keep up with Kamille as she dashed and dodged around each of the turns they had to make.

None of them had time to pay attention to the increasing smell of rotting corpses or the sounds of more creatures running after them, nor did they stop and turn to see what was following them. Their lives depended on their need to control their frightened curiosity.

"No!" Liz whimpered as her breathing grew heavier. Ayela looked back at them with anxiety all over her face.

"Liz!" She barked, slowing herself down enough to run beside her and Jack. Kamille stayed in front, leading them through the sewers. The rushing waters were louder than before. Jack hoped that meant they were closer to an exit.

The creatures behind them roared in a distorted unison, announcing their pursuit throughout the entirety of the sewers. Kamille shrieked, running even faster than before. Jack didn't know what to do. His heart pounded in his ears, and his legs burned with energy as he pushed himself even harder to run faster and faster. The thought of losing Liz made his heart beat irregularly. Pain began to swell in his chest. He couldn't let that happen. He wouldn't let that happen. He refused.

Then, all of the sudden, his world turned upside-down.

Liz tripped.

She fell hard onto the ground and rolled forward a couple feet, her arms and legs sprawled for a moment before she collected herself and tried to run. She knew she wouldn't catch up in time. She was going to die. She looked back at the horrors, seeing them in closer detail as time began to slow down all around her, and the noise and clamor quieted to a muffled volume.

Observe. A familiar voice chanted to her mind. That same voice... The one that helped Jack and her escape from the tower... There it was at the time of her death.

Observe, see what man cannot.

She looked on at the creatures, many of them with distorted flesh. They looked as though they once had ears, but they rotted away. The tallest one that they saw earlier approached slowly, its steps shaking the ground a little. The other creatures had empty eye sockets and toothless mouths. Were they once reman? How were they still able to move?

Observe the truth which was lost.

Then she saw it: they didn't have empty eye

sockets. There was flesh covering the holes, and while most of their teeth had fallen out, they still retained what she assumed were their canine teeth – the sharpest ones. They were once reman, but something changed them into the things that charged at her. They were blinded to all sentient senses and reduced to carnal craving. They were animals; wild, vicious, and no longer cared for truth or lie. They only sought blood and to fill their ever-empty stomachs.

Observe, oh human...

Moving with all urgency, Jack leapt in between her and the creatures. He just couldn't leave her. In their slowed state, he ran back to her and stood in front of her and the beasts, facing them with courage and clenched fists. She saw it; his heart. There was nothing he could do, nothing she could do. They were going to die there, but Jack was ready to fight his hardest. He drew his pistol and unleashed a barrage of bullets onto them, though it had no effect. Within seconds, there was a clicking sound, and he knew he had no more shots to fire. He wouldn't let them get to her without a fight, though, standing and raising his fists as if he could do anything to fend them off.

Then an expanding wave of radiating energy, bending and warping the dim light that passed through it, shot forth from Ayela as she landed in front of them and gently pressed her hand to the ground. The creatures were frozen in place, and Jack was gripped with awe once more. It was her second display of incredible, unexplainable, reality-warping power. Ayela stood to her feet, and without missing a beat, spun on one foot like a ballerina before stomping her other foot down as she faced them.

In one fluid motion, she moved her arms in dance-like rhythm, and then thrust her right hand forward. On cue, they heard a subsonic boom, and a flash of intense light emitted from her open palm in a split second, packed with enough force to shake their environment a little. The blast consumed the creatures without leaving a trace. Ayela paused and examined the area, making sure there weren't any surviving monsters, and rested on her knees to catch her breath. Satisfied, she turned to help Jack and Liz up. There was silence once more, save for the rushing waters.

"That was…" Liz began as they followed Ayela back over to Kamille.

"Something she shouldn't have done," the stern leader answered curtly.

"They were in danger," Ayela defended.

"It doesn't matter now, but next time, find an alternative."

"There was no alternative, Kamille," Ayela said defiantly. Kamille stopped and whipped around to get into Ayela's face.

"Then let them die! There's too much at stake, Ayela! Too much! You can't use divine logic here, and you know that! You can't dance! Imperial Operatives know how to track those energy outputs, and dancers are so rare, they'll pick up your signature in an instant! You'll jeopardize our entire operation if you let them get their hands on you!" She yelled. Ayela was silent as she looked down and held her arm, shame and guilt written all over her face. Kamille, however, was hardened.

"We haven't had any luck since we let Tallie die... And then these two come along, and things change for us. The first alien species that didn't outright attack us, and even more – a species that looks like us... I can't just let them die," Ayela said, still looking down. Her voice was quiet and solemn.

"All of our sacrifices could be wasted, Ayela... We can't make ourselves targets like that. I know your heart, and I value it so much. But if it means the survival of our people and the end of the

empire, I will break it over and over if I have to…
Please don't force me to…" Kamille said softly,
raising Ayela's face to hers. "…As much as I want
to show you some kindness being here, there's a
lot going on you're just not privy to. I know you
didn't mean for that to happen… But if you want
to move with us, you're going to have to keep
up. Do whatever you need to do… But I can't
stop to make sure you're not getting yourselves
in trouble… Now let's go."

They silently accepted her rebuke and pressed
on. As hard as she was, Jack knew there was a
deep reason for it. They'd lost as much as he did,
he had no doubt…

…But how much more did he have to lost before
she shed a little mercy on him?

Scaling The Mountain Of God

They squinted their eyes as they emerged from the wide opening onto a cliff-balcony on the outer edge of the towering city, which sat on a massively high mesa. Rushing water poured out into a waterfall that misted into the air before it had a chance to hit the ground. The wind was loud and strong as it blew across the mesa's rocky wall, threatening to take anyone not paying close enough attention.

"We're going to need to climb down! There's small caverns along the way where we can rest and break and eat so it's not just a straight shot!" Kamille warned. Jack took a deep breath as he looked out over the horizon, taking in the breath-taking view. The landscape was a sea of grass with patches of forest along some of the edges of the horizon. He could see some wild creatures dashing along the open plain with a freedom only animals knew. There were no mountains in the distance; just flatlands all the way through until it reached the forests of massive trees… trees that could dwarf any tree on earth.

"It's so beautiful!" Liz commented. Their sun was making its descent, splashing beautiful color into the blue skies that painfully reminded them of earth. It was a vivid array of oranges, pinks, purples, and blues.

"We only have hours to make camp and get a fire going! If we don't, some of the hawks will nest in those caverns! Let's move now!" Ayela barked as she and Kamille began to descend gracefully down the rocky wall. Liz didn't hesitate in following, but Jack continued to scour the skies for what they were talking about.

Then he saw them; massive birds all flying in the distance high above and far away from the city walls. They were like eagles, from what he could see. But he was sure they were their own breed of wicked.

They climbed as fast as they could, scaling down the vertical formation with tact and care as they carefully planned each placement of their feet and hands. Ayela and Kamille were faster; they had clearly been doing it long enough and knew what to avoid and what not to. Jack was unfamiliar, but he spent many years scaling walls as a kid with less to grab onto. Liz, entirely inexperienced, focused her efforts in being careful rather than being quick. Jack made sure he was near her so that he could help her to safety.

"Don't worry about any airships! We're too small for them to see and they're too high up! If any of those Mjurdöks fly close, though, don't move; they hunt for things that are moving!" Kamille shouted up at them. As if on cue, the sound of massive engines spewing out burning flames and exhaust soared overhead as a militarized, boat-shaped airship flew over the city walls. Liz clung tightly to the wall, nervous that the shear sounds of the engines would shake her loose from her grip. Jack placed an arm over her to reassure her that he was there.

Once the ship had passed, they continued their descent. Jack trailed behind to keep an eye on all of them and on those massive creatures, what he assumed were the Mjurdöks, flying around in the open skies. Just below, he could see the mouth of one of the caverns Kamille was talking about. They were close to their first stop.

"Just a little more!" Ayela yelled over the rushing winds. Jack's skin was growing numb from the cold, but he couldn't imagine how Liz felt. They'd been descending down the mesa for at least an hour or an hour and a half, and the lack of sunlight was making that apparent.

Jack began to rush. Both the elvish girls made it to the cavern, now it was just Jack and Liz. "I'll go start the fire!" Kamille yelled, dashing into the cavern.

"Try to move faster!" Ayela yelled. Liz, being that she was closer, carefully leapt onto the ledge where Ayela could catch her and help her balance. Jack was the only one left.

He was about to drop down as well until he heard a grotesque shriek from behind. He looked over his shoulder to see one of the birds of prey directing its flight towards him. "RUN!!!" He screamed as he dropped down onto the ledge. He leaned forward to regain his balance, then turned to face the creature as it darted towards the cavern. Ayela and Liz ran deeper into the dark of the cave where they wouldn't be seen. It was just Jack and the monstrous hawk.

What do I do??? He panicked as he looked around at his surroundings. There were plenty of boulders big enough to hide behind, and it was an open enough area that he could leap, dodge and roll. Perhaps he would just need to find a way to wear it out.

Then he noticed something metallic glistening in the fading sunlight; a sword. That would have to be his only way of killing it. the pistol he'd cleaned of ammo was left in the sewers, and who knew where Liz left hers. He had to move quickly, though. The hawk was seconds away from the cavern, and it was just barely enough time for Jack to leap to the side and roll behind one of the boulders.

Everything happened quickly. The creature was confused after he slammed on to the cavern's floor and his head smashed into one of the boulders. Jack was able to get a good look at it in their limited sunlight; it had two green eyes on either side of its head, and its black beak was lined with sharp teeth. The creature had to be at least ten meters tall, and its feathers were a slate color. It had patches of white and blue fur all over its body, and when its wings were folded, it treated them like forelegs with claws at the outermost folds.

When it got back on its feet, it shrieked with a blood-curdling sound, and scoured the room for Jack's presence. The sound was disorienting, but he focused all his strength into fighting the haze that its jarring sounds inflicted. He was sure the creature had spotted him by now.

Angry that it missed, it reared its head back and glared at Jack, who maintained his position. He slowly backed away and towards the sword on the ground. The bird let out a demonic growl as it slammed one of its feet forward and moved its head closer to him. Jack was cautious, unsure of what the bird was trying to do.

Without warning, the creature tried to peck at Jack again, but as the adrenaline kicked in, everything began to move slowly. Jack leapt to the side once more, dodging another near-death encounter, and dashed towards the resting blade. He leapt at it, and once his hand wrapped around the handle, he rolled onto his feet. He faced the bird with the sword in his hand, poised and ready to strike. His heart was pounding in his head, reminding him that he was indeed alive and wasn't dreaming of his own death.

The bird didn't wait to strike again, and nearly hit Jack when he side-stepped out of the way. As the bird's beak was near, though, he swung the sword down with an angry force, lodging its angular, single-edged blade into the beak so hard, cracks descended even further down. Jack refused to let go, ignoring the ear-piercing roars and shrieks of the creature as it reared its head back in pain. Jack pried the sword loose once he balanced himself on the creature, re positioned so he was facing the opposite direction, and then rammed the blade into the creature's eye socket.

It was a fatal strike. The bird instantaneously

collapsed on the ground and threw Jack forward. He slammed into the rocks in front of the bird. He grunted and wiped away the blood from his mouth as he stood to his feet, his heart pounding in his throat so hard he thought he would have a heart attack. He held his side, bruised from the fall, and breathed in deep.

Just in time, a flickering orange light began to emerge from the deep recesses of the cavern, with Kamille, Ayela and Liz accompanying it. They paused, awestruck he was able to slay the mighty beast with nothing more than a sword. Ayela and Liz ran over to him, anxiously checking if he was alright. He gripped his side almost as tightly as the sword, unable to ignore the throbbing pain that darkened his flesh.

"How did you manage to take down this beast?!" She exclaimed.

"You'll notice an eye is punctured," Jack grunted as he went to sit down and lean his back on one of the boulders.

"I've only ever known one other person killing one of these with nothing more than a sword before..." Ayela said as she looked down at the sword. Then, as if whispering the name of a fabled hero, she exhaled, "Captain Lunar..."

Jack spat out a mouthful of blood before looking over at her. "I know you told me who he is," he said, "but I still don't hold much to this man's name."

"And you're spitting out blood," Kamille said as she set the torch and the wood down and rushed over to him. "This isn't good."

"It'll be fine," Jack snickered. "I only-"

"Let me see your chest."

"Listen, Kamille, I-"

"Jack, please," she begged calmly. Jack sighed as he pulled his arms away and let her lift up his dirt-stained hoodie. On his chest was a dark area near where he landed on the rocks. "You're injured... But I don't think it's fatal."

"It's a bruise. Humans do that with relative ease. I also hit my chin on the fall down," Jack revealed.

"You need to be careful as we continue our descent tomorrow. If you make any wrong move, you could damage something important," Liz commented. "Don't force me to lose you. I already lost my home."

"Aye, lass," Jack said with sarcasm. Liz gave him a stern look in response. "I'll be careful, Liz. I promise." He swore as he gently held her hand.

"Be more than careful," she shot back. "I can't lose you, Jack... Please don't tease me about that," she begged.

"Don't play with her heart," Ayela warned.

"I promise I'll be careful... I promise," he swore, looking into Liz's eyes. She took a deep breath and exhaled in relief as she positioned herself beside him. He placed his arm over her.

"Rest up. Tomorrow, we have a long descent... We'll take some of the meat from this beast to make it through the day," Kamille ordered as she set up their fire. Jack yawned and took off his pack and pulled out one of his spare hoodies as he folded up the dirty one and put it away. Before he got comfortable, Kamille pulled out a tall bottle of sparkling, golden liquid that glistened in the light of the campfire.

"You humans drink?" Kamille asked as she bit the cork that sealed it and yanked it out with her teeth. Jack smirked.

"It's about time something went positive besides our skins getting saved," he commented as he sat down beside her. Craving set in, and he took a large gulp. It was strong, fizzy, and one of the most refreshing things he'd had since they got there, aside from Ayela's finely cooked meal.

After they each took a couple more sips, they laid down, with Ayela agreeing to stay up for a first watch of the night to make sure the fire was stoked and they were safe. Within seconds, the exhaustion of their eventful day finally took its toll on him. As he fell asleep, though, he felt the nagging of that voice, urging him to see something that he was missing… a key piece to this entire puzzle that he wasn't grabbing a hold of…

Jack…

Wake up, Jack…

X

Imperial Lands of Peaceful Danger

*Wild is she, the nature and wood of
Enthedrill, that she would gore her people
in prejudice.*

A Trance Of Elvish Humanity

"Wake up," Kamille ordered sternly as she nudged Jack's foot, startling him awake. He gasped as he sat up straight and rubbed his face, and squinted at the bright, white light of the sun. He grunted as he stood, clenching the bruise he received from the previous night's battle. He looked over at the corpse of the massive bird and observed it in greater detail now that there was light.

"That's one big damn bird," he commented. He slung his pack over his shoulder and picked up the sword he used to slay the beast. Once he saw that there was nothing to carry the blade, he took out his dirty hoodie and tied it around his waist, and then shoved the blade through tight and snug.

"Here," Ayela offered, pulling out a couple of pins from her bag and handing them to him.

"Stick these through the knot of that hoodie so that it won't come undone." He obeyed.

He climbed up and over the corpse of the bird. He looked out at the grand landscape below and clenched tightly once he looked down. They were still very high up, and he could feel the air pressure was increasing as they got closer to the ground.

"How often do you both make this trek?" He asked, looking back over at Kamille and Ayela.

"We've made it maybe six or seven times. Affording passage on a shuttle out is too expensive, so we take this route." Kamille answered. He could tell she was lying through her teeth, though.

"Alright, look-"

"I know what you're about to ask," Ayela said as she approached him, holding up her hand as if to stop him from moving forward. "You want to know our secret... Clearly, we could afford passage if we wanted, but now especially, we have to keep our identities secret. The Empire is particular about who comes and goes from Bavylune. The more we're seen, the more danger we're in. We take public transport rarely. Usually, we can get through the sewers safely, because we know how to hide ourselves from those creatures."

"Why, though? Why do you have to hide? No one who is a lawful citizen of any nation should have to be so secretive, even on earth," Liz pointed out calmly. "You can trust us."

"Let's get to the plains. Once we're at Shamol, we'll explain everything... but if you prove to be a threat at all, we'll leave you behind in the dust, am I clear?" Kamille threatened.

"Crystal," Jack agreed.

"Good. Now let's get off these cliffs. No doubt Bavylune officials are preparing to scour the sewers for what happened yesterday."

"As you command," he submitted as he let the girls begin their descent first, and quickly followed behind them.

The day passed by when descended the mesa. They were all exhausted, but especially the humans. Ayela pressed on to the dirt paths that etched their ways through the plains. Jack made sure to stay close to Liz in case she began to feel unwell. He noticed that his own stomach began to hurt a little, but he just credited it to the massive amount of physical activity they accomplished.

"My friends; welcome to the plains of Enthedrill," Kamille exclaimed as she held out her hands to the open ocean of grass around them.

231

The forests they had seen above were so far away, they couldn't see them over the horizon.

"Our first stop will be over there," Ayela revealed, pointing to a small town miles off in the distance. "Don't worry; they're sympathizers with anyone who opposes the Empire. People who are on the run can go to this town too; they're a sanctuary town. City officials rarely venture this far below unless it's to escort a convoy of supplies, but even then, they get most of their goods from other towns."

"How do we afford to stay so hidden here?" Jack asked. "Wouldn't the Emperor simply threaten to destroy the town or establish some sort of martial law?"

"They're well prepared for such occasions. Besides, sanctuary towns are an establishment within the founding documents of the Empire – no Emperor has the power to overrule it. If they violate the clauses that permit the solitude and privacy of sanctuary towns, they are removed from office under compulsion of the senate of house, or by force if they refuse to step down," Ayela explained.

"It was smart of them to establish a town like that so close to the Capital," Liz commented. She looked up to the massive city atop the mesa.

Kamille reached into her pocket and pulled

232

out a stack of bills similar to the dollar on earth. "None of you may have any sigil, but I do. They aren't looking for me either, which means they haven't seized my cardchip. I can buy us anything we want or need. Do you all understand?"

"I still have some sigil in my bag too. They might have seized my accounts by this point, but I can at least chip in a little. I always kept cash from the jobs I worked here in each visit," Ayela chimed in.

"Do you know how much?"

"About eleven hundred total."

"Sigil?" Liz asked.

"Money. It's the currency in Enthedrill. They use sigil here and in Dominov, klaks in Durinveii, uim in Sangriveii and the Latvian Isles, and weyts in Korok," Kamille explained. "We've tarried out here too long. Come on, it'll be nightfall before too long, and we want to be within the walls of the town before then." They obeyed and followed her as she led them on, pushing through the exhaustion of having just descended a mountainside.

Finally, they arrived at the tall metal gates of the walled town. Bright lanterns at the gate kept things lit as the sun began to set behind the horizon. The light would help to keep any predators that hunted in the dark away. The sounds of strange insects in the plains around them cricketed and announced themselves louder and louder than before, signaling the arrival of twilight hours. Jack's legs hurt, and he couldn't imagine that Liz's were doing much better. He kept a strong expression, though. He had to. There was no room to show any weakness, not in their predicament.

"Open the gates!!!" Kamille shouted to the top of the walls. A couple of heads peered over, examined them for a second, then disappeared just as quickly. The very next second, the metal doors in front of them groaned and creaked loudly as they began to recede into the walls. Behind them, a man approached with an ebony-like complexion similar to Kamille's, and with a build as slender and athletic as Jack's. He was handsome and agile.

"Kamille, my love!" The man exclaimed with outstretched arms. He quickly rushed over to her. His accent was as thick as hers.

She said nothing as she embraced him just as eagerly, and then motioned for them all to follow. He led them into the town with his arm around her. Jack let the ladies precede him first, but he hesitated. He felt an overwhelming sensation that he was being watched closely. He turned to survey the horizon while there was still light yet saw nothing. He heard nothing except the strange howls of canine-like creatures in the distance. No one followed them, and yet the feeling grew stronger by the second.

"Jack?" Ayela asked as she placed a hand on his arm, startling him. He sighed as he looked up at the others, who were watching him as if he were going to have a meltdown.

"I'm fine. Probably just weariness," Jack said plainly.

"C'mon. Let's get in and get some rest before any animals decide that we're their next meal," Ayela warned as she turned to walk with the others through the gate. Jack paused for one more moment to look out over the darkening horizon. He was certain they were being watched. He felt it. He shook his head as he turned to follow the others into the town.

Then, uncharacteristically, Ayela stopped dead in her tracks and looked around as if she were confused by her surroundings. She slowly looked at everyone, as though she was a stranger in her own lands. Everyone was startled, but he felt the most uneasy. In the light of the city gates, he could see it; her eyes were different. Rather than their vibrant purple color, they were a deep chestnut. But what startled him wasn't the color…

It was their *humanity*.

He saw the eyes of a human woman, confused by what she saw, and most frightened and awestruck once she laid eyes on him. It was as if the sight him brought shocking revelation. And then, just like that, she blinked, and her eyes were normal again.

"Ayela?" Kamille asked with concern in her expression.

"What just happened?" Ayela asked, looking around with even more confusion in her face.

"You tell us, love," the man that came out to meet them stated. She didn't answer. She just looked at Jack and stared into his eyes. It was like she was hoping for an answer from him that he couldn't provide.

"Let's just go. We had a long day, and we need to get some rest," she said, still looking at Jack. With that, they all turned to enter the town. Jack followed but watched Ayela with suspicion. There was so much going on, it wasn't a surprise that things continued to get stranger and stranger. The gate closed behind them as they entered the safety of the town's walls, protecting them from alien dangers that threatened to keep them from ever making it home...

...From making it to his brother.

Shamol, Haven Of Heathens

"My name is Thillan Otash."

Kamille snuggled up to him and rested her head on his shoulder. Her love for Thillan resonated strongly in the room, and Jack felt safe. He hadn't seen any of them in a comfortable enough place to express their hearts as freely as Thillan and Kamille did then. Peace permeated the air in the oaken room, lit by warm amber lights that reflected off a glossy round table in the center. Weariness wafted over him like a woven quilt, tugging at his eyelids with force. Another emotion and sensation stirred in his chest, though, when he gazed over at Liz. Peace, love, and the passionate desire he felt for her.

"Hello, Thillan," Liz finally said. He could read the same emotions like a text scrawling on her face. His heart pounded in his throat with eager anticipation, one that he stayed for the sake of their company. "I'm Liz, and this is Jack. We're humans from a world called Earth."

"Pleasure to meet you. I assume you're wondering who we are exactly," Thillan stated plainly. Jack pulled everything together in his thoughts, puzzling over every instance and clue he'd analyzed since meeting Ayela. His mind was quick at work, piecing things together - Ayela's disposition towards the Empire and its socially unequal ethics; Kamille's bitter defensiveness of their secrecy; connections and secret routes to major cities; the need to stay undetected by destroying anything that could lead back to them- Theirs was a fight that took place in the shadows.

His response was curt, "You're a band of rebels. Whether or not you're of the same brutish breed as this Captain Lunar and the Majjai or not is yet to be seen, but I get it now. You're enraged by the Empire's treatment of any of its poor and hard workers. It's almost as if you yourselves have been on the receiving end of it – or know people personally who were – and are standing up because they can't-"

"Jack-"

"I'm not finished. See, the first person we met here was a little girl who gave us the same shocked expression we gave her when we met.

When the empire captured all of us, we were treated like animals by them. I can't imagine what that little girl must have been feeling, and then she was shuffled off to a family she doesn't know. I *feel* the anger. Not just over my brother, but how they treated us, how they dismissively passed little Zesha along.

"Then we met Ayela here – someone who truly made us feel like we could have a friend on this world – and then Kamille, and then you. I see it now… your fight is political. It's social. You're so involved with the individuals of this Empire – specifically those who have been given misfortune at the hands of this empire. It's made you so bitter against anyone who even slightly resembles them.

"But let me be clear; my reasons for having any vendetta against the Empire are different than yours. You stand up for the ones who don't have feet to stand up with. I stand up because they took one of the only people I have left after my home was destroyed. They put a wedge between us and the only one – a child – that could have helped us make sense of anything. And they have sought to take our lives for no readily apparent reason at all."

"So, you couldn't care less about what happens to our people?" Kamille spat. Ayela was silent.

240

She watched Jack intensely, staring into his eyes for some sort of emotion or response that he was unaware of.

"It's not exactly a priority of mine, no."

"I knew we couldn't trust y-"

"But that's not a fair question, and you're making an enemy where there isn't one. Listen..." Jack stood up and pushed his seat in. "My world is full of problems that seem very similar to yours. I suppose I could relate to your people very well. But we were brought here without cause, without explanation, and without direction. We were raked up into a war that we weren't initially involved in, and forced to pick a side we don't even know if we should believe in. Liz here might feel for you, and I may understand, but I refuse to be bullied into a cause I don't know if I believe in while it seems as though I'm only going to be an outsider of it. You either look past my differences to your people and try to trust me, or you let me go my way... But don't force me to put everything on the line for something I wasn't involved in to begin with."

Tension started to build, replacing the peaceful atmosphere. He'd brought tension that he had not intended to. While he knew in his mind he was right, he couldn't help but feel in his heart that he was wrong. He wondered what his mother might have thought if she'd heard him now. He was always a fighter. He always stood up for those who had no one to do so. Why was this any different?

Perhaps it was the expression he wore that softened Kamille's response to him. Perhaps she read his emotions, and sensed that he realized he was wrong in his statement. Perhaps she could see through his pride and self-centered goals. "Look," she said softly, "you're here now. And you sniffed us out from simple observation. You're correct. We are a band of rebels. We're called the darklings, based off an old mythological creature of some ancient civilization from our people. We stick to the 'shadows,' meaning no one knows who we are. We are able to hide our identities, even with such advancements in technology, and we're good at what we do. And yeah, you have the same skin color as the asses that oppress my people, but that's not why I don't trust you. You've got a self-centered mentality, and you act like your problems are the only ones that matter at the moment. We've all got problems. All of us. And really, what you're feeling right now... The problem you've got at the moment... My people have been dealing with this for hundreds of years in this empire- longer, even. To say it's because of our physical differences is a really generalized assumption, honestly. The content of your character looks like shit right now, and your brash attitude could compromise what we do," Kamille revealed.

"Which is what, exactly?" Jack asked.

"Exposing the government. There's so much tension because of our work. We have the same cause as Captain Lunar, but we're non-violent: which means we don't kill. We fight, we incapacitate, but we do not execute. We leak information to the public and weaken the Empire's regime, and when someone becomes dissatisfied enough, our leader – Ruat – recruits them and they become one of us. Our goal is to turn three quarters of the population against the Empire, because by that point, they will have no choice but to dissolve and make way for new leadership," Ayela answered.

"How do you know that will work?"

"What do you mean?"

Jack took in a deep breath. "You're talking about overthrowing a government – a nation. Do you really know what that means?"

"...Yes?" Kamille asked more than answered.

"Not everyone wants the Empire to fall. For plenty of people, even the ones you fight so hard for, this nation may be the one thing they rely on to keep going... It may be the only thing they know. If you take that from them without warning and plunge this nation into chaos, are you prepared for the consequences?" He pointed out. There was silence. "Are you prepared to not be prepared? Can you expect unexpected outcomes?" He added.

"We... I... How can we let someone as wrong as the Emperor remain in his position of power?" Ayela complained.

"Because the one who comes after him could be even worse than him," Jack stated plainly.

Kamille cleared her throat. "There's nothing that could be worse than him. And if you'd ever grown up here, you'd know this government was set up to benefit certain people. This isn't just a flash-moment decision; this has been years and years and years of oppression, injustice, civil unrest... The only ones who would want this government to stay the same are the ones who benefit off it- and the ones who *think* they benefit off it."

The tension loosened, but there were still questions in his mind. Were they right in their cause? Could he trust that there would be a better leader after the emperor was dethroned? How could they be so certain? Sure, he agreed with the motive of their cause, but what if the end result left their world worse off than when everything began?

Still, though, he saw it in Kamille's eyes. There was pain. Pain, torment, and a longing for things to be better. She longed for good lives for everyone the empire walked all over. He could see it all just from the dim glint that sparked in her pupils. Even ones that looked like him suffered under the empire's oppressive rule.

But what could he do?

Trust in me. The familiar voice that had been appearing when he least expected whispered to his mind.

How can I trust in someone whose name I don't even know? Jack responded mentally. There was silence.

"We've all talked about Ruat," Jack said, changing the subject, "but Liz and I don't really know anything about them... Who are they? Aside from your illusive leader, I mean."

Thillan took a deep breath. "He- She- Whoever they are, Ruat is the one responsible for bringing us together. We were all recruited by them the same way; a message on our phones or some letter delivered to our mail without a return address, each saying one short phrase; You were chosen. The only one who got more was Ayela."

They all looked over at her. "Mine said *You were chosen. You are the last, dancer.*"

"'Dancer?'" Liz asked. "Like what you mentioned in the sewers. What are dancers?"

"Practitioners of divine logic."

"It doesn't matter for now. We've had a very exciting past couple of days. We have our mission now, and we need to begin arranging for our next move... We can't stay here for long, either," Thillan answered.

"Why not? Isn't this a sanctuary town?" Liz asked.

"Yes, but we don't need to put anyone in danger. It would be good for us to throw off their scent. We'll stay here until we get in contact with Asher, and then we'll carve a route to follow to get to him," Thillan suggested. "Once we've gotten to Asher, we can begin our search for Ruat. Once we have Ruat, we can get your brother back. And once we've made it to your brother, we-"

"We could use this. We could show the Empire that the government is eager to execute anyone – even visitors from another world – to instill fear in the hearts of the people."

"Wait, what?" Jack protested.

"This is good," Thillan finished. Liz reached for Jack's hand and held it tightly under the table. She was on the same page with Jack. *This is stupid.* He thought.

"If you go through with this," Jack began, "I will

not help you."

"What do you know, *ivory?*"

"ENOUGH!!!" Thillan barked. "We'll think about it. Alright? Nothing is set in stone. For now, let's just focus on getting to Asher. Once we're there, we'll plan our next move..."

"I agree," Ayela said, breaking her silent streak. "Let's all just go to bed now. I'm tired, and today was long."

"Agreed. Jack and Liz, you two have beds in here if you'd like," Thillan offered.

"Thillan-"

He threw up his hand, silencing Kamille before she had the chance to protest. Jack was thankful.

"Can we have our own room?" Liz asked politely, not letting go of Jack's hand. Thillan smirked as he turned to walk out the door.

There was a silent electricity in the air as they sat beside each other on the bed. Liz held her arm nervously, standing in nothing more than her underwear and a tanktop. Jack gently dropped his hoodie and shirt on the other side of the room, and gently traced his hands down her shoulders and to her own. He held her tightly, and kissed her neck.

"...We haven't had a chance to be alone for so many days, Jack..." she cooed. "I need you right now… You don't have to say anything. Just give me this night and hold me in your arms. Remind me that you're my man, and that I'm your lady."

"Always," Jack promised. "As long as we both live."

"Take me, my love…" she whispered as she pressed her lips tightly to his. His heart skipped a beat as they kissed. He let himself go as they took each other into the night, comforted by each other's loving embrace. They dipped deep into each other's love, and for that moment, they forgot about their pain and loss of being stolen to another world and only focused on how they felt for each other. He remembered the one thing he held onto that brought happiness in his life…

He was so in love with Liz…

XI

When Peace Has Fled

Under Gorvon Komin, no sanctuary will be left alone in his pursuit of power.

The Tension Of Rest

The intoxicating aroma of brewing coffee permeated the air in the room as Jack and Liz took their seats. Sun rays beamed through the dusty atmosphere, pouring in morning light that negated the need for any other illumination. Everyone was dressed and ready, joking and talking while the two of them sat awkwardly. There wasn't any uneasiness save for their uncertainty. How do they fit in? How do they relate to a group of people they've only just met?

Breaking the casual morning, Kamille cleared her throat. "Let's focus. Right now, we have to talk about our plan," she urged, disrupting the casual chatter. Ayela started to delicately eat the food on her plate as they talked.

"Right. Our first objective is to find this Asher, correct?" Jack reminded them.

"Correct. Like we've said, he's currently in D'Vnora. That's about all we know," Kamille answered.

Thillan stroked his chin inquisitively. "How do we know that exactly?"

"It was his prerogative when we last spoke that he needed to secure a connection for the darklings in D'Vnora. He said there were valuable persons there who had a wealth of inside knowledge of some of the government's deepest secrets: cover-ups, espionage, kidnappings, cult practices of some of the higher officials, and even records of sightings and signals in deep space. I was in Lythia at the time, preparing to make a trip to Ih'Dejj to recover some artifacts of the ancient order, and then our precious Ayela contacted me about these humans and said it was more important than anything we'd find there."

Ayela cleared her throat. "That's a very generalized retelling, but accurate, nonetheless. So, Asher went to D'Vnora. Did he drop off the grid again?"

"Presumably," Thillan interjected. "That's how the man operates."

"Risky as hell, if you ask me," Kamille commented as she sipped on her coffee.

"It's what's kept him alive and in charge. He's the only one who still gets any sort of orders to give out to people – orders that keep us a loose organization and not just random people who are all using the same name."

"I sent out a call to someone this morning before you both woke up, someone who knows Asher very well and will let him know we're planning on visiting the city soon, and then he will be on his way here. That gives us a few days here to catch up with these fast-moving times and get to know each other a bit, wouldn't you say?" She set her eyes on Jack and Liz at her last comment.

"I don't have a problem with it," he shrugged.

"What I wanted to hear," Kamille said with a smirk.

Ayela looked over to the window, losing herself in her thoughts now that they came up with a plan. Jack couldn't help but notice her expression; alone, wounded, offended. Was there something that happened while they were getting ready? Did something happen that she didn't agree with?

"Liz," he whispered. The conversations Thillan and Kamille entertained weren't important in that moment. Something in his heart drew him to her pain, something he felt an urge to ease. Perhaps Liz could offer her a break from her life for just a little while.

"She looks really hurt," she commented in a hushed tone.

"Yeah, she does... Do you think you and her go for a stroll around town? I'll stay here and let them give me this harsh interrogation," Jack suggested. She smiled and kissed him, and turned her attention to the scarlet-haired elf.

"Want to get out of here for a little while?" She offered. Ayela smiled in relief and stood to her feet.

"Let's go," she agreed. She turned to the others. "We're going for a walk around town."

"Try not to stay out too long. There's a bounty on your heads, and there's no reason-"

"Let them go, Kamille. They'll be fine," Thillan interrupted. "They're adults, and you're not a babysitter."

"Sure feels like it sometimes... What are you going to do?" She asked Jack.

"You said you wanted to get to know me, so here I am," he retorted as he slouched in his chair and folded his arms across his chest. "Ask away with your questions."

Kamille rested her chin on her hands. Her inquisitive demeanor pierced through his eyes. "You're a character, I'll give you that much... Alright, have fun you two. Don't stay gone too long, and if there's any danger, make it back here immediately and let us know."

"With utmost obedience," Ayela submitted as the girls hastily left the room.

A Foreboding Invasion

Chatter filled their ears while the sun shone brilliantly in the morning sky. Liz enjoyed Ayela's company, listening while she shared extraordinary stories from her unusual adventures, even for elves. She imagined the intense visions of her spirituality, the stories of the gods her former religion regaled, and her own encounters with such majestic calamities. Her faith in the divine seemed to permeate her former religion, ascending to a limitless battle between agents of good and evil in cosmic realities existing beyond their own. The gods they revered seemed to grow beyond religious dogma, and drove her to a form of devotion that strayed from, as she described, conventional practices.

It was so similar to home, and her heart throbbed with pain as she recalled the church her parents raised her. It wasn't too far of a stretch for her to believe in the supernatural, but after everything she'd seen, the idea of an elder man on a golden throne seemed childlike in its fantastic setting. Here, she entirely accepted that the supernatural was far more strange than she'd thought. Perhaps it could be explained with science, but how could she or any human know? How could they comprehend a place of pure white, veiled by an endless abyss of darkness? How could they comprehend that the spiritual was so much more grey than their narrow black-and-white perceptions?

"We aren't so different, you know," Liz said with a smile. It was true. Elves were just as clueless as humans, despite their advances in technology and science.

"What do you mean?"

Liz paused. The words escaped her, but she knew the thoughts she wanted to share. "It feels like you're a race of people just trying to understand their place in the universe... Like you're just trying to exist, love and grow. You want to understand this universe, understand each other, but the wrong kinds of people are the ones making decisions for your people as a whole... Those leaders treat the lives of those under them as though they were merely ants under a boot. It's a lot like our people on earth. At the core of it, though, you just want to live and build relationships."

There was silence between them for a few moment. The noise of the cars passing by and the people walking and talking around them saved them from deafening obscurity, but she could tell Ayela was deep in thought. "You're absolutely right," she finally said. There was a depth to that short confirmation. Ayela had experienced the heartlessness of her empire firsthand, and in so many ways, it showed itself to everyone else around her.

"I hope you find love, Ayela. I hope your life gets easier, and I hope you find someone to love you deeply for who you are. I hope you find someone that can take you away from the troubles of your world," Liz encouraged. And it was a true, heartfelt encouragement. This crimson-haired elf wore her heartache on her sleeve, and it was a deep heartache. Loss, abandonment, and uncertainty seemed to follow her like an infection, and Liz was all-too-familiar with the sensation. With the weight.

"Thanks, Liz... I'll be honest, I envy your relationship with Jack. I had a few smaller relationships that sizzled out, but there were two... Two times, I fell deeply in love... Two times I had to watch them be taken from this world in horrible ways."

"I'm so sorry to hear that... I can't imagine what that feels. If that happened to me, I don't think I could love again."

"Yeah... So, how *exactly* do relationships work with your people? Is it just a choice to get romantically involved? Do your kind have ceremonies, or make a big deal out of it? How does your relationship with Jack work?"

"I mean, for the longest time, in a lot of human cultures, marriages were arranged. I guess it depended on what class you were born into. I mean, sure, sometimes the couples fell in love on their own and pursued their intimacy that way, while aristocrats and wealthy families arranged unions for their children for political and financial gain. My relationship with Jack is very pauper, and simply being romantically involved prior to a marriage relationship is a bit more frowned upon... How about remans? Do your people have more than just... Seeing each other?"

"Yeah, we have marriage too. It's a pretty serious occasion. It starts with a courtship, where the girl will take the guy's hand and place it over her heart. It symbolizes the connection she wants to have with him."

"What happens next?"

"If he traces his finger down the center of her breasts and drops it by his side, he's rejecting her. It means either he has no interest, or his interest is purely sexual. If he traces his finger upwards to her forehead, and then rests his palm on her forehead, it means he accepts the connection and wants both her mind and her heart. The gesture doesn't really change in same-sex relationships."

"Wow…" Liz said, amazed at her culture's beautiful traditions. Ayela paused in front of a general goods store and looked up at the sky.

"That's so beautiful," Liz added.

Ayela smiled. "If he accepts her interest and returns it, they begin a courtship process. It usually lasts about a year or two, and they take that time to plan their lives together as a married couple, prepare for it, and get to know each other. This process is as important and sacred as marriage in elvish culture and is so unbreakable that if they do split apart, neither would be willing to find someone else. It's a total commitment. It even requires a splitting certificate to break up, or else they're still considered courting. No matter what country or land you live, this practice is the same, even if the marriage ceremonies are different."

"So, you have to know for sure what you're committing to before you even consider offering interest?" Liz asked, though it was more rhetorical. "Is it strict? Do couples even keep from kissing each other during that time?" Ayela almost laughed.

"Well, not exactly. Some couples just happen without the ritual. Most courted couples have sex, if that's what you're wondering. Some are religious and wait until the night of the ceremony, but most couples have sex. They figure since it's so intense, and since they're practically married once they enter a courtship, it doesn't hurt. I mean, the only real danger is if the girl gets pregnant and they aren't living together, which happens a lot," she explained as she led Liz into the store.

"Humans are a little different... I think a revolution is coming in the way humans view love and marriage..."

Here eyes drifted to the racks of goods lined up in the store, and her arms instinctively reached around some of the things Ayela was picking up. All sorts of things caught her attention; candies, food, clothes. Her skin felt numb, though, when she noticed locked racks behind the counter, full of rifles and pistols of all shapes and sizes.

"They sell and carry weapons so freely here?" Liz asked.

"Yeah. We have a freedom of arms in this country, though our weaponry is nothing compared to the government's," she commented. "Dominov is the same way, and so is Korok. Songriveii allows you to bare small arms like close range weapons and handguns, and Durinveii depends on the state you're in."

"We have pretty strict laws that are starting to let up a little. In the eastern cities, there's more freedom to carry, but most towns and cities make you leave your weapons with law enforcement if you're visiting, but a lot of those laws are changing. A lot of places are making you get a license to carry a firearm," Liz explained.

"...Are humans really that violent?"

"From what I hear, your people aren't so different," Liz retorted with a gentle tone. Ayela hesitated to respond. Liz paused and mulled over different topics, her mind buzzing with curiosity. She found so much so new and interesting, but she didn't know where to begin. Eager to break the silent tension, she asked, "How old were you when you were kidnapped?"

"Since I can remember..." She revealed. Liz blinked in surprise. How did she survive? Was it so traumatic that she knew what evil was even at a young age? "I grew up in an orphanage run by an old poor hermit that had a self-made hut in a small town called Thallia; a port-town that runs the northern island off the coast of Enthedrill.

Once I was old enough to go out on my own, I earned my citizenship, and I traveled from city to city trying to help people in need. I gave food to the poor and helped to take care of widows and orphans. I worked and only kept enough to survive while I helped as many people as I could. I spent a lot of time training, learning and mastering martial arts and several dance styles from different cultures- especially from my native country. I guess that's what attracted Ruat's attention and was offered a place with the darklings... That, and the fact that I'm a dancer." She revealed in a hushed tone. "I only ever used divine logic to heal people, and it wasn't often because of the bounty on dead wielders. I trained hard, though. I learned some of the most elegant dancing techniques of my people, and I studied martial arts since I was a young girl. I've also practiced meditation."

"That's... Such a strange life," Liz commented. Ayela shrugged as she led the human to the register to pay for everything.

"It's the past, now. Anyway, I'm making you try some of these treats," Ayela ordered.

Before Liz could respond, the crowds outside began to grow larger and shout a little. In a heartbeat, a man burst into the store who knew the cashier and blurted, "Imperials are here!

They're trying to make a public arrest!" The cashier handed Ayela her change and made a mad dash to the front door, leaving the girls confused as they looked at each other with panic and dismay.

Soldiers lined the streets, confronted by an angry mob of confused citizens. The girls' hearing was so sharp, they could hear the conversations they were having outside. Their minds buzzed and burned with anxious intensity, pushing them to the brink of action. Did they not honor their own laws? Did the empire truly care so little about the tenants their founding fathers instilled? Liz clenched her bags in her arms instinctively, and flinched when Ayela gently urged her to back away from the window.

"We're here searching for two known fugitives that pose a threat to our national and planetary security, as well as an accomplice whom we have evidence is aiding their infiltration of this great empire! Your cooperation will be appreciated, but if you refuse, we will enact clause number two forty-three of the ordinance of Emperor Somso the Second, which allows us to detain any resident of a sanctuary town we know to be a criminal, and will hold them until your cooperation is offered to us!" The man yelled to the crowd. Ayela's eyes widened as he spoke.

"You can't do that!" A girl from the crowd yelled defiantly.

"Actually, we can, and we can also accuse anyone of treason and terrorism under the law regardless of whatever bloody town they reside in! Don't test me! Just do as I ask! Comply, and we will leave you be!" The man retorted curtly.

"You can't make us! Your empire took enough from us!" The same girl yelled back. The man sighed and rubbed his temples, then motioned for some of the men to retrieve her from the crowd. Two of the soldiers obeyed, forcing their way through the crowd and seizing the petite woman that spoke out against him. They kicked the backs of her knees, and trained their rifles to the back of her brunette head. Her hands shook with fear, and her curly locks fell in curtains in front of her face.

Ayela gasped as she covered her mouth. "They wouldn't! They fucking wouldn't! They better not!"

Without warning, the officer who questioned them pulled out his pistol and held the barrel to her forehead. Liz could see the girl sobbing moments before he pulled the trigger.

BANG!

The girl's body fell limp.

His expression was cold, heartless.

"I. Will. Not. Ask. Again," the man growled. Liz saw the knuckles on Ayela's clenched fists turn white as her hands shook with anger.

"We can't, Ayela," Liz begged, stopping her before she had the chance to storm out of there. The redhead didn't answer, though. Instead, she opened her palms and jerked her head to the side. Liz watched as the man's head whipped to his right the moment she moved, and he collapsed to the ground, screaming but motionless.

His screams...

Screams from someone as motionless as the woman he shot...

His pained screams haunted her, etching an eerie sound in her mind.

"Let's go!" She ordered, grabbing Liz's hand and rushing to the back door of the store while gunshots could be heard. Liz turned her head and watched as some of the crowd fell to the ground while others ran. She couldn't tell if they were just maimed...

...Or if they were dead...

Run

"...That's a tough story to hear," Kamille commented, leaning back in her chair. There was a bittersweet emotion in the air, and Jack felt as though they related a bit more to him. Or, at the very least, they empathized with his life's story. They certainly went through a great deal more than him, and he reflected over his attitude towards her with scrutiny. He was harsh, cold, and he conflicted with his own passions and drive by passing them off the way he did.

"So, you're some sort of hero for the people," Kamille more said than asked.

"I'm just a factory worker. I drink, I work, I fight sometimes. I don't really pray anymore, not like my brother. I have a drive to fix my mistake... To make up for the error I made when my fighting got my mother killed... I find it difficult, because if I don't work, I starve, so I have to pick and choose my battles. Not everyone can be rescued, and I know that. I'm no hero. I'm no savior. I just want to make things right."

"Yet, you'd let the people of another species be enslaved to a tyrant-"

"Kamille, seriously, stop it! I've had enough of this taking shots at someone for seemingly no reason!" Thillan shouted. "The guy just shared his entire story, and even opened up about his beliefs, and you just mock him!"

"Babe-"

"Don't babe me! You know it's messed up," Thillan interrupted. His gaze quickly turned back to Jack. "Look, I won't lie to you; there's a lot more opportunity here for you than where you're from because of how you look. Does it make us hurt? Sure. But we're not trying to be your enemy, here. I know Kamille is harsh, but she truly does have a heart for people. She doesn't want to see anyone suffer. She just wants things to be fair for everyone. If you can get behind that, you're alright in my book. If you can be yourself, not put any of us in danger, and play on our team by our rules, there's no quarrel. I see your fight, and I think your mission is noble... I just don't want to pick an ally for our side of this if we don't know that we can trust you."

Jack paused and mulled his response over. It wasn't that he didn't want to align with them-quite the contrary. He agreed with them. His heart hurt for the struggles they endured. He just didn't want to say something that would come across as something he didn't mean. "I'm not going to hurt you, Kamille," he said, addressing her clear and appropriate mistrust. "I'm not going to try and say I've had it harder than you... Hearing your stories, I get it. In a lot of ways, I empathize. There are other ways I know I can't. But I... I see where I was wrong. I still want to go home, but you've both already trusted me with a lot. I'm sorry for how I disrespected your integrity and your position. While I'm here, and even after I get my brother back, we'll fight alongside you until we can leave."

She folded her arms across her chest, grazing him up and down with her inquisitive stare. She had every right to be suspicious, but he could see it in her eyes; she was starting to trust him a little. "Alright, Jack. I'll take your word. We'll help you and you'll help-"

The sound of the gunshot echoed in their ears longer than they liked. They scrambled to the window, carefully peering at the platoon opening fire on unarmed civilians. His heart sank, and his gaze refused to leave the lifeless body of the woman that the soldiers eventually marched over. Some carried away a screaming corpse, and he immediately knew what was going on; the empire was scouring the town for them.

"We have to do something!" He demanded.

"Like what?! We'll be killed on sight if we step out there!" Kamille protested.

"But those people are dying!" Jack interrupted.

"Jack- *pick your battles!* What do you think will happen if we, a group of unidentified rebels, goes out to face an armed platoon of soldiers from the empire? There's nothing we can do. Ayela can't even fight off the overwhelming forces that would drop down if she started to fight them. We're outmatched," Thillan cooed, trying to talk him down from his anxiety-induced panic.

"Didn't she fight an aethril? Didn't she redirect the bombardment of missiles from a warship? Didn't she shield herself from the explosions in the desert against Tallie? Or was all of that a ruse? *How* could they possibly overpower her?" Jack protested.

"That was one ship when she was at the most primal form of her power, her stopping an aethril was only with the help of a now-dead divine logician, and she was bed-ridden for days after the fight in the desert! Her power has tolls, Jack. She might be strong, but she's no goddess. The

270

empire would unleash a fleet from the capital off of that *very close* mesa just to decimate this town, and you can bet that her shielding everything here would push her to death's door. That's *if* she managed to avoid getting stuck by debris or shrapnel from the explosions! The empire *will not hesitate* to eliminate any possibility of a resurgence of the divine logicians."

They were silent as the gunfire continued in short bursts off in the distance. After a few moments, a siren sounded from deep in the center of the town, signaling that they were under attack– and truly they were...

"...We can't, Jack... I'm sorry... It's too much... Their blood isn't on your hands: it's on the empire's," Kamille cooed. "It's on the ivory's who think they're the only true elves in the world... Of all people, Ayela, Thillan and I understand what you're feeling. Of *all* people."

"What are we going to do? Are we just going to wait here?" He asked in a calmer, sober tone.

"For now... Ayela is a smart girl. She and Liz are safe, I know it," Thillan promised. Jack knew that already, though. He didn't think of Liz as a dainty little girl that always needed his protection. He knew she needed it sometimes, and he would always stand up for her when she couldn't stand up on her own, but she was a

271

strong woman that held her own for years before they met... And he knew Ayela was the same, if not more so.

"Jack..." Kamille said softly. He looked out the window once more and watched as the some of the soldiers stayed by their vehicles. The rest, he assumed, scattered throughout the town, no doubt in search of him and Liz. There were only two options for them to take; hide or run, and he was less keen on hiding.

"We need to-"

Before he could finish, the door burst open as Ayela and Liz frantically rushed into the room, panting heavy breaths after running for their lives. He rushed over and quickly embraced them.

"You're both alright," he declared. "Thank God."

"We won't be if we stay," Liz answered as she marched over to the window and peered through. Ayela untied her hoodie from around her waist and threw it over her tank top.

"We need to run, now," Ayela affirmed.

"Well, hold on-"

"We. Need. To. Run. NOW!!!" Ayela yelled angrily as she marched to Thillan's face. They all looked at Jack, and then back at Ayela. She was on the same page with Jack.

It was time to run…

XII

The Imperial Witch Hunt

When the threat of the divine logicians surfaced, his response was genocide, not a willingness to cooperate.

Marshal Law In Lawlessness

The sun had set, and the stars shone brilliantly in the evening sky as the twilight faded. They'd left the inn, paying the innkeeper for his silence and constant cover, and once more stuck to the alleys and shadows as they sneaked by soldiers patrolling the streets. Despite her power, Ayela couldn't cloak them with her profound magic, not without signaling their satellites. There were too many of them this time, and the concentration it required would exact a heavier toll than they were willing to pay. It was time to rely on the shadows to cover their escape.

Distracting him from his thoughts, Kamille threw up her hand before they could emerge on the streets. "We're almost at the northern gate," she said in a hushed tone as she peaked around the corner. "So far, no soldiers have been spotted.

We're in the clear for now."

"Where are we going to go? Actually, how the hell are we going to get anywhere outside of this town?" Jack asked.

"We're going to flee to a town northwest from here called Asiat." She said. She motioned that it was okay for them to move ahead, and they quickly dashed across the residential street.

"Asiat?! That's the opposite direction we need to go! Asher is in D'Vnora!" Ayela protested quietly.

"Well we can't go to Cassum or D'Vnora right now, can we? Especially being so close to getting caught ourselves! We need to throw off their scent," Kamille whispered curtly.

"How long of a journey is it?" He asked. They all had their gear; backpacks filled with food and clothes, pouches with money in it, and an extra hoodie each tied around their waists. Jack had the sword he found in the cavern on the side of the cliff dangling at his hip with a makeshift sheath that Thillan helped him craft. Kamille had been kind enough to empty out her accounts of all her funding, and Ayela threw in her money to a pool that they distributed among the group evenly.

"About a week on foot if we were to go it on foot," Kamille answered after peaking around another building. "But we're not doing that. We're going to catch a ride there once we're far enough away to walk near the open roads."

"How do you know who you can even trust? Any time I've seen those big vehicles drive by, I can't ever see through the glass windows because they're so dark," Liz pointed out.

"Any hauler will do. Remember, the government isn't looking for me or Thillan. We can sneak you three in through the back. But we can figure out the details once we're out of town. I hope you're ready for a long night," she warned.

"Hey!" Yelled a mechanical voice from behind them. They all turned to see a soldier with a rifle trained on them, and just as quickly ran away from him, barely dodging the open fire as they ducked and dashed around the corner. They could hear the heavy footsteps of the metallic boots pounding against the ground as they ran.

The wide road they emerged onto led straight to the gate, and it seemed like they were going to make it. It should have been an obvious thought, though, but they didn't consider that there might have been guards stationed at the gates as well.

"SHIT!!!" Thillan barked. They were rounded off by the inevitable. Soldiers moved from their stations and cut off their exit.

"Stop moving!" Their pursuers shouted. Hope

dwindled, and it seemed their journey had come to an end. Jack and Liz wouldn't make it home after all, and his stomach churned with sickening momentum. He cursed their cruel fate in his heart, wishing and hoping for a drop of Ayela's power. It was too late, though...

...Or so he thought.

"Do you trust me, Jack?" Ayela asked in a hushed tone. He whipped his head around and looked at her with a confused expression. Why was she asking him?

"Ayela, no-"

"Shh! I was asking Jack," she interrupted. "They found us, Kamille. There's no sense in hiding it now."

"Jack..." Liz urged before the arguing could begin. He knew the answer he needed to give. He looked at her once more, seeing the fire in her violet eyes. He knew in his heart he could trust her...

He trusted her more deeply than anyone else he knew. He couldn't explain it, but there was something in her eyes that felt familiar, comforting, and consuming. There was a connection that lingered, like they were two souls that knew each other deeply, but had been apart for centuries-millennia, even. Whatever it was, he let his heart convince his mind, and he gave into that connection.

"I trust you," he said, and it was as though his voice was the only one that echoed in his ears. No other sound trembled his eardrums. No other sensation distracted him from this new, yet ancient resolve. Ayela smiled, and then moved her gaze to the guards who were approaching them.

"We're who you're looking for!" She yelled out to them. Kamille and Thillan hung their heads as they heard the words escaped her lips.

"You're Ayela Rhexa? And those two teenagers are the humans?" The soldier asked. *Obviously,* Jack thought to himself.

"Yes. If we turn ourselves in, you'll lift the marshal law on the town?"

"Yes."

"Then we surrender," she declared as she got on her knees. Jack and Liz followed suit, and then Thillan and Kamille with heavy sighs.

"Smart woman. Who are these accomplices?"

"Bystanders. I threatened them so that they would escort us to Preston in the south," she lied. Kamille looked up at her.

"How do you feel now that you're going to the Emperor's tower?"

Ayela looked over her shoulder at the two soldiers behind, and then back at him. They had gotten close enough, exactly where she wanted them.

"You can tell him yourself, when you approach him wreaking of your failure," She smirked as she quickly threw her palms down. It came with struggle, and he could see it in her shaking arms. They resisted her magical control, but she was clearly stronger. Their rifles fell to the ground, and the slowly levitated, as if unseen hands had clenched their bodies and immobilized them.

With a quick thrust forward, the soldiers were flung into the distance. He had not time to marvel, but the image burned in his mind.

"Okay," She gasped as she collapsed to the ground, breathing heavily. "Grab the weapons. Let's go before they send the trucks," she ordered. They silently obeyed.

The wind rushed past their faces, but biting at their cheeks with the cold of night as they dashed to the gate. It was surreal, the feeling of surviving so many moments where death or capture was right at their heels. Yet, there they were, running towards a fateful escape from the clutches of the empire once more.

How familiar this feeling was to him, that he found himself once more running from the grasp of those who would lord their power unfairly over a people undeserving of their hatred. All at once, he remembered running from the police after distracting them from a couple minding their business. He remembered running from the law every time he stopped them from beating people that didn't reflect their pale, English hue. He remembered running, fighting, and standing up against oppressors, trying to live in repentance for causing his mother's death.

Their exit was cleared of any other guards for the moment, and rightly so. The guards were flung, and it would take time for them to gather themselves again. At this point, though, they knew Ayela's name. They knew Kamille and Thillan's faces. They couldn't turn back now, even if they wanted to. The only way was forward, into the dark, into the wilds of the unknown. The only voices they could trust were their own...

And the one who'd been guiding them this whole time...

Jack...

Open your eyes, Jack...

...Nothing is as it seems.

XIII

The Horrid Wilds

How should nature respond when something akin to cancer is threatening its life? Well... How do we respond?

In The Dark, A Weariness

Despite the stars that dotted the sky, despite the beauty of the moon high amidst their glittery presence, terror kept their weary gazes fixated forward. Their path had taken them to the edge of the black woods, and their nerves were sensitive to the cool, brisk winds that whipped across their skin and through their nappy hair. They'd spent hours running, only stopping for short rests when they were sure that the empire's trucks were thrown off their trail.

The only lead the soldiers had was Ayela's deterrent, but now their identities were exposed. All of them. Kamille and Thillan had the misfortune of being accomplices, whether or not Ayela's declaration of hostages had any effect. They would all be noticed if they made the wrong move. Things couldn't have gone more wrong.

But nevertheless, there they were, flirting with the edge of the dangerous wilds the girls had warned Jack and Liz so much about. There, in the cover of night, their lives ever depended on the rifles they carried, and they could only hope whatever gods the elves worshiped wished favor upon them.

Jack's head was on a swivel, keeping an anxious tally on everything that moved in the darkness besides their ragtag group of refugees. He could only hope whatever alien creatures that dwelt in those woods weren't curious or hungry enough to give them chase. His heart pounded in his throat, refusing to grant him any relief to the hunger or thirst that threatened to exhaust him.

"We can stop here for a moment," Kamille ordered. The others were too quick to stop and rest beside the treeline, but he couldn't. If it wasn't the animals and creatures of the night, it was the soldiers that were vigilantly searching for them.

"Jack, it's okay," Liz cooed. He couldn't submit to that, though. Kamille stood with him, rifle in hand, watching and waiting for any danger to make itself present.

"We're in one of the most dangerous parts of this country. I think we're anything but okay," he said curtly. It wasn't that he was trying to be rude or dismissive, and she knew that. They'd been on high alert for so long, the idea of them being able to stop and rest even for a moment seemed like a fantasy that was too far out of reach.

"I was just trying to ease your nerves."

"I know… I'm sorry. It's easy to act out of my tension and anxiety right now…"

"It's okay, my love… Don't wear yourself out in your anxious state of mind, though," she said, gently holding his face as she stared into his eyes. She peered into his soul, reaching the depths of his being with such concern, all time seemed to stand still. He had to get them home. He had to rescue his brother. They needed to survive this. He couldn't let this be *another* failure to add to his growing list.

"I will try, for our sake," he reassured. He couldn't tell, though, if he was lying more to himself or to her.

"Look alive, Jack. It's going to be a long night," Kamille ordered.

"Aye, Kamille. You don't have to worry about me falling asleep."

It was true. His heart beat so violently in his chest, and his nerves were so sensitive to every gentle brush of the cool air, there wasn't a chance his body would let him succumb to his weariness. He fought off his panic with every fiber of his being. He couldn't believe these things were happening, but clearly reality didn't care. They were happening whether he wanted to believe or not.

A snapping twig from deep in the woods caught their attention, but after a few tense moments of silence, they cautiously returned to what they were doing. Silence. That was what Jack thought he needed. Silence. In that silence, though, something felt off.

What was it that drove him to such perilous readiness? What was it about the silence that had him fully aware of his surroundings? The dark seemed to lighten a little, showing the various shades of black in the woods as outlines of different objects. Those objects were imposing, too; the trees, the bramble, the fallen branches that littered the forest floor- all things he instinctively paid attention to. There were no details, only the barely lit shades that hid in the dark under the canopies.

But what if it was the silence that his subconscious was so wary of? Not just the silence, but what it implied? What was the natural response to a threat? To hide away. The make your presence unknown in the dark forest of the universe. To make yourself so unnoticeable, even demons and spectres wouldn't have been aware that you existed.

Then it clicked.

The silence was a warning.

All the creatures around them made not a sound.

All the insects that had been chirping their mating sounds had fallen to the stillness and quietness of the night, and the snapping twig was a blunder. They weren't alone.

"Everyone needs to get up now," Jack whispered urgently. They gave him wary looks.

"Why, do you-"

"Just get up and get your weapons ready! We need to start moving again," he pressed. They obeyed, quickly packing anything that was unpacked, and readying their rifles. There was no hesitation. They pushed forward, careful to keep any noises to a minimum, and kept looking over their shoulders as they hovered near the treeline.

Jack's eyes were glued to the depths of the woods, though. He scoured and scoured, memorizing the differences in shapes until he no longer had to question if he was looking at a tree or a branch. If anything moved, he would know.

And then it happened.

A hulking shadow silently moved behind the trees, carefully stalking them like the predator it was. There was no earthly creature he could compare the silhouette to. It was a shape of ferocity, brutality, and terror.

Sheer.

Utter.

Terror.

"Everyone keep doing what you're doing, but we're being followed," he informed. He was sure they all felt the urge to turn and look for what it was, but they obeyed his direction.

"What's going on," Liz whispered in a panicked tone.

"Trust me; you don't want to see," Jack answered. There was no way to make that sound reassuring. There was no way for him to ease their panic. But he needed it to think they were unaware. If they tried to look, they would already be dead- of that, he was certain.

He kept his gaze fixated on the forest, doing his best to maintain his behavior. He wanted it to think he hadn't noticed, but he didn't know how long he could prolong it. He just needed it to get closer.

Closer.

Just enough for them to get a clear shot.

"Jack," Ayela whispered. He refused to look over at her. "Tell us what you're seeing."

She'd been in the wilds before. There was a certainty in her hushed tone that gave it all away.

Whatever terrors she'd faced in her past, she knew a thing or two about being in the wilds.

"You can't use your divine logic here, Ayela," Jack pressed. "It'll bring the empire on us."

"I won't, I promise. I need you to describe its shape, though."

He roiled his tension into a long, dramatic exhale. "It's big. Bigger than those vehicles the empire was using… It's long, too. A long body. I can't tell where its head is or what it looks like. For a creature of its size, it's moving too silently."

"Ayela," Kamille panicked.

"We need to run!" She said.

It was all a flash. From the moment Ayela said run, everyone broke out into a mad dash. It was impulsive, but he trusted her. There was no reason why he shouldn't. But what was the creature? What haunted them so carefully, that its mere description pushed Ayela to break their cautious stride into a run for their lives?

He turned to see, and immediately wished he hadn't. Its slimy body slithered on the ground, rushing at them with speed they couldn't outrun. There was no face, no definable limbs. It was a massive worm with a carnivorous apatite for any creature that moved in its presence. It was only a matter of time, and the idea of breaking into a dash only put them in greater danger.

He stopped and turned, his rifle poised. In a split second, he opened fire. The noise of his rifle pierced his eardrums, but he pulled all of his mental focus into ignoring the ringing pain and unleashing a barrage of bullets into its body.

The creature roared with a blood-curdling sound louder than the rifle, and reared its faceless maw to a towering height as it stood over him. His heart dropped, and he watched as memories of his entire life flooded his mind. Was this it? Was he destined to die a wanderer's death at the hands of an alien nature?

He wasn't sure what was worse, though; the thought of him dying by this creature, or what actually happened. Liz rushed to his side and pulled him out of the way of the worm's descending grasp just in time, but they didn't see the small stones behind him that tripped them both onto the ground.

Her screams pierced his eardrums as the creature latched onto her foot, and try as he might, he couldn't grasp her hands quickly enough. She was yanked away from him, and in one quick, fluid motion, its maw wrapped around her head and quickly swallowed, frantically trying to make quick work of her before moving onto its next meal.

Something snapped in him, though. Something that refused to let this be his lover's end. Its toothless mouth had reached her hips and kicking legs when he rose to his feet. The sword he'd picked up from the cave had been strapped to his hip, and proved to be just the tool he needed.

He drew the sword as he ran to it with as much speed as he could muster, and with all the force his muscles could push, he sliced at the base of its neck, cutting halfway through. The creature grunted and dropped Liz from its mouth, and quickly backed away from its assailant as he pried the sword loose. He wasn't going to let it get away, though; he leapt into the air, and with a precise downward stroke, finished his incision.

The severed head flailed alongside the body, spraying blood and mucus everywhere while the others rushed to Liz. He took deep breaths, ignoring the putrid smell from its opened corpse, and rested on his knees as he dropped the blade.

"Ew, ew, ew, ew!" Liz panicked, frantically trying to wipe the saliva and slime from her body. She sobbed and clung to Ayela, and Kamille used her shirt to get as much fluid off of her as possible. Jack wasted no time picking his weapon up and returning to his partner's side, helping Kamille with his spare hoodie.

"We can't take too long," Kamille gently urged.

"That was a brave thing you did."

Somehow, the compliment meant even more coming from her. He smiled and wrapped Liz in a tight embrace. She gripped handfuls of his shirt in tight fists and cried.

"It's alright," Jack cooed. "You're alive. We're all alive."

"We won't be for long unless we get moving," Thillan pushed. "I gotta say, though, that was the quickest *and* the longest minute I'd ever seen take place… Next time, don't stand directly in front of us. We'd like to shoot the monsters, too."

He snickered for a brief moment, but his attention quickly turned back to Liz. He took off his other hoodie and handed it to Liz, and then scoured their surroundings for any other threats waiting in the dark.

It seemed their moment of relief would be short lived, though, when a pair of headlights zoomed around the corner accompanied by the low rumbling of a massive truck's engine. His heart sank, but he couldn't wallow in despair. He picked up his rifle and trained it on the truck, ready for a fight at a moment's notice.

Just as quickly, though, Kamille rested her hand on the barrel and shook her head. "I can't let you, Jack. We wouldn't be able to help you any further if you did."

"Damn your rules!"

"Don't, Jack!" Ayela shouted. "Look! It's not the empire!"

His head whipped back around as the truck approached and slowed to a stop. It was bigger than the military trucks from the town, and a trailer was attached to the back. "It's our ride! He came!" Thillan exclaimed, quickly picking up Liz and rushing over to the driver's door. A larger man climbed out and immediately embraced Thillan and Kamille, and Jack stood there motionless.

He looked down at his rifle and paused, wondering what would have happened if Kamille hadn't stopped him. He'd grown so used to fighting first, so accustomed to having to resort to violence, his instinct had adapted to combat as his solution before communication. He was so used to needing to survive over others, he needed to consciously stop himself before hurting anyone. If she hadn't stopped him, he would have took someone's life. He wouldn't have even thought about it.

The thought sickened him to his core.

"Jack..." Ayela said, stealing him from his thoughts. He looked over at her, and even in the dim light, her violet eyes pierced into the depths of his being, as if that was where she belonged.

"…You can breath now. We're safe."

He looked back over at the others, not even noticing that Kamille had helped Liz over to the truck's cab. Could he breath? Were they truly safe? Ayela's hand gently rested on his shoulder, and her caress on his bare skin invoked a strange sense of peace and comfort. Not even Liz's touch offered him the same break from his strange reality.

"Thank you," he said. He couldn't look back at her though, fearing what emotions her gaze into his eyes might evoke. He loved Liz, and his goals remained the same; get his brother, find a way home, and help the elves along the way…

…Right?

XIV

The Toll Of A Home Lost

There is a severity to the mind robbed of its home, stranded on a strange land. A severity, and an unpredictability.

Arrival In Asiat

The hiss of the engines rattled Jack awake, if not the force of the truck stopping. He hadn't realized how badly he needed a good night's sleep until the groggy feeling of waking gripped his joints and slowed his process of sitting up from his makeshift bedding on the cab's floor. It was a tight fit, but they all made it work, with Liz taking the only bed the trucker had. There was plenty of yawning and stretching, and he was sure they all felt the soreness of the floor's unforgiving sleeping conditions that he felt.

"Good morning," Ayela murmured, her discomfort evident in her tired tone.

"Morning," Jack mumbled as he rubbed his head in an attempt to garner energy quickly.

"We arrived at Asiat just in time, it would seem. Our driver told me last night that the

Imperials just cleared out of the town in order to double search efforts in the southern towns. We seemed to have thrown them off our trail effectively," she revealed. He looked past Kamille and Thillan who gathered their things, and out the window towards the various buildings and homes that littered the horizon instead of trees, hidden behind a towering wall like Shamol had.

He reached down to grab his backpack, and then looked up at Ayela only to find her staring back at him. She looked into his eyes inquisitively. He felt awkward, but let it happen rather than waste the energy in probing for answers. He predicted he would find out soon enough.

He looked over at Liz and picked up her bag and gear. She smiled, and then rubbed her tired eyes and continued waking herself up. She needed a good night's rest for once, and he could see it. He hadn't thought of it much before, but he began to wonder how heavy the strain must have been on her. She was someone like him, though her life must have been quiet and peaceful before he entered it. He felt pangs of guilt for roping her into everything, even if they never predicted what would happen.

"Welcome to Asiat, humans," Thillan declared as he stretched his arms and legs. "You'll find no shortage of wonderful foods and diners in this most eldest of townships."

"I certainly hope so after the past few days' excitement," Liz said with a deep yawn.

"We'll be best with a room for the night before we catch a ride to Cassum. We need to be careful here that we don't give ourselves away. Friends are few and far between," Kamille ordered, bringing direction and urgency to their morning.

Jack watched out the window and noticed the massive gates they had to pass through to enter the city. There were no check-in's, no security guards asking to inspect the vehicle, just passage in a line of cars from what he could see in front of them. The doors at the rear of the truck had no windows.

This town was smaller and homely. The buildings were humble and quaint, and as Thillan declared, there were restaurants and diners that lined the busy streets they now drove through. He watched the people from the window, paying attention to how friendly they were when they greeted each other and how at peace everyone who sat at the tables seemed. It was like Asiat was unaffected by the chaos of their country at war.

"Peaceful, isn't it?" Kamille pointed out as she sat by his other side. "Look, we can relax a little more, alright? Be careful and stay out of sight, and remember, the Empire's looking for us elsewhere. Ayela did a good job throwing off our scent, so you can breathe a little now. I know you and Liz haven't really gotten a chance to be with yourselves for a long while now..."

He paused, noting the calm atmosphere even in the cab. For a brief moment, it felt like they could let their guard down a little. "Thanks," he offered, looking out the window with her.

Liz had moved over to sit beside Ayela, who entertained her need for conversation, while the truck came to a complete stop. Their driver turned around and yelled from the driver's seat, "This is as far as I go. Good luck, you guys. I'll be heading down to Preston to meet with a group that's been researching the gramatoginon, so we probably won't see each other again for some time."

"Thanks!" Thillan offered as he made his way to the door and swung it wide open. The noise of the chattering crowds and rumbling engines filled the quiet cab, inducing the reality of their long-awaited arrival. Then, without a word, they were off. It truly was brief, his momentary peace and relief. Seeing the crowds of people, he felt like he did on earth; cautious and afraid. Who could they truly trust? The empire violated one of their oldest tenants in pursuit of the *dangerous* humans. How would this town be any different?

After all…

Just like his guiding, unpredictable voice of help had said over and over…

…Nothing is as it seems.

The Soulless Elves

"Shh." Ayela ordered, interrupting Jack as he was trying to explain to her once more that he was a common factory worker on earth. Her eyes narrowed as she looked into his. Jack noted the likeness in her features as she analyzed him; she was human in almost every way except that her ears were longer and her eyes were violet. Her hair was scarlet – a brighter red than any human he'd seen - and her skin was perfect. She was beautiful, prettier than most human women on earth. He admired her ethereal appearance, her elegant figure, and her even her freckled complexion. He felt the pangs of conviction in his heart, realizing the infatuation he suddenly caught for this girl while being so emotionally tied to Liz.

He quickly put it away from his mind and

ignored it. He refused to become that kind of man. Society frowned upon the kind of man that was given to their passions, the kind that wasn't loyal and kept eyes only for their lovers. But then, as he wrestled against his fleshly impulses, he wondered if that was exactly the reason why so much infidelity occurred among humans. What if the harsh rules of purity and societal standards created that very atmosphere where men were given to their violent urges, regardless of the harm it caused? He wasn't gawking at her, nor was he trying to indulge in fantasies. He was admiring her beauty. Perhaps it wasn't about restriction, but about controlling the impulses he felt as a man; to admire and appreciate her appearance, and leave it at that. Even then, he wondered how she felt with his gaze upon her. Did it make her uncomfortable? Did it-

"There's something different about your kind," she blurted out, distracting him from his appraisal. He was carried back to reality. Liz and Kamille were chatting up a storm on the other side of the room while Thillan read through scrolling text on a glass screen built into the table he sat at near the girls. They had secured a spacious penthouse on the upper floor of a hotel deep in the heart of the town. It was like a bigger, richer version of Jack's apartment, except cleaner and not as expensive as he would expect. He and Ayela sat on the other side of the large living room, near the windows that overlooked the smaller buildings of the town.

"Care to elaborate?" He asked.

"Your eyes... In remans, there's a lifelessness we can't explain in the eyes of the men. The women aren't as bad, but the men are almost... Soulless. It's not that we aren't loving, or that we don't have emotions, but there's this... Energy in your eyes that isn't present in the men of my race... There's only one other person I've known who had that same look in her eyes..."

"Thillan seems pretty lively to me," Jack commented sarcastically.

"It's not some glisten, or some physical appearance, you idiot. It's an energy. It's a spark of life that looks different than ours," she retorted as she leaned back and took one of the cups of coffee. Jack didn't know how to respond. "It's much more carnal in our men... You... If all men are like you, casual factory man, then there's something deeper about your kind."

He paused as he thought about what she said. "What's that book you were reading earlier?" He asked, changing the subject.

"This?" She asked as she pulled it out of her bag and looked at it longingly. "It's called The

Alldweii. It's a religious title that is tied to the faith I belong to..." She said, running her fingers over its cover. His heart pounded with excitement, though he didn't know why. She was just telling him about her beliefs. Perhaps it was that he was getting to know her a bit more, and to him, that meant she trusted him. His eyes darted to the cover of the book, which had characters and letters that rang with familiarity, though he didn't quite know from what.

"How many other religions are there on Thearv?" Jack asked as he picked up a cup of coffee and took a sip, only to be taken aback in surprise from its unsuspecting sweetness and smoothness. Ayela snickered. She stood and walked over to the dresser on the wall, rummaging through the first drawer.

"There's too many to count. The faith I am a part of is called Korism. Its concepts are littered throughout our society with the naming of those alien creatures 'aethrils,' to even using Rök's name as a petty phrase of digress. Korism is one of the most famous. Aside from that, there's Zadism, Khebreh, and Grogam as the next three largest organize beliefs structures. Zadism shares religious background with Korism, and Khebreh is a belief built from translations of a dead langue. Korism and Zadism gets their roots from it. Grogam is a belief in... Well, they believe that we are gods and that to unlock our power, we must live a certain way on Thearv.

"Aside from those four, there's also Nastim, Zevlyim, Ishism, Sicireanism, and Klothanism – all of which believe in so many gods, you couldn't name the categories for them. Those are the bigger ones. There's a lot more, but smaller organizations," she explained.

"...What's so special about your faith?"

"...Well... I believe that when I die, Rök will preserve me in his jar of memories, and the gods will chant my name and the names of the others in the great halls of the Blind Eternities."

"You don't believe in the concept of an after-life?" Jack asked.

"Afterlife?" She quoted with a raised eyebrow.

"Yes. Life after death. Don't your people believe in spirits?"

Ayela tilted her head to the side in genuine confusion. "Well, yes, we believe in spirits – but we are not spirits. We're remans. Are humans spirits?"

"No... Some of our religions believe that humans have spirit copies of themselves that continue to live on after our physical bodies die... In fact, mostly all religions in my world believe this. One group of people, as far as I know, don't believe in anything supernatural," Jack explained.

"Such strange concepts... No, we do not have an 'afterlife,' per say. In my belief, while we may die and cease to be, Rök keeps memories of those who believe in him in a jar by his throne in the heavens, unable to be touched by daethrils or any who would seek to destroy them. We believe that one day, Rök will wash away this world with the waters of recreation, and give us new life when the world is recreated..."

"...Fascinating..." Jack admitted as he stared into her eyes.

"And what are your beliefs?"

Jack sat there for a moment, unsure of how to answer. His brow furrowed, and then he looked at her. "I suppose my belief would be closer to those on my world who don't believe anything... At least, I *didn't* believe in anything... But now, I'm not so sure. I believe in what I can see. My mother was a faithful Jew, and my father was a devout Catholic... Which are a group of people that took my mother's culture and religion and made one of their own out of it. As for me, my mother taught me as much as she could while she was alive, but once I was old enough to pick my own belief, I stopped attending either of their meetings... I've always been bitter towards the Catholic religion after what they did to my mother's people- *my* people. I don't exactly practice my mother's old religion, but I identify with them nonetheless."

Ayela listened intently, and expressed her compassion when he explained his feelings. "Whether you believe in gods or not, something brought you here – and apparently saved your lives, if your tale is true. Perhaps science will help you understand… But are you sure you really want to?"

"Ignorance may be bliss, but even if it fills me with bitter wrath, the truth will set me free," Jack said cryptically as he looked over at Liz. "I've seen countless unimaginable things I could only dream of seeing. If I'm going to survive, I need to understand. Whether it's a god or a person or something else, I want to be free from the puppeteer pulling my strings."

"Freedom. I wonder if anyone truly understands what that word means," Ayela commented as she looked out the massive window and observed the borderline cityscape.

They sat and pondered what they talked about, and shared a deep connection that transcended their backgrounds, their worlds, their races, and even their times. He hadn't stopped for a moment before he arrived on thaerv to really think about his beliefs before. He was always busy working unmanageable hours at the factory, the only thing he really had time for afterwards was drinking, eating, and sleeping. He and Liz had the beneflf of working together, and they cherished what time they could spend with each other.

"Oi, you two ready to talk a bit about our next move?" Kamille called to them, stealing them from their deep thinking.

"Yes," Jack agreed. They made their way to the table the others sat at.

"Good," she said as Thillan sat beside her. "I was thinking that we leave for Cassum tomorrow."

"How far away is that from D'Vnora?" Liz asked.

"Half a day's journey on foot. About the same distance as Shamol is to Bavylune. To Cassum from Asiat, though, is a two-day ride in another truck," Thillan revealed.

"This is quite the venture… we've not really stopped to catch a breath," Jack retorted.

"These trucks… These vehicles you use… How do they work? We've seen so many different kinds, and the wheeled transportation we have on earth looks much different." Liz asked, raising an eyebrow. "With boats that float in the air and are powered by massive engines, and then small screens you put in your pockets that play moving pictures; why would you still need to travel in something that rolls on the ground with wheels?"

"Well, how do yours work?" Thillan asked.

"They're a fresh invention on earth. They're fueled by gasoline. We've only gotten so far in scientific advancement. After all, we also just discovered how to harness the power of electricity. Humans, compared to remans, are – simply put – apes," Jack clarified. "So forgive our misunderstanding of your rather elaborate terms."

Kamille's brow furrowed. "Then how on Thaerv did you make it to this planet?" She asked after staring at them. "You know what – it doesn't matter right now. What does matter is that we get moving. Once we make it to Asher, we can plan our next course of action."

Liz cleared her throat before she spoke. "So Cassum… We leave tomorrow. Once we get there, we go to D'Vnora. Once we get there, we look for Asher. Once we find him-

"We search for Ruat, and once we find Ruat, we… Figure out a way to get my brother free… We can find a way home." Jack finished. Emotion began to swell in his heart. He could hear it beating in his throat. It seemed like it was going to take so much longer to get his brother back.

"He's just fine right now… I can feel it. We just need to adventure a little longer." Liz said, trying

to offer some comfort.

"We've been on quite the adventure already, haven't we?"

"The adventure isn't over until we're home."

"Yes, that may be the end goal for you two, but we need to have an actual reason for looking to find Ruat. It isn't justifying enough to break into the Emperor's tower to free your brother. You forget; we're at war," Kamille explained calmly. At first, Jack felt the stress tugging at the strings of his heart. She was right. Once again, he felt the conflict that pushed his heart into his throat. He felt his internal turmoil, wrestling between getting everyone home and staying to help them fight. It was what he did; fighting for the ones who couldn't. Fighting to right his wrongs. After everything they did for him and his companions, how could he justify packing and leaving?

"So, what do you suggest?"

"Well... Let's assess your situation first. We're helping you get your brother. That's clear and evident by this point. So, for us helping you, we ask for your help in return..."

"What do you want from us, Kamille?" Liz asked, leaning her elbows on the table.

"Well that's the question, isn't it love? What do we want from you... I'm just going to put it plain and simple and speak for at least Thillan and I;

we want you to help us overthrow and replace the Emperor."

Jack blinked in surprise. He suddenly felt transported back to conversation they had at the inn in Shamol. "Why- no, *how* are we supposed to do that? Why do you need our help?"

"I've been putting some thought into it," Kamille began. She looked over at Thillan, who shrugged and let her continue. He could see his submission to whatever she was designing. "Once we find Ruat, we need to find a figure who is literally the polar opposite of the Emperor... A person for the people. Someone who values reman life above all else. Someone who is a strong leader, but also someone who can respect opinions and leadership from others... We need a hero of the people. We need a hero who can fight off even those aliens that are destroying our towns."

"It sounds like you want Captain Lunar to be your emperor," Jack pointed out.

"Maybe," Kamille agreed... Mostly. "If he fits that persona, then certainly. But you, Jack... We've watched you. We heard you. We hear the stories you share of your life on your world. We saw how quickly you were willing to go out and fight the soldiers that attacked Shamol... Even saving Liz from that creature... You're a fighter, Jack, but you're also a *good man.* You'd do anything for the ones you care about, like your brother. Or Liz... Or..." She paused, and then looked over at Ayela. "The point is, if it's not you that can be that face of hope, then you could help us find that face. It could even be the all three of you... It could even be... Well, if she had the backing of an armada to accompany her divine logic." Jack saw it then, and he couldn't agree more: of all the people who fit her description most, Ayela was the girl that could do it.

"What? Me? No, I'm not a leader, Kamille."

"Ayela, I *know* you're not about to belittle yourself or downplay your accomplishments... Look, we don't need to betray our values or secrecy to make this happen. We just need to find someone who can stand up to the emperor and rally the people against him." Kamille explained.

"What do we do when we find this person? And how are we going to make them the Emperor?" Ayela asked. Clearly, she picked up on Kamille's thoughts as well.

"We need to convince this person that they are what this nation needs. We need to purpose them. And then, we need to convince the public that they are what we need. As for how we're going to make them the Emperor? We're going to find the dirtiest, most unruly secret that could damage

Emperor Gorvon the most, and we're going to reveal it to all of Enthedrill. And then, when the people want Gorvon gone, we'll sit our hero on the throne, and restore the reman race to its place of unity…"

"…But who that person might be, we'll just have to figure out."

A Breaking

"Alright, we're here to get supplies for our trip and get a move on. Jack's sword in the hotel room is the only weapon we've got in our possession at the moment, so let's do our best to not draw any attention to ourselves. Got it?" Kamille ordered as they stood outside the hotel. Their objective was simple enough, and they did everything they could to make themselves as unrecognizable as possible. It was strange, the sensation he had when he looked at how they were all dressed. He wasn't sure how he could describe it.

Liz wore a flowy white shirt with long sleeves and a hood, which she had pulled over her braided hair. Her pants were the same style as what she wore in the capital, paired with black boots he'd expect to see on soldiers. Ayela's attire was probably the most different from everyone else's, but still managed to fit in nicely with the surrounding crowd.

She wore a white, cropped tank top with a pouch-less bandoleer that wrapped around her torso snuggly. A navy skirt wrapped around her waist that draped down to her shins, with golden charms dangling around the waistline. A slit parted up the thigh and revealed her own black leggings, and she wore tightly strapped sandals on her feet. She wore long, fingerless gloves with mismatched gauntlets. Her hair was braided into long pigtails that she draped over her shoulder, with her bangs parted and tucked behind her ears, the left of which was adorned with a fine earpiece pierced on several places, with ornate gold chains linking together.

As she put it, it was one of Songriveii's only styles that was popular in the empire, and since she was in such mixed company in Asiat, she felt comfortable expressing her native culture.

In a similar manner, Thillan and Kamille dressed themselves in styles from Korok. Thillan wore a white shirt with a black, sleeveless jacket over top. A gaudy belt was fastened around his waist with a few silver chains attached to it. His pants were black and baggy, but tucked into his gray boots. His hair was braided, as well as his beard.

Kamille wore a tight, purple jacket with buckles and fasteners arranged in an ornate pattern down the front. Her belt was similar to Thillan's, but given a more feminine touch. Her pants, like the other women, were tight and black, but she wore boots like Liz. The shoulders of her jacket were padded, but it wasn't too distracting from her appearance. Her long, curly hair was tied into a pony tail, with several other ties at intervals until it reached the bun at the tip. Like Ayela, she wore an ornate earpiece that matched her outfit's color palette.

As for him, the driver had a hard time finding something that would work for him per Kamille's instructions when they were making contact in Shamol. Somehow, it worked, though. He wore a white shirt with a gold-plated pauldron and gauntlet over his right arm. He wore a thick leather belt with a long, black cloth draped down to his shins, parted in the middle. His pants were. baggy like Thillan's, and he wore black boots. His shirt had a hood that he wore, and fingerless gloves similar to what Ayela wore.

They were dressed like characters from an epic tale of magic and adventure, and ironically, their lives seemed to match the look. He felt a little awkward with an empty set of buckles meant to holster his sword, albeit exposed, but he figured no one would stop to ask any questions.

"…And we've got to make sure we don't try to pick up any high-powered rifles. Only pistols, got it?" Kamille finished. There was more than a lot of instruction he missed, but he didn't want to make her repeat herself.

"How much sigil do we have left?" Ayela asked. Jack did what he could to remain focused, but something deep in his heart burned with anxiety. He couldn't help but to feel a sense of impending doom.

"We have more than enough to get us to our meeting with Asher. Once we're there, I'm sure he'll have found a way to get us more resources."

"Seems like we have our work cut out for us," Liz commented.

"More than enough, that's for sure. Alright, Ayela, you and Jack go get the food, drinks, and anything else we might need for clothing. Liz, you come with us for the rest," Thillan ordered. They all nodded, and without a clue to what Kamille's directions were, Jack sheepishly followed Ayela.

There was a heat Jack was unfamiliar with as the sun reached its highest point in the sky. The pair had indulged in deep and meaningful conversation while they were running their errands, as though they were old friends that had been separated and reunited after being years apart. He was invested in her beliefs and her values, and his heart throbbed with empathy for the things she'd been through.

"I'm sorry for Rhaja's death, Ayela," he said with a comforting tone. She'd told him about the tragedy briefly before, but to hear the staggering details of what happened and how it led her to join the Darklings added many more layers of depth. "I can't imagine what it must have been like to have gone through that... For a second time, no less."

"I've since healed from it, but every so often the scars remind me they're there. You never really fully recover from something like that... You *especially* don't forget it. It changed me, for sure, but I don't want it to be an excuse to behave horribly."

"I can understand that- no, I *feel* that. When my mother was killed, I swore to do what was right by the people most oppressed to make up for my actions that caused it... I still make mistakes, of course, but I think she would smile down upon me knowing that I'm doing what I can to help others."

"I don't have any doubt of that, Jack," she said with a smile. "Liz is lucky to have a man like you in her life."

"I don't know about that," he chuckled nervously, adjusting the backpack full of the things they'd bought. "I've brought so much chaos into her life... She wouldn't be here now if it weren't for me."

"You can't do that to yourself. She loves you, and you love her. You have to look at the happiness you've brought to her life. She's told me all about how you stand up for her, fight for her, and how you stood up to your boss when he threatened to take her pay away. That's not something people really do, from what I hear. Your mother would be so proud of you, sticking up for people- especially women where you're from. She raised a good man... And as for mistakes, we all make them. Human and elf alike. I mean, I slept with the very woman who killed Rhaja because I was drinking my pain away. Justified or not, whether I knew it or not, it wasn't right... It wasn't healthy."

He was all too familiar with turning to a bottle instead of facing his demons directly. Even the few bottles of ale they bought to enjoy a little that night, he could almost *feel* them pulling at his impulses, tempting him to take a drink. And then another drink. And another. All until his problems faded with the dizzying sea of drunkenness he was so accustomed to drifting in.

"...Still..." He continued. "...She would have been better off with someone less prone to such destructive behaviors... Someone who had stability in their life. My life was miserable and unpredictable- *is* unpredictable. Sure, she makes it brighter... But she suffers from it, too. I can tell."

Ayela paused for a moment, with the sounds of their steps and the crowds around them filling the silence. "I know how you feel," she said, and in that one statement, he felt a familiarity in her tone and a connection to her he hadn't expected. There they were, two wandering souls swimming through a sea of uncertainty and unpredictability in their lives. There they were, connected by their shared experiences, lives so innately similar yet so different. But their experiences left them in that place together, and neither of them had felt the comfort of familiar company like they did in that moment. For once, neither of them felt like they were alone anymore.

In a moment of pure instinct alone, he reached for her hand and intertwined his fingers through hers. It was too late, he didn't catch himself in time, but the response... The response was what caught him off-guard. Instead of pulling away and rebuking him like he expected her to do...

...She held his hand back.

It was brief, and when they realized what they were doing, they gently let go of each other. The sensation of her skin against his, though... Even if it were just their fingertips... It lingered. Pleasure and another sensation he hadn't expected stuck to his fingers like a coat...

...Love.

But they couldn't. He was with Liz. And he loved Liz... He loved her... She encapsulated all that was his desire, all the good he wanted to keep in his life. She was worth his affection, and that wasn't something he couldn't share with anyone but her...

Her...

As he looked over at Ayela, his heart panged with emotions he hadn't experienced before.

Her...

He did what he could to keep his mind fixed on the one he loved... But that's who he was looking at, wasn't it?

Her...

Ayela...

"I'm sorry," she said, nervously tucking loose strands of her bangs behind her ear and looking down at her feet.

"There's nothing to apologize for, Ayela," he

said with a gentle tone. "I reached out for your hand. It was my impulse."

"I didn't push back, though," she admitted. He stopped and calmly placed a hand on her shoulder. She looked back into his eyes, and he stared into her violet iris's with compassion.

"I'm sorry I put you in that position. I won't do it again, as long as Liz and I live," he said, with all the sincerity he could muster from his core. "Please forgive me."

"I forgive you, Jack. I know you're not the unfaithful type. Let's just promise not to let ourselves be grouped together alone like this, yeah?" She asked with a smile. Her response, though, invoked feelings of guilt.

And those feelings were entirely justified. He was committed to Liz, and he refused to break that commitment... He refused...

"Yeah," he said, returning her smile.

If only, as the hour had gone by that they traveled to return to the others, he could shake those heavy feelings. He hid them well, kept their deep and engaging conversation going, but he felt them nonetheless. He had to bear them silently, but at what cost?

They met up with the others, and while they were discussing the supplies everyone picked up, his mind began to spiral. His world began to spin. What was going on with his life? How did he end up here instead of crushed under the remains of his apartment? Were they truly alive, even? His mind was spinning, but his body remained present. His heart was beating with chaos and anxiety, but there he stood, doing his best to hide it. He just wanted to be home…

But a lingering question continued to remain; what was home anymore? Home was where the heart was, and he found himself at a loss, not understanding where his truly was. His head pounded as the deep thinking continued, and he started to feel nauseous.

Then, Jack couldn't handle it any longer; he slung the bag over and shoved his hand in, gripping the bottle with aggressive firmness and yanking it out of the bag. Without waiting for anyone, he pulled off the cap and threw the bottle back. Everything was too much, and he couldn't take it anymore. The mission, the fact that their lives were so at risk, Ayela's hand in his- he couldn't take it. He was spiraling, just like the ale that spiraled down the bottle and into his mouth.

"JACK!!!" Ayela shrieked, rushing over to him from the group that he sneakily lingered behind. Even Liz had stayed with them, but by the time she turned and called out his name, Jack had drank two thirds of the bottle. He didn't even allow himself to savor the sweet flavor and energizing burn as it glided down his throat.

Before anymore could be drank, Kamille smacked the bottle out of his hand. It shattered loudly as it hit the ground, spilling the rest of the golden liquid everywhere, and nearly hit a couple as they passed by warily, staring at him all the while. The anger was evident on her face, but Jack felt no shame. The alcohol on Thaerv was stronger than earth's, and it worked through his body too quickly.

"You bloody drunk! What the hell is wrong with you?!" She barked as she grabbed his collar. Ayela and Thillan were quick to pull her off, while Liz stood in front of him and held him up. Her expression fell with disappointment.

"What can I say, girly – I'd 'ave drowned my sorrow in my hubris would it have the potency of a damned grapevine," he spat as he leaned on Liz's shoulder.

"What are you thinking?!" Ayela cried, frantically looking around and making sure they weren't drawing too much attention. Liz saw her wounded expression and mirrored it, feeling the pain of Jack's failure.

"C'mon, mate; you see the looks the girls are giving you? Do you even care?" Thillan shot.

"YES!" Jack shouted, demanding their undivided attention. "I DO care! Thas the problem wit' you! You seem to think I only care about myself!!! But what would YOU do if you were taken from your home, and put somewhere you didn't know or belong with some alien people, and your brother was taken from you by this people's *fucking* government – and then som'more of 'em wanted your help?!"

Kamille was silent. They were all silent. They could hear the despair in his voice, but he was too drunk to notice their concern. Tears began to swell in Jack's eyes, but it wasn't from sadness. His brow furrowed, and his scowl sharpened, anger twisting his features.

"I killed a massive *fucking* bird, ran around some future-alien-city-poppycock-*shit*, and got yelled at and threatened by some girl playing *fucking* sergeant with a group of pacifists, and watched my brother get kidnapped! So maybe leave the drinking thing for me to handle, 'kay? 'Kay," Jack said as he slung the bag back over his shoulder, quickly wiped the tears off his face, and threw his hood over his head. He didn't wait for anyone but pushed his way through them and left them to deal with the crowd of onlookers.

It was Liz, though, that chased after him.

"Wait!" She shouted, tears streaming down her

cheeks. "Jack, please, wait!" He stopped in his tracks. She didn't say anything or even try to make him turn around – she simply wrapped her arms around him from behind and embraced him.

"Y'know what the worst part of this is, Liz?" Jack asked without turning to face her. "I don' even know if we're gonna get to go home after all."

With that, he gently broke free from her embrace and continued on, occasionally asking a random citizen where the northern gate was. He needed to be by himself.

He needed to drift in his sea of drunkenness...

XV

How To Make A Logician

Divine logic and dark logic are kindred magics; one doesn't simply make one... Do they?

The Human Of Intrigue

Four sat at the black, round table with Kozek. Four inquisitors. Each of them were given their own domains of authority and jurisdiction. Each of them wielded a form of the ancient magics the elvish people mastered... Each... Except for him. There were many things he had to learn, to adapt to and to accept in his new role. He'd met each of the inquisitors individually before their meeting that day, and he found them to be the most peculiar of individuals.

There was Banïl that sat across from him, positioned a little to the left. He was the most mysterious and intimidating of all the Inquisitors. He was the most infamous of mysterious figures of high military position, despite not having a name that anyone knew. When he arrived in any town, city, or government installation, they were just given an order from the Emperor preceding him that he would have full access and control. He commanded respect, because if that requirement wasn't met, he would enact a vicious and painful retribution. He maintained loyalty to the Emperor above all else and was powerful enough to topple governments by his strength alone.

But it wasn't just strength and skill in methodical torture that set him apart; he was a genius. His intellect was rivaled by no one. He was the mind behind many of the secret branches of the Governmental structure that handled the many behind-the-scenes operations. Many rebels were discovered, apprehended, and even executed by him. He was the Emperor's closest advisor.

To the famous inquisitor's left was Jürdæ, and until Kozek, she was the newest member of the inquisitorial staff. She wielded a strange magic, as ancient as divine logic itself. She was a pretty woman, for a blood elf. He didn't care much for women that weren't ivory like himself, but she was as rare an exception as this Ayela Rhexa that they were hunting. Ruby irises adorned her eyes, glistening with mystery and secrecy. She proved herself a powerful witch, routing out dissidents within imperial ranks and subjecting them to the emperor's harsh sentencing. She wasn't someone he wanted to find himself standing against.

Next to her was Körok, A tall, solid, olive-toned man of brute force and an even stranger magic than his blood elf companion. There were rumors of a government agent that couldn't be killed. In fact, whatever tried to kill him, he was able to replicate its effects to some degree. He was sure those were just rumors, but the fact that he didn't indulge Kozek on exactly *what* his magic was capable of created a sense of discomfort and anxiety within him. No one really knew what happened to his victims, and very few people ever saw someone that identically matched his description. They were only rumors.

The fourth and final inquisitor sat to his left...

A woman of exquisite beauty and gentle grace, but who wielded a power over energy he still didn't understand...

...Semus

"Inquisitors," a disembodied voice commanded, deep and powerful. It was the voice of the Emperor, Gorvon, that demanded their undivided attention. As he spoke, Kozek examined the two women and two men who offered their presence with him. "We have an unprecedented urgency in our laps that demands our fullest attention."

"We presume it has nothing to do with the wars?" Asked the gentle-voiced Semus. She was among the most beautiful women he'd ever laid eyes on. Had the Inquisitors been known to the public, he was certain her face would be the most recognized and celebrated by all the nations – even the closed-bordered kingdom of Korok. Her face was elegant, adorned with emerald-hued iris's in her eyes, and exquisitely attractive features. Her body was a work of artistry, a perfect hourglass figure. She kept herself fit and in shape and took great care of her appearance. Her hair draped down over her shoulders in large, chocolate, bouncing curls, and bangs curtained over her forehead.

All her beauty hid a dangerous reputation among those of their clearance within the Empire. No one knew her name. No one knew her face. But there were rumors of an unnamed woman with unrestricted Imperial clearance that was the most perfect extractor of information and secrets. Her victims were always memory-wiped of everything, even their identity, and not a single person recovered what they lost. They were forced to begin anew. There wasn't a document on record observing her existence. She was the very definition of an enigma.

"You presume correctly, Semus. No, this matter is related to something else entirely... The dispatch of units sent under the orders of General Himathian on the southern continent has vanished without a trace... All but one. And that one has returned with an important message," the Emperor clarified.

"...It can't be..." Banïl whispered with his hands firmly planted on the table. Kozek's attention was turned towards the screen in front of him, scrawling with images and texts. Each of them had their own screen built and angled to them at their seats. Images appeared in empty slots of a snow-covered pyramid with an ominous gate at the base, towering into the sky many kilometers away from whoever took the snapshot.

"This is the temple of the Daethrils!" Jürdæ declared with terror in her voice.

"Correct, Jürdae," The Emperor answered plainly. "We have discovered the temple. Of all the fascinating, supernatural phenomenon to occur from ancient mythologies, this is the most threatening. Therefore, I now have an objective for the inquisitors."

"Proceed, Your Highness," Banïl calmly requested before adding, "We eagerly wait for our instruction."

"Banïl... You may now reveal to your fellow Inquisitors what you've told me in private. I agree to the bulk of the plans and will reveal what I want done additionally afterwards."

Banïl nodded humbly as he stood up, running his hand over his slick black hair before placing them both inquisitively behind his back. He stepped around his chair and walked to the place in between Körok and Jürdae, placing his hands on the table as a devilish grin crept across his face.

He inhaled deeply before speaking, "Fellow Inquisitors, may I present to you one of the humans we had maintained to keep, of the three that escaped."

The blood drained from Kozek's face, and the clenched fists at his sides only tightened. He could see the jaw muscles in Körok's face tighten as the curly, dark-haired human entered into the light beside Banïl, bearing a stance just like the Inquisitor that introduced him, and dressed in similar clothing. This was what Banïl was up to for the past few weeks; training a human in the ways of an Inquisitor. If he stood there before him, it meant this human was able to learn as quickly as he was, more even, for the lack of any formal reman militarized or disciplined training. Kozek honestly found it fascinating.

"What is the meaning of this?" He demanded. Semus gently placed a hand on his clenched fist, commanding his attention for just a brief enough time for her to shake her head, warning him not to act out. Kozek settled back into his seat.

"I know you four are alarmed at this sight, but rest assured that he is on our side as much as we need to be on his. This plan is vital to ensure the success of the Empire in the wars against Durinveii and Songriveii, and the possibility of crushing the rebellion and those pathetic hackers called the Darklings. Dominov has been our long-standing ally in trade, and we've continued to negotiate further allegiances so that they might bear our flags, and the Kingdom of Korok continues to remain elusive in this war, announcing every chance they have that they aren't apart of any global conflicts or affairs. As far as I'm concerned, that is their decision that we can respect until they decide they want to change their minds," Banïl explained.

"What's your angle?" Körok asked, leaning over in his seat.

"Simple," Banïl began, his slick and velvet voice in stark contrast to Körok's. "We are going to put a swift end to the wars with the nations and focus intensely on the rebellions. We're going to strengthen and confirm our relationship with Dominov, and we're going to establish the Empire of Enthedrill as a global dominance that has the Kingdom of Korok as its lapdog. To do this, my fresh colleague here suggested that we focus our offensive efforts against one nation at a time, while we keep defenses at the forefront of the other fights we have going on. Our first target... Will be Songriveii."

The human cleared his throat as he began to speak. "It's quite simple, really," he started. "I have looked into reports about Songriveii amidst my training as an Inquisitor. The nation is split at the seams. There are four territories; north, south, east, and west. The Sovereign has been working hard to promote economic growth and environmental safety as imports from Durinveii threaten their most sacred forest. Unfortunately for him, his Supreme Judges have cornered him at every turn despite the protest of the people because of their fear that their economy will crash if they place embargos on any Durinveii imports. So, the Sovereign has been trying to find any other means available so that he doesn't have to declare martial law.

"What's better is that there is internal turmoil with his own household; an infant of his was robbed from her cradle and mysteriously vanished twenty years ago – fresh after she was born. There have been no signs of her appearance until recently, not even a trace of her even being alive. With the royal house in disarray to this day because of his daughter missing – and no body recovered living or dead – and the decaying state of their nation's infrastructure, it makes them ripe for a desperate attempt at making peace with us.

"Since their war with us is about the missing princess to begin with, we just need to paint the picture that we happened upon her, and then we have a good chance of ending it with them by presenting someone who could be the possible young heir to the Sovereign's throne, we have a proposed plan to either send in someone to pose as the daughter, or find her ourselves and return her," he explained. There was silence for a moment as they pondered his words.

"How do you propose we find this girl, and ensure the reality of this plan?" Semus asked.

"We have an idea of who she is already," he revealed as he pulled out a phone from his pocket and flicked whatever was on the screen into a holographic projection hovering over the table. It was an image of the red-haired girl that accompanied the other two humans in Bavylune when they escaped.

"There's no way…"

"We ran image comparisons of our databases of all the citizens of Enthedrill, and there's only one match; Ayela Rehxa, an orphan. Turns out, this girl grew up here, and was discovered at the doorstep of the orphanage around the exact time the princess went missing. Emperor Gorvon is convinced; Ayela Rhexa is Tsana Renn. Her being a divine logician- the one that sent our satellites pinging with locations in the capital and in Shamol- only solidifies this fact," Banïl explained. "Assuming we're right, she's in league with the humans. She was working a small job here in the Capital and quit about the time this image was taken. After that, she fell off the grid."

"So, we find her, we possibly give Songriveii a deal they can't refuse. Meanwhile, we do what we can to crush down their forces. This way, they won't have anything to fight back against our proposal," Semus pointed out. "That's great for Songriveii submitting to our rule, but what about the other warfronts? What about their governing structure? And how do we recover the trust of their people once we've taken their nation?"

"I'm glad you asked. Songriveii will be our primary effort, and then the others after. We will be effectively breaking off and enacting carefully crafted orders that, if followed exactly, will dissolve their governments, assert control over their people and ensure that they will willingly submit to our rule, and bend these territories to submission. As it stands, Körok, who resembles the natives of Durinveii the most, will travel to that country and blend in with its people and government operatives. We have left your directives in your personal quarters and will effectively dispose of them once you've memorized them.

"Jürdae, because you are Songrivan, you will begin your mission in the land of your ancestors. Your operations are also left in your personal quarters," Banïl explained. Finally, his eyes rested on Kozek and Semus.

"You two have special directives," he began. "Emperor, if you could please elaborate."

"Thank you, Inquisitor. Kozek, you and Semus will be hunting for the remaining humans, and you will end the war with the Darklings. We have observed their tactics and have an idea of how they operate now. Since they have made their primary target myself, they will be punished appropriately. You two are going to be public faces, now. You are going to begin attempting to observe the Darklings, route out their members, and expose them if they have any other criminally incriminating pasts. Where the Darklings assert a public presence, you will do the same, and you will expose them in front of all their supporters. Gain their trust. Detach yourself from any Imperial influence and show that you're one of them. Once you have them in your grasp, crush their efforts and execute their leaders in front of me," the Emperor commanded.

"What are we to do with the humans?" Kozek asked.

"If they have joined the Darklings, their punishment will be the same as theirs."

"Which is?"

"Death," the Emperor declared.

There was a tense silence, even in front of one of their own race. Kozek observed the human to see his reaction but was disappointed to find no expression present. Disconcerted, he courted a half-smile as he looked over at Semus, who kept her gaze forward. He was looking forward to working with her.

"Once their public face is defamed, the public won't really care if they die," Banïl explained. "In fact, they'll probably welcome it."

"The disintegrator chambers will be active once more," Kozek said with excitement.

"What will you and this human be doing?" Semus asked.

"We will first be traveling to Dominov for positive propaganda, and then we will be going to this newly discovered temple on the Southern Continent," The human answered, his voice cold and robotic. "I am Adrian, by the way. I will be joining your ranks as Inquisitor. And we believe that this temple appearing is no coincidence with all the happenings concerning the Aethril judgments on vulnerable towns, and with my fellow humans and I having suddenly appeared."

"And how do you feel about your human companions being killed along with the rebels they may or may not be helping?" She asked as she leaned forward and rested her elbows on the table.

"It's their choice to make. They still believe they can make it back home. I've accepted our fate," Adrian answered curtly, looking Semus in her eyes. The woman seemed to lean back out of intimidation. Kozek was impressed.

"Such heartlessness..." She commented.

"Sometimes, that heartlessness is required," The Emperor commented. "Inquisitors... You are dismissed."

A Lady Of Desire

Kozek and Semus walked side-by-side down the winding, curving halls of the upper floors in the Emperor's tower. They kept their gazes forward and the tongues silent. Kozek preferred the silence. It helped him think. That silence, however, would not last. He welcomed the sound of her voice as a pleasant interruption, though.

"Emperor Gorvon has asked me to do something to you that will hurt and leave you incapacitated for a while…" She said, distracting him with a soft, gentle voice. "I am going to be endowing you with magic. The process will painfully alter your body so that you can properly use it. Once you're relieved, would you meet me at the entrance to the tower on the bottom floor for dinner? Does the Promenade sound appealing?" Semus asked politely. She stopped him in his tracks and stood in front of him with eager eyes full of intrigue and desire. With intensity, she offered a look of longing that seeped into his heart. It pounded in his chest – he'd never experienced such powerful emotion driving him towards such an exquisite creature before.

"Most assuredly, Semus," Kozek agreed. She smiled pleasantly and closed the distance between the two of them a little.

"We need to bear different names. I've been thinking of mine, but perhaps you would like to think of yours? Also, we'll need to wear more casual clothing as we'll venture out. I don't think our mission will be successful if we go in our Inquisitor garbs."

"I agree," Kozek responded. He tried hard to keep his focus. He admired her even more that she was so forward thinking.

"Good," She said with a smile. "We're going to get along well, Kozek. At least, I hope we do." With that, she turned and continued down the hall and led a breathless Kozek to his chambers. He savored every moment, even as she walked farther ahead, and captured mental snapshots of the sway in her walk. She was smooth, slick, and as deadly as he expected her to be. He yearned for the sensation of his hands tracing the contours of her body, and his heart burned in his chest with lustful passion.

They stopped in front of his quarters, where he made his permanent abode, and faced each other. He opened the door and waited for her to enter. Instead, though, she placed a hand over his head and closed her eyes, then whispered an enchantment in a language he'd never heard before.

Then...

Then he began to feel a sensation, painful and writhing, as if tendrils of some unseen entity began to dig their way into his head from her hand. Before he had the chance to scream, she shoved him into his quarters and closed the door.

Pain.

Pain gripped every fiber of his being as he succumbed to whatever cursed enchantment she spoke over him.

Kozek had spent the past three hours in utter pain, groaning and even screaming from its torturous crawling. Guards positioned themselves outside his room, ordered by Semus, to ensure that he would be undisturbed while he concentrated on maintaining a steady heartbeat.

But as time passed by, the pain would only grow worse.

When would it end?

When would he be free?

He hoped the Emperor saw his loyalty for enduring such hardship without question...

Five hours passed, and then the pain slowly left his body. Kozek sat on the edge of his bed, dripping sweat down from his brow and breathing heavily. He could feel it, though; power coursing through his veins. As a test, he reached out his hand to a steel cup resting on the sink in his small quarters' humble restroom section. The cup flew to his hand as he commanded it in his mind. It was as if he moved it with invisible hands, and then crushed it effortlessly, as if it were made of paper. Kozek grinned. Now he could be an instrument of his Emperor's will. And an effective instrument he would be. He stood to his feet and readied himself for his prior engagement with his new, paralyzingly beautiful coworker. His heartbeat with newfound excitement and motivation.

What chance did even the gods have?

XVI

The Adventure Of Unknowns

*What adventurous tale can be told from a
bed of comforts and a hearth daily lit?*

Sobriety To Hidden Destiny

Jack was sober before he knew it. He started to regret his choice to guzzle down a rather large bottle of alcohol. The sun was getting ready to set, and no one found him. No one searched for him, as far as he could tell. His desire to be left alone had been painfully granted. It left him in a sniffling, emotionally unstable mess. Before he knew it, he was already suffering the panging headaches of a raging hangover.

His thoughts turned to his late mother. He missed her so terribly. His dad was a fighter, tried and true, from Waterford in Ireland. His mom, though, was a gentle spirit. She was a devout Jewish woman. She would always know what to say and how to react to every situation; "Just pray to Adonai. You don't always have to fight." She told everyone that, but she especially stressed it to him. If only he could believe what she believed so readily. If only he had a deity to vent to like she did. If only he had something greater than himself that he could trust in.

But as he looked around it the world he was trapped in, he saw that turmoil and trouble wasn't just confined to the human race. That torment was what made him question if there was a creator that was all good. How could that be? How could they be all good if there was so much pain and death?

"Jack?" A gentle voice whispered. His gaze drifted to the entrance of the secluded alley he hid away in.

He looked up, his brow furrowing in confusion at the sound of Ayela's voice. He noted the expressed concern on her face. Why did she care? What did she see in him that drew her to him?

"There you are..." She cooed with a gentle expression. Calmly, she walked over and sat down beside him.

Still confused, Jack asked, "Why did you come looking for me?"

"Because I'm worried about you," she admitted. "Because Liz is worried about you, and Thillan and Kamille are worried about you too."

"I would say not to worry about me, but I think we all can agree that would be unwise," Jack said in a somber voice. He rested his head on the gray-colored brick wall behind them.

"We all agree on that... Liz was the one who told us to let you have your space... That was the hardest thing I've ever seen that woman do, but she was confident it's what you needed. I think I agree with her," Ayela revealed. Jack blinked in surprise. The Songrivan looked away and added, "She loves you, Jack. She loves you so deeply."

Jack looked down at his dirty hands, wondering how many times he stumbled over and fell before finding this alley. "I don't deserve it," he said.

"No one ever does..."

"Isn't that the truth."

"Yeah," Ayela snickered. "Why do you do this to yourself?"

Jack paused, unsure of how to answer her. "I'm not sure I understand what you mean," He said transparently.

"Seclude yourself... Let me preface by explaining that I know how much stress you're under, and I won't negate that, but why be alone at such a vulnerable time?"

"It's how I am... Even while my mother was alive, I found it easier to think when I was alone. It's how I clear my head and organize my emotions... It's how I'm comfortable expressing my emotions. No person could really do that for me. No god could ever do that for me," he explained. Her brow furrowed.

"God? How does a religious belief fit into this?" She asked.

"I don't know, I just... I always remind myself about my mother's belief for some reason... Even if I don't really believe it..."

She paused for a moment and took a deep breath. "Rök is the name we give to the one we believe is the creator – at least, those of our faith. And though he loves us, we chose to separate our lives from him and make our own law of life. But the thing is, even though we walked away and carved our own path of life, he never left us alone... I guess, what I'm trying to say, is that even though you may not believe in a god, that doesn't mean that he doesn't believe in you."

"I guess... But it still doesn't make any sense to me, really. I don't know. Let's get our minds off this. God's the last thing I want to think about right now."

"We'll have plenty of time to talk about him in the days to come..." She said calmly. Then, without saying a word, she gently put her arm around him and pulled him closer to her. He didn't fight it, and rested his head rested on her shoulder. He couldn't keep it anymore.

He sniffled as the tears began to stream down his cheeks. He cried voiceless sobs on her shoulder. It didn't matter that they came from different worlds, and it didn't matter that they were different races. They crafted a bond over those barriers through the common understanding that death, trouble and suffering happens to all, and when it happens, others would be needed to soften its blow. True suffering was to suffer alone.

"Let it all out," she said as she caressed his head. He obeyed as if it were an order, and let the tears flow as the setting sun turned the baby blue sky into an amber hue.

Relief

"There you are, you bloody idiot," Kamille cooed. There was no aggression. No anger in her tone. He'd expected the same sort of violent reprimand his brother would have offered, but instead, he only saw compassion, empathy, and worry on their faces. He saw the concern of close friends.

His gaze rested on Liz, and his heart sank with the pangs of guilt and shame. Her carefully crafted makeup streaked down her cheeks from the tears she'd cried. Her expression churned a brutal concoction of emotions, from sadness to anger. The most eye-opening for him, though, was relief. There was relief on her face when she saw him. It was like the clouds of a storm parted, allowing the rays of light and hope to shimmer in her eyes.

She nearly leapt out of her chair and wrapped

360

him in a tight embrace, one that he quickly returned. It didn't take much for her to start crying again, but it was his own tears that carried the weight of realization. His own actions caused this. His own desperate need to sooth his anxiety and panic drove him to act on his impulses, to escape while everyone else was left to deal with their harsh reality.

He was weak.

He slowly sat down across from her, but before he could speak, her hand smacked him across the cheek so loudly, it almost echoed. He didn't say anything. Instead, he looked down. It was justified. The pain didn't stay on the surface of his skin. No, it sank to the core of his being. He felt sick to his stomach. He felt the sharp sting of regret.

"You're all I got, Jack," she said in a quaky voice. "You're it. No home to go to, no family, no job… Nothing. It's only you, Jack. Don't you dare try to take yourself away again, you hear me?"

Jack paused. He didn't know what to say, so he let out a pathetic, "I'm sorry." There was silence as they all heard his words. Leading up to that moment, there was self-justifying, self-pity, and self-concern. Something inside of him needed to change. He needed to dig deep within himself and find out who he was. He needed to find power within himself and find strength within himself to be not only what he needed to be, but what she needed him to be as well. He was the only one who could do it, and while he had friends to help him, only he was able to make the choice to grow up.

"What?" Thillan asked, shocked. "Did you-

"I said I'm sorry, yes. And I meant it. It's not right that you have to worry about if I'm going to drink myself sick or go and do something stupid that could get me hurt or killed. It wasn't right, Liz..." Jack admitted as he looked into her eyes.

"We'll work on it together," Liz said. Without saying anything else, she pressed her lips to his.

"This is touching and all," Kamille started, interrupting their moment, "but we have to go. We secured a ride, and we're lucky the driver agreed to take us at night. Let's get our things and get ready to leave."

"We have a long ride ahead of us, and we have a lot of explaining to do before we sleep on the ride there," Thillan said. Without saying anything more, they grabbed their things and traveled together to the gate they had meant to go to the next day...

It was a fateful walk...

…One that would change Jack and Ayela forever.

XVII

A Villain Willing

To the patriot, the concept of being a villain is not scary, because their love of country pollutes their view of what's wrong and right.

When Is It Too Much?

The breeze blew, offering a cool caress on Anæsïa's skin. She left one loose, curly strand of hair on the right side of her head dangling against her face while the rest was tied in a bun. She nearly squeaked and jumped as a loud truck's exhaust erupted with the sounds of hydraulic pressure releasing, startling her while she tried to admire the city of Laviport. She and Kozek had been stationed there to follow a lead on darkling activity. Kozek's raging hormones and relatively simple intelligence made it easier for her to hide her true objectives, though... Something only Banïl was aware of, and a secret he would take to his grave.

She wanted to laugh, to smile, to glower at her cunning. The emperor saw nothing. The others... Only Kozek and the dwarvish inquisitor were loyal to the emperor. The Songrivan was a recent addition, and while she was able to exercise her power over the others, it didn't work on Anæsïa. It didn't need to work, though. They were on the same side...

Her thoughts turned to Kozek, and she almost pitied him. He was proud, patriotic, and an utter imbecile. Why the emperor decided to reward his failure, she wasn't able to comprehend. What was he good at, save for tormenting and torturing the people of the empire? What use would such brutality have in the highest office of government authority, second only to Gorvon himself?

There was only one possibility that came to mind; his relentlessness. He didn't stop until his goals were achieved. He swore his life in servitude to the empire, and Enthedrill has never known a more fierce achiever than Kozek. Perhaps that was why the emperor chose to rely on him. Despite his blunder, his previous achievements were nothing short of superb- if not violently brutal. He was exactly the kind of pawn Gorvon would want at his disposal.

She shook her head, though, and returned her attention to the physical world around her. She admired the bridges that crossed over above the towering complexes and structures in the heart of the city. The roads she walked beside led to the open oceans that stretched across the horizon. Airships soared high in the air. Her heart yearned for a people free of Gorvon's sinister rule, where peace and life could flourish. If she'd sat on his throne, she'd ensure that would come to pass. Her bloodline would instill security and freedom for Enthedrill, and she would make sure they never tried to take over the world again.

"'Scuse me, miss, but are you lost?" A man called from behind her, catching her as she held her hand up to block the sun.

"No, I'm fine," she said without looking over at him. Without warning, his arm wrapped around her waist and forcefully pulled her in, his grip painfully tightening with every attempt she made to get away. She grunted and groaned in a panicked tone as he forced her to walk with him, pressing her body against his.

"You're quite lost, miss. Lemme help you around," he nearly growled. She looked over at him, seeing a man with a pale face and dark hair, dressed in a light-grey suit and tie, with a white shirt underneath. His coat trailed down to his knees, identifying him as a man of stature. "I can tell you aren't from around here." She wished she wielded the power she had given Kozek, but her religion had forbidden enchantments like that on the user's self. To her dismay, if she unleashed the extent of her power there and now, so much would be altered that it would leave a trail and expose everything. She was bound by the code and rules she instilled in the very order she founded, and couldn't leave any room for them to be discovered.

All would be lost.

"What. Do. You. Want?!" She barked as she finally shoved him away from her, causing a commotion that stole the attention of those nearby. She clenched her open hand into a fist while tightening her other hand around the package.

"You're new to Laviport, so I'm here to show you around. After all, judging from your rather heavy accent, you're Dominovan, aren't you?" He assessed as he straightened his posture. "You're wise to come with me instead of forcing me to make a mess on these fine streets."

She knew his kind: he was a kidnapper. He was a trafficker. She was a fine prize, and a suitable target; a 'foreign' girl looking as clueless as ever traveling alone with nothing more than a small package to her person. She snickered.

Then, all the pieces fell into place. Her power granted her such unlimited access to the empire's databses, she knew everything. That paired with a photographic memory, she could recognize anyone that came across as a person of interest in imperial records. This man was exactly that. He was a mafioso, a ciminal overlord. He wasn't like the leaders of the murder gangs to the west. No, he was much more sophisticated and methodical than that. His operation was clean, clever, and the crimes his people committed left barely any trace in official records.

"No, I'm not new to Laviport, sir. And I know what you are," she said as she looked into his amber eyes. "I know who you are... It's a surprise to see you so far from D'Vnora, Mister Jhryde."

"Keep a civil tongue in that pretty little mouth of yours, lassy. You might know my face, but you don't know the man that wears it. Shame your airship dropped you at this snide port instead of one of the northern gates of the city. I own this portion of Laviport, and my industry's growin'. We don't squabble with those petty murdering thugs in the Corpse Grinders or the drug peddlin' Resin Razers anymore. We've grown more industrious," Jhryde spat. The people around them simultaneously turned around and began to walk away from them. Aæsïa noticed, and her heart began to pound in her chest a little harder. If only she'd chosen a school of combative magic. If only she'd focused more on defending herself instead of power over information and minds.

Sure, she could stop him, but again…

…The cost would be too great.

She would need to rely on the public eye, and what little bit of self defense she learned for her military position. Against a man as skilled and deadly as Jhryde, though… His reputation preceded him. There was a reason he was at the top.

"If you're going to take me, you're going to die," she warned.

Jhryde erupted into laughter. "You think you can stop me?" He chuckled as he stepped closer. "I've gotten my hands in some of the deepest reaches of the gov that money can buy. There ain't a power in the universe that can relieve me of my position."

"You haven't met me yet," Said another voice. Anæsïa sighed in relief. Kozek defiantly stopped behind Jhryde and pulled the hood he was wearing off of his head. He was a perfect assassin, unnoticed and just like any other passerby until he was close enough that it was too late. In that moment alone, he was a hero.

"Who're you, love?" The crimelord spat.

"A god you don't want to defy, if you know what's good for you… Leave the girl alone," Kozek threatened.

"You're serious?! No- you know what, I've got

one better. How's about you walk away now before I make a call," Jhryde began as he pulled out his phone, "or I make my fuckin' call and the street is swarmin' with my guys in seconds?"

"What makes you think you'll survive long enough to make that call?" Kozek asked rhetorically.

Never before had she witness such raw savagery.

He raised his open hand, palm up. As he did, Jhryde straightened stiff and began to levitate off the ground, groaning and grunting in excruciating pain. His face turned upward, and the veins in his neck began to bulge. She started to hear cracking and popping, and his groans became worse. The sounds were jarring, sickening. She couldn't take it anymore.

"KOZEK!!! STOP!!!" Anæsïa shrieked as she ran over to him and tried to pull his arm down. He obeyed, and slowly he lowered his hand. Jhryde was released and crumbled onto the ground, screaming in intense pain.

"You would stop me from killing the man who threatened your own life?" He asked, confused. She looked over at the pathetic mess writhing in pain and had pity on him.

"I would keep my hands clean from shedding any blood," she admitted. "I'm known for extracting information, not for killing. As long as I'm present, any life will be spared."

"…Curious…" Kozek admitted as he eyed her with slight suspicion. Then he knelt down beside Jhryde.

"I've got a couple options for you," He began as he held his hand over the mob boss's head. An ambient glow illuminated from his palm, and suddenly, Jhryde was fine as if nothing had happened.

Frightened, he smacked Kozek's hand away and jumped up to his feet. "Freak!" He spat.

"Such a simple statement from a man who's encountered a concept too grand for his puny mind," Kozek said curtly. "Listen carefully. You're going to walk away. In fact, you're going to leave the city and take your clowns with you. Go back to D'Vnora while you can. Better yet, migrate to Songriveii while it's still its own nation. Don't come back. Or, you can stay, and you will suffer."

Jhryde looked at the both of them in horror that slowly twisted into anger. "No one tells me what I can and can't do in my city! I earned my keep here! I made the moves and killed the other crooks that thought they could run the scene here, and I took the throne myself! You think just because you're some warlock that you can tell anyone you want to come and go? I got news for you's! You fuckin' can't!"

Kozek sighed and rubbed his temples in frustration. Before he had the chance to speak, though, Anæsïa placed a hand on his chest. "You're right," she started. "We can't. But there are consequences, and he just laid them out. It's your choice."

Jhryde's response was an action; he unlocked his phone and tapped his thumb on the screen and held it up to his ear. Both the inquisitors sighed.

Before he could call, though, his body repeated the painful process it had gone through just moments ago. This time, though, it was much worse. Kozek strained his fingers, gripping some invisible object with such force his hand shook.

There were screams. Agonizing screams. His body shook and convulsed as it hung suspended in the air, and a smile crept across Kozek's face. He watched the worm cry and grovel like the insect he was, and the inquisitor felt justified. Men like this interrupted everyone's good lives. Men like this preyed on the defenseless. Anæsïa's silent observance only affirmed his actions. He couldn't see the anguish in her face, though. She hid it well. She didn't want to kill anyone, but this man... She forced herself to watch him suffer.

It was justified. It was retribution. For her, and for every woman he ever stole.

"That's enough," She declared. Without question, he let the criminal loose to curl on the ground, sobbing from the excruciating pain he was in. Death was too easy for him. He needed to suffer, and she was more than willing to leave him as the mess he was. "We need to go," She said.

They turned and carried on their way.

She moved on...

Driven to make a world free of men like him...

The Shock Of The Truth

"Are you alright?" Kozek asked. She was still shaken from the encounter, but she managed to compose herself. Her emotions were a whirlwind of disgust, anger, fear, and guilt, but she couldn't let them control her. She had mastered herself long ago, and she was no stranger to the guile and uncontrolled impulses of the common man. Even one as endearing as Kozek had been couldn't be entirely trusted. Men like him... When they didn't get what they wanted through kindness and being 'good,' they resorted to harsh insults towards her character and her identity as a woman. There was a selfish darkness inside of him, and it didn't take much for her to see it.

"I'm fine," she said. "And I'll be fine... Thank you for not killing him."

"Such a gentle spirit for an Inquisitor," he

commented as he pulled her eyes up to his. She stared, gazing through the windows to his heart, trying to read the script that drove him. She hid her discomfort well, knowing that in a moment's notice, he could utilize his newfound power against her as well.

Then she looked away. "You don't truly know my history," She said. Her cryptic response was intentional, but it wasn't untrue. He truly knew nothing about her. He knew nothing of the depths of her betrayal to his beloved empire. To her, though, the emperor and his loyalists were as cruel as the mobster that tried to steal her... The mobster... Jhryde...

Her stomach churned, and even more with the thought that citizens were left unattended under the oppressive rule of criminals and greedy thieves. She questioned the government for allowing such travesty to occur in the first place. How could Gorvon be so apathetic? How could the governors of the holds be so uncaring? Her thoughts turned to the Kult of Salom'Sileyu, the ones the emperor aligned himself with... That was her answer; *them*. Though Tallie, their former leader and highest witch, was dead, they still functioned as if she never existed.

"You're right," Kozek agreed as they slowed their pace. "You don't know mine, either," he added as he held her hand. It was like a stain that his skin left on her hand, one she equally enjoyed and was stung by. She couldn't deny that she craved a lover's touch, but from him... From someone so comfortable and supportive of the emperor's regime... "You don't know why I feel so strongly for my Emperor, or why I care so much for my nation. So, don't feel so alone, Anæsïa... I'm right there with you."

There was a sense of darkness to what he said that she couldn't deny. Maybe it wasn't that he was a simple man, but that his intellect was wasted on worthless causes. Though his failure should have ended him, he was given a place among the inquisitors. He was cold, calculating, but also perhaps there was some genius that lived in that mind of his.

Whatever emotion there was in his heart, it was densely wrapped under layers of callous. She was heartless when she needed to be, but she made an effort not to take life if at all possible. But him... He was a different kind of heartless. In that encounter, she saw the Interrogator side of him. But now, in his arm, she could see a tenderness in him that sought to keep her safe. For some reason, he was offering her a glimpse at the reman in him – the man driving the machine.

"I'm sorry," she offered, her face downcast.

There was guilt. She'd judged him without knowing him. She assumed he was like all other so-called patriots. Under his political views, under his deeply held convictions, there was a complex elf that experienced all of the joys and pains that shaped him into who he was now. He offered her a window into his heart, so she would offer him the same in return. After all, they were partners in a long and arduous mission.

He lifted her eyes once more to his, and she saw it; passion. He viewed himself as a simple man with simple goals, but he wasn't after all. He was a passionate believer. He believed in his country, its people, and its leadership. He believed in what they believed and offered himself as a willing vessel for their deeds – good or evil. He didn't let himself get in the way, but this one time... The one and only time... She saw it in him. She saw a shift in his passion, and that focus now rested on her; she was now the center of his desire and affection. For him, it was love at first sight. For her, though, he was not... They could never be, and there wasn't anything that could change that...

...What a dangerous place for someone's heart to be...

"For what?" He rebuked as he looked forward.

She thought to herself silently and wanted to answer him, but she couldn't. It would reveal too much, and she wasn't ready for him to see that yet. She hadn't let anyone close to her heart except the Emperor, and there was a reason she would never do it again. Kozek wasn't the exception to that rule yet.

"Now, are you going to tell me what's in the package yet?" Kozek asked as they turned another corner.

"Yes," she began as she looked around to make sure no one was following them or close by. "I apologize for the secrecy, but if we must maintain it, then I must wait for opportune moments to tell you anything."

"Of course, Anæsïa."

"I have spoken to the Emperor in secret," she lied, "and he has agreed to send me hand-written pages to include in a specially bound copy of a particular religious text that was outlawed not too long ago."

Kozek stopped and faced her, his expression intense and serious. "Even with our high government stature, we technically don't exist, and would still face-

"You entirely misunderstand the position of an Inquisitor, Lïam," Aæsïa interrupted in a hushed tone. She observed their surroundings to make sure no one was eavesdropping. "If any federal workers were to detain us, we express the highest authority with observable access, and present overrides to any security measures they place on us – and we do so as ghosts. Imperial detainers will submit to our authority without question. That means that we will have access to any contraband they relieve us of as well. Don't be so quick to worry or judge, my friend. I am well aware of the risks, and for our mission, we must take those. Our roles must be believable."

"I understand, Anæsïa, but, I assume, it's an Alldweii? This is a bold move..." Kozek pointed out as he stroked his chin and placed his other hand on his hip.

"We needed incriminating evidence against our Emperor," she stated plainly as she dusted off the package. "This will prove to be quite in-criminating indeed. He outlawed many religions, including this one, and yet there's a religious text belonging to that faith of his own personal library... And once the people side with us, we will expose our enemies for what they truly are."

"How will you explain obtaining it?"

"I've been putting thought into it. He regularly and wastefully has workers clean out his shelves of books he no longer reads or has an interest in. Perhaps one of those workers stumbled upon

382

this and tossed it? The books are transported via armored transport to Ih'Dejj and burned in the Uri'Kai's Execution Chamber. Since the first floor of the Emperor's tower is open for guests and tourists to freely visit and sight-see, I could say that I noticed it on the ground and picked it up, saw what it was and waited until I was safely away to show it to the public."

Kozek stroked his chin. "That's a pretty well-thought-out plan, but a lot of people are going to call it out as fraud. They have never been that careless when disposing of anything in the library."

"And yet two aliens escaped and are out in the world," Aæsïa pointed out.

"Good point."

"I'd like to believe so."

"And once that is accomplished and we have those who war against us, we will execute those gutless bastards that skulk in the shadows," Kozek declared defiantly. She winced inwardly at his choice of words. Then, suddenly, his face turned to dreariness and doom with a sudden mental revelation; "The humans know my face."

Her mind worked quickly to think of a solution. "Then you will remain a villain," she suggested. She looked up into his eyes, which emulated confusion.

"How will that work?" He asked.

"Simple; you will continue to attempt to thwart our efforts, and when we have them where we want them, capture them and reveal the truth to them. Right now, we're hunting ghosts. Let me become a ghost with them, and at the right time, I will bring you in. That's when you'll make your move. Until then, you continue to carry out his majesty's orders and hunt them with heartless vigor," Aæsïa suggested.

"I suppose we don't have a choice," he submitted.

They waited patiently for a taxi to arrive. Aæsïa's eyes drifted to the scenery of the city, shying away as police vehicles drove past with speed to where Jhryde was last seen.

Then, distracting her from her thoughts and feelings, her ears perked at a conversation from the citizens walking up to the post with them. "I think it's crazy the Government hasn't come out with an official statement about it. I mean, seriously; their number-one enemy slaying an aethril in plain sight? It's crazy!" The one girl said to the other.

Before her friend could respond, Aæsïa looked over at them and interrupted, "Could you repeat that?" She asked.

"What, about the aethril? You didn't hear?" Her

friend asked.

"Apparently not," Kozek retorted. Aæsïa elbowed him sharply, reminding him to express some politeness.

"Who defeated an aethril?" She asked with urgency.

"Captain Lunar and that darklings who're wanted by the Empire."

Aæsïa was awestruck. "You're sure about this?!"

"Yeah, it's all over the news."

She was without words. Rather, she turned and started walking away from everyone. Her world was rocked at the sudden event that aethrils could not only be stopped, their enemies were the ones who accomplished it. A decade of attempt after attempt, and yet the Empire failed the only one attempt they made that could halt their advances. Their adversaries in this war, however, just found the biggest advantage over anyone who stood in their way – the power to stop an extraterrestrial threat. They were an even bigger threat than before. What no one else could tell, though, was whether she was panicked...

...Or excited...

Conspiracies

Jhryde sat at the table, casually eating his freshly prepared meal at a rather exquisite diner when two figures dressed in black suits sat down across from him. He smiled, recognizing the faces of Banïl and the human Adrian, whom Jhryde agreed to offer a wealth of services only he could provide in return for healing him so quickly.

"I congratulate you on your successful recovery," Banïl began. Jhryde didn't respond with anything more than a grin as he set his utensils down and gave them his attention.

"We will see to it you are rewarded handsomely for your efforts," Adrian added. "With our priorities presented to you, we can proceed to our next objective. As we stated before, payment and resources will be credited to you once the job is complete."

"As expected, fine officials," Jhryde said as he looked over at the waiter standing by the front door and gave him a nod. The waiter instinctively closed the blinds on the windows, then calmly ushered all other guests to the next room, refusing to answer any of their confused questions. Once the room was clear, Jhryde leaned forward on his elbows and eagerly awaited their next request.

"We need to locate the other humans and their darkling friends... And Captain Lunar as well," The brooding elf suggested. "I need you to not only locate them, but also ensure their safe arrival to Dominov. They may have entered D'Vnora already, but once you have them, make sure they are safely transported. Once you do so, we will arrange for your transportation as well, and move you to Vör so that you may begin to make a presence there. Distract the ones looking for them. Mislead them. Do whatever it takes."

"Anything else?"

"Yes," Adrian declared. "Make sure someone tells my brother that I'm alright, and that he's on the right side."

"That all?" The criminal overlord asked. Banïl smiled.

"Just make sure you don't tell anyone what we're

doing."

XVIII

The wrath of a God and Their Gods

No one knows the true nature of the aethrils, save for the Seers of the once-multitude, the Divine Logicians, the Uri'Kai.

A Multiple of Constants

Cassum

3 days ago

The Day of Judgment

"Wait! We already bought our tickets!" Ayela yelled as the group ran screaming and shouted. A run down, rusted truck with roaring engines began to roll forward. They had to rush after arriving in Cassum so early that morning to make it to the only transport on its way to the city of D'Vnora that day- only to get there too late. Jack was just as uninterested in prolonging their trip as the rest of them were. His stomach felt heavy and churned within, but such was expected when he dashed like a madman immediately after waking and eating.

"Come on!" Kamille complained as the vehicle picked up in speed and left them behind in seconds. "Assholes!" She barked as she slowed to a stop and kicked a rock on the road in its direction. Sweat glistened off her forehead, and she rested her hands on her knees as she tried to catch her breath. Her clothes were a mess, but so were the rest of them. They hadn't bathed in days and didn't exactly have the chance to change clothes that often.

"Well, that puts a thorn in our plans," Thillan declared as he placed his hands on his head and caught his breath. Liz doubled over, resting her hands on her knees as she breathed heavy.

"So now what?" Jack asked as he walked over to the rest of them. His vision started to get hazy and his stomach hurt worse than before.

"You need to sit," Liz ordered as she stood up straight and took a deep breath. He threw up his hand in protest and dismissed her unwarranted concern. He was in better shape than she gave him credit for. She rolled her eyes at him. "So now I assume we just start walking. You said it was half a day's journey or something, right Kamille?"

"More like almost a day. It's going to be risky. Some animals are day hunters, especially

392

the further away we get from the capital city," Kamille confirmed. They stood just outside the Cassum gates, and glowered at the massive city that hazily loomed over the horizon. The town was small, with only a few shops and refueling stations, and a few inns and apartments. There were homes closer to the eastern and western sectors of the town, and then the walls rose high above the buildings around the borders. It was small enough that they could make it back and forth between the northern and southern gates several times in one day.

Jack looked up at the clear skies and felt the rising heat of the day as the sun slowly climbed higher above the horizon. "Well, I'm not sure how much worse the day could possibly get," He complained. Kamille snickered.

"Let's just hope we don't get any mauth doogs or some other rabid creature to chase us down," she retorted.

"If one does, at least record the chase it gives me on something," he joked as a cool breeze picked up. It was subtle at first, but he started to notice how strikingly cold it was.

"That's strange," Ayela commented as she looked at Jack and Liz with furrowed brows. She seemed confused.

"I assume that's not normal weather."

"Obviously," Kamille spat. "I don't like it. We should move."

"Wait," Liz interrupted as she scoured her bag. "I can't find any water bottles."

"We have more, now-"

"Actually, love, we don't... We drank them already," Thillan corrected. Kamille sighed in frustration.

"Hell. I guess we need to go and get what we can while we're here," she iterated with and irritated tone. "Let's go."

"I mean, I'm sure we could make it without any-"

"No, I'm not risking someone passing out and us being stranded in the wilds just because we decided to be stupid," she declared as she stomped her way passed them. The rest followed suit.

Ayela stopped dead in her tracks, though, and stared into the sky with eyes wide with fear. Jack noticed her while the others continued past and walked back over to her. He followed her gaze and then noticed it: gray clouds that seemed to have appeared from nowhere slowly filling the sky. They were patchy at first, but as they thickened, dread filled his being. He knew what it meant. He knew what was paralyzing her with fear. The unimaginable was about to happen.

Before they could take another step, though, the wind started to pick up. It wasn't instantly, but they didn't make it too far before their slow breeze turned into strong winds throwing their hair about wildly. The sky darkened as clouds steadily took shape overhead. Jack's heart began to race as a sudden storm appeared, blue lightning crackling and thunder roaring where there wasn't any only moments before. At first strike of the alien lightning, the crowds panicked and ran for the closing gates.

"WE NEED TO RUN!!!" Thillan screamed. Terror twisted his features. The wind was howling, and flashes of memories of their first arrival to thaerv flooded Jack's mind with each peal of lightning. They ran, the only thing they knew they could do amidst the loud chaos and confusion of screaming crowds and booming thunder. Rain poured down overhead without warning, drenching them as they dashed for the gates.

He looked at the town behind them as he ran with Ayela and Liz, and saw the darkest portion of the clouds over the center. Lightning flashed, and both Jack and Liz saw the silhouette of a being they couldn't comprehend. They didn't understand what they saw, and it filled their hearts with terror. They didn't truly see the being; they felt it. They felt it walking forward, as if their senses were suddenly opened to it, and translated the presence as corresponding emotions deemed most appropriate to describe it. No words could do it total justice.

It was as if the being itself wore the storm clouds as its body and took the shape of what they assumed was a man. Its arms hovered where its shoulders should have been, and its legs were long and limber. Its head appeared as though it wore a mask concealed in the clouds and hovering above it was a halo ring made of the purest white light. Its rays gleamed through the storm that enshrouded it.

The gates were closing, but they made it out in plenty of time to escape the ensuing carnage that the aethril was about to wreak. The people of the town weren't going to make it before they closed, though. As she recognized that reality, Liz stopped dead in her tracks just outside the gate and looked back at them. Time seemed to move slowly. Everything seemed to move slowly. Her world paced longer as a vital question rooted itself in her mind.

"What about the people in that town?!" Liz shrieked. Jack and Ayela stopped, but Kamille and Thillan kept running. They knew what staying in that town meant, and they were right to keep going.

"Where are you going?!" Jack screamed after the two.

"HIDING! There's nothing we can do! If we stay, our mission is over!" Thillan barked back as he ran after Kamille. Ayela poised to run with them, but paused when she saw Jack stand beside Liz, and then she looked back towards the looming terror that spelled the doom of Cassum. Ayela had dealt with their kind before, and there wasn't a doubt in his mind that she was prepared to do it again.

"We have to do something!!!" Liz yelled over the whipping wind. He knew she was right. He wanted to run with the others, and Kamille and Thillan were right; if they died there, their mission was for nothing. For all logical reasons, their mission needed to come first... But...

"Then let's go!!!" Jack urged. He followed his lover into the fray of chaos. Ayela sighed in fearful frustration, and then rushed in after the humans, knowing that at the very least, her divine logic would prove of some use against the scourge of Enthedrill.

To Fight A Storm

It took seconds for the sky to darken, leaving no trace of sunlight to illuminate their path. The only source of visibility they had came from the streetlamps that dotted the sidewalks, but who knew how long those would last. The crowds that tried to rush out of the gate had dispersed, and they stood on an empty street, facing their godly opponent.

The winds whipped past their faces with a bitter cold bite, but adrenaline pumped through Jack's veins. The terror they stood in front of offered no chance to find a way to keep warm. His heart pounded in his chest with ferocity, and he scoured his mind for ideas to fight the celestial being.

The aethril didn't wait for them, though. They could hear the dying screams of the people in the distance as lightning struck. Everything happened faster than he needed it to, but he couldn't stop. He needed to do something.

"Listen, there's little time and too much to do!" Ayela began, shouting over the roaring winds. "While we're unnoticed, we need to get the gates open and these people out of here! Jack, come with me! Liz, go to that guard's tower and find a way to open the gate! Press all the buttons! Do whatever it takes!"

Liz didn't wait. She ran as quickly as she could and followed Ayela's instructions. Jack and Ayela, though... What could they possibly do in the face of such awesome terror?

"Jack, listen to me," Ayela said, grabbing his shoulders, "This is going to be the most dangerous force you've ever encountered! You're not going to be able to stop it, and neither am I! Our goal needs to be the people of this town."

"What are we going to do?!"

"Go around the town and get as many people as you can before it's too late! I... I'm going to fight it!"

For the briefest moment, he saw her memories flash before her eyes. Her trauma, her fear, her maelstrom of energy and anger... Who knew what he meant to her in that moment, but it didn't matter. For the briefest moment, her affection became clear. She made sure Liz wasn't watching, and did exactly what they promised they wouldn't ever do.

She kissed him.

And as quickly as she did, she ran towards the dark god with all the haste she could muster. He was struck, frozen in place and time. He looked over at Liz, conflict and conviction swirling in his heart as violently as the storm above. She hadn't noticed, focused on her objective at hand. He wanted to run to her, to run to the woman he forced himself to believe he loved, but it felt too late. The unthinkable had happened. The promise was broken. In the face of death, the truth was made known.

So he ran into the town, obeying Ayela's instruction as he frantically followed the sounds of screaming and terror. A flash caught his eye, though, and he saw the divine logician leap into the air unnaturally high. The light warped around her, and blades of invisible energy slashed at the aethril with such force, thunder clapped with deafening volume.

He struggled to maintain his balance, but he refused to be stopped. He refused to let this be the end. Would his mother be proud of his betrayal?

Would his mother approve of the crimson-haired elf that had entered his heart, and forced a shared space with Elizabeth? He never stopped to ask, though, if she would have even approved of Liz either.

Would she approve of such drastic risks to save the people of this town, though their efforts were seemingly in vain? A loud clap of thunder stole his attention, and he watched as Ayela flung to the ground, surrounded by an orb of energy. Lightning struck where she landed over and over, threatening to end every atom of the dancer's being, but it failed. The ground rippled towards the god as though it were a wave from the ocean, and exploded underneath it.

She leapt into the air once more, repeating her earlier attack, but when she finished, something unexplainable happened. From her outstretched palms, a beam of light with black at its core erupted, piercing the chest of the aethril with violent force. It was over almost as quickly as it began, but the aethril had not vanished. It was wounded, miraculously wounded, but the fight was not over.

His attention turned to an alley he nearly passed, though, when he heard crowds crying and shouting behind the buildings. Survivors. They amassed safely away from the fight, watching in awe and wonder at their hero. He wasn't sure how big the crowds were, and he didn't care. They were his objective.

"Come on!" He shouted, rushing over to them. "We need to move! Come to the north gate!"

"Are you crazy?! Do you see that thing out there?! Half the town is already dead!" A woman shouted above the chaos.

"We're safer here!"

"No-"

"LISTEN TO ME!" Jack screamed at the top of his lungs. "That thing is going to knock these buildings down on all of you if you don't move! Let's go!"

They listened, rushing behind him and pouring onto the streets as they frantically ran to the un-opened gate. Liz struggled, just as he'd predicted. How could they have hoped to have it open in time? They didn't understand their technology, they didn't know how to command their vehicles or their gates, they didn't understand anything.

"The gates aren't open!" Someone panicked.

"They will be, come on!" He barked, ignoring their fear.

They reached the gate suddenly, and Jack forced his way into the guard's tower to Liz. "It won't open, Jack!" She panicked. "I pressed the button over and over, hit every possible override, pulled every lever! It's stuck on something!"

He peered out the window and fought off his despair when he saw the pole lodged through the top of the gate. How did he not notice it? How could he have overlooked such a glaring and obvious obstacle?

"I've got it," Jack said, drawing the sword from its buckled holding at his hip. "When I yell to open, open it!"

"How in the Hell are you going to pry that thing out?!"

"I don't know, but I have to try! We have to try!"

"You don't have to do it alone," Thillan said, bursting through the control room's door with Kamille. He didn't have time to stop and ask how they made it over the wall, he was just glad they were there. "Let's go, Jack! Kamille will help Liz!"

He sighed in relief and smiled, and they rushed out of the tower to the walkway at the top of the wall. Charred bodies littered the path, struck by lightning when they weren't paying attention. They rushed around the corpses, and when they were close enough, they dropped onto the pole and started to work.

Another thunderclap stole his attention, and he watched as Ayela stood in the middle of the street against the aethril. It was an epic scene, one reserved for mythologies and ancient tales of heroes facing against impossible odds. Her stance was fierce, brave. Slowly, she lifted her arms.

It was a choreography orchestrated by the gods of fate and time. She lifted in the air, held by unseen strings of a cosmic puppeteer, and then the roads beneath her rippled. Arcs of the ground pierced through the road, and imitated the ripples under her.

With fluid motion, reciting an obscure dance as she hovered in place, pieces of the erected arcs flung at the aethril with blinding speed, paired with blades of wind and energy. Her power was truly divine, and she lived up to her fearsome reputation. The sounds from the aethril as it grunted, though, were unlike anything his mind could comprehend. There was nothing to compare it to. Clearly, her strange magic had an impact, but how far that impact was, he was unsure.

"Jack!" Thillan shouted. He quickly returned to his task, shoving the blade in the gate's wound, but try as they might the pole did not budge. When all hope seemed lost, in another impossible turn of events, a ship roared overhead with rope ladders dropping into the crowd. "YES!" Thillan shouted. "Captain Lunar!"

Another set of ladders dropped with a ragtag group of armed vigilantes clinging on. At the bottom of the crew was a man cloaked in a torn cloth with a hood over his head. Jack watched with hope in his heart as he drew a sword, glowing with a cyan hue, and slashed at the aethril without hesitation. A blade of energy resonating with the same color flung from his swipe, and struck the dark god with a thunderous blow.

He couldn't have prepared for or expected what came next. Its ethereal, indescribable sounds pierced all of their ears, and with lightning striking in any direction from its wound, it fell to the ground with such force, the world beneath them shook. The clouds quickly dissipated, and from where it fell came a beam of blue energy that shot straight into the sky.

In a single moment, the aethril was defeated. What had been described as an unstoppable horror had met its end by the hands of the ones it plagued. His gaze drifted down the street, watching as an exhausted Ayela limped towards the group. His heart jumped in his throat, and he followed Thillan back to the tower where the others waited for them.

In a single moment, things changed for the people of Enthedrill.

In a single moment, the tides had turned in the wars against the elves of thaerv.

In a single moment, Jack saw that there was something he, a mere mortal, could do for the people of this strange world...

He started to see it all...

Nothing was as it seemed...

A Moment's Peace

Only a couple hours had passed. They lingered longer than they liked, but they couldn't just leave the people of Cassum to pick up the mess and chaos by themselves, so they agreed to help for a little bit. It seemed like the chaos was unending, as if no matter where they went, something was bound to happen to cause mayhem and destruction. Everything from the pursuit in the capital, to the occupation of the sanctuary town, to the aethril raining down the wrath of the gods.

Jack felt the weight of the tragedy as he looked around at the rubble in the distance, the plumes of smoke rising into the sky. The Majjai agreed to help keep a watch for imperial ships as long as they were able, but once they were in radar, they would need to leave. The darklings would have to do the same.

"Jack," Liz said, calmly walking over to his side. He set down the pile of rubble he was carrying, and looked out once more at the wounded citizens that the Majjai and the darklings were helping. "Jack, I need to talk to you..."

He looked over at her, bearing his emotion in his expression. It was clear something was bothering her. Something beyond the noise and bitter destruction of Cassum around them. "What's going on?" He asked.

"...I saw what happened before Ayela went to fight the aethril." She revealed. His heart sank with despair. What was going to happen? How should he respond? Did he need to defend himself, defend Ayela? How could that at all be fair to Liz? Guilt shook his heart violently, and he hung his head in shame.

She lifted his eyes to hers, though, and searched his soul for something he couldn't possibly understand. "...Why?" She asked, tears welling up in her eyes. There was a sting on his lips. A sting on his hand when he reached for Ayela's in Asiat. A sting in his heart, knowing he betrayed the woman he loved, the woman he wanted to marry and spend his life with. How could he forgive himself? How could he possibly heal any of the wounds his actions left?

"I... There is nothing I could say that would

make it right," he said.

"No, there isn't," she answered honestly. "It hurts, Jack, I won't lie. I trusted you. I love you... But I also know you. I know that what we're going through... It's enough to make even the most noble person to think and act irrationally... I guess, what I'm trying to say, is that I forgive you. There's consequences for this, but I forgive you."

Tears started to fall from his cheeks. He didn't deserve it. He didn't deserve to have a woman like her in his life. She deserved so much more than he was capable of offering her, but she still stayed with him. Perhaps it was because she felt like he was all she had. Perhaps it was that she felt like there wasn't anyone else on earth that she could see herself with. Regardless of the reasoning, she pardoned him from the unpardonable, and wanted to work things out.

"Thank you," he said. With every ounce of compassion in her body, she wrapped her arms around him and held him as tightly as she could. He returned her embrace, and savored that moment.

"I love you, Jack. So much. Please don't betray that love," she cooed.

"I hate to break up this touching moment, but there's someone you need to meet," Kamille said as she walked over to them.

Behind her was the one who struck down the aethril, the hero of Enthedrill. He was tall, with an imposing stature. His shoulders were broad, and he could see the solid elf underneath the cloak and light armor he wore. He pulled back his hood, and a smirk crossed his rugged face. His nappy blonde hair was tied into a bun behind his head, with his bangs swept to the side out of his sapphire eyes.

"It's a pleasure, Mister Owens and Miss McOwens," he said with a thick accent akin to an Australian. "I'm Captain Lunar, leader of the Majjai."

It was like shaking hands with a hero out of a grand fable. Both Liz and Jack gawked with awe, amazed to meet such a legendary figure. "The pleasure's ours," Liz said.

"Ayela has told me much about you both. The first aliens to meet us aside from aethrils, and from a world not as developed as ours, no-less. It's quite the tale," Lunar commended. "I've discussed things with Thillan and Ayela. I have business with Asher too, so I'll be joining you."

"Glad to have you along," Kamille said with a smile. Then, with a sharp inhale, she picked up the pile Jack was carrying. "I'm going to finish taking this to the garbage pile. We're going to need to wrap things up soon and head out of here."

"Agreed. The empire's likely not far away now, and we don't need to bring a warfront to this town after all this. I'll have my people let the townsfolk know and we'll head out in fifteen minutes. Do you all have your things packed?"

"Yes. Thillan and Ayela made sure everything's ready to go at the tower," Kamille confirmed. "It wasn't easy carrying everything after these two and Ayela ran off to play hero," she added with a smirk.

"Good. Let's wrap up," Lunar ordered.

The ship's engines roared with intense volume, and the group watched from far outside the gate as it surfed through the skies with blinding speed. There was a loud pop as it burst some unknown bubble in the air, and before too long, it was little more than a speck on the horizon. Jack sighed in relief, and looked over at everyone as they began their trek to the looming city in the distance. It wasn't easy, and it wasn't anything that he could have ever expected, but even with the messy madness of their lives, he couldn't have imagined a more perfect cast of characters to take down a dark emperor.

They were outcasts, downtrodden and exhausted. They were each of them a mess in their own ways, with their problems in full display for everyone to see. But despite their problems, despite their disagreements and mistakes they've all made, they stuck together. Jack and Liz were among their number now too, and he pressed that question ever more in his mind, wondering if the answer now was different than when they first arrived...

...Did they truly want to go home?

XIX

The Illusion of Wealth

D'Vnora, an ironic image of the divide between those who hoard wealth, and those who suffer beneath their heavy feet.

In Search of the Undefinable

Sin. Debauchery. Dirty, dark, and wreaking of industrial stink. D'Vnora had reminded him more and more of earth in the ways that shouldn't have mattered. They'd been there for a few days, having snuck in similar to how they snuck out of the capital so long ago. Kamille used her connections to find them a safe place to hide out in while they searched high and low in the undercity for their illusive leader, Asher.

There was a haze in the dim amber streetlamps. Most people walked around, but there were a few cars and trucks that occasionally passed by. They had spent the better part of that day visiting bar after bar, and diner after diner, asking whatever tender stood behind the bar if they'd seen the whereabouts of anyone matching Asher's description. Most were clueless, but a few were able to point them in the right direction.

Lunar casually led them into his favorite diner and to a round booth in the back. Their feet ached once they sat down, but Jack paid it no mind. There were a few other patrons there with them, puffing away at cigars and slowly eating away at whatever meal they'd ordered. There was a little bit of chatter, but paired with the smooth music playing quietly on speakers above, it made for a good background noise.

"We've searched all over," Kamille complained. "I never understood how you two met up with each other as much as you did without communicating."

Thillan smirked. "Part of the practice, love. We can just, you know, read each other's mind."

"Right. And I'm Gorvon's daughter."

"Ooh, Ayela's got jokes now, does she? C'mon, then, let's hear some more Songrivan humor."

Ayela glared at Thillan playfully, but before they could continue their banter, Lunar cleared his throat, demanding their attention. "So what's the plan? You all just wanted to find Asher and then what?"

There was a moment of silence, but Kamille was the first to break it. "We've got a plan, yeah. It took a bit of planning on the go, but we think it might be just what we need to tip the scales of this war further in our favor, and it involves our guests here."

"Let's hear it, then."

"These humans… They're evidence against the empire's barbaric acts against the people and anyone who might usurp their regime. We plan to find Asher, and then get a hold of the leader of the darklings and show the humans to the public. Our leader, Ruat, is the only one we think could have the connections enough to verify the validity of this exposure to the public, and Asher is the only one who speaks to them," Kamille explained in a hushed tone.

"…That's it? You're going to do what you've always done and hope this one is the big break you've been needing?" Lunar said, almost chuckling from his disbelief. "Look, we've been fighting different battles for the same goals, but at some point, you've got to try something different. Your exposing of the government's involvement in sparking war with Durinveii did nothing to sway the people, almost. Sure, there's been protests and petitions, but the empire shut those down with brutal force. If anything, we've been a lot more active in fighting along the border, while you've had to take even more steps to stay hidden. Showing the citizens their emperor's dirty secrets isn't working like you think. You

417

need to flex your moral code a little."

"We just don't do that, mate," Thillan said. "We refuse to shed elvish blood. It's more than just a code. How can we say we're better than them if we're willing to resort to adding more violence?"

"I've liberated towns where they were too quick to join our cause, Thillan," Lunar said indignantly. You'd be surprised how few share your values. People have been walked on for far too long over far too little. A lot of them are past the point of peaceful protests. They want to take action, to pick up rifles and show the empire the pain they've been feeling this entire time. The only ones who are *really* seeing your messages are those in a place of privilege, and they don't want to upset their already upset lives. They're clinging desperately to what they have, because they know that this system benefits them over everyone else. They're not willing to let it go."

"...We have to try," Kamille insisted.

"Try as you might, you're focusing on the wrong people. It's not the smaller, wealthier ones in society that are going to achieve the change you seek; it's the ones they walk all over. The ones that the empire looks down on, and the ones who support the Majjai. In theory, sure, you've got a sound plan. All our factions could use a little more support and resource from the ones who have it at their disposal. In reality, it's just not going to work... Don't get me wrong, I'm not saying to kill them or something extreme like that, but unless they see a means of survival and prosperity in turning their backs on the government, they won't. They're safe. It's the ones under them that aren't. Take a look around in the undercity; it's easy to think that these are the ones you're reaching, but so many of them don't even turn on the TV to watch the news or the circus show that's running this country. They're trying to survive, trying to work, trying to stay under the radar so the cops don't come knocking on their doors. The gangs offer better protection for them than the darklings..."

They were silent, chewing on his words like they were a bitter meal they needed to survive off of. The truth was never easy to hear, but in that moment, something seemed to clear the smog in their minds. The gravity of the situation that the three of them found themselves in started to weigh, and Jack felt more pressured to find a way to salvage their conversation. The fact was, though, that Lunar was right. They were trying desperately to find a non-violent solution, they were almost deluding themselves...

But what if the darklings were right? What if Lunar was wrong, and more people would incline their ears to such an exposure? What if the knowledge of humanity to the nation helped to sway the public, especially after such violent efforts to recapture them?

"I trust in the darkling's plan," he said. They gave him more attention than he was comfortable with. "I think there's an underlying belief that the government isn't inherently honest with the public, sure. A lot of exposing their deeds wouldn't be enough to sway them, especially after suffering extreme attacks from these gods your people once worshipped. But what if we were exposed? What if they saw us fighting off the ones who wished the people harm? I was there with Liz and Ayela to fight an aethril, and the people saw us. There's no doubt in my mind that it left an impression. So what if they kept seeing things like that from us? It would let the pieces fall into place, especially after the news of the attack on Shamol by its own government."

"Oh, that story didn't make the headlines. The government is very good at picking what stories they share and don't share, and they're good at silencing anyone who speaks out and shows what happened."

"Except they haven't caught or stopped the darklings or the Majjai," Jack pointed out. "Captain, you and the darklings have some pretty deep access to imperial records, it sounds like. You get news of things that don't even get shown to the public. Is there a way you can make any of these headlines offical-looking?"

"No, not really… But whoever is running the darklings might be able to. Isn't that right, Thillan?"

"We've never tried before… We mostly do the work ourselves, or we infiltrate their broadcast networks. We've never tried to forge a leaked document before, though… The only one who would know the answer to that question is-"

"Asher, right?"

The answer came from a deep, velvet voice behind Jack. A man stood, tall and slender, with black hair finely combed and gelled. His face was clean-shaven, and he carried himself with more confidence than the ruler of the empire. He wore a gray hoodie, clean jeans, and stylish shoes he'd expect from someone who lived in the uppercity.

"Bloody brilliant timing!" Thillan exclaimed, rising from his seat and giving Asher the tightest hug he could muster. They laughed, and Asher pulled up a chair.

"Imagine my surprise when I heard my favorite group of people arrived and were poking around for me," he said as he sat down. "And with guests."

"It's a pleasure," Jack said, reaching out his hand.

"I'm Jack, and this is Liz."

"Hello, Jack and Liz. You could have guessed at this point that I'm Asher," he said with a half-smile. He leaned his elbows on the table and pressed his fingers together. "So... Why have I been summoned?"

"You're aware of what these two are, right?" Kamille began.

"I've heard chatter."

"Then you know the empire's after them with utmost urgency."

"Honestly, I'm surprised you've made it this far. The empire has no shortage of resource, and to have evaded them when the remaining efforts they can muster are being spent in this eager pursuit is impressive- even for darklings... And now we have you two. Humans. The second alien contact our world has experienced. The biggest question I have is why? Why search me out, and why does the empire want you two so badly?"

Ayela cleared her throat. "...The empire was planning to torture them when they were captured."

"Yes, I understand that, but why? What significance do these two have to the empire? I certainly hope you've thought this through," Asher rebuked. "Is there more to this plan than to just reunite with me?"

"Yes," Thillan said in a hushed tone. "We're hoping to make contact with Ruat."

Asher nearly burst into laughter. "You risked exposure, capture- even your very lives... To speak with Ruat?"

"To be totally honest, Asher, the empire's pursuit of these two has been making quite the upheaval in government activity. Part of their plan was fleshed out here and now by Jack, and I actually think it could have an impact," Lunar added.

"Alright, let's hear it."

Jack took a deep breath before he began. "The empire is convinced we're a danger to the empire. I have no doubt they would try to frame us as such if we were exposed here and now. But what if there was footage of us helping the people of the empire? Some already know our faces with what happened in Cassum, so it's reasonable to think they would be eager to spread the word on our good nature. Perhaps if we were to aid in fighting some of these organizations plaguing the undercity here, or if we were to join some sort of outreach group and help give to those in need, we could make an impact in a way that would not only give a positive view of us, but also of the darklings."

"Perhaps… But this is a big plan that requires a lot of steps. Additionally, we have the imps to look out for. Their officers and soldiers will not hesitate to take you in if they have a chance… But my question is why? Why would you help us when you have no real obligation to?"

Jack paused for a moment and mulled his response over. There was a lot that came to his mind, but the first and foremost was his mother's death. He lived his life to try and make up for what he did, and perhaps this was the underlying drive. Perhaps he could fight without fighting, and she would look upon him from paradise with pride.

"Look, we've lost a lot even before we arrived on this world. I've been fighting my whole life for those who can't fight for themselves, all to right wrongs I've made in my past," he admitted. Liz reached over and held his hand. "This is a chance to do something different… Maybe if I stop raising my fists for once and start learning how to give, everyone can benefit from it."

"So you're trying to be a better person by helping out a group of people you don't know," Asher retorted. "There's a huge number of organizations out there that do things for communities everywhere. What makes your idea any different? Why would it matter if two aliens joined them and helped the people out? You'd get exposure, become famous for your actions, and then what? Have the whole world see your faces and the *good people* you actually are? I'm sorry, but there's too much risk in this plan, and it'll only serve to put you both in the spotlight. I've seen what happens when people do good in the eyes of others, and while there would be a benefit, you'd likely end up dead and the empire would be ever closer to its goals of a single global nation under its banner... We've all seen the power those behind the scenes wield. We've seen the power of those who avoid the spotlight, who work in secret like us. You're just not a match for it."

Jack wasn't sure if he should have been offended or not. "What do you propose then? How are we going to cripple the empire and break the people's trust in it if not by showing how very wrong about us they are?"

"By not showing them anything. The people are safe right now- or, at least, as safe as they can be. The organizations and charities that help the people do so with legal standing, and they operate in full view of the public. They have reputations, ones that can be easily fractured if we give the empire ammunition such as aiding wanted criminals. The people they help would lose their only support."

"Asher-"

"No, Kamille, I cannot support this plan. These two have *no idea* about our world or how things work here. They don't realize the consequences for actions like this. They're warriors seeking to be peacekeepers... If you're on our side, Jack and Liz, then we need you here with us. We need you to stay out of sight and out of mind. The fights you participate in are grand in scale; taking on an aethril, leading the empire to break one of its eldest doctrines, and working to usurp the throne. The ones who are helping the public are the ones who need to be helping the public, not you. You don't know just how many dangers we face here, and with what you've been taking on, the empire would have a hard time trying to vilify. Reports within the imperial networks show the scale of your actions; aiding in the stopping of a nearly undefeatable aggressor, fending off the attack of a sakworm, and escaping the clutches of an imperial arrestor squadron."

"So what do you propose, then? Answer the man's question," Lunar urged.

"What do you know of the criminal organizations in Enthedrill?" Asher asked. Jack shrugged.

"Gangs, mobs, and larger groups. Not much, really."

"There's more than just that. Those groups

break down further. For instance, we've got murder gangs that cause mayhem and chaos in the towns outside the city. The worst of them are the Corpse Grinders; thugs with machines they designed themselves that go around and destroy towns if the mayors don't give into their high demands. No one knows where they hide at, and no one knows when they're coming. If a mayor spreads the word, they attack right away and hunt down any survivors. Fight a group like that, and you'll not only achieve your goal of publicly proving the empire's claims about you wrong, but you'll be a good person righting your wrongs-whatever they may be. You've got a sword at your hip, Jack, not a pencil or a pocketbook."

"The Corpse Grinders? That's a pretty tall order, there," Lunar snickered. He folded his arms across his chest and leaned back.

"Didn't they sack Nora'Vidale not that long ago?" Ayela asked. Asher shook his head and looked down.

"Nasty business, that one. The mayor was the only survivor. He was exposed for money laundering and sexual misconduct shortly after. Been rotting in prison since- and no, not the prison of Tai'Daloma."

"They've been getting bold lately. Nora'Vidale was a major trading town. There were darklings stationed there," Kamille said. She rubbed the base around her neck, as if to calm her anxiety about the thought of an attack by the gang.

"How would we fight against something like that?" Liz asked.

"Don't know, yet. It's not like we can just call the Majjai and go looking for them. We need to do some research first-"

Before he could finish, the door to the bar burst open with a man leaning on his knees. "THEY'RE HERE! THE BLOODY CORPSE GRINDERS ARE HERE!!!" He screamed when he caught his breath.

Panic set in, and the patrons scrambled to escape. Jack looked over at the others, all with wide eyes and paralyzing fear freezing their bodies. It was like they couldn't believe what they'd just heard.

"We need to move! Let's go!" Lunar shouted, rushing out of the booth. They all followed, and as they emerged from the bar, the most grueling, ear-piercing sounds erupted from the streets. What was he going to do? Evil didn't wait for him to prepare, it didn't wait for him to gather his weapons or his courage. It was there, now, rushing to snuff out his light. This was the moment Asher talked about. This was what he was meant to do. It didn't matter how he would accomplish it, it only mattered that he stood his ground and fought, no matter the outcome…

…The warrior within him was ready to awaken.

XX

The Gore of it All

Of the gangs that plague the empire, none are as ruthless and feared as the vicious and visceral murder gangs of the east.

Grinded Gears

Though the noise and chaos filled Jack's eyes and ears, and the stench of fumes from the churning and twisting of machines filled his nose. He couldn't pay attention to anything except the massive machines erupting from the ground only a couple miles away from them. They were massive and adorned like machines of death, rolling on six wheels each the size of a single truck, and armed with massive spiked grinding pins spinning wildly on the front, and already covered with blood. The screams grew louder as they quickly mowed through crowds, spraying the blood of whatever poor souls were in front of its path. They crumbled buildings, caring not for the damage they caused. No one really knew where they came from or left to, but they were all too aware of the damages left. In the distance, with demonic engines revving as they started carving a path through the city, Jack found himself paralyzed by fear.

"LET'S GO!!!" Ayela yelled. She shook him free from his frozen state and dragged him with her. The others, save for Liz, were far ahead of them. He turned and followed them with his heart pounding in his throat and adrenaline pumping through his veins. The shrieks and cries of absolute pain and horror behind him made his skin crawl. He wished that it wasn't reality. He wished that he didn't have to witness carnage like that.

Liz looked over her shoulder for a brief moment back to watch the machines plow through the crowds in their direction, and let out a panicked, shrill scream. It was her worst mistake; it caught the attention of one of drivers. He flipped open the hatch above the cockpit and observed them through a looking glass like they were from the dark ages and pointed straight ahead.

"Don't look back! Just keep moving!" Ayela panicked. They ran even harder, slipping through the stampeding crowd and leaping over obstacles that would have otherwise tripped them to their doom. His heart sank as he listened to the sounds of people being ground and reduced to nothing but puddles of blood and chunks of flesh. He looked around, hoping to find something to hide the others in.

They turned around onto a wide road and saw Asher and the others waving them into a hidden alley just out of the way enough. Jack only hoped the Grinders wouldn't chase after them. Only some of the crowd turned down the road with them. He looked back and made sure they were out of the line of sight of any of the Corpse Grinder's machines.

Just in time, they slipped into the alley, and they all rushed to the far end safely away from the road. His heart pounded as he heard the engines of carnage pass by the road they were on and then quickly fade into the distance. Then he noticed out of their group that Lunar was missing.

"Where's the captain?" He asked.

"He... He went to fight them off," Kamille explained between breaths. Suddenly, Jack's stomach churned at the thought of them hiding in safety while everyone else were being slaughtered like cattle.

"I'm going out there," he declared. Ayela grabbed his hand as he tried to walk out and held him back.

"Jack, what can you do?! How can you fight them off?! Captain Lunar is just one man, and so are you!" She shrieked. Her violet eyes were watery with panic, but his heart was settled. Memories flooded him of his brother and his parents, and stirred his emotions. He felt his warrior's soul itching to stop the menace before it could wreak anymore havoc.

"What are you planning on doing?!" Kamille panicked.

"Stopping them."

Thillan shook his head. "What do you think one man's gonna do against all of that?!"

"Sometimes, all it takes is just one man," He declared defiantly. Then Liz stood up and made her way over to him. Tears started to fill her eyes.

"You better come back to me," Liz demanded as she pressed her lips to his. Ayela gave her a mortified expression as tears began to stream down her cheeks. As soon as Liz pulled away, the redhead dashed over to him and held him in a tight embrace.

"Don't... You heard Liz... Don't die, Jack, or else," she threatened with a quivering voice. He could tell she wanted to say something else.

"I promise," Jack declared as he returned her embrace. Then, without warning, he turned and dashed out of the alley and into the chaos. He saw Ayela sobbing as he lost himself in the crowd. He wondered if Liz felt as heart-wrenched as she was.

But now, he was alone with no one there to have his back. No one came with him to watch over him or offer their aid- No, it was time he had the backs of others. He thought about what his brother would have done in his situation, and it wouldn't have been to hide while others were senselessly murdered by a rampaging gang. Adrian also wouldn't whine if there wasn't anyone there to help him or assist him. He never sought to be served, but rather, sought to serve others as best as he could.

As he ran towards the sounds of danger, he realized that he didn't have any plan. People only survived moments like this one in fiction, and even though his reality was almost a pure fantasy, it was still reality. He knew he wasn't likely to make it out alive, and fear began to numb his mind and heart. He felt helpless. He felt like he just wanted to let them grind his body into dust and just be done with everything. The pressure of acting without thinking along with the weight of its consequences began to sit heavy on his shoulders.

Don't give up.

It came at just the right moment, when the

familiar feelings of failure and self-deprecation began to settle, encouraging him to press on. It was the same voice that reminded him that nothing was the as it seemed, and the same voice that warned him his brother would be captured. It was one of the few things he was beginning to trust, and now it was telling him to not give up. Whether the owner of the whispery voice was a reman or something else, at the moment at least, it clearly had his back.

He ran as quickly as he could with resolve in his heart. No longer would he be held back by his plague of heavy emotions. He wouldn't stand by while others were in danger of suffering horrific death.

He focused, tracking the sounds of the engines of carnage as they rampaged through the undercity. Then, an explosion rocked the ground, nearly knocking him off his feet. He presumed something happened and caused one of them to crash. The other engines continued their pursuit; they weren't far. Even though he didn't know the city at all, he knew how to navigate crowded buildings and tight alleys. He ran across streets, dashed through passes between apartments, and leapt over street vendor's carts as he hunted the hunters. The sounds of screaming and grinding started to grow louder as he neared, and instinctively, he drew his sword and held it in a tight grip.

Turning a final corner, where the noise was the loudest, he found himself standing down the road from the Corpse Grinders, who were stopped from proceeding any further. He quickly found out why as a beam of bright, yellowish light zipped past and pierced the head of one of the pilots through a cracked windshield. Blood splattered against the glass, and the other machines' engines revved in response. Jack turned around to see the hero, Captain Lunar, holding a powerful rifle and unleashing a barrage of gunfire on their enemies, causing them enough chaos that the pilots needed to retreat into the machines and halt their progress for a moment. He was impressed at Lunar's tact and precise aim.

The crowds had just enough time to move on and safely escape their field of view – at least, most of them did. There were still enough that Jack saw the need to do something. But Lunar's wild attack on the murderous gangsters afforded him the time he needed to think and plan, and then come up with a backup plan.

He quickly scoured his surroundings amidst the carnage of bodies crushed by the trampling stampede, and the blood splattered all over buildings and the road from the machines merely a few hundred meters away, and saw a bike. He knew there was a bounty on his head and on Liz's, and surely the gangs knew about it or they wouldn't have obnoxiously pointed at Liz when she shrieked. He would use that to his advantage.

The gunfire stopped, and Lunar made a mad dash towards Jack. When he finally caught up, he kept his rifle trained on the machines. No doubt, they were waiting to see that Lunar wasn't present before they kicked their contraptions into gear again. It was clear that they feared Lunar, and perhaps they weren't confident that they could do anything to stop him even with their massive vehicles. Jack noted Lunar's impossible speed and dexterity, and wondered if Lunar was a practitioner of divine logic, like Ayela.

"What's the plan, human," Lunar asked.

"There's a vehicle over there," He began as he pointed to the motorcycle, though he didn't know how to pilot it. "I'm going to get their attention and have them chase and lead them away from the people. You lead the people to safety; I'll lead the Corpse Grinders down a different road. Don't forget Liz and the others; they're-"

"Hiding in that alley, I know," Lunar finished. "What if that plan doesn't work?"

He didn't hesitate. "I'll find a way to get onto

one of their machines, and I'll crash it into the others."

The sound of one of the massive engines of the grinders revving up again pulled their attention back towards them. Jack turned to see one of the pilots through the cracked windshield with a sickened grin on his face back into the cockpit.

"Boys, get the disclaimer goin'!" He yelled. "We got a high bounty prize to chase today!"

"You know what to do. I'll cover for you," Lunar offered as he popped off another couple of shots at them. The creatures erupted in laughter as some of them dodged his bullets. Others were pierced and fell limp either inside the cockpit or hung over the hatch at the top.

Jack didn't wait. As the rest of the citizens vanished in the broken-down, steel jungle, he rushed over to the bike and hopped on.

"The big blue button right in front of you! Pull the right trigger to go, the left trigger to stop after you let go of the right one!" Lunar called out as he unleashed another barrage of bullets. Jack followed his instructions and pressed the large, silver-lined blue button. The engine roared to life, filling his eardrums with a low, rumbling hum that revved ferociously as he pulled the trigger. Without hesitating, he knocked the kick-stand back and zoomed off down the streets.

It was just in time, too, as the machines growled viciously and gave chase to the plucky rider, barely missing Lunar and ripping off the faces of the buildings they rolled past. Jack's heart pounded in his throat as the adrenaline kicked in, and his focus became hyper as he plotted each move. It was luck that he didn't run into any dead ends.

"Thank you for attending our feature, ladies and gentlemen," A voice called over a loudspeaker from the Corpse Grinders. The casualness of his tone sent chills down his spine. *"The provisions of our presentation today may cause heavy stress and induced cardiac arrest, as well as painful lacerations and intense negative nerve stimulation. Wavers are handed out by special uniformed recruiters at various locations, and safety measures are to be performed at your own discretion. Failure to comply may result in serious medical injury and death. We excite you today by introducing a special guest with a high net value and look forward to posting his mortified image all over vid screens around the city later this day! Thank you, and good luck!"*

Luck.

That was what he needed.

Just a little bit of good luck…

A Reincarnated Revelation

The crowds died down, and the sounds of the machines grew dimmer as they rolled off in the distance. The announcement from the Corpse Grinders' contraptions in the distance filled Liz's ears, and her heart sank at the thought of his death, but she stayed behind for a reason. She knew him. She knew he would find a way out of his situation, and she knew he would make it back to them. But her mission now was to ensure the safety of those with her.

"The roads are clear," she declared. "Let's move."

"Lead the way." Kamille urged.

She peaked around the corner, and when she saw no one else, she led the darklings in a mad dash in the direction the crowds went. Without declaration, Lunar dropped down in front of them, rifle in hand and a sly grin on his face. Her heart skipped a beat, and her mind raced with frightened thoughts of Jack's well-being. She was sure, though, that if he wasn't okay, Lunar's expression would have looked much different once he saw her.

"Follow me," he commanded as he turned to run. She didn't have time to ask questions, only to follow his lead. She relied on his knowledge of the city's layout. Her heart burned a little as he took charge though. She felt the energizing effects of being the hero that everyone followed and didn't appreciate having that role suddenly taken from her. As soon as those feelings emerged, though, she batted them down. He knew the city. He knew thaerv. More than that, he'd been fighting this war longer than she'd been a resident on his world.

True to her gut-feeling, he quickly led them through the undercity and even away from the crowds. They all kept their heads on a swivel and made sure they weren't being pursued by anyone or anything out of the ordinary.

"Did he have a plan?" Kamille asked. Lunar shook his head no, and then held up a hand, causing them all to silently come to a stop. Liz peered around his shoulder and checked the surrounding streets of the four-way intersection.

445

There wasn't a soul in sight until she peaked around the corner he was looking down. Down the street were men dressed in fine suits, talking amongst themselves as if they were searching hard for someone amidst all the chaos.

"Who are they?" She asked as she stepped back and brushed loose strands of hair out of her face.

"Other gang members. They're not with the Corpse Grinders... They're too armed and finely dressed. These guys might be here for a different reason," Lunar assumed.

Asher didn't look up as he spoke. "Grey suits, high powered automatic rifles, and slicked-back hair. Am I right?" Lunar nodded in affirmation. "They're Jhryde's men."

Thillan's eyes widened. "Jhryde? Are you-

"I am serious. They don't show up in the undercity either unless they're hunting. Perhaps we can make an ally out of them," Asher suggested. Liz tied up her hair into a ponytail and placed a hand on Lunar's shoulder, getting his attention.

"Perhaps one of us distracts them while everyone else sneaks off?" She offered.

"Why?"

"What if they aren't friendly?" Liz asked, looking back over at Kamille. "We made it this far, and Jack and I are the ones putting all of you in so much danger. Perhaps we remove

446

ourselves from this equation, and you live to fight Enthedrill another day."

"No, it's not an option anymore," Ayela defied.

"Why are you so Hell-bent on protecting them?!" Kamille growled, pinning the red-haired woman to the wall abruptly. Lunar and Asher placed hands on her shoulders and gave her firm looks. Kamille didn't back down this time.

"...Because... Because it's the right thing to do," She stammered as she looked over at Liz. "They didn't do anything wrong... They got us to finally move forward with something other than hiding and revealing petty secrets to the public, and they motivated us to find our founder... And I... I... I think I-"

"Ayela, they're making choices that are compromising our objectives! They're throwing themselves into danger, and while I admire their motives, they risk exposing us, and destroying everything we've worked so hard for! Is that worth the risk?! Is it worth it to save these humans over and over again, when they rush into danger like children?!"

"Yes! They didn't ask to come here! It just happened! Maybe they are an answer to our problems! Maybe we're an answer to theirs!" Ayela defended.

"You try too hard to protect them, Ayela..."

Thillan said in Kamille's defense.

"...It's not even that... I know we've all suffered, but for me, it's more... It's more than just a mission, and it's more than exposing an evil man. It's justice for the lives of people who have the same skin color I do. And it's hard to trust anyone who hasn't put any thought into their actions..." Kamille explained. Liz's heart sank. She knew the darkling was right.

"You see too much evil in everyone you don't know," Asher barked back. Kamille threw their hands off her shoulders and stepped back. Liz kept her wounds internal. She refused to let them see the hurt they caused. It was clear they didn't trust either of them yet, and she didn't blame them. Her loyalties were entirely to Jack. If any of them were dying, and she had to choose between them or Jack, she would choose him.

"And you?" Lunar asked as he looked at Liz. "What do you see in all of this? This squabble between supposed allies? Two of them fight against harsh social injustice, another fights to protect everyone because she can't bear to see people be hurt, and the other shows no emotion at all. Meanwhile, we sit here on the sidelines and watch them pick each other apart."

They were all silent as Lunar spoke. Each looked down in shame. He spoke a bitter truth that was hard for them to swallow. Even Asher expressed a little shame in his actions. "While you were all bickering, those gangsters moved on and headed in the opposite direction," Lunar added. "This is a fragile time, and things are being set in motion that cannot be undone. Fighting with ourselves... Dividing ourselves doesn't help anything. Either stick to the mission or leave. But if you're just going to attack each other, I will gun you down myself. We don't have room for traitors."

"You know what I see?" Liz started, demanding all of their attention. "I see a group of people who were hurt in some way, and don't want others to hurt like them. I see people who are trying their best in the only way they know... I see an inspiration for myself, who only wanted to go to a home she doesn't have anymore. Now I want to fight for a home others can go to... One that others can call a home. To help people keep something that Jack and I lost... That's what I see."

"None of us are perfect. That's why we need each other," Ayela pointed out as she stood beside Liz.

"And you?" Liz asked, looking over at Lunar. "What do you see?"

"People who need to find out who they are on

the inside, and why the universe chose them," he responded effortlessly. Liz saw Ayela cringe a little at his statement, but she hid it well. "Let's keep moving," he said, urging the group to press on. She noticed the sounds of the machines of the Corpse Grinders still plowing through the city.

"What happened with Jack?" She asked.

"He hopped on a bike and led the Grinders on a chase. He's a capable man. You've got yourself a keeper," he encouraged. She smiled warmly. Her Jack was still alive and was giving them something to chase. At least, that was her desperate hope. "Now let's get going."

"Actually," a sly, slithering voice said from behind the corner. The gangsters, all dressed in their slick grey suits and armed with their powerful rifles, stepped around and stopped them before they could take another step forward. "We would like for you to come with us."

"You all work for Jhryde?" Asher asked, his fists clenched and ready to fight. The man snickered.

"Yeah. But you don't gotta worry," they reassured. Liz watched Lunar relax a little and take his hand out of his pocket. "We're on your side. We're here on special orders from friends in high places, and we're to deliver you to the sovereign nation of Dominov to meet with contacts there."

They all looked at each other with confused expressions. Perhaps Ruat had grown tired of waiting for them to find the phenomenon of a leader and sent lackies to collect them. Liz didn't have the slightest clue. Ayela looked over in the direction of the sounds of the Corpse Grinders with concern written all over her face, then she looked back over at Liz.

"Hold on, there's only one of the humans... We need the other one, and we're on a time crunch," the gangsters revealed. "Where's he gone to?"

"Hear the machines in the distance?" Lunar pointed out.

"You're serious?! They still chasin' him?!"

"Yeah."

"We can blow their machines to bits and-"

"No! No death. You might be able to do that on your own terms, but we won't have blood on our hands," Asher protested with urgency. The leader of the gangsters raised an eyebrow.

"You sure? We won't make it in time otherwise," they suggested. Ayela looked down for a moment, pondering their options. Then she looked up towards the machines.

"I'll go get him and bring him to Dominov," she declared.

"Ayela, no-"

"There's no time! You all have to leave..." She

said. She refused to give in to their concerns.

"You might die, Ayela," Liz said, gently grabbing her hand. Ayela turned to see the concern in her eyes.

"I know," she said. She paused for a moment, and with a wounded expression, added, "He's a lucky guy... And you're a lucky girl. If I were in your shoes, I'd want someone to bring him back to me safely too," she said with a forced smile. Then, without waiting for a response, she ran off towards the sound of danger... Liz stood there with shock. What kind of signal was she giving her?

"We need to move now. There can be questions later," Asher said, shoving past them and following the gangsters. Liz followed urgently as they dashed around the corner. She was confused. Her heart was torn. She wanted Jack to be protected, but all she could think of was the kiss Ayela gave Jack. Her heart burned, and she panicked. Was she going to lose Jack, too? Was he going to be taken from her by Ayela? Was she trying to admit those feelings to Liz? She didn't want to believe it, but after spending so much time together and getting to know each other so intimately over the past few weeks, it started to make sense...

…Ayela had fallen in love with Jack…

XXI

The Nature of Reality

None promised to confuse the nature of reality like the dancer - a divine logician capable of warping the fabric of space and time to their supernatural will.

Mercy For the Merciless

The wind whipped past Jack's face with ferocity and left him barely able to keep his eyes open. He'd been riding for nearly an hour, and the Grinders relentlessly pursued him past what he thought they'd be willing to. And they were relentless indeed, greedy for the bounty that laid on his head – dead or alive, he presumed. But he wasn't going to give in. He'd gotten this far, and he was sure Liz and the others were safe. It was time for him to make it to safety and find his way over to his people.

The hour he'd been riding gave him plenty of time amidst the panic and anxiety to study the bike, though he couldn't read a single letter of the language written on its gauges. He had gotten used to its feel, its weight, and the way it rode. Eventually, though, it seemed it would end up turning off. There was a gauge he'd noticed that slowly shifted from one end of the meter to another. He assumed it was meant to represent fuel or power.

"You're gonna give up soon, kid!" One of the pilots chasing him yelled. Jack only responded by holding up his middle finger to them and pulling the throttle harder. They were right, though. He felt exhaustion draining his body of the energy he needed to keep the chase going. He was determined, but he didn't know how much longer he could keep it up.

He watched as a ship lifted into the air off in the distance and quickly flew past him overhead. He couldn't shake the feeling that he should have been on that ship, but he was stuck running from the monsters that forced families to evacuate their homes. As far as he was concerned, he was alone in his flight. Eventually, though, his run would come to an end. He just hoped that there would be some sort of rescue before that end rushed to meet him.

Then he noticed a flash in the distance and ducked his head as a blast of red energy seared past him and slammed into one of the machine's grinders, piercing it through and emerging out the other side. The machine stumbled and quickly rolled to a rough halt as the remaining two machines closed in to fill the gap and fit snug into the shrinking confines of the street he led them down. It was as if someone heard his despair and had an answer for it. He looked in the direction of where the blast came from and saw the silhouette of a woman on top of one of the buildings with crimson hair flowing in the wind. His heart skipped a beat. He recognized her fiery mane anywhere.

He watched as Ayela performed a highly chore-ographed dance. As thrust her hand downward, a ripple flowed from the building she was standing on, and then past him as if the road were an ocean he was on the surface of.

Then, in an instant, the ripple exploded under the machines and violently tore the wheels, tines, and grinders from under them until they plopped onto the ground and slid to a grinding halt. He continued forward, but not before looking back to see if any of the gangsters were killed in the wreckage. Much to his surprise, they were all in prime condition as they crawled out of the hatches. While he was considering their miraculous survival, he became keenly aware of an alarming fact; Ayela used her powers. That meant that somewhere, the government caught them on their sensors.

He wasted no time and pressed on, leaving the

gangsters to deal with their own. It was only a few moments before he arrived at the building she'd vanished into. Quickly, he got off the bike and ran through the front door, and almost right into Ayela in the same manner as when they first met.

She smiled and sighed in relief, and then embraced him in a tight hug. "Don't go running off to meet death so quickly, you idiot," she scolded. He snickered, but before he had the chance to speak, the ground began to rumble and shake.

Jack swore as he looked out the front door. One last Corpse Grinder emerged from the ground directly under where his bike was. Though the machine was much smaller – only big enough for one and only one pilot – it consumed the bike entirely in its silvery grinders. The hatch folded back behind the pilot, and light flashed off its red paint as it spun around, headlamps flickering to life as it searched the slowly darkening surroundings and inside the buildings for where Jack might have gone. He hadn't realized that night was beginning to fall.

He didn't wait for them to find the two, though. He grabbed Ayela's hand and rushed into the dark, unlit halls of the abandoned building they stood in. Ayela turned to see the survivors of the wreck pointing their comrade towards the building Jack went into, and yelped as they rammed through the front door. "RUN!!!" Jack screamed as he shoved her out of the way and leapt into the air. He landed on the pilot as the small grinder whipped past her and slammed into the far wall.

The wind was knocked out of her when she was thrown on the floor, and she was confused for a moment when the small explosion happened after the Grinder bike crashed into the wall. Scarlet locks fell over her face in a nappy mess, and dirt covered her clothes and her skin, but nothing compared to the dread that poured from her heart. As her vision cleared, her sights settled on the flaming wreck. Her heart sank. Numbness instantaneously struck her body. She feared the worst.

"...Jack?" She yelped pathetically, hoping the impossible happened. There was no response.

"Jack?!" She panicked. Tears swelled in her eyes as she tried to stand to her feet, but she groaned as pain shot up her arm. She looked down to see a piece of shrapnel pierced through her forearm. Every movement she made was excruciating. The pain was so intense, she didn't see the pilot who survived the crash. She winced as she stood to her feet, and then began to panic when she saw the Corpse Grinder stumble to his feet and crack his back. His angry gaze rested on her.

She stumbled back and then tripped over a chunk of debris and fell. The jerky movements jostled the shrapnel and sent pangs of searing pain up her arm. She grunted and grit her teeth as she held her arm. She didn't notice the pilot as he marched his way over to her. He pinned her down, and clenched her throat with an iron grip that tightened as the seconds passed by.

"Yer gonna pay for that, street urchin!" He barked in pure rage. She gasped for breath. His voice was muffled in the pain, and only worsened as she struggled for air. Her heart sank further at the realization that he got up, and not Jack. She was truly scared.

Don't be afraid.

A voice whispered to her. It meant nothing if she wasn't going to survive. Her heart throbbed. She felt awful that she let herself feel so strongly for him... That she wished she was the one he craved, that she was the one he pursued his affection for...

Then, at the last possible second, when everything in her vision started to get dark, Jack tackled the pilot to the ground with an angry battle cry. Blood streamed down his head from the crash, but he seemed to ignore it as he threw the pilot off of her. There he was; a human man that was dwarfed by one of the worst criminals on thaerv, had brought down the hardened murderer with his sheer brute force. Humans were packed full of surprises she couldn't begin to predict. Without hesitation, he drew his sword, much to her terror. He didn't hesitate, rushing at the grinder while he drew a pistol.

Jack quickly side-stepped as the pilot fired his first shot, and then swung the sword at his arm before he had the chance to re-aim at Ayela. The arm plopped on the ground in front of her, blood splattering all over. Her stomach churned at the sight and her heart throbbed with panic. Tears swelled in her eyes as Jack poised the blade to impale his screaming and agonized opponent. She couldn't bare to see him meet his enemies where they were at. She couldn't bare to see him coat his hands with the blood of his enemies, like so many heroes had done before. She wanted to cling to his innocence, to help him retain his spotless soul.

"WAIT!!!" She cried, jumping up to her feet and dashing in front of Jack. "Don't do it! Please! You're not like them!"

"MOVE, AYELA!!!" He barked.

"NO!" She protested, holding out her arms. "Your point was made! Please don't do this!"

He huffed angrily, but then his senses came to him as he listened to the Grinder's screams. Her sobs quickened. He noticed the piece of metal piercing her arm and watched as the wounded reman fell to his knees holding his wound.

"I can't feel my arm!" He cried pathetically. "Please, have mercy on me!"

Jack's bloodlust faded, and his humanity returned to him... And then there was shame. He was ashamed that he'd become so violent. Tears filled his eyes as he sheathed the sword and gently ushered Ayela away from him.

"I'm sorry," he said to the pilot as he held her hand and led her towards the rubble of the front door he'd crashed through.

"It hurts so much," she complained. Her face reflected how she felt, and she held her arm tenderly as if it would make the pain go away.

"We're going to get some help," Jack promised. As they left the building, though, they saw flashes of white-and-red swirling lights. Law enforcement rode up to the crash sight of the biggest Corpse Grinders vehicles. Without warning, they opened fire on the cops with weapons they'd kept hidden in their pursuit. It seemed they savored death by their machines more than by rifles that could have easily saved them from Lunar's attack. A firefight between the two groups began. Ayela and Jack hid behind larger piles of rubble.

He looked down the street and saw more officers approaching in armored trucks, and saw an opportunity they may not have gotten elsewhere. "No," Ayela protested. "They'll arrest us." He pulled away and gave her a confused look.

"You're wounded, Ayela. Don't be stupid," he spat. "Besides, the guy in this building needs help too."

"You don't understand; we're wanted! They will take us directly to the people who want us captured! Look," she demanded as she ripped the piece of shrapnel out of her arm with a blood-curdling scream. After a few seconds, when she collected herself just enough, she encouraged him to escape; "Just wrap it up and let's go!"

He looked at her eyes, so full of pain and sorrow, yet full of heart and passion. Her face was dirty with the tears that streaked it, catching particles of dust that filled the air from the wreckage. He saw a woman who was desperate to see her people free and wouldn't give in to those who wanted to change her vision, even if it meant that she would suffer.

465

He looked back to see how much time they had, then drew his sword. He carefully sliced the cloth around his waste and used the scraps to wrap the bleeding wound on her arm, despite her whimpers and tightened grip on his arm.

"Your head-"

"Let's go!" Jack ordered. He pushed her in the direction they were escaping in, and then looked back at the cops who were just arriving. He screamed and waved for them to check inside the building they just left. Once they heard him, he turned and followed after Ayela, and vanished into the steel jungle of the undercity, where they hid away from a violent world that sought to taint their hearts and spill their guts...

A Silent Admission

Hours passed, and nightfall hit D'Vnora. To be fair, the undercity never saw much sunlight to begin with, but they got enough that they could tell when it was day and when it was night. Streetlamps illuminated the empty roads, and vehicles were just barely starting to roam the streets once more. People were wary after the trauma they were forced to endure. Families grieved openly on the sidewalks, and others did what they could to repair the damage caused. A lot of people talked about Jack and Captain Lunar, and their valiant efforts at detracting the gangsters until law enforcement arrived and, eventually, the military. The Corpse Grinders that attacked the city were quickly put down, and their bodies were disposed of along with their deadly vehicles.

Since the attack of the Corpse Grinders, law enforcement constantly checked the streets for anything that could resemble an uprising, and wily citizens remained indoors at the preservation of their lives. Jack and Ayela were hiding in one of the abandoned apartment buildings, occasionally peering out of the window while they waited, leaving only the light from the streetlamps outside to let them see around the room. Everything was silent save for the occasional car or truck that passed by. Not even a rodent or insect peaked in to bother them.

"Thanks again," Ayela said as she leaned her head on Jack's shoulder. They had made small talk every so often, but Jack encouraged her to rest and recover.

"It's no problem, Ayela. Thank you for coming back for me," Jack said. "You said the others are going to Dominov?"

"Yeah. Some mobsters from Jhryde, a powerful crimelord, came and picked them up," Ayela answered truthfully.

"I think I saw their ship leave... How were we planning on getting to them?" Jack asked with a sigh.

"I didn't think that far ahead," she revealed. "The plan was really to make sure you weren't minced meat."

"At least we've got that going for us," Jack said with a chuckle. Ayela tried to chuckle with him but ended up whimpering from her arm. The pain wasn't as sharp for her now, but it still ached enough that she needed to be careful. He felt bad. "We'll probably stay the night here, if I had to guess."

"What, in this apartment room? …I mean, there's not really anywhere else in the city we can go either…" Ayela pointed out. A small police dropship passed by, rumbling the building as it drew close and flew away.

"Right. Why is this kind of craziness allowed in this city? Why is this a major hold?"

She sighed at his question. "It's the Empire…" She started to explain. "We're pretty sure they let it get like this on purpose. It's not just here, either: every major hold has something deeply wrong with it. Here, it's violence. Murder. People just get so angry here, and there's so much stress because of poverty. The upper city isn't so bad, but there's still enough that it's not exactly everyone's first choice to move here. People usually move here out of financial necessity… And this city doesn't handle newcomers very well."

"But why allow it? Why does the Empire let it happen? And can't they just move to a town or a village or something? Hell, let them leave the country even! This is madness…"

"…I don't know… I mean, there's government servers in this city with pretty deep secrets, but it doesn't explain why there's allowed to be such gaps in our social climate… Here, most people are poor… Scavengers, even. There's a few in the working class of citizens that make a decent living. They try to make things comfortable in pockets of society in random places, but those are few and far between. The richest live in the capital or in Laviport… The other cities have their own issues. It's like our Emperor just doesn't care."

Jack was silent as he pondered her revelations. "I don't understand either… What does the government gain from all this?"

"Control, I'd guess… I mean, there is something else we've uncovered."

"Oh?"

"Yeah. They're older documents from two Emperors ago… About thirty years. They detail this plan to 'reshape the Empire under a new regime.' One that would bring all people into one belief, one mindset, completely obedient and submissive to its whims. But its methods of getting there looked so different than what we have now… It's like the Emperor is trying to

470

let everyone destroy themselves," Ayela observed. "And we can't understand why."

"Hmm... I don't see why either, but here's an idea: maybe he's trying to thin out the herd, so-to-speak."

Ayela raised an eyebrow at him. "What do you mean?" She asked.

"I mean, he's waging war with two nations, trying to take them over, while also carelessly waging war with a violent rebellion in his own country. As a leader, he would still need to tend to domestic affairs, but he doesn't. It seems intentional, and perhaps it's meant to let the lesser classes – the poor, homeless, and needy – kill themselves off or die out... I'm not sure, even that doesn't make sense," Jack said. He realized he contradicted himself. Ayela chuckled and winced.

"Nothing he does makes sense. If it did, today probably wouldn't have happened... Violence isn't even the worst thing that happens in D'Vnora."

"Do I want to know?"

"Drugs are prevalent here... And sex trafficking," she revealed. "It's disgusting, and you'd never know who's guilty of it."

"I believe you," Jack said. "I can't imagine how rough that is."

"Yeah… What's your world like with things like this?" She asked. He took a deep breath as he thought of where to start.

"It's… It's got its ups and downs… I guess, even you'd miss your home if you'd lost it the way I did," he explained. She was silent, not knowing how to respond.

"We'll get some food in the morning and then head out. We'll have to find our own way to Dominov, and we need to be as cautious as we can, and we can't get discovered by anyone."

"You got it," Jack confirmed as he laid down beside her.

She was silent as she pondered what he'd told her. Her thoughts were swirling and buzzing with everything that transpired that day. He survived. Because he survived, she survived. She pondered the feeling in her heart. She had affection for him. She wanted to be with him, but she started to believe that it wasn't wrong. They'd spent so much time together, constantly with each other, and she'd gotten to know him well. As she drifted to sleep, she whispered a truth in her mind that she wondered if it had always been there…

…I love you, Jack Owens…

XXII

Children of Destiny

The laws of destiny and prophecy have gathered those to their fates - for life, for death, and the adventure in between.

An Inquisitorial Patriot

News spread quickly in Enthedrill, especially if it involved one of the major cities of the mainland. D'Vnora was no exception. Kozek watched in horror as the vid playing on his phone flashed images of destruction and chaos wreaked across the undercity, caused by one of the most destructive gangs that surfaced in his beloved nation; the Corpse Grinders. He knew the Emperor was intentional about allowing some of the cities to fall into the muck and mire of crime, corruption and death, but when was it too far? When was the sigil and power not worth it any longer? Or was there another reason that the Emperor kept to himself?

Never-the-less, he remained loyal to the throne, no matter who sat on it. He worried about Semus, who left for D'Vnora after she saw what she believed to be the faces of a human and the blood elf all over the news, claiming that they were there. He couldn't deny the energy readings; there was someone there with divine logic, and they used it to fight off the criminals. There were only a few people registered in the Imperial watch list, and Ayela's face was compared to recordings of a girl in the distance with strikingly similar hair performing a routine characteristic of dancers.

She was going to meet up with them there somehow and begin the plan he set in place. Meanwhile, he left for Dominov to follow reports and sightings of the other human. It seemed the group had split up, since the reports mentioned that Ayela and the brother of their human friend were missing from the group. He wondered how long they thought they would stay hidden.

He stared out the large glass panes of the bridge he stood in – a massive cockpit for the Empire's massive airships that soared through the skies of Thaerv over Enthedrill. Movement was all around; pilots, navigators, technical officers, and the Captain. The Captain was a woman nearly a head shorter than him, but just as strong and capable a leader as he was. She had dark brown hair, crystal colored eyes, and tanned skin. She was a native to Durinveii, but moved to

Enthedrill at a young age. She enlisted as soon as she was able, and now sits comfortably as captain of a fine airship.

"Captain Caelee Khost," Kozek declared as the woman, dressed in her most elegant uniform, emerged from the captain's quarters and walked up to his side.

"It's a pleasure... I'm sorry, they never told me your name or rank," she responded rather awkwardly.

"I have none. Technically, I don't exist," he revealed as he fixed his long Inquisitor's coat and smoothed some of the unwanted creases out. Silence followed.

"Captain, we will be arriving at the Dominov port-city within the hour," One of the navigators declared. Kozek grinned with eager anticipation. Soon, he'll have his escaped prey back into his caged grasp, and he'll have redeemed himself to his emperor.

"Good. Begin the docking procedures. Hail port control with our clearance codes and military signature, and make a request for replenishing supplies and fuel," Caelee ordered.

"Aye, ma'am."

"Master, shall we begin detailing your visiting plans?" Caelee asked, turning to the inquisitor.

"There's no need, Captain. My stay in Dominov will last longer than yours. You may depart without my presence. Thank you for transporting me; the Emperor will recognize your service and reward you richly for it," Kozek declared as he turned to exit the bridge. He hoped they attempted to resist. He hoped he had a chance to make them suffer before bringing them back to the one who wanted their heads. There would be violence in Dominov. The darklings would suffer at his hands for the ways they hurt Enthedrill's citizens. And once the Emperor was finished with them, he would end them slowly and painfully.

Oh, What Cursed Fate

He quickly made his way through the dense crowds after stepping off the boarding ramp. The inside of the terminal building where all docks and gates connected was massive, and yet, it was more packed with people than the busiest streets of D'Vnora's undercity. The building was large enough that it took him nearly a half an hour just to navigate through to the long and winding halls just to get to the tram, and even getting into the trams was difficult. He'd been to Dominov plenty of times, and had even traveled into Port-City on almost every visit, but it was never as crowded as it was this day.

As he examined the tags on people's bags, the clothing styles, and even hair-styles, he noticed something startling; they were mostly Enthedrillan citizens that were entering the city, and mostly Durinvan and Songrivan citizens leaving. Were these people trying to escape the Empire? Was their opinion of his powerful and sovereign government so low, that they wished to revoke the security and safety of Imperial control? His heart began to sink with heaviness, though he betrayed no emotion.

He stepped off the tram and made his way to the front doors, where a government caravan was waiting for him. There was no delay in driving off and entering the busy highways of the massive city – a city big enough to rival Bavylune. He was glad to be out of the noise and uncomfortable heat of so many bodies close around him. In the cabin of the vehicle, even the hum of the engine was silent, and the smell was fresh and pleasing. He could think clearly.

Before they got too far, though, his phone vibrated in his pocket. He pulled it out to see a message from Semus, detailing that she found their location and was in the process of setting up a meeting with them. He grinned as his plan was coming together, glad to finally have at least two of the largest insurrectionists to the Empire securely pressed under his thumb. They weren't even aware of the pressure they had found themselves in.

"Sir," the driver called from the front seat.

There was a window in a wall that separated the driver's cabin from the passengers, but he had rolled it down to talk to him.

"What's the news," Kozek asked, getting straight to the point.

"We have the location of the darklings," he revealed. "We're heading there right now. Would you like us to send law enforcement to detain them?"

"Excellent idea. Move forward with your objective," he commanded. Things were moving along as he had hoped, and before too long, he would not only have redeemed his name in the eyes of the Emperor, but also solidified the regime's presence in Dominov. They would learn that there was no place too distant, no place too hidden that an Inquisitor could not find them. He would even scour the metropolis city-continent of Durinveii to achieve his objectives.

"As you command. We will intercept them within the hour."

"Good. Let's take our time. I want to savor this victory," Kozek ordered. He smiled as he looked out the window. With the darklings gone, they were one step closer to crushing all who threatened the peace of his beloved nation.

And So it Begins

Liz followed Thillan and Kamille through the streets of Port-City, a bustling metropolis where people of all colors and backgrounds melted together into one functioning society. Lunar and Asher had other matters to attend to, and had left the group behind. It was a utopia, but as Kamille explained to her, it was all because of strict laws that Dominov enforced more than usual. The moment one person stepped out of line, everyone would make sure they were reprimanded and disciplined accordingly. There was no tolerance for violent people that ridiculed others for silly reasons. Liz couldn't say that she disagreed with it; Dominov was a republic – no, a democracy. They believed in power for the people, and did what it could to ensure their safety. It was the closest to home that she'd seen since she had arrived on Thaerv, and for once she felt she didn't have to hide herself from the public eye.

"Liz," Kamille began, "I want to apologize for how harsh we've been towards you and Jack."

Liz smiled gently as she thought of a response. The city's noise and atmosphere was content; not too loud and not too quiet. It smelled like San Fransisco, even. "You've no need to apologize, Kamille. I promise. We put you all through so much Hell… I'm sorry for that…"

"Thank you, Liz… We've been so mean to you… We've treated you like you're reman, but you're not. Your society, your culture… You're so far removed from it, and we treated you like you were in your element. I know you're new on this world, but we haven't been a very good example of the good this people here can be," Thillan explained. "There's enough squabbling over petty things here, and treating you like we would-

Before he could finish, they stopped in front of a little girl standing in the middle of the sidewalk who was ignoring the crowd around her and had her eyes solely fixed on Liz with amazement. "It's you!" the girl shrieked as tears ran down her cheeks. She ran to Liz and attempted to tackle her in a tight embrace. Liz's heart melted. She immediately recognized her…

Zesha

"What are you doing here, Zesha?!" Liz cried as she fell to her knees and embraced the little girl. Tears rolled down her face, followed by a heart-warming smile.

"The men from the Empire took me here and dropped me off at an orphanage, but I didn't wanna go there, so I ran away," Zesha explained. Liz's heart dropped. She wondered how long Zesha had been roaming the streets, scavenging for food and living out her childhood having to grow up and act far older than she actually was.

"You know this little girl?" Thillan asked. Kamille's expression, though, was one of shock as she realized what their reunion meant.

"This is the girl from Liz's story..." Kamille stated plainly, disbelief striking her expression.

"That's right," Liz said with tears in her eyes as she stood and picked her up. Her expression was suddenly determined. Zesha's presence sparked something in Liz's heart; a fierce resolve, and a bright spark of hope. "And she's been here this entire time, searching for a home."

"My home was broken by aethrils," Zesha corrected. "I don't have a home... The Empire kicked me out. Now this is my home."

"Oh my gods," Kamille spat as tears filled her

eyes. She looked away, unable to see the little girl as anger towards the Empire began to permeate through her being.

"It's better here," Liz said. "And it's better that you ran into us."

"No… It's better that you ran into me," Zesha corrected. Liz cocked her head to the side in confusion. "I have something to give you."

She pulled out a golden necklace with a heart-shaped charm on it. The charm had a cross etched into it. Liz held the necklace in the palm of her hand with a shocked expression, recognizing it immediately. It was a necklace that her mother had given her just before she died when she was little.

"How-"

"A really nice lady gave it to me and told me to give it to you. She's been taking care of me, and today, she let me go walk around the city by myself," Zesha said with an excited grin, proud that her caretaker let her have such awesome privilege. Liz was wrong. They were wrong. "She said today was gonna be a special day for me, and a really sad one too."

"Did she say why?" Liz asked.

"Nope," Zesha said as she looked down. Liz stood to her feet, wondering how anyone was able to get their hands on something so precious to her... When she started working at the factory, before she met Jack, the boss had taken her and assaulted her. She tried to get away, but he grabbed her by that very same necklace she held and tore it from her neck. He threw it out the window, and she never saw it again.

Then Jack showed up one day and treated her with such kindness that she'd never seen. Sure, he drank, swore, and got in fights, but he always held her when she cried and walked her home at night. He was always a good friend, and listened when she needed to talk. He defended her when men got violent and brutish. She smiled as she remembered a silly promise he made her one day, 'I'll get that necklace back, Liz. I swear it.' She never told him that he raped her, only that he got mad one day and threw it away...

But now she stood there with that necklace in her hands. *Who brought us here?* Her question burned evermore in her mind, culminating the entirety of her mental strength to find answers to that question; a person who spoke in a voice without a sound to her, Jack, Adrian, and Ayela. A person that brought them to Thaerv when they should have died in the wreckage of San Fransisco. A person who knew them so intimately, they held onto insignificant, yet all too important artifacts from their pasts... But someone that also began a revolutionary pacifist rebellion against a tyrannical Emperor. What kind of power did this person possess? How was this person able to reach across the universe to pick the three of them to bring to a world consumed by war? Was divine logic truly that powerful in those who possessed it?

Her questions would have to wait, though, as the red and white lights of law enforcement flashed in her vision, and the powerful engines of police vehicles filled her ears while they surrounded them. Her heart sank further than ever at the realization that quickly set in; they were caught. But the worst sight she saw was a familiar face walking up to them from around the corner; Adrian, bearing the insignia of the Empire on a badge, dressed as a high-ranking official. Tears began to fill her eyes as anger gripped her heart with a fiery touch.

"What is this?" She asked, dreariness evident in her voice.

Adrian held up a hand and winked. Her emotions were sent into a state of confusion. Kamille recognized the stature of human males, and deduced Jack's brother before Liz had a chance to introduce him.

"Don't tell me you sided with the Empire," Kamille spat. Beside him was a elvish man who carried himself as though he held a power like no other creature alive. Liz could sense from him that he had every right to walk like that. She could tell he was dangerous.

"Adrian... Why?" She asked.

"Greetings, darklings... Hello, Elizabeth. I've heard much about you," the elf answered, not allowing Adrian the chance to speak. "You will be coming with us."

As he spoke, law enforcement officers emerged from their vehicles, weapons trained on Liz and the others. "Darklings; you are here by detained until your Imperial escort arrives, under the authority of the Republic of Dominov!" They called out. Adrian's friend raised an eyebrow in confusion.

"I am here already, officer. I will be taking them with me," he declared.

"I'm sorry, sir, but I have to decline. We have our orders from a high-ranking government official of Enthedrill, and we were told not to allow them out of our sight until their caravan arrives," the officer said, denying his order. Liz's heart pounded in her throat in nervousness. There was no chance that Adrian would have simply received authority like he did without help from the elf who stood beside them, but the fact that someone else ordered them to detain utterly until they arrived sent chills down her spine. She could only wonder who was coming to meet them.

On cue, a black vehicle– slick and beautiful, but professional and with the insignia of Dominov on its doors, pulled around the corner slowly. Zesha whimpered as a man stepped out, dressed in a long black coat that descended to his knees. His black hair was greased back, and he wore dark-lensed glasses on his face.

"Hello, Zesha," he said with a sly smile. The little girl gripped Liz's pants tightly as she hid behind her. "And hello to you too, Liz. And, of course… The darklings."

"Who are you?" Liz asked, confused. "And how do you know my name?"

"You don't recognize me, and that's okay. But surely you remember the soldiers who captured you when you found that little girl?" He asked. The blood drained from her face as the memories returned to her mind. The town that was burned… The gramatoginon… And the terrifying airship that soared overhead. He was the one Jack mentioned from when he woke up. Interrogator.

"You're the interrogator," she declared. He smirked.

"You're correct. But that was in a past life.

489

Now, I'm the one who will return you to our glorious Emperor. But first, I need to get a hold of your… Lover," he revealed with a sinister grin. Her immediate thought was of Jack. The emotion she felt at the thought that they may never get to hold each other again… The thought of him falling into harm began to tear her heart in two.

"You'll never get a hold of them!" She screamed as she hicked and sobbed. "You might as well kill me!"

"I will. But I want to do it in front of the last two that are wanted," he barked.

"Kozek-

"Ah, yes! Banïl, and Adrian; the human who joined our cause!" Kozek declared as he turned to face them. "Thank you for bringing me my objective! I invite you to watch the show… In fact, your Emperor would most certainly wish for you to do so as well… Lest he be concerned that your hearts are suddenly turned against him," he threatened. It became clear to her; Adrian and his friend were attempting to rescue them, but they needed to remain under cover… Was the Emperor truly that powerful?

"…With pleasure…" Banïl growled. Liz looked over at Kamille, who began to shed tears. Thillan held her in his arms tightly. Even the police officers looked over at Kozek with pale faces,

490

not sure how to react to everything. She looked down at Zesha, who clung tightly to her leg, and then knelt down. "Go. Run back to the woman who's taking care of you," she whispered.

"...This is what she meant by today being a sad day..." Zesha sobbed. Liz didn't respond with words. She hugged the little girl tightly and sent her on her way. The officials were considerate enough to let her pass and run away to her home. Kozek smirked as Liz stood back to her feet.

"Good. Officer, will you take the darklings and the human girl? I'll invite the other Enthedrillan officials in my caravan," Kozek ordered, keeping his eyes on Adrian and Banïl.

"...Sir?" He asked with a quivering voice. Kozek rolled his eyes and then held his hand in the air. He closed it into a fist, and a with a loud pop, the officer's neck snapped to the side. The man fell to the ground, dead. Liz and Kamille gasped and looked away, while Thillan glared at the official.

"Do I have to repeat myself to you?" Kozek asked as he laid eyes on the female officer nearest to the one he killed. She shook her head quickly, scared of his sudden display of power. "Good." He said as he quickly turned his wrist. All of the other officers except for her grunted in pain before cracks and pops resonated from them, their necks also twisting in unnatural ways. Their bodies collapsed, and all that was left was the frightened blonde-haired officer who submitted to his terrifying authority. Liz's heart pounded in horror, not knowing how to react to him.

Before she could ask any questions, though, the officer quickly ushered them into her vehicle while Adrian and Banïl entered Kozek's. The doors shut, and the frightened girl revved her engine as she threw it in gear and waited for Kozek's truck to move.

"O-Officer?" Liz stuttered.

"Shh! Don't make me lose my life too, please! I have a husband and daughter at home," she sobbed and begged. Liz cupped her hands over her mouth as guilt and emotional pain wrecked her body. She couldn't stop the tears from pouring down her cheeks.

"...I'm so sorry..."

XXIII

The Beginning of the End of the Beginning

And here we stand, observing the spark that will save those who're meant to be saved, and abandon those who're meant to be abandoned.

Master of the Darklings

Her heart sank. As Anæsïa read the message on her phone, her plan to extract the darklings and the human girl before Kozek had gotten to them clearly failed just a couple days before that moment. There was nothing she could do or say at that point without revealing her true identity or compromising Banïl and Adrian... Or herself. She'd seen the atrocities of the Empire and did nothing about it for far too long. Tears filled her eyes as she looked down at the contraband she'd ordered.

But now... Now, those faithful and strong leaders she'd banded together under her revered title were in the clutches of a man entirely too devoted to his emperor. He was a man who purposefully allowed the wickedness of dark men and women, and the pain and sadness of unfortunate situations feed and grow into the sacrifice he desired. It was a sacrifice to appease the fallen beings he'd acquired his majestic authority from... The fallen gods.

The Towlål.

She was so close to meeting with Ayela and the other human man she traveled with when she received the message. She was so close to enacting a "genius" plan Kozek dreamed up – a plan she fully intended to subvert to her own whims. She was going to use it to their advantage, but now things have changed. She couldn't afford to hide any longer from those she recruited. She knew they would search for her, but now she needed to seek them.

She stood in front of an abandoned hotel, torn down and ravaged in the undercity. Some homeless would use it occasionally to sleep in and would often get away with it due to the city's laziness. It remained tall and barely functional. She'd been in D'Vnora two days and found her darkling with relative ease. She saw them pick food from the open markets and produce stands that dotted the side of the streets, and watched them return to this very building and leave only to scout out the docking bays for low-security ships – no doubt to find a way out of the city. Hitching rides off run-down trucks was a difficult process, especially when they didn't know where they were going, but these two managed to make it just fine. Anæsïa was proud... Though, she figured she'd need to use her true name with them at this point.

"Ayela!" Anæsïa called out from the front entrance. After a few moments, the Songrivan's recognizable fiery mane poked through one of the windows three stories up, looking down to see who called her name. "Could you come down please?" She asked, waving at her.

After another fifteen minutes, Ayela and her human friend emerged from the aged doors of the hotel cautiously. The darkling leader expected as much.

"You're going to tell us who you are?" the human asked, his hand gripped firmly on the hilt of the sword at his hip. He was dirty, obviously from not having showered for a few days and having fought fiercely against the dangers of the crime capital of the Empire. Ayela's crimson locks were a tattered mess, but her violet eyes were full of hope. She was in good hands with the human.

"You two look like you've been through hell," Anæsïa pointed out as she carefully took a step forward. The two backed away, concern and tension tightening their features, and they were right to. She was dressed in fine Imperial clothing; a long black coat that hugged her figure with a maroon shawl stitched into it, and glistening black boots and black gloves. She looked like a high official.

"You didn't answer his question," Ayela retorted.

"I... I am Ruat," she revealed, her face downcast. "And I can no longer hide myself from all of you, Ayela."

The blood drained from their faces at the revelation, but the human didn't seem to trust her. He drew his sword and held the tip at her neck. "Prove it," he spat.

"I can't prove anything to you," she said, gently pushing the blade aside. Jack repositioned it at her neck and pushed forward, forcing her to take a few steps back.

"Incorrect. I'll give you one more chance," he warned.

"Jack..." Ayela cooed, gently resting her hand on his, forcing him to withdraw the blade. Her eyes never left Anæsïa's face.

"I... I am the one who wrote to her, Kamille, Thillan, Asher, and the rest of the darklings... I am the one who told her she's the last and showed her I know she's a dancer... And I know your brother," She revealed. "My true name is Anæsïa, and I am an Inquisitor of the Imperial throne. You don't know what Inquisitors are, and that's understandable, so I'll explain it to you: we are the elite of the Empire. We are just under the Emperor's rank, and do his bidding in a more unofficial capacity. We are his hands and feet, his eyes and ears... But what he doesn't suspect is that two of us are also the knives in his back... And that one of them has successfully brought in one of the humans he fears so greatly."

The clanging of the sword rang in their ears when it hit the ground, and it took Jack a moment to collect himself and pick it up. "You work for the Empire... What happened to Adrian?" He asked. Shock consumed Ayela's expression.

"It all makes sense... But... You sent letters to Jack... You were in our heads?" Ayela asked, trying to make sense of the past. Anæsïa cocked her head to the side.

"What do you mean? No- it doesn't matter. Right now, there are more pressing matters," Anæsïa said.

"But you just showed yourself to us! You just revealed your identity, answered so many questions, and then gave us so many more! You can't just leave us in confusion like that!" Ayela complained.

The Inquisitor held up her hand. "I'll explain

on the way. For now, lives are at risk, and if we can prevent any more loss of life, we must. It's the mandate of the darklings."

Without giving them the opportunity to ask anything more, Anæsïa turned to walk the direction she arrived. They had no time to waste, and quickly caught up to her. The city was silent, still recovering from the carnage of the Corpse Grinders. Barely any cars drove on the roads that day, and most of the busy commotion was in the upper city, where a lot of the poor attempted to retreat to out of fear. It was customary; a gang would attack the lower cities, they would flee to the upper cities, and the upper cities would give them what they wanted/needed so that they would return to the undercity.

"So, you've been giving Asher, Kamille and Thillan access to government servers this entire time?" Ayela asked, disrupting the tense silence. Jack kept his hand on his sword, keeping ready just in case Anæsïa decided she really wasn't a friend.

"Yes," she answered plainly, not giving away any more information as she flagged down a taxi-driver.

"And you've been sending messages-"

"What I don't understand is how you're able to do all of this… Doesn't the government suspect you at all for treason? Doesn't the Emperor ask questions to those in its structure?" Jack interrupted. Anæsïa sighed before turning to him, an emotionally pained expression twisting her features.

"I am... Like Ayela," she revealed. "Divine logic directs the beings of certain individuals. I are one of those beings. We are the remnant of an ancient order called the Uri'Kai, though I belong to a smaller, different one. We have more... Senses than the average man or woman, and more abilities than others. It's almost like we function in a higher reality than others. My gifts make me smarter than almost any other person, and I have emotion deeper than most. I feel for the lives of my people, and our Emperor does not. I am able to hide in plain sight from him. I am able to outsmart him at most turns, and I fully intend on dethroning him for the safety of my people."

Ayela first paused to take it all in, but then started to analyze her tone of voice and the air she held herself in. "Are you truly doing this for your people, though?" She asked in a quivering voice. "I'm sorry, I've met so much disappointment in my life that I have come to expect it... It almost sounds like you're trying to take the throne from him to prove something to him..."

They were all silent for a long while, then Anæsïa spoke up. "Whatever my motives," she began, almost admitting to what Ayela pointed out, "a man who seeks to sacrifice nations of people to dark celestial beings so that he can become a god should not be sitting on any throne of power… Let the people rebel against me, for all I care; he must be stopped."

"…Are you sure a seat of power is what you need right now, Ruat?" Jack asked, loosening the grip around his sword.

"I'm sorry, who are you again? Jack? You're an outsider in my world. In my world, outsiders don't meddle with seats of power-

"I'VE HAD ENOUGH OF THIS!!!" Jack screamed, anger twisting his features. "All you darklings have done, except that wonderful woman here standing with us, is push me aside and talk down to me!!! I've had it! I've had it with feeling like shit just because I'm a different species! SO WHAT if I'm an outsider?! Truth is truth, and just because you can't stay your pride for just a moment doesn't mean you shouldn't accept it!"

Ayela made her way over to his side and stood between the two of them, facing Anæsïa. "He's right… Just because he's an outsider to our world doesn't mean he can't see what's in someone's heart... We trust you... But there's no throne waiting for you if you can't be better than Gorvon Komin... If you can't calm your desire to rule..."

Anæsïa had no response. Instead, she flagged down a truck, managing to get them a ride to the docks. "Regardless of who I am, we have to leave. Your brother's life, the life of that human girl and the lives of the darklings are at stake here, and time is not on our side-

She stopped to answer her vibrating phone, vehemently demanding her attention. As she checked the screen to see the message that waited for her, the blood drained from her face. Jack knew it in the depths of his heart; things had gotten worse much more quickly.

"Aye, you three getting' in?" The driver called from the cab.

"Yes," Jack responded, his eyes trained on Anæsïa. "Just give us a moment."

"We need to leave now," she said, looking into Jack's eyes with a desperate fear. "If we get there in time, we might just be able to save your human friend's life."

Jack put a hand on her shoulder, forcing her to look him in the eyes. "What's happening to Liz?" He asked.

"We need to move."

"Answer his question, Anæsïa," Ayela pushed,

stepping in front of her before she could get into the truck. Anæsïa inhaled quickly as tears began to swell in her eyes. Jack could see the remorse in her eyes. He could tell; she knew she'd made a grave mistake.

"He's gained access to an ancient chamber in the city of Ih'Dejj called 'the executioner's pole.' It was used by the Na'Tzeth– enemies of the Order of the Uri'Kai– to execute its rival's members once they were caught... He plans on using it on your human girl," Anæsïa revealed. Panic quickly set in Jack's brain.

"Who's *he?* How long do we have?" Jack asked.

Anæsïa paused.

"There's no time left. Kozek is preparing it now."

XXIV

A Sickly Chamber for Death

Oh, what tortured history surrounds the Execution Chambers of the ancient Uri'Kai, that they would still be of use for a more brutish generation.

The Bruised and Assaulted

The chamber was a sickly color, cold and ancient. Her hands were chained above her head to a large metal pole that stretched from the floor to the ceiling. Her clothes were filthy, but now there were splotches of blood on her white, thin-strapped tank top and black tights from the torture she'd been subject to. Kozek made sure she had just enough water and food to survive, but he fed her himself. Her chocolate-colored hair was a nappy mess that fell down her back. Dirt particles clung to her face, revealing the tear streaks that were flowing down her cheeks.

Liz hadn't felt as violated and defeated as she did since her old boss at the factory on earth. She missed Jack. She wished like hell he was there with her, and sniffled as her heavy emotions began to bubble up again. She knew he would

507

come to her. She didn't care about anything any longer. She longed for Jack. She missed him so terribly.

Beneath her bare feet was a grated floor made of cold metal, and painful for her to keep standing on. It was more painful, however, for her to dangle by her hands, so she continued standing. She learned that day just how weak humans were compared to the elves. They were built the same, but so much stronger. Kozek hit hard regardless if he used a torture tool or not. Each strike was only half his strength, but it felt as though she'd been punched by the strongest man in the world. She was sure one of her ribs were broken, and there were cuts and bruises all over her body. Her lips were cracked, a blood that had dripped from the corner of her mouth was dried now.

Then, distracting her from her pain, the door directly in front of her slid open with a screeching sound, causing her to wince. Kozek stepped through and entered the dimly lit chamber with Adrian and the other elf. After them came in Kamille and Thillan, chained and arrested, walking like prized catches after being hunted in the wild by vicious beast tamers. Their faces were as downcast as hers, but their expressions fell even worse once they saw Liz.

"You didn't fail me," Liz said with a cracked,

508

pained voice.   She was so dehydrated, she couldn't cry anymore. Kozek erupted in laughter as he turned a rusted nob on the wall, raising the lights and igniting a churning, groaning mechanical contraption beneath the grated floor. The others safely stood on solid ground. She didn't know what it was, but if she had to guess from the slight raise in temperature, she assumed it was some sort of furnace.

"No, they did. They failed you. Adrian failed you. Your lover failed you... My colleague is on route with both him and Ayela right now as we speak... You all failed," he spat.

He calmly made his way over to Liz and lifted her face to his with brute force. "And you see that friend beside Adrian? You know why he doesn't aid you? Because he doesn't care. You're all pawns to him. No, he will pay in another way," he whispered. A scowl twisted her features as she looked into his eyes. Hate began to fill her being. He snickered at her reaction as he traced his fingers down her neck, then to her breasts, then down her stomach. She flinched at his touch, and before he could do any worse, she shoved her knee in between his legs. He grunted and doubled over, then she spat on his face with what little saliva she had.

"You..." He growled as he straightened himself.

"I'm going to enjoy watching your lover's face when he watches you die."

"You bloody *fucking* monster!!!" Kamille shrieked. Her voice was desperate and pained.

Kozek ignored the insults of the darkling as he walked over to a chair seated atop a raised platform. "Banïl," he began as he sat down. "The Emperor will be watching this take place. He wishes to congratulate you on the vast amount of propaganda and promotion you've been doing for the Empire," he added. "What I want to know is how you were able to learn the location of the darklings and this beautiful human woman, and intercept them before I had the chance to take them in?"

"You are quite perceptive, Kozek. A brilliant addition to the Inquisitors," The reman began. "But you're mistaken, I assure you. The Emperor and I have spoken indeed, and he wishes to congratulate me, most assuredly... But not for the reasons you think."

"We shall see. My associate should be arriving any moment, now," Kozek grinned as he crossed his legs and stroked his chin inquisitively. "By all means, if you seek to attack me; you can do so now. We-"

"I have much more in place than a petty move of violence directed at another Inquisitor," Banïl

510

interrupted. "There are times for violence. There are also times for... Other ways."

"I'm intrigued. No matter. The Emperor is far superior than you are, regardless of your magnificent prowess with dark logic. I'm sure he would not appreciate the death of his newly appointed, or the treacherous convincing of one of his other most powerful and intelligent Inquisitors," Kozek spat. He grinned wildly as he checked his phone. "Let's put these trivial matters behind us. The humans have plagued our world long enough; let's end this chaos now and focus our efforts on more immediate and powerful threats..."

A Sharp Revelation

Jack's heart raced as their small transport rolled up to the front entrance of the massive, dome-shaped structure in the sectioned, abandoned part of the walled woodland city of Ih'Dejj. The city would have been a sight to behold if they weren't in such a desperate rush. There were tamed animals that roamed free in most areas, but were kept safely out of the residential sectors. Some parts of the city, like where they were, had been sectioned off to anyone except government officials.

"Everyone follow my lead," Anæsïa warned as they exited the vehicle and marched toward the building. Jack looked over to Ayela with desperation in his eyes. She grabbed his hand and took a deep breath, reassuring him that she had his back no matter what. Then he noticed her stealthily shove the inquisitor's phone in her pocket.

"What should we expect?" Jack asked.

"Empty ruins except for the executioner's chamber. There we'll find everyone except Asher and Lunar – the two who were absent when everyone was captured."

"Probably for good reason," Jack commented.

"They will be here to extract us once we're safely away," Anæsïa clarified. "Now let's disrupt this execution."

The sounds of insects and other forest-dwelling creatures filled their ears until the massive rusted doors of the dome groaned and creaked, opening slowly to a dark foyer that appeared as though it once was bustling with life and activity.

"These ruins…" Ayela commented, looking at the various racks and shelves that were turned over and broken, leaving a path in the mess that led directly to the large doors in the rear of the massive foyer.

"Shh! Don't speak. Remember everything I told you," Anæsïa said, silencing Ayela's fascination. She obeyed.

Jack observed the many weapons that laid on the ground; swords and spears, as well as a few older-looking rifles and pistols sprawled

513

everywhere. There were also books and many different statues amidst the mess piles. He set plans into place in his mind, keeping many options open once they would make their attempted escape. He knew as well as any, though, that the future was an unpredictable variable. Little else mattered in his heart; get Liz, get his brother, get the darklings, and escape with everyone alive. He wasn't going to shed anymore blood... At least, he hoped not.

Anæsïa opened the door to the large chamber, and Jack looked on in horror: Liz was chained to a long pole, beaten and bruised and a tattered mess. Blood stains littered her shirt, and her clothes looked torn. He could only imagine the things the monster seated comfortably on the executioner's chair did to her. Anger began to burn in his heart. Anger that was steadily turning to blind rage.

"Welcome, Semus! So glad you could finally make it with our straggling renegades! Shall we begin this process?" Kozek announced in a sneering tone. Anæsïa casually walked over to Ayela, clapping handcuffs onto her wrists exactly as she said she would. Jack watched as she pulled out a second pair, noting the cracked notches that were made of a weaker material on his and on hers. He knew what needed to happen; Anæsïa needed to convince Kozek that it would be better to execute Ayela before Liz, and Ayela would escape containment. She ensured him that she could inhibit the abilities of others gifted in dark logic– something she made sure no one else knew was possible, not even the Emperor. This meant she could cut off the telekinetic powers of Kozek before he had a chance to stop them.

Jack knew the hard work Anæsïa and Banïl poured into their stealthy subversion of the emperor. They carefully infiltrated the Empire's highest order and were working hard to ensure his removal from office in a non-violent manner, though their objective was quite difficult. Perhaps, once they escaped, they could help. Jack found himself getting more involved in his rising desire to help the people of this world.

"Welcome to you as well, Jack and Ayela!" Kozek announced as he stood to his feet. He pulled his phone out of his pocket and flicked his fingers across the screen, tossing a larger holographic projection into the air. Hovering above was the eager face of the red-eyed, dark haired emperor.

"Your majesty…" Anæsïa said with a respectful bow.

"Greetings, Semus. Kozek has informed me of the result of all of your ventures. Well done.

515

And you as well, Banïl. Your work at improving the standing of the Empire in Dominov and improving our relationship with them. Good work indeed... Now, for the matter at hand," The Emperor began with a sinister grin as his eyes settled on Liz. "Before we begin with the execution of the traitors to the throne, I offer you, humans, amnesty on the condition that you either return to your homeworld, or you pledge allegiance to me as your new sovereign."

"You think we'd surrender to you?" Liz spat before Jack had the chance to respond. "Our answer is no."

"Then execution it is. Kozek."

"Yes, your Majesty."

"Wait!!!" Anæsïa shouted, demanding all of their attention. "What if we don't execute the humans first?" She suggested as Kozek made his way over to Liz, drawing a large knife from his coat.

"Kozek, wait," The Emperor ordered. "What do you suggest?"

"I suggest we execute one of the darklings first. Let's give the humans an understanding of the pain they would feel at such horrific death. Perhaps it will change their mind," she said, pushing Ayela forward.

"Tsk. Such a waste of such great power...

I know about you, Ayela... The *lost princess* to the Sovereignty should have more wisdom in her current predicament, don't you think, *Tsana Renn?*" The Emperor scolded. Jack's eyes widened as he looked over at Ayela, unsure of how to respond to the revelation of her noble blood. She looked just as confused as he did. "Kozek, do you have any objections?"

He paused, looking Anæsïa intently in her eyes, as if trying to find an alternative motive to her suggestion. "Forgive my hesitancy," Kozek began. "I've been suspicious of traitors even among the Inquisitors... So, to have such an idea occur just after such an emotional outburst... And to have it timed as it was... I wonder if my partner is truly making this suggestion for the benefit of the Empire, or for the benefit of these weak humans..."

"Hmm... What do you suggest?" The Emperor asked. Kozek didn't answer.

It was the longest second of Jack's life. He watched in horror. Everyone's screams were muffled. The commotion moved slowly. Every millisecond slowly passed before his eyes, and he felt powerless as the blade sunk into Liz's chest. The blood seeped around the hilt slowly as she cried from the pain, and Jack's body became numb from the sound. She gasped and coughed as blood began to drip from her mouth. His emotions were a mixture ready to explode like a chemical reaction; sadness, pain, despair, fear, and anger. His eyes ached as the tears forced their way around them, and he didn't stop them. He desperately looked into Liz's eyes.

"NO!!!" He finally cried. Kozek, grinning at the obvious havoc he unleashed, pulled the knife out and made his way back to the seat as he pulled out a remote controller from his pocket. Jack didn't even notice the increased heat. His only focus was Liz, who breathed heavy as blood poured from her gaping wound.

"KOZEK!!!" Jack growled angrily. The Inquisitor laughed with wicked pleasure. The Emperor, seemingly unimpressed, gave Banïl a nod and then turned his end of the video-call off. The hologram vanished without a trace.

Jack didn't notice the commotion afterwards as he fell to his knees. The other two inquisitors were busy getting everyone else out of the room, while Ayela and Adrian picked up Jack by his arms and attempted to pull him out.

But he protested, snapping back to reality, fighting against his friends and snapping the cuffs at the weakened link. "No, Jack, it's too late! We have to go!" Adrian protested. "We cannot end his life! Anæsïa won't even allow Banïl to do it!"

"I DON'T CARE!!!" Jack protested in rage. Then, Liz's coughing distracted him.

"Jack," Liz called out weakly. He looked up at her to see a pained smile. "It's okay… You can let go."

"No, Liz! Please!" He protested.

"I love you, Jack… I always have," she said amidst her coughs. "Now go! Bring down Kozek another way… Anger isn't the answer."

"Listen to her, human! This is the only time I'll simply let you all escape!" Kozek taunted. Then he laughed.

He taunted.

He laughed.

He taunted.

And Jack's vision turned red.

The Power of Creation

Elizabeth... The voice whispered into her mind's ears. *You're dying...*

I know... She answered back mentally. Time moved slowly. It almost seemed to pause as she held her conversation.

You've been searching for a way home this entire time...

I know... She responded with pain in her heart. She would die without a home.

You've lost so much...

I know...

Let me be your home...

I don't know who you are...

Yes, you do...

...Ruat? She asked. There was silence, and then an answer clear as day.

You know who I am... He said. His voice was

clear and as audible as Jack's. Her eyes widened. She tried to envision his dark face, the white robe, the golden crown of thorns upon his head... The one so many claimed to know intimately, and the one who's name so many more abused... The avatar of the Grand Creator... *Do you trust me?* He asked.

...Yes...

Suddenly, she felt an energy course through her body. It was a power unlike any she'd felt before. Colors began to brighten, and her senses became hyper as a presence filled her being. Then she knew. He was the one above all. He was the master of all the gods they'd heard of, and the one hiding behind a veil of eternity.

You are given the same power that can raise the dead... What will you do with it?

She knew the answer was clear. Even though she could come up with a number of ways to use this power, there was a reason she was given it, and there was a reason it was given at the time it was given in. No matter what she wanted, she knew that he needed to be there. His place was on thaerv, bringing the fight to whatever was tormenting it. Thaerv was Jack's home, and the one who filled her with such power wouldn't let

521

her use it to bring them back to earth; that much she was sure of.

And she thought of the way Ayela looked at Jack... Liz loved him, but her place was never meant to be at Jack's side, no matter how much she longed to be there... She wasn't meant to be with Jack...

...But Ayela was.

So instead, she reached out with her consciousness and took hold of the force of power that nested itself in Kozek's heart, and ripped it out of him angrily. She smiled as she gave up her life, knowing that they would all make it out alive because the one who sought them with a power not his own was finally brought low. That was how she was better; she could give up her life for the ones she loved...

She could give up everything...

...And in return, she would gain so much more.

Death's Wrathful Vengeance

Then, without warning, Kozek pulled up on a hidden lever on the side of his chair. Jack could hear the churning of a massive machine underneath Liz and could see the sudden rise in temperature as heat waves distorted the air around where she was tied.

It took only seconds. With a loud pop, a blast of quick, loud, and concentrated fire blasted from the floor beneath Liz and into the air as doors on the ceiling above them opened up. They were thrown through the doors into the messy foyer filled with weapons and books, knocking the doors off their hinges with them. Everything was far away, but even Kozek was thrown from his chair onto the wall behind him. Nevertheless, Jack could hear her screams of pain through the fire as she was consumed.

Once it was over, the fires immediately ceased, and all that was left was a glowing pole from the heat, a glowing grated floor, and empty, glowing shackles that once bound the wrists of the woman he loved. She, however, was gone. Liz was gone. His heart was torn in two. One half was shattered and broken, lost and without direction. The other half...

He didn't wait for permission, and he didn't care. He threw himself up and ran to the pile of weapons that were once wielded by the ancient warrior culture. After picking up one of the old swords, he dashed into the room where they were thrown out of. "Jack, no!!!" Ayela cried from behind him, but he ignored her plea. Only one thing burned in his mind; revenge.

He ran up the steps to the platform that Kozek had sat on, and seeing the confused reman rise to his feet, he leapt in the air. Everything moved in slow motion once more. He didn't notice the desperate Ayela chasing after him, nor did he understand the sacrifice Liz made when she suppressed Kozek's power. He didn't think of anything else or feel anything else as he held the sword above his head with the blade poised to pierce his enemy's heart.

In an instant, it was all over. The blade made a loud *shunk!* as it stabbed through Kozek's chest. He grunted as he looked down and then looked up at Anæsïa. Tears filled his eyes. He started to understand how truly alone he was. He realized that even his emperor didn't remain behind to watch him finish his task. It was almost as though the emperor knew he would fail and wasn't impressed enough to stay and see the rest. Jack saw the realization fill his eyes, which were red from the pain he felt.

"You..." He began as his life started to escape him. "...You will never go home..." He swore as he attempted to reach for the knife that laid on the ground a few feet away. Jack gritted his teeth as he twisted the sword, listening to the Inquisitor cry from the pain.

"Your empire will fall, Kozek... If it's the last thing I do," Jack swore as he stepped back and pulled the sword out of his chest. Then, Kozek fell lifeless to the ground.

Kamille shrieked at what she saw after entering the chamber with Asher and Lunar. Ayela sniffled and sobbed as she looked at the chamber, seeing that Liz was truly gone, and that Jack had committed the unbelievable act.

"Let's go! This place will be crawling with Imperials before too long!" Lunar warned. Everyone left except Ayela and Adrian.

"Aren't you going to fly with them?" Jack asked,

not able to look away from the act he'd just committed.

"We're not going without you…" Ayela said, looking up at Adrian, who nodded in agreement. Pain emulated from their expressions. "We're standing beside you, Jack."

"Why?" Jack asked as he looked up at her. He didn't feel accomplished by killing Kozek. He didn't feel avenged. Instead, he felt much worse.

"Because when everyone ran, you turned back to fight an aethril. When we all hid, you turned to lead away a group of murderous gangsters from a city's population. When everyone would push you for being an outsider, you pushed right back… And right now, Jack… you can't be alone…"

"The darklings are going to exile me," Jack warned.

"Then they're exiling me too. We'll figure it out… But for now, let's get out of here… Let's live to fight another day," she beckoned. Adrian, who had been silently agreeing with her the whole time, placed a hand on his shoulder as he began to hic and sob.

"I'm not leaving you behind again," he promised as he held him in a tight embrace. Ayela grabbed Jack's hand as he sobbed into Adrian's shoulder. "Now c'mon; they're going to leave without us."

The Journey Has Just Begun

The shuttle lifted off into the air, a shuttle that belonged to Lunar's capital ship. It had a unique feature that allowed it to hide from Imperial radars, which let them slip away undetected from the obnoxious activity that occurred at an abandoned sight. It was going to be a long journey for all of them. They sat there in silence, unsure of how to address everything that had just happened. Jack slumped in his seat, his gaze fixed onto the floor as he drifted into his thoughts.

"We're aware of what happens when a darkling kills," Asher stated. Kamille wiped her eyes as she looked at Jack sympathetically. Thillan grabbed her hand and caressed it.

"It's not fair," She protested. "He lost the love of his bloody life… He had to watch her die."

"That's the one law of the darklings, Kamille.

This has happened before. Do you remember Xidokk and his wife? Or Shior and her daughter? They received the same treatment... Exile," Asher responded curtly.

"He wasn't born into our way. None of them were. They aren't even from Thaerv... It's not fair," she protested again. Then Anæsïa cleared her throat.

"Fair or not, Asher is the current leader of the darklings," she declared. They all gave her shocked expressions. All except Jack.

"I'm sorry? We all acknowledge-

"Ruat, I know," she said, interrupting Asher. "I am Ruat." There was tense, shocked silence at her statement.

"...Ruat?..." Thillan asked in a nervous voice.

"That's right... And I gave Jack his plan to kill Kozek," She lied. "This means I now relinquish control of the darklings to Asher. He's your leader now," she said. Jack looked up at her, impressed at her willingness to humble herself, though he didn't think she needed to lie about anything. "This is irrevocable."

"But wait, we have so many questions!"

"I know, Kamille. But this is our way. While we're together, I will answer as much as I can. After, though, I will depart with Jack..."

"I will be returning to the capital to answer to

the Emperor about Kozek's failure, and throwing him off your scents," Banïl offered.

"And I will take Jack and Anæsïa with me and the Majjai. We'll take care of them there," Lunar revealed. Tears began to flood Kamille's eyes.

"...I'm going with Jack," Ayela declared.

"So am I," Adrian added.

"What? No! You aren't exiled! You're still one of us!"

"I know, Kamille... But I need to do this," Ayela answered.

"Adrian, are you sure about this?" Banïl asked.

"Yes, Banïl. I'm sure. I'm not going to leave my brother behind again," Adrian answered. The inquisitor nodded in approval, releasing the human from Imperial control.

"Alright, then... Jack, as my first official act as Master Darkling, I hereby exile you from our ranks, and relieve Anæsïa from her noble position for breaking our only law... Ayela, I hereby release you from darkling obligation, and permit you at your own risk to a life free from our direction. Though this exile is in effect, however, you can still call us friends," Asher declared. Jack began to sniffle as everything was set in motion. They all surrounded him and placed their hands on him, and then Ayela wrapped her arms around him and rested his head on her shoulder as he sobbed. He felt worse than he ever had; the violence of war took Liz's life, and in his anger, he took the murderer's life as payment…

…He just wanted Elizabeth back…

XXV

Memories of a Mystic High

How would a human react, when confronted with such strange visions? They would try their hardest to find a rational solution to an irrational problem.

The Soul of the Reborn

London England, April 19, 2021, 2:00AM

It was as if her name were being called from a great distance, like she was marooned on a solitary island, and her rescuer were calling from a ship many hundreds of miles away. It was all she could hear, though her mind was swirling with the sounds, smells and sights from the memories she spent the last two hours witnessing. She fought to pull herself from the memories, and she was filled with regret from drinking the glowing solution, worried that the effects would be so dramatic that she wouldn't recover.

But she couldn't give up. She couldn't explain it, but she was the right one who would drink it. She had to be. She drank it, so there was no going back now. Perhaps God knew she would do it. Perhaps fate just aligned itself so, that even with his power, there was no way he could intervene to stop her from drinking it. It was the obvious truth, because even if it wasn't the his plan, something knew she was going to be the one to drink it. Because of that, she couldn't give up. She couldn't let the intense sensations and reality-warping visions she witnessed overtake her and end her. She would be victorious.

But there was more, and she knew it. The visions weren't at an end. She blinked her eyes, realizing she lay on her back as the colors and familiar setting of the room she collapsed in returned to her in blurred vision. It was only for a moment, though. Tears streamed down her cheeks as he bent over her. She could feel his hand lift her head off the floor with a gentle caress as he adjusted her onto his lap. She couldn't see clearly at all, but she could tell from his body language that he was emotionally distraught. Was he crying? For her?

Her vision faded from reality into more memories and strange sights, luring her and promising to teach her the deep secrets of creation and the blind eternities that existed beyond the boundaries of the universe. As her consciousness drifted back to that strange realm, she saw herself floating momentarily in the blackness of space.

She witnessed the beauty of the stars around her, and a nebula that extended upwards like a hand.

The three fingers on it turned and faced her, filling her heart with dread as celestial beings formed themselves from them. They appeared like men made of pure blackness with a single red star as an eye on their heads, and they were draped in ragged, terrifying hooded robes that were made from the nebula clouds. She wanted to scream, but fear gripped her vocal chords.

They simply stared at her, and she stared at them as they too faded from her sight. Then, she felt herself plunge back into the exciting memories of that world of mirage. There was a long journey ahead of her, and she could tell from those three figures…

…Nothing is as it seems…

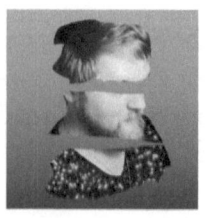

About the Author

Zachael is a writer with a love for fantasy, science, and the allure of religious myth and cosmic theories.

You can connect with me on:
- https://www.zachaeltjp.com
- https://www.twitter.com/JZachael
- https://www.facebook.com/zachaeltjpresgrove
- https://www.instagram.com/zachael.the.writer

Subscribe to my newsletter:
- https://www.zachaeltjp.com/forms